ALL IN
GOOD
TIME

ISBN 979-8-9889961-0-1 (Paperback Edition)

This book is a work of fiction. Names, characters, places, and incidents either are products of the author's imagination or are used fictitiously. Any resemblance to actual persons, living or dead, events, or locales is entirely coincidental.

Edited by Shannon Cave
Front cover art by Talia Aden
Cover text design by Talia Aden
Interior design and formatting by Talia Aden

Printed and bound in the United States of America
First Printing, 2023

ALL IN GOOD TIME

TALIA ADEN

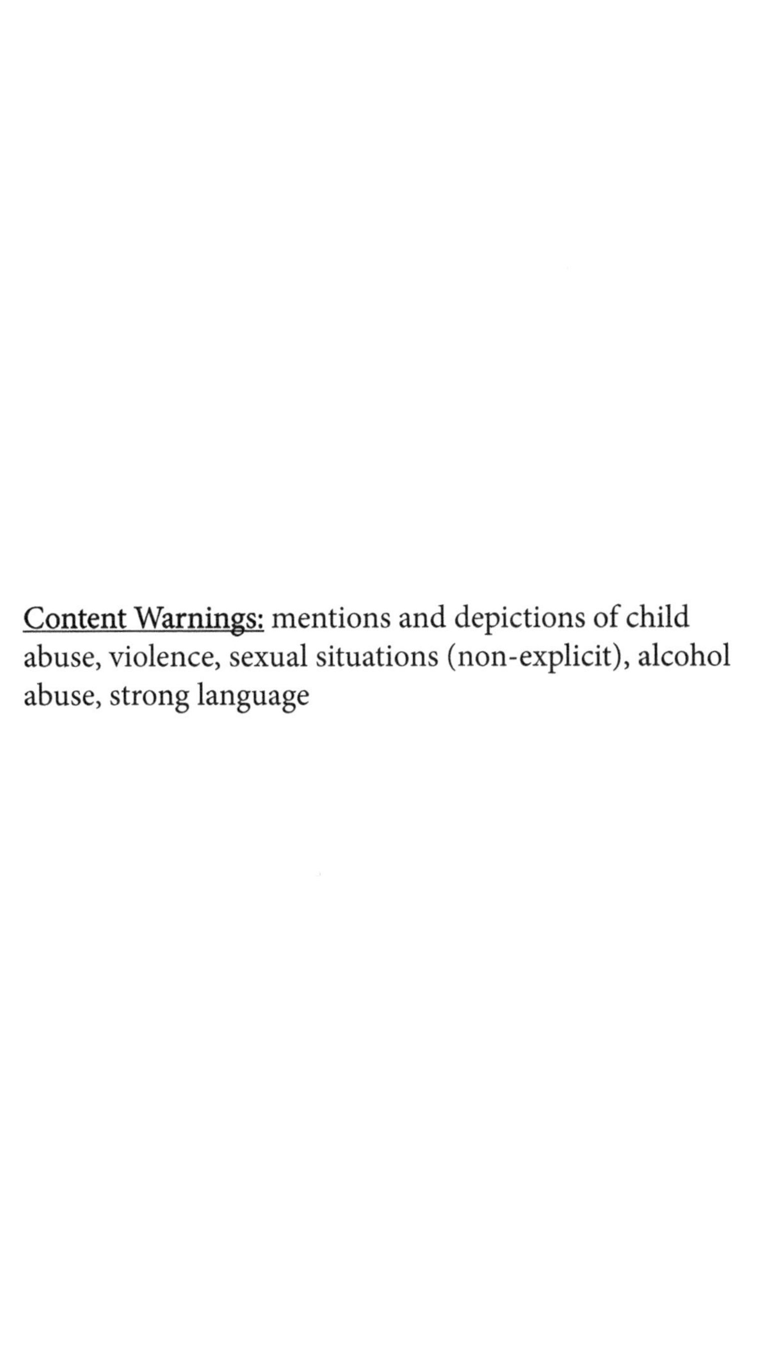

<u>Content Warnings:</u> mentions and depictions of child abuse, violence, sexual situations (non-explicit), alcohol abuse, strong language

1
SEPTEMBER 1985

"I'm sorry, Derek."

He didn't seem fazed as she said it. Instead, he just pinched his cigarette between his thumb and pointer finger. A stream of smoke slid up from his lips and past his nose. He looked at her only through the corner of his eye, so he probably couldn't quite see the way her brows were furrowed in worry.

He pulled the stick away from his lips, licked them, then pulled it back. "Sorry about what?" There was no curiosity or concern in his voice; it was relaxed. She knew it took a lot to rattle him, and this wasn't anything new. But that bubble of fear rose in her chest, because she knew once she said it, he wouldn't act so careless.

She knew that he would be far, far more than worried. And it would be her fault.

Becca Lewis had run the words over and over in her mind, barely getting any sleep. Knowing that what she had done would mean a change in Derek's life. Just a simple call would alter everything for him.

Logically, and perhaps emotionally, it was 100% the right thing to do. After everything he had said and everything she had seen, she knew this was necessary. But it hadn't made her any less terrified to do it.

And it didn't make her any less petrified to see how he would react.

"I had to do it."

That piqued his interest, if only slightly. His brow raised, but his attention remained on the end of the cigarette, puffing in the corner of his mouth, as he pocketed his hands. His head rested against the brick wall behind him, his eyes fully on her. They squinted slightly.

"You can go a little faster, sweetheart. I'm not a quick learner, but you know I'm also not very patient. Get along with it. What did you do?"

She swallowed, once, twice, then the tears started to form. They pinched at the corners of her eyes, and she had to close them as she finally said it, wincing. "I had to tell them about your dad."

Her eyes stayed shut for a few seconds, but unlike what she'd expected, there was only silence. She had expected him to curse and yell, punch a wall or something. Instead, nothing.

That alone made her open her eyes. She wished she hadn't.

The cigarette was still in his mouth, but it was frozen. The smoke that had been seeping out seemed to stay in place, as if there was no air to move through. She might have thought time had stopped if it weren't for the slow, disconnected blink of Derek's blue eyes, or the stony, hard stare behind them. The same way he was when he showed up after a bad beating, with a purple bruise on his chin.

"Told *who*?" It was less a question and more a threat. There was a clip at the end of the sentence that cut into her.

A shudder ran down her shoulders, and it took everything in her to fight the urge to shake. "People who can help you, and Mal too." She hadn't planned to say much, expecting him to storm away before she could, so she hadn't prepared a thorough explanation. Instead, hurried reasons flooded before she could think. "That place isn't safe for you, and you know it. Jennifer obviously has no intention of helping, and I've seen how you leave that place. I've seen you, Derek, and I can't stand by and watch you pretend you're okay when you're obviously not. It's not normal, you know that, right? It's not normal to leave your home with new bruises every single day, and—"

She was interrupted by a smaller sound. A light flutter on the ground as the cigarette fell from his lips and hit the dirt. He made no move to put it out. The white and red end continued to burn.

And he was on her, his hands on her shoulders. His eyes grew wide, rabid, blue, and ringed with red, which added to the insanity behind them.

Despite it, his grasp didn't hurt, but it was firm. His fingers dug into her shoulders, and he towered over her. "*What* exactly did you tell them?"

He was cruel. Both to her and himself. She knew he already knew, but he was forcing both of them to relive the things never said aloud. Until now. "Derek—"

"What the *fuck* did you tell them, Becca?"

She squeezed her eyes shut again. "I said that I know your dad beats you to the point of drawing blood. That your stepmom watches it happen, and that I watched him punch you right in front of me. That Mal is in just as much danger, if you aren't around."

The pressure on her shoulders disappeared, and she opened to a sight entirely new to her. She had seen Derek Stokes at his worst. Scared and sad and broken. Crumbled on the ground and shaking, bleeding from his lips or nose.

But she had never seen him like this.

His eyes shifted, and he grabbed at his hair, pulling at the dirty-blond curls. He mumbled something she couldn't quite hear, but it sounded like the curses he had mumbled and screamed before.

The look in his light eyes, it wasn't the stony or broken look she was used to when he was afraid. She knew he hid so much, and his eyes were the closest she would ever get to fully understanding it. But when she caught a glimpse of them now, it was like a dam had been broken and everything Derek Stokes hid in that mind of his had burst into insanity.

"Why, why, why?" he muttered, his voice rising each time he said the word. "Why, why, why?" Louder and louder, and she couldn't help but take a step away from him, as he was practically screaming now. She'd never been afraid of Derek, but this was unpredictable. She had done something very, very wrong—and it finally broke him.

"Why would you do that? Who said I needed that? Who said anyone needed to know that? You promised you would keep your mouth shut."

She swallowed something heavy and bitter that caused her words to come out quiet and shaky. "I did it to help you."

He laughed a laugh so unhinged, she flinched, and her back hit something smooth and cool. She hadn't realized she was already backed against the bleachers.

"I didn't ask you to help me!" His scream burst over her face, and she whimpered.

Part of her expected him to grab her again, but all that was left was a cold space where he had been, and he was back against the opposite red brick wall, leaning forward, as if he might be sick.

She usually knew how to handle these situations, but now she was unsure.

She reached out her hand and laid it warily against his shirt, which had become damp in just the past few seconds.

He flinched when touched, and in a second, was on the other side of the hidden area behind the bleachers.

"Derek—"

"Get away from me."

Her heart shattered. "Derek—"

"I never want to fucking see you again. You are *nothing* to me."

A deep shuddering flinch racked her entire body, and she stumbled back a few steps. Derek was scared.

He had always been scared—but what she did had brought it all to the surface. He was scared of what his dad would do once he found out someone had been told. Scared of how people would look at him once they realized where those bruises came from. Scared of everything there was.

She knew all this. He had told her these things in the dark of the night, when he couldn't even see her face in the forest or her bedroom. The only times he could truly open up were when it was too dark to see anything else.

But she had brought all those fears to reality. He had trusted her more than anyone else in the world, and by making that call, she had committed the ultimate betrayal.

"Get out."

2
SEPTEMBER 1985

After

Derek was not at school the next day. Or the next. Or the next.

Derek Stokes had vanished.

She only knew he wasn't just avoiding her, because Mal had shown up at her house in the evening two days after it happened, panting and red-faced from running.

"Mal." She took in Derek's younger stepsister's appearance and led her into the house, closing the door. It echoed slightly off the walls; the way doors only do in an empty house. It did that even when her mom was home, but since it was just Becca alone with Mal it resonated a little louder. "What's wrong?"

Mal took a few heavy breaths, then tears started to pour down her tan face. "Do you know where Derek is?"

Becca furrowed her brows. After that day behind the bleachers, she had done the last real thing she could for Derek and just stayed away from him. She hadn't tried to reach out. Hadn't tried to explain her side anymore. As far as she knew, Derek simply wasn't coming to school.

"He's not at home? I thought he was there."

"He hasn't been home in a few days." Mal's voice choked as she said it. She sat on the couch and buried her face in her palms. That's when Becca saw the marks on her wrist, bruised and angry. "Mark's real mad too."

Becca felt like she was back on that forest road a year ago, when she had first met Derek sitting on the side of the street.

Middle of the chilly autumn and he had a bloody nose and bruised face left behind by his father Mark. She blinked and shook away the memory.

Sickening guilt started to build in her stomach. She should have checked in on him, should have at least tried to figure out how he was doing instead of avoiding him. She should have made sure everything was okay for him and Mal. That was the point of her reaching out to someone in the first place, she'd wanted to help them both.

"What happened?" Her voice shook as she gently grabbed onto Mal's wrist and pulled the sleeve up to expose the full extent of the bruise. Long, thick, dark lines wrapped around the entirety of it. Becca's breath caught, and she thought she might puke. She was asking the obvious. If Derek had not been home since she told him, Mark needed someone else to turn his attention to when he was angry.

"Someone came to the house a few days ago after school. They were asking questions about Derek and me, asking if we liked it in Highburg. If everything was okay." She paused to sniffle a bit and pulled her arm out of Becca's hand. She pulled the sleeve down and grasped it in her fingers to hide the array of reds and blues and purples. "After they left, Mark was pissed, throwing things around. Then he realized Derek wasn't home and started asking me what was going on. I didn't know, so…" She shrugged, her eyes stuck on the wood-paneled walls as her hand picked at a frayed thread from her denim jacket. "Whatever. I just need to find Derek."

"You don't have any idea where he might be?"

Mal finally met Becca's eyes, her eyebrows knit and expression desperate. "You know him better than anyone. I thought you would."

"I—" Becca faltered. She had been avoiding questions about Derek at school, trying to not bring more attention to either of them. But this was not something she could avoid. "We had a fight. He wanted me to stay away."

Mal's dark eyes went wide. "Is that why he's gone?"

Becca sighed and tried to will back the tears that were begging to come out. "It's part, I'm sure." She got up for a moment when neither of them seemed like they could think of anything else to say. She gave Mal a moment to herself and went to the kitchen to grab her a glass of water.

With a wall between them, she finally let the biting tears out. As water from the faucet flowed into the cup, she pressed a hand over her mouth and let the sobs free, muffling them as best she could.

This was partially her fault. Would it have been better to just keep quiet or to not tell Derek what she had done? It was hard to say, but it wasn't hard to realize that, no matter what she chose, someone would get hurt. Now Derek was missing, and Mal was bruised, and she didn't even know if the people she had called were going to do anything like they said they would.

It only took three seconds to fill the cup, but she cried in the kitchen for close to a minute as the water hid her gasps. Mal might be fourteen, three years younger than Becca and Derek, but she wasn't stupid and soon would realize what was going on.

Becca pulled herself together as best as she could and shut off the tap. She stared at the half-dead floral assortment her mother had bought last time she was here until her breathing slowed. Becca didn't know why her mom always brought flowers home when she was never around long enough to take care of them, leaving the responsibility to Becca. She wiped away the tears and blinked to clear her eyes. Before she left the kitchen, she grabbed the flowers and chucked them into the trash then slapped a small, soft smile on her face and reentered the living room.

Mal watched as Becca crossed the room and set the full cup of water on the round wooden coffee table. It made a dull clunk that broke a tense silence between them. She knew Mal caught the lingering redness in her eyes when she saw the sympathetic frown on the girl's tan face. Mal shouldn't be concerned about Becca, she had other stuff to worry about.

"Mal." Becca pulled herself together, sat down on the plaid-upholstered couch, and gestured for the girl to take the glass.

Mal did so out of politeness.

"Those people that came to your house, did they say who they were?"

There was a pause as Mal slowly sipped at the liquid. Then she pulled the glass away and nodded. "Child Protective Services. They pulled me aside without mom and Mark and asked if I felt safe with Mark. Then they asked if I knew where Derek was." She stared at the water.

"What did you tell them?"

She shrugged, nonchalant, but her tense shoulders gave away her anxiety. "I told them I was fine, and that I thought Derek was just out with some friends."

"But that's not true, is it?"

Mal sighed and put the water back down. "I'm sure Derek is off doing something crappy, but I couldn't tell them about Mark. What if he overheard it? It would only make things worse around that place anyway." She reached out, and Becca jumped as small, cold fingers wrapped around her hand. "You have to help me find Derek. I'm sure things will get better if he comes home. Mark thinks that Derek is the one who told them, so if Derek just comes home and tells him he didn't do it, he'll calm down."

The desperation was palpable. Her eyes begged with such intensity, Becca froze.

Mal was not stupid, no, but she also hadn't been the main victim of Mark's abuse until now. If Derek went home, things wouldn't get better. They never did. If Derek went home, things would only get better for Mal, but they could become worse for Derek. If Mark thought Derek was the one who called CPS, there was no way he'd believe him, even if he claimed he wasn't the one who did it.

Becca shuddered at the thought of what would happen then.

For the first time, Becca was glad Derek had disappeared, because it meant he was safe from his father's wrath. But it didn't change the fact that not everyone was—Mal was still there, and she wouldn't be able to hold up against her stepdad the way Derek did.

"I'm sure Derek is fine, wherever he is, but I'll try and find him. Why don't you stay here tonight? We can ask Jane if she wants to join too." Becca had introduced the girls to each other half a year ago, and they'd become fast friends. It might help Mal to have someone with her while she went through this.

"I'll have to call my mom and ask."

The same mom who stands by and lets abuse happen. Becca kept the bitter thought to herself and smiled at Mal, who smiled back. "Okay, you can use the phone. Call Jane too. I'll make you guys some popcorn while you pick out a movie.." She gestured to the wall where she'd stored her assortment of favorite VHS tapes for the days when the house was a little too quiet without her mom around.

"Thank you, Becca."

Becca ran a hand over Mal's tousled black hair and nodded. "Anytime, Mallory. You know you're always welcome here."

***

Becca jumped when there was a knock at the door. It drew her attention away from her thoughts, and she realized she'd bitten her nails down to the point of almost drawing blood. It had taken her years to break that nasty habit, yet only a few days for it to come back at frightening speed.

She brushed the raw tips of her fingers against her jeans and answered the door.

Becca smiled at the short-haired girl who stood there. Jane grinned up at her. In her arms was a small overnight bag and a pouch of what looked like some sort of snack.

"Hi, Becca," Jane greeted her, entering when Becca stepped aside.

Becca tried to give the girl her attention, but, really, she was more focused on the faded blue truck that sat idle in the driveway. Sheriff Winston Wade watched them through the windshield.

"Hi, Jane. Mal is upstairs washing up. Why don't you join her?"

Jane nodded enthusiastically and dropped her belongings on the ground before rushing up the stairs.

Normally, Becca would have just waved Winston away to let him know his daughter was inside safe, but today she stepped out onto the porch and closed the door behind her. Today was different.

Her body language must have given that away, because once he realized she was walking toward his car, he shut off the engine and stepped out. He raised a single brow in a wordless question.

Aside from her mom, Winston was the only other adult in this town she trusted. He and Jane were like family to her. When her mom started taking out-of-town jobs, Winston became Becca's caretaker while she bounced back and forth between her house and his until she was old enough to remain home alone for longer periods of time. Now, he came by once or twice a week to make sure she had enough food or to bring Jane over for sleepovers with Mal ever since she introduced the girls to each other.

"Hey, Winston." Becca greeted him.

"Hey, kiddo." He nodded in greeting. "Where's your mom at now?"

"She's in Michigan for a few weeks. She said she'd be back soon. That's what I get for having a traveling nurse as a mother." She shrugged and tried to sound unbothered. And really, she wasn't. She was used to it by now. It had helped when Derek showed up and they were able to keep each other company.

Which didn't seem like it would be happening again anytime soon.

Despite her smile, Winston's frown made it obvious he knew something was off. He wouldn't even need police training to be able to decipher that. "Okay, what's up?"

She sighed and dropped the carelessness she tried to wield

while easing into the subject that was pushing violently on the back of her mind. "Have you heard anything on Derek Stokes?"

He frowned. "Nothing past what I helped you with last week." Aside from the CPS call she had made, Winston was the only person she told what was going on in the Stokes home. He had been the one to give her the number and the encouragement and the statistics to show her how serious it was to get in contact with the right people.

When she'd told him Derek wouldn't admit anything to the police, all he said was that the police could do nothing without evidence. So the next best thing was to turn to the people whose name was literally "Child Protective Services."

We would need to be there in the middle of Mark Stokes beating his kid, he had said, *Otherwise, it would be easy to talk his way out of it.*

Becca hadn't wanted to sit around and try and catch a moment where Derek was getting beaten to a pulp to call the police. She wanted something to be done *now*. So she had made that call.

"You haven't heard anything?" Her mind went blank.

"Was there more to hear?"

She swallowed and bit her lip. "Derek has been missing for a couple days…I thought they made a report or something."

"That long?" Winston sounded shocked. He pulled his hat off and rubbed at his unruly hair. "Jesus, Becca, why didn't you tell me that earlier?"

"I just found out myself." Her defenses rose and her hands twisted into fists. Winston might be a constant in her life, but he really had a hard time with kids, even with a daughter of his own.

"I thought he was your best friend. Wouldn't you notice your best friend missing?"

"He is my best friend! Or he was…" She sighed and glared at him. "We got into a fight when I told him I called CPS. He told me to leave him alone, so I did. I thought he was avoiding me, but apparently, he hasn't been home since. And now Mal is here, and Mark has hurt *her*, because Derek isn't around, and

I don't know what the *hell* to do, Winston. My best friend is missing, and his little sister is terrified of her house, and those damn CPS people you told me about went and then left her there alone after everything. And I...I..."

Everything she had been holding in since her conversation with Derek two days ago came out in earth-shattering sobs that echoed off the suburban houses around her. Tears streamed down her face and dripped from her chin onto the dry concrete under her feet. Her legs could no longer hold her up and she dropped into a crouch, burying her eyes into her fists.

The very first promise she ever made to Derek was that she would simply be there for him if he needed it. Somehow, she had single-handedly managed to ruin that to the point where he didn't want to be anywhere near her for anything.

She stayed for what felt like minutes, but, in reality, was probably only seconds. A heavy hand came down on her shoulder, and then a few moments later, two strong hands pulled her back to her feet and into an awkward but warm embrace.

Winston was not the affectionate type, but Becca appreciated the effort.

He shushed her sobs for a few moments, his hands finding something to do by patting the back of her head. "Hey, kid, I'm sorry, okay?" He stepped back so she could look at his face and see the genuine regret at his words. "It's not your fault, alright? Nothing about this is your fault. You saw someone who was hurting, and you wanted to help them. You've done good."

"But it hasn't helped anyone. It only hurt them more."

"But it isn't over. Listen, I'll get people on the lookout. For now, look out for yourself and that girl. See if you can find anything about where Derek is. Who knows, he might be closer than you think."

Becca took a deep breath and stepped back, letting Winston's comforting hand fall from her shoulder. She sniffed and brushed away her slowing tears. She didn't feel better, but she didn't feel like complete shit. He was right. Maybe Derek could be found easily, if she just started looking.

She nodded. "Thanks, Winston."

He smiled. "Anytime, kid."

She turned and walked back toward the house.

"Oh, and one more thing," he called out to her.

She stopped and peeked over her shoulder.

"Can you at least stay in tonight? I don't want my girl running around at night looking for someone."

She smiled, loving the protective side of this father for his daughter. "Alright."

"'Night, Rebecca."

"Goodnight."

She turned back and walked inside as his truck roared back to life and left the driveway.

When she was back inside, the girls were already situated in front of the TV. There was a wash of relief to see that Mal was safe for now, smiling softly and enjoying *Bedknobs and Broomsticks*. She took note of the long-sleeved shirt Mal had picked to wear from Becca's closet as pajamas, then locked the front door and left the girls to safely enjoy their night alone.

She, instead, grabbed a notebook, a phone book, and headed to the telephone. While the sounds of upbeat trumpets played on in the background, she settled into a stool at her counter and began dialing the numbers of anyone who might know where Derek Stokes was.

*****

"Becca."

She gasped and rose from where she had fallen asleep. For a few moments, she forgot where she was. There was still no sunlight coming in through the dark windows, and once she took in the surroundings, she realized she was exactly where she had been before—sitting at the kitchen counter, with the phone book open to page three hundred, which had become her makeshift pillow. The phone was off its hook and in her hand—the dial tone faint away from her ear.

Mal was looking at her, her mouth open in surprise, since Becca had popped up so suddenly from her uncomfortable slumber. Becca glanced at the clock on the wall. Ten o'clock.

"What?" She stood up, alarmed. "Are you okay?"

Mal nodded. "I'm fine." She said in a low whisper.

Becca relaxed and sat back down, rubbing at her eyes. She must have been asleep for half an hour, and her lower back ached from sitting at the kitchen chair for so long. "Good."

"What's that?" Mal pointed at the open notebook with scribbles lining the page.

Becca's handwriting had been hasty, so even she could barely read the names of people she had scrawled in the off chance they would be someone to contact about Derek, and it was even messier from where she had scribbled out several others. Becca covered it with her hand.

Becca felt low. No one knew where Derek was. Even Brent and April, who were the only options she thought might lead somewhere, had just said that Derek's favorite whore should be the one to keep track of him and hung up. She knew it was a long shot, considering they'd not been friends with him for a while, but at this point, she'd been desperate. Only one person had seen Derek, but it was the day of their fight, and they couldn't remember what time it was. Plus, nothing they gave her was anything to go off of.

Dead end after dead end after dead end.

"Why are you awake?"

"I couldn't sleep, and then I remembered something. I think I might know where he is." Mal's voice was cautious, a little nervous.

Becca's heart spiked the same way it did when Mal woke her, and her sore back straightened. "What? Where?"

"I saw a map in Derek's car the other day. I didn't think anything of it then, but it was a map for Madison, Wisconsin."

As quickly as her hopes flew, they lost the momentary momentum and plummeted down deeper into the pit than before. Becca sighed, as she hid her helpless disappointment behind a halfhearted smile.

"That's my map. I put it there for him to look at. I was looking at the college there, and we were thinking of visiting for a little bit. That's why it was in his car."

Mal deflated. Her hopeful eyes lost their spark. "Oh."

"It's a good thought, though, Mal, but—"

A thought. A small one, like the simple passing of a fly, buzzed through her head, and she stopped. Madison, Wisconsin. It was about two hours north of Highburg, and a direct route by freeway up across state borders. It was about as direct you could get to anywhere from this town.

The one person who had seen Derek the day of the fight. They'd told Becca they saw him driving north out of town toward the freeway. It sounded normal to Becca at first. Derek had driven that route day after day to get home.

But Derek never made it home. What were the chances of him continuing two hours north, all the way up to the same city they had been talking about?

"Becca?"

Her entire body nearly lost connection to her brain. She jumped and grasped the edge of the table as the world seemed to fall from under her. Mal was looking at her, lips turned down in confusion. "Madison."

"What?"

"I think you're right."

Mal's eyes widened and she inhaled sharply. "I am?"

The ache of her back disappeared, and her exhaustion evaporated under the rush of adrenaline. "He's in Madison."

Mal blinked rapidly, looking urgently at Becca for anything else she could give her. "What do we do?"

Becca picked up the phone that was still lying beside her. "I need to make some calls."

OCTOBER 1984

Before

Halloween was either the worst or best part of the year in Becca's book. This year could arguably be considered the worst of the worst.

That damned party had left her standing alone at damn Ruby's house, as the rest of her friends disappeared. She managed to find her friend Marty as he stormed out, with his new ex-girlfriend, April, on his heels, begging for forgiveness. Not much time to ask questions and receive answers.

Not long after, the cops arrived while she was trying to find a ride, and she had been left hiding in the forest behind Ruby's house until the lights of the cop cars disappeared. The only solace in the entire situation was that she had dressed as a cute rabbit rather than a sexy one, so she wasn't entirely freezing in the dark.

But that was where the relief died, because it would take about an hour to walk back to her house from there, and her mom was out of town—again.

She cursed as she began the trek from the northern side of town to the southern. She passed through some of the nicer suburbs, similar to where Marty lived, and then through some of the more run-down areas. But her own house was on the other side of a forest, and while walking straight through it would have been quicker, she had seen enough of those slasher films to know that it was the perfect way to get slaughtered. So, instead, she stuck to the road that wound around the deepest part of the woods and connected her subdivision with another.

Cars sped past her, and she regretted her outfit choice. A damn bunny. No one wanted to pick up a damn bunny on the side of the road, and if she tried to stop anyone by standing in the middle, she would just end up roadkill.

So she stuck to the edges and cursed throughout the entire dark part of the area—and pulled off the ears once she realized they were still on her head.

Halfway home, she saw a car sitting on the side of the road. She paused and looked at it from a distance. She could tell it was something nice, and more than that, it was something familiar. She just couldn't place her finger on it quite yet, but whoever it was, maybe they would give her a ride the rest of the way home.

She approached it cautiously, trying to see if there was anyone in there, and when she was next to the driver's side window, she cupped her hands and peered inside. It was empty. But from the heat of the hood, it hadn't been there very long.

She tried to open the door, but it stuck. Locked.

"Dammit." She kicked at some pebbles, and turned back to the road, ready to walk the rest of the way. Who the hell left a perfectly good car on the side of the road like that?

Then she saw him. Leaning against a tree, his head tilted back against its trunk.

She didn't recognize him at first, and from the distance she thought it might have been a dead man. But then he coughed and spat something onto the ground, and she realized he was very much alive.

"Hello?" she called out.

It was so dark she couldn't make out any features, but she could see him flinch at the sound of her voice. His head leaned forward, and she could feel the moment his gaze landed on her. He didn't say anything.

She walked closer to him, and realized he was wearing a leather jacket and a pair of acid-washed jeans. A step closer, she realized he wasn't wearing a shirt. Certainly not suitable for sitting on a roadside in the middle of the night in October.

"Are you alright? Is this your car?"

Only a couple yards away, and she finally recognized him. Those long dirty blond curls, that face. It was surprising that it took her so long to figure it out. Even the car made sense now, since she'd seen him driving it every day to school.

"Derek?"

He looked up at her, then his eyes glazed down over her costume and back up. "What the hell are you supposed to be?"

She frowned and held up the ears in her hand. "A rabbit."

He didn't laugh. In fact he barely showed any emotion. At least that she could see. "It looks stupid."

She already knew that, but she still rolled her eyes and crossed her arms. "At least I dressed up. You're not even wearing a shirt under your jacket. *That* looks stupid."

She didn't know much about Derek. In fact, this was the first time she had ever spoken to him. But she knew he was a major flirt, who targeted any girl or woman he came into contact with. So part of her expected that he would make a remark about how he looked better without clothes or that women were dying to see him tonight.

He said nothing.

He just leaned his head back against the tree again, and Becca realized he was looking up at the sky.

She followed his gaze and saw the stars. Millions of them— absolutely extraordinary. But not what she would expect Derek Stokes to be admiring, half dressed in the cold.

"What are you doing out here?" She stepped closer, and when she did, he flinched slightly. She stopped. "Are you alright?"

"Jesus, don't you have anything better to do?" he snapped.

She stepped back, putting more distance between them. With it went the clarity she could see of his face. "Sorry, it's just…the party ended, like, thirty minutes ago and now you're out here alone, and it's freezing, and…" She almost didn't say what she wanted to, but the darkness gave her more courage than she would have if they could see clearly. "To be honest, I thought something might be wrong."

"As you can see, I'm perfectly fine. Now move along and leave me be."

She sighed and backed away some more. "Sure. Whatever."

There went her ride.

She was about to turn when another car passed by, just quick enough for her to catch the way the headlights hit Derek's face and illuminated the answers for her. She gasped, and in a second the lights were gone, but she had already seen everything.

"Holy shit."

He seemed to realize he'd been exposed. The blooming bruises under his eye, on his cheek, and his jaw. The dried blood coating his nose and the few drops staining his bare chest.

He rose from his spot and shoved past her, heading toward his car.

Becca knew she had about three seconds to decide. It only took her one to move.

She grabbed his arm and pulled him to a halt, spinning him so he was facing her. This time, she was close enough to see the damage, even in the darkness. "Holy *shit*. What happened?"

She had watched from the sidelines, countless times since he moved here, as he pummeled others and received a punch or two to his own face, but she had never seen him walk away from a fight with more than a small bruise. Now, his entire face was an array of colors.

He tried to pull out of her grasp, but she was stronger than she looked and pulled him closer as her hand lifted instinctually— fingers lightly touched the spots where red littered across his jaw.

He hissed as they connected, and she paused. When he didn't push her away, she continued to examine him. She was no doctor, but being raised by a nurse had taught her a little.

"I told you to mind your own business," he said again, but his voice didn't hold the same venom as before. Now it sounded defeated, as if whatever fight was in him had vanished the second she stopped him.

"This is my business now."

He didn't respond, and she reached up with her white fuzzy sleeve and wiped away the almost-dried blood under his nose. She didn't care about stains at the moment.

His nose wrinkled at the feel of the fake fur brushing against it.

"Do you have any bandages?" she asked. "Or water or something? You should really clean these."

"I know what to do."

She didn't like to think about what that insinuated, so she ignored him and continued trying to catch his eye for an answer.

He sighed and relented. "In my car. Passenger side."

Becca pulled him with her to his car and told him to wait right outside the passenger side. He unlocked the car for her and leaned against the hood of the Monte Carlo, looking up at the sky like before.

She found a few fast-food napkins in the compartment, along with a half-empty water bottle. She wet the napkins and walked back over to him. His attention turned to her, following her every movement as she got to work patting the injuries. His nose was easy to wipe up. There wasn't much she could do about his bruises, but there were a few cuts on his jaw that needed cleaning. He was lucky nothing was broken, which she checked by prodding around at his face.

When she was done, she wadded up the dirty napkins and threw them in the cupholder to be taken out later.

His eyes didn't leave her the entire time.

She closed the car door, and they once again basked in the silence and darkness of the forest road. Him leaning against his car, her standing there, unsure of what to do now.

"How does it feel?"

"Like hell."

She shrugged. "I guess that makes sense."

Silence.

A million thoughts kept it from being too quiet, and she wondered what she should say. Should she just give up on getting a ride at all? Maybe just walk away? Should she ask for a ride? Instead, she settled on something different.

"What happened?"

He didn't answer. She realized maybe that was the wrong question and backtracked.

"I mean, you don't have to—"

"My dad."

She frowned, surprised. "What?"

"He's an asshole."

It clicked in her head, and her breath caught. "Your *dad* did this?"

His gaze finally left her. No longer studying her, he stared at his feet, which she just realized were bare. The sight of him, bruised and beaten and lightly clothed…it stung her heart more than she cared to admit.

His dad. She hadn't seen her deadbeat dad in nearly ten years since he left her and her mom behind without a word. Horrible as he was for that, the little of him she does remember would never have done something like *this* to her.

"Jesus. Why would he do that?"

"Came home late, didn't like that. Was drunk, didn't like that either."

"That's it? He did…*this* because of something like that?"

"He's an asshole."

She scoffed, nearly to the point of laughing. Not because it was funny, but because of how extremely absurd it was—so shocking she wasn't quite sure how else to respond. "Yeah, no kidding."

He paused. "Did you just laugh?"

She froze. "No. I mean, yes, but not because it's funny. It's just…" The unwelcome laugh slipped out again, and she covered her lips as it if would stop it. "It's just one of those situations, where you aren't sure how else to react, and you know you should be serious, but you can't help laughing because you need to be serious, and then it makes things worse, and then I look like a total idiot and—oh, god—I *sound* like a total idiot, don't I? I'm sorry, this is really messed up. Please don't think I think any of this is funny, because it isn't. I just want you to be okay, because your dad is an asshole, and you don't deserve what he did and—"

She was cut off by a chuckle, but it wasn't her. Derek was smiling right at her, a small, amused huff coming from him. Now that she thought about it, she didn't think she had ever heard him laugh before. At least not like this. A laugh that you couldn't help, one that was completely inappropriate but just happened anyway. And he had a smile on his face—not a smirk, not a frown, not a sneer. A smile.

She blinked. "Are *you* laughing?"

"Obviously."

Another inappropriate smile forced its way to her lips. "Why?"

"Because we shouldn't."

Her fingers covering her mouth no longer worked to keep her amusement in. "We really shouldn't." She giggled and moved to lean against the car next to him.

In a matter of seconds, she was caught in an unfortunate case of unstoppable giggles. Both of them were. For a few minutes, all they could hear were the two of them laughing at nothing.

She bent over, grabbing onto her stomach as the enjoyable pain ached in her gut. He leaned back, staring at the sky as he chuckled.

Becca was able to take a breath again once it slowed, and they both gained control of themselves. All that was left was heavy breathing. She wiped invisible tears from her eyes and glanced at Derek, who was looking at her.

He wasn't smiling the way he'd laughed, but he didn't look upset. He looked, if anything, at ease for a short moment.

Becca couldn't deny that Derek Stokes was the most beautiful boy she had ever seen in her life—his dirty curls and dark blue eyes made him a topic of interest to most girls in this town. Even more so standing in front of her with bruises on his face and a peaceful smile lingering for a moment. She could *really* see what was great about him when she saw him like this. It was a completely new Derek Stokes.

She cleared her throat and stepped away from the car. "What are you going to do?"

He shrugged. "Go home."

"Is that okay?"

"It'd be worse if I didn't."

"Okay." She looked down the road. She wasn't sure what time it was, but she was lucky her mom wasn't at home. She would have been worried, too, but she wouldn't have reacted the way Derek's dad did. "Well then, goodnight." She gave him one last awkward smile and turned.

She got all of three steps before he called out, "Aren't you going to ask for a ride?"

She sheepishly turned back to him. "I…I mean I wasn't planning on it."

He gestured to the car and walked to the driver's side. "Just get in."

She wasn't going to say no. She hopped into the passenger side as he revved the engine to life. Neither of them said anything else the entire way. What had been said was all that needed to be. She didn't want to push it by asking more questions, and he didn't seem like the type to offer up unnecessary answers.

Every now and then she peeked toward him, but he was focused on the road and didn't notice. When she pointed out her dark house, he pulled into the driveway.

She opened the door and stepped out, fully intending to offer him a quick goodbye before rushing inside. But something stopped her. "Can you wait a moment?"

He looked at her a second, then nodded.

She hurried into the house, fumbling with her keys until the door unlocked, and ran to the kitchen. In the notepad by the phone, she ripped out a small piece and jotted down a few quick things:

Call if you need anything. I can sit quietly and listen or laugh with you. Whatever you need. She quickly signed her phone number.

Was this a smart move? Honestly, she'd had no interest in Derek Stokes before now. She was worried he would take this wrong. She didn't want to be a fling. She saw a boy hurting alone, and she knew how it felt to be alone. She wanted to give him a companion and nothing more. But only if he wanted it.

Even if he ripped this paper up, right in front of her, at least she'd tried.

Like he promised, he still sat there waiting. This time, there was a cigarette in his hand. His face was illuminated by the porch lights, and he watched her run up to his window. He rolled it down and looked up when she reached her hand in.

"Here."

He took it but didn't open the folds to read what was inside. He only watched her carefully. "Thanks."

"Good night."

He smiled again, a puff of smoke rising from his lips in a way that would soon become very familiar to her. "Good night to you too."

She watched Derek Stokes drive away from her house at two a.m., and she had no idea if he would ever open that paper.

SEPTEMBER 1985

After

The phone rang, going to the answering machine two times. Sure, Marty was an early sleeper, but he had always been good at picking up the phone, no matter what.

Sure enough, on the third try, there was a click, followed by a groan. "Hello?"

His voice was groggy, detached, and hoarse.

"I need your help, Marty."

"Oh, look who it is. If it isn't Little Miss I Can't Make It Because I'm Too Busy Moping About Derek Stokes. You know, I picked out your favorite movie and Nicole and I were left to deal with it alone. I hate *The Karate Kid* and you know it."

Shit. She had completely forgotten she'd had plans with her friends that night. Marty didn't know what was going on with her, because she couldn't tell him the full extent of what happened with Derek, but he had tried to make her feel better. Movies made her feel better, so he had invited her over for a movie night to get her mind off stuff.

Then Mal had arrived, and Becca had forgotten.

"Shit, I'm sorry Marty. I totally forgot."

"Clearly." He sighed, and she could imagine him running his hand over his face. "So what, did you find that asshole? Still don't understand why you like being his friend so much, but I'm guessing he's the reason your phone was busy all night."

Derek was the reason her phone was busy all night. But not because she was talking to him. "That's actually what I'm calling about."

"This doesn't sound promising," he mumbled.

She ignored him. "I need you to drive me somewhere."

"Right now?"

"Yes."

"Where?"

She hesitated and bit her lip. She knew he wouldn't take this well. "Madison."

"The fuck?" he blurted, and there was a muffled rustle on the other end. "Madison? Why the hell do you need to go to Madison at—" there was a pause and the sound of him moving for a second, "—eleven at night?"

"It's a really huge favor, and I can explain it all, but the faster we get going, the better."

"Why can't your pretty little Stokes take you?"

She squeezed her eyes shut. "Because that's where he is, and I need to find him."

He groaned, sending out a few curses as he did so.

"If that's too much, can you at least come over and watch Mal and Jane while I find a car or something? I need someone to watch them."

"Oh *hell* no. I'll drive you to Madison, find someone else to watch those punks."

"They're not punks."

"Whatever. I'll be there in thirty."

Becca breathed a sigh of relief. "Thank you, Marty."

"Yeah, yeah, whatever."

The line clicked dead, and she hung up the phone. She was spoiled rotten in terms of friends. And now she really did need to find someone to watch the girls. She settled on a quick call to Winston's house, where he picked up quickly. He always stayed up late watching the television and sitting next to the phone when he wasn't working. A hazard of being sheriff is never really being off the clock.

She explained everything, and he understood. He would come get the girls, and they would spend the rest of the night at his place.

When she hung up, both Mal and Jane were awake and peeking around the corner at her expectantly.

"Both of you go gather your stuff up. Jane's dad will be here soon."

Jane left first, but Mal stayed behind. "Are you going to bring Derek home?"

Becca smiled gently. "I'm going to bring him back to Highburg. But I don't know if he'll be going home."

Mal's brow furrowed, a slightly angry look on her face as she crossed her arms. "So he can't go home, but I have to? It's not fair."

"No, it's not. That's why you need to stay with Jane for tonight while we figure stuff out for now, okay?"

She didn't look convinced. Becca sighed.

"It isn't fair to you or Derek. Neither of you should have to put up with any of that. We're going to try and help you."

Mal paused, looking into Becca's face, searching for something. Mal and Derek were not blood related, but there were some things similar about them. They both had that same stubborn streak and the same intuitive eyes.

"It was you, wasn't it?"

"What was?"

"You called those people."

Becca's breath shuddered, because, for a moment, she expected the same reaction she got from Derek. She wouldn't be able to stand it if Mal said even remotely the same words that Derek had.

But Mal and Derek were not that similar.

"Yes."

Mal nodded like she already knew that. "Then I'm expecting you to bring him back."

Becca's voice caught, and she didn't answer, because she couldn't give Mal the answer she wanted. She couldn't promise to make sure Derek made it home…where his father was.

Mal turned and walked from the room to follow Jane, and

Becca still couldn't say anything.

***

When Winston arrived, he helped the girls load up what they had. The kiddish excitement over a sleepover had mellowed out to tired, serious faces. Becca was glad she at least knew that Mal would be safe with Winston, probably more than anywhere else.

Becca had no plan for when she got to Madison. She expected to drive around the entire city until she found Derek's car, and if, for some reason, he didn't have his car, as implausible as that sounded, she didn't know what else would work.

She looked over Winston's shoulder at the girls staring at her through the windshield. Jane waved. Mal didn't.

"She has bruises up her arm, and they're recent. You've got to be able to do something with that."

He nodded. "I can try. At least I can start another report and get some eyes on the house." He paused to take in Becca's tired eyes. "You sure you should be heading there right now?"

"I have to try."

He sighed and reached into his back pocket to pull out something. He motioned her forward, and she reached out her hand as he put a crumbled twenty-dollar bill into it. "For gas or something. I dunno, whatever you need."

She smiled down at the money, grateful for his support right now. She had been worried he would push back against it, but instead, he gave her the proper backing. He believed her ridiculous story and even came to help out with the girls. "Thank you. I don't know how long we'll take, but I'll keep in touch. Just, make sure she's safe. See if there is anything you can do for them."

"Whatever you say, kiddo." He dropped a heavy hand on her shoulder and nodded. "Just don't tell your mother I had anything to do with this. She'll kill me."

"I won't tell her if you don't."

"Deal."

She waved as they left the driveway, but with the headlights in her eyes, she couldn't tell if they waved back. Their lights disappeared the same moment new onescame into sight, and a second car pulled into the driveway. Marty left his car idling as he got out and walked over to her.

"Jesus, you look like shit." His hands were in his pockets, and his dark, naturally textured afro was flattened on one side from sleep.

"Thanks for doing this."

"You owe me big time. You know I hate getting involved with that dickhead."

"I know." She smiled fondly at him. He talked big, acted real tough, but her best friend was a sweetie. There was nothing he wouldn't do, and she would gladly take a bullet for him as well. "I'll make it up to you later."

"You better."

"Let me grab my stuff."

She ran inside and turned down all the lights before grabbing the duffel bag she had stuffed with a dozen things she wasn't sure she would need. A single outfit, every dollar she had saved, and an array of medical supplies.

In Marty's car, she saw that he had also packed a bag, which she placed her own next to.

"You ready?" he asked, yawning and running a hand down the side of his face.

"Ready."

He nodded and put the car in reverse. "Let's go get that asshole."

NOVEMBER 1984

Before

After Halloween, it was like that night with Derek Stokes had never happened.

Becca never got a call, and when they returned to school, there was no sign that he even recognized her. While she watched him in the halls, not once did his eyes meet hers.

The only thing that proved she hadn't made the entire thing up was the torn notebook paper she had ripped out to write her number down for him.

She sighed and buried her face in her hands during Ms. Carmine's English lecture. She couldn't stop thinking about their encounter, and now she only felt like an idiot for giving him that paper. He probably threw it out as soon as she went inside.

There had been a few times she felt like someone was watching her—in the cafeteria, in the parking lot—but when she turned to look, Derek wasn't even looking remotely in her direction.

So she decided it was a lost cause and chose to forget it ever happened, just like he had.

Until that night.

Her mom was gone for only a week this time, and she had left in the morning. Becca decided that she wouldn't be doing anything fun for the day and hunkered down under a warm blanket with a cup of tea and David Letterman.

It wasn't uncommon for Marty or Winston to show up, even at night. So, when there was a knock at the door, she had expected

Marty to be standing there on the step—maybe looking for something to do, since he often complained about being bored after he broke up with his cheating girlfriend. Not as many girls were interested in him lately.

She pulled the door open, with some sarcastic remark already falling off her lips. "Oh how nice of you to—"

She stopped when she realized that Marty wasn't standing there. She hadn't turned on the porch light, so the figure was bathed in darkness, only lit from the bluish glow of the TV screen in the other room.

She sucked in a harsh breath—Derek Stokes stood there. Well, "stood" wasn't right. He was leaning one arm against the doorway, the same way she had seen him lean over girls against their lockers. But, despite the darkness, she could tell this situation was entirely different. He was swaying on his feet, his head bowed forward like he struggled to keep it upright.

Immediately her assumption was that he was drunk, and one strong whiff told her she was right.

"Derek?"

"You said to call if I need anything." His words were slurred, an incoherent mumble that she had to strain to decipher.

She looked behind him at the street. His car wasn't there. He moved slightly, and finally looked up at her, which made her wince. Once again, his nose was bloody, and he had a small welt under his eye. It wasn't as bad as it had been before, but it wasn't good. Not to mention he looked like he might collapse at any moment.

"You're the only person I could think of."

He tried to take a step in but swayed heavily to the point of almost falling over. She caught him just in time. And lucky she did, because he weighed a ton. If he had fallen, she would have struggled even more than she did trying to walk him from the doorway to the living room couch.

She forced his arm around her shoulders to give him a crutch, and he used it—leaning more than half of his body weight on her. She grunted and threw him onto the couch—wiping her hands together as he groaned against the cushions.

"Gentle." His hand came up against his forehead, rubbing at the skin as if to will away some foreboding headache.

"Jesus Christ, are you all right?" Becca asked, as she helped him take off his boots before he placed the dirty heels on her couch. "How did you get here?"

"I walked."

She could have guessed from the mud on him. "Where's your car?"

"I dunno." He closed his eyes, drifting off.

"Hold on there, cool guy." She patted his cheek gently to keep him from dozing, and he groaned again, but opened his eyes and shifted his head so he was lying against the armrest. "Let me clean you up before you pass out."

He grumbled something, but pushed himself into a sitting position while she ran into her kitchen and grabbed the first aid kit her mother kept there for emergencies.

When she came back into the room, Derek sat slightly more alert. He observed her movements as she prepared a swab for his bleeding nose.

It didn't make a whole lot of sense to her. He had ignored her for a while now, and suddenly he couldn't seem to look away. Luckily, she still hadn't turned on the lights, so the darkness made her feel more comfortable under his intense stare.

There were all sorts of new smells floating from him. Some strong cheap cologne, the musty scent of dirt and metallic blood. The tar of cigarettes.

"What happened?" She was gentle as she tended to his face.

"Too much." Okay, so he didn't want to go into detail. "But I can't go home."

She nodded. "Stay here then."

Derek didn't agree or object, he just watched as she unwrapped a small bandage and covered a scratch on his chin. He didn't move when she reached behind herself and grabbed a mug off the table and held it out to him. "You like tea?"

He shook his head, and she turned to put the mug back down.

A warm hand on her arm stopped her before she got rid of it, and she paused as he reached out and plucked the drink from her hand. "But I'm thirsty."

While he sipped on the hot beverage, Becca cleaned up the supplies, and for a moment, she was reminded of the other day when he'd stood against his car as she cleaned up the wet, bloody napkins.

They let several minutes of silence settle between them. The only sound was the quiet white noise of the television that went static during her aid. She hadn't bothered to turn it off.

"Want to talk about it?" Her voice was gentler than before, and she watched him carefully as he set down the now-empty mug.

Leaning back against the sofa, he sighed and shut his eyes again. "No."

She nodded and rose from her spot, carrying the dirtied supplies with her. "Okay, another time then."

She left him alone for a moment, put his mug away, and going to the closet where the spare blankets and pillows were.

When she came back, Derek was lying back on the couch with his maroon shirt unbuttoned to reveal his whole smooth chest, even more so than what had been exposed before.

"Come on," she said, and his head raised—taking in her arms filled with an assortment of blankets.

"Where?"

"Your bedroom for the night." She turned off the television and headed up the stairs. There was a groan as he shifted on the couch, and then the shuffling of him moving after her up the steps.

Down the hall and to the left, she opened the door to the empty room across the hallway from her own. It had a couple pillows on the bed, matching the floral quilt, but if Derek was anything like her, it wouldn't be enough, so she dropped the pile she'd brought with her onto the mattress and stepped aside.

He took in the area, still not fully sober, but not totally out of it.

"I don't have any clothes that would fit you, unfortunately, but there's a bathroom right there." She pointed at the room at the end of the hall, right between theirs. "You can wash up. Everything is in there, but if there's anything else you need, just let me know. I'll be in there." She pointed at her room.

A curious glint lit up his eyes as he stared at the bare outside of her door, but he didn't say anything.

There was nothing else to say. He obviously didn't want to talk much and that was okay. It was better he was here and quiet rather than somewhere he might get hurt. She wouldn't wish that on anyone.

"Okay." She backed away, toward her room. "Goodnight then."

"Is no one else here?" He asked.

He must have noticed that in any other circumstance, a concerned parent would wonder why their daughter was walking in with a random boy. But that wasn't the case in this household.

"It's only my mom and I and she's gone for a couple weeks. My dad's not around anymore." Understatement of the century, which he was free to interpret as he liked. She didn't even care if people assumed her dad was dead, it made her feel less abandoned to think that too.

"It must be nice to have this place to yourself."

She looked around the hallway, at the wood doors and the pictures that filled the place. Only a few of them were of her and her mom. "I don't know." She faced him and shrugged. "It's kind of nice having someone around."

They separated after that, and she closed her bedroom door softly behind her. She followed her normal nightly routine and sat in bed reading the book she had grabbed earlier that week at some small shop. But she meant what she'd said to Derek.

For so long, she had gone to bed in that house with just the sound of her own breathing, but now there was the sound of a door opening, and then another one closing. The hush of a shower turning on and running.

These sounds, while simple and insignificant to others, were more comforting to her than anything else. It used to sound like this before her mom started her job, and she missed those days. The words of her story were lost on her as she wished, a little selfishly, that this wouldn't be the last time Derek Stokes needed something from her.

After

"Beck, this is going to end up taking hours if we take one more wrong turn. I would rather turn around now than go to Madison anyway." Marty said, groaning as Becca adjusted the map in her hands to see it better.

"Not an option anymore, sorry."

"He's not *my* friend. I don't know why I'm being dragged into whatever trouble he's gotten into."

"He hasn't gotten into anything. Okay? It's my fault he's there." They were both exhausted and cranky from the first half of their journey, but she wasn't going to let even Marty Parr talk bad about Derek. Not when he had no idea what was going on.

"Then I should be thanking you that I haven't had to deal with him in class."

"Marty." Becca sighed, running her hands over her face.

He let go of the wheel and raised his hands defensively. "Okay, sorry. But a little explanation is needed now."

A numb sickness rose in the back of her throat, the truth bubbling there but unsure of whether it was okay to reveal or not. Maybe this was the least she owed him—but was it fair to Derek? "Derek, he…he has a difficult home life. I tried to get someone to help, but he freaked out and ran. His dad is not a good guy, and I'm scared I made things worse."

Marty was quiet, but his dark fingers threaded up into his hair as he took a deep sigh. "That's heavy." He shook his head, and she knew that she'd made the situation clear enough for him to realize the gravity. "Why didn't you tell me before?"

"Because Derek didn't want anyone to know."

"Have you talked to the sheriff about it?"

"Yes, and we are trying to figure out what to do, but right now, Derek isn't safe out there on his own, and we need to bring him home. Then we can figure everything out."

He sighed, shaking his head. "He shouldn't have dragged you into his shit. If that asshole hadn't left—"

"It isn't his fault. He's scared. You don't know how scared he is of his dad. Don't you dare blame him."

"I'll try, but you don't deserve any of this."

"*He* doesn't deserve it either, Marty. He's a kid too."

He stayed silent, his hands wrapped tightly around the steering wheel. Sometimes it was easy for all of them to forget that they were all really just a bunch of kids at seventeen. None of them knew how to really live on their own. None of them knew life without school and leaders and parents and security. It was hard to admit to themselves that none of them knew what to make of the future.

They were all moving parts of some story, and the things of the past were a result of something none of them could change. Luckily, they could do something about it now.

"How far?" He pressed on the gas, pushing their speed ten above the limit.

Becca lifted her map, using the signs and markings to understand exactly where they were. "Exit in three miles. We're almost there."

NOVEMBER 1984

Before

When Becca woke up the next morning, Derek wasn't there. She didn't realize it at first. She quietly opened her door and leaned slightly toward the guest room, trying to hear if he was awake.

When she heard nothing, she assumed he was still asleep, and went downstairs to throw together a quick breakfast for the two of them, including a pot of hot coffee and a glass of cold water with a couple of painkillers for the hangover he was sure to have.

The breakfast sat on the table in front of her, untouched, for nearly twenty minutes before she decided it was a good idea to go check on him. Surely, he wouldn't mind being woken for some food.

There was no answer when she knocked on the door, nor any sound. After ten seconds, she pushed the door open to see an empty room, with no sign of anyone having been in there at all.

She might have assumed their interaction had been a figment of her imagination. The bed looked untouched, the pillows perfectly fluffed and placed back where they always were. Like before, the only thing validating the entire experience was the small piece of paper on the nightstand, which looked like it had been ripped right off the corner of an old receipt, with a single word on it: *thanks.*

That was the last time Derek acknowledged her that year.

***

Something shifted after the new year in January. Her mom was always busiest in the winter months, so even though she was stationed "nearby" in Indianapolis, Becca had only seen her briefly on Saturday before she had to head back to the hospital on Sunday morning. Aside from that it was only a collect call or two for company.

Becca was always the loneliest during the winter months. Especially the two-week break from school, when Marty was away half the time in some tropical land and she was at home, like always, alone.

God, she wished she had made more of an effort to make other friends. Especially now that Marty had broken up with his girlfriend. Even when he was here, he was out a lot of nights on dates that went nowhere, and Becca had no desire to play third wheel.

So winter walks became her thing. Bundled in her heavy coat, face covered in a scarf, and hood hiding all her dark hair, she would walk about two miles a day in the freezing cold, just because it was better than sitting in that warm home alone.

As usual, on this day, she'd walked through the neighborhood and turned the corner down Maple Street, only to run directly into someone coming toward her at high speed.

"Shit," a soft voice said, as they both fell hard onto the sidewalk.

A very icy and unstable sidewalk, apparently, because as soon as Becca hit the ground, a sickening crunch sounded from under her. For a moment, she thought it might be her body, numbed by the cold, but when she realized she could move without any pain, she looked down to realize she had not fallen on the sidewalk at all, but a skateboard.

"Shit," the voice said again.

Becca looked up from the board to see a young girl with black hair and dark olive skin eyeing the broken board with a frown on her face. Both stayed still on the ground, and Becca bit her lip as sheepish guilt welled in her.

Great. She'd broken a little girl's skateboard.

If the universe wanted to make things even worse for her, the girl would start crying and make her parents come demand payment for breaking her board.

Becca bit her cheek and shifted uncomfortably. "I'm sorry."

By some miracle, the girl didn't cry. Instead, she just stood up and wiped her hands on her pants, before holding one out to Becca. "It's not your fault, I knew the ice would make it harder to stop."

Becca paused, then put her hand into the girl's, letting her help her up. She winced slightly at the tug on her wrist.

"Are you hurt?" The girl must have noticed Becca's strained expression and eyed her wrist from where she stood.

"Just a little twist. I think I'll be fine." Becca smiled to reassure her, and the girl didn't look like she wanted to argue. Now that she was standing up, Becca noticed the girl looked about thirteen or fourteen, older than she originally assumed because of her short height. Probably a freshman she'd never noticed. "Are you okay?"

"I'm fine." She stepped past Becca and picked up the now flimsy board. "But this isn't. I hate winter."

"I'm really sorry about that. I should have been paying attention."

"You don't happen to have a car, do you?"

"No." She smiled sheepishly. She could drive, but her mom wasn't willing to buy her her own car just yet. Extremely inconvenient, especially in times like this. "Sorry."

"It's fine." She waved it off. "I'll see you around."

With a piece of the broken board in each hand, the girl started to walk away. It was only then that Becca realized she was wearing barely any layers. Only a semi-thick jacket. No gloves or hat or anything.

"Wait!" Becca called after her, already removing her own gloves to hold out to her. "It's way too cold to be walking around without a coat. Why don't you take these to keep warm?"

"I'm fine. It's not too far." Clearly, this girl was the independent type.

"Please, it's the least I could do," Becca said.

The girl took a moment to think about it, but she still didn't look entirely convinced.

"Or at least let me walk with you so you don't pass out from hypothermia or something."

The girl's lips lifted into a small, amused smile. "Fine."

She turned and Becca kept pace next to her, the two of them taking up the width of the icy sidewalk. Becca kept her gloves in her hand though. It felt wrong to be the only one bundled up when the girl was probably freezing to death. She shoved them into her pocket.

"I'm Mal," the girl said first, not looking at Becca when she did.

"What?"

"My name, it's Mal."

Becca's brows raised. "Oh, I'm Becca. It's nice to meet you, Mal."

"Yeah." She still sounded a little awkward. "You too."

"Why were you skateboarding just now?"

She shrugged. "I like it."

"I mean, why when it's so cold out? People don't usually go out when it's like this, much less skateboarding or riding a bike."

"I used to skateboard all the time during winter in LA."

Becca turned to look at her. "You're from LA?"

"Yeah, we moved here a few months ago."

Apparently, there were quite a few people moving to Highburg from California recently. "Huh, I know someone else who moved from California."

She finally turned to look at Becca, her interest piqued. Perhaps the idea of someone else from her home state was exciting. "Who?"

She doubted that he and Mal would really have much in common. "Just a classmate of mine."

"Huh." Mal turned her attention back to their path.

A nice silence settled between them. Sometimes silence was deafening, awkward with an intense need to fill it. But now, it was comforting. Maybe it was because Becca was just glad she wasn't walking alone for once.

"You know, you don't have to walk me all the way. It's actually a lot farther from here. I kind of lied about it being close." Mal didn't look annoyed by the fact that Becca was walking with her, but she did look sheepish, maybe a bit embarrassed to admit she had lied about how far away her house was.

"Don't worry about it. I like walking."

"I would usually have a ride, but he said he was busy."

"Who did?"

"My stepbrother."

"Maybe you should have waited for him. It would be better than walking in the cold."

She scoffed. "No thanks. He's kind of an asshole, so I'd rather walk when I have the chance."

Becca smiled and laughed, the air creating a steaming visual of her breath.

Their brief conversation was cut short by a honk and the rev of an engine coming up from behind them. Both girls jumped in surprise, and Becca turned to see a familiar dark blue Monte Carlo approaching them. Her entire body tensed, and her eyes widened in surprise.

Meanwhile, Mal cursed under her breath and rolled her eyes. "That's him. Asshole."

Derek Stokes pulled to the curb right next to them, his fogged-up window rolled down to reveal him inside as a puff of smoke came from his mouth. His eyes were narrowed at Mal, not even noticing Becca right away.

"Get in. Thanks to you I missed out on a very important—" His hard eyes shifted to Becca midsentence, and he halted, freezing as he recognized her standing there. She wasn't sure if she should smile or wave or acknowledge him—instead she didn't react at all. He tapped his barely smoked cigarette into the side of the car door and dropped it into the road. "Rebecca."

Becca didn't realize until that moment that Derek had never said her name before. She also realized that she didn't even know he knew her name. Not until he said it with his voice light and surprised, his eyes conflicted.

Mal turned to look at her. "You know him?"

Becca tried to say something, but her throat was frozen shut. She wasn't sure how to answer.

Derek did it for her. "We're friends."

Friends. Becca and Derek had a…confusing relationship, to say the least. One she didn't fully understand, one she didn't really know existed. But friends? She was as surprised as Mal.

"Right." Mal looked between the two of them, clearly not convinced.

"Get in the back." Derek ordered Mal, taking his eyes off Becca for a moment to make sure the girl got his command. His noticed Mal's board. "And throw that out."

"I'm gonna fix it."

"Just get a new one. That one is shit now."

She groaned but walked around the side of the two-door coupe, opened the passenger door, slid the front seat forward, and slipped into the back.

Becca still didn't budge, and Derek turned his attention back to her. "You get in too." His order to her was much softer than it was to Mal.

Becca finally found the willpower to clear her throat. "Oh, uh, that's alright, I'm not far from here."

"I know where you live. I'm still not letting you walk home. Get in."

She saw Mal watching her from the back seat, waiting for her to get in, the door left open for her on the other side. She nodded and walked around, sliding in and shutting it.

They were moving the second it closed, and Becca was in Derek Stokes's passenger seat for the second time.

She expected Derek to take her right home, but he didn't. He continued along the way Mal had been leading her, and Becca hadn't recovered enough from the term "friend" to figure out how to ask where they were going.

The music on his radio filled any awkward silence with Van Halen's guitars and drums. He tapped his fingers on the steering wheel.

It was hard not to stare at him from the corner of her eye. This was the first time she had seen Derek Stokes this close in daylight, and all she wanted to do was search his face for some sort of answer she was sure she would not find there.

Instead, she stared straight ahead and focused on the road, giving her hands something to do by rubbing at the soreness that started to swell in her injured wrist as it thawed in the warmth of his car.

The movement caught Derek's attention, and suddenly his hand wrapped around her forearm. An outsider might think the grasp looked tight, but his touch was gentle as he pulled her coat sleeve up to look at the area her hand had rubbed red.

"Are you hurt?"

Mal answered for her. "She fell on my board and hurt her wrist."

"I told you not to ride that thing when it's icy out," he said over his shoulder.

Mal crossed her arms and leaned back with a frown.

Becca pulled her arm out of his grasp, and he let her. "I'm fine, really, it wasn't her fault I wasn't paying attention to where I was walking."

The car slowed down next to a new curb, in front of a small house.

"Get out. I'm gonna take her home," he ordered Mal, who, surprisingly, did not object. With a little seat shifting from Becca, she slipped out of the car and threw a small wave to Becca and flipped her middle finger at Derek.

"I didn't know you had a sister," Becca said, watching Mal walk up to the house and in the door with the broken skateboard still in her hands.

"Stepsister. And she's a pain in my ass."

"According to her, you're the asshole."

"Of course, she told you that."

"Well, are you? An asshole?"

He looked at her, his eyebrows raised and lip twitching with amusement. "What do you think?"

What *did* she think? Before Halloween she would have said, yes. Absolutely. Derek was an asshole of the highest degree. He picked fights with anyone he could, he didn't care about anyone but himself. But, then, after Halloween, her view of him shifted seemingly overnight—Derek Stokes was an asshole with scars and bruises up his body, and she wasn't sure how deep they went. "It's still up for debate."

He huffed a small laugh, and put the car into drive, turning back the way they came and toward her house.

He drove like he had driven it a million times. The road between their houses was long, with many twists and turns she wasn't sure she would remember. But Derek did it with ease.

"Why did you tell her that?" Becca bit her lip.

He leaned one elbow against the bottom of the closed window while the other hand settled on the top of the wheel. He peeked over at her for a moment then turned back to the road. He knew exactly what she was asking about. She half expected him to pretend he didn't, but he just shrugged. "Was it a lie?"

"I didn't realize you thought of me as a—"

"Friend?"

"Yeah. A friend."

He shrugged again. "Friend or not, you've seen more of me than most people."

Becca resisted the overwhelming urge to blush. She looked out the passenger side window to hide her face at the way that sounded. "I doubt that." She murmured, and he laughed.

"If you're having doubts, we can fix that."

Her head whipped around toward him, eyebrows furrowed in shock. But he didn't look as seductive as his words sounded. He grinned at her, delighting in her reaction. A bubble of scandalized laughter rose in her chest, and despite trying to hold it back, it boiled over. She shook her head and rolled her eyes. "Yeah, I'll pass."

"Your loss."

They were in front of her house soon enough, pulling into the driveway as the early evening rolled in with a winter breeze. He put the car into park and the heavy engine reverberated through her as they sat there. She felt like she was back to that first night they'd met, sitting in the dark in her driveway. The night she gave him her number and told him he could come to her when he needed to.

"You never came back." She cringed at the sudden words that burst from her before she could stop them. There were a million questions rolled into one: What happened? Why did you never call? Are you okay? "After that night," she clarified, as if it made things better.

He paused, staring at his steering wheel. His posture no longer held the swagger she saw in the hallways. Next to her, his back was straight, his knuckles tight, his face serious. She wondered if she would regret bringing it up.

"I didn't want to bother you."

Becca shook her head. "If it bothered me, I would have told you so. I never say anything I don't mean."

"You don't deserve to be the one dealing with it." His voice was low, barely above a whisper. Gone was the smirk, the chuckles, the bedroom eyes.

"And you are?"

Blue eyes met hers, and she held her breath, waiting for an answer. She got one in the form of a look. Of a sadness buried so deep it was visible for only a second. *Yes.*

"I don't like being alone either, Derek. We could keep each other company—if you'd like."

He pursed his lips, unsure and conflicted. He finally gave one quick, reluctant nod.

"Call or come over whenever you need. Just like I told you." Or rather just as she'd *written* him…on the note he probably threw away.

She opened the car door, a cutting breeze slicing through the warmth the enclosed space had provided. She stepped out, but he caught her again by the arm, lightly, right about the wrist.

"Where are you going?"

She furrowed her brow. "Inside."

Softly, he pulled her back and reached across her to grab hold of the door. He pulled it shut. Before she could ask what he was doing, he grabbed the familiar first aid kit from the glove compartment and placed it onto the center console.

With curiosity, Becca watched as Derek silently lifted her sleeve once again, looking lightly at her wrist, eyeing a small scratch and pressing gently at the swelling. In a quick few minutes, her hand had a small bandage on the scratch, and her wrist was expertly wrapped to help prevent unnecessary movement and further any damage.

It all happened so quick, with the only sound of Derek rustling and Van Halen playing through the stereo.

Giving one final look over of his work, he nodded in approval and met her eyes once again, a decision made. "It's about time I get to do something for you."

SEPTEMBER 1985

After

Becca had never been to Madison. In fact, she barely went anywhere. Despite her mom being around the country at any given time, Becca was forced to remain in her humble little town. So Madison was a shock. The streets, even at one a.m., had people on the sidewalks, cars passing them. She'd heard that cities never rest, but she wouldn't have imagined that they truly never rested. A city twenty times the size of Highburg—any other day she could enjoy it.

Instead, her hands nervously wrung together as she paid attention to every single dark car that looked remotely like Derek's Monte Carlo. She had hoped it would be easy to spot it, but despite it being one of the most recognizable in Highburg, it would barely stand out here.

"Any idea where he would go?" Marty asked, driving as slow as he could to look at the passing crowds without infuriating the people behind him.

Becca bit her lip. She had no idea, but she might be able to deduce some possibilities. The first thought would be a hotel. He would need a place to stay. But even a summer of lifeguarding at the local pool wouldn't make him enough money to stay in a hotel in a bigger city like this for very long.

It pained her to think it, but he was probably sleeping in his car.

So where else? Where else would he go that could pose as both shelter and a distraction?

"A bar." Before he met Becca, he liked to go to the few bars there were in Highburg a lot—according to him. He told her once, when they were sitting quietly in the dark and she couldn't see his face, that drinking had been the best way to distract himself from everything else. After they met, though, she didn't see him drinking a whole lot. "Or somewhere he can drink."

Marty hummed and slowed the car at a red light. "He picked the right place then."

"What do you mean?"

"I mean, in a college town like this, in a state where all anyone does is drink—it would be easy to find plenty of bars that won't ID him."

"So we just need to look for places like that?" Becca nodded. "How do we do that?"

Marty smirked at her, then started to drive again as the light turned green. "You're so lucky to have me."

***

Marty knew someone who knew someone who said that the best bars for kids their age was in any college town. Apparently, all the bars that didn't ID were right by the university area, and the people they wanted the most were the students, who were desperate to live out the American college experience.

This wasn't an issue in Highburg, because nearly any bar let anyone in.

Becca's hopes were rising, and she had more energy than before as they pulled into a gas station parking lot. Marty parked and went in, saying he was going to grab a map of the area.

While he was away, Becca went to the pay phone against the building and rummaged through her pockets for some spare change so she could make a call.

Winston wasn't happy to get a call so late, but when she said her name, his voice softened slightly over the line. She quickly explained the situation, giving him a small update on their progress and asked for an update on Mal. She was fine—asleep and safe with Jane in her bedroom for the time being.

Becca sighed in relief and leaned her forehead against the metal of the booth. There was some good news. Hopefully, she would have some more in a short while and she could really relax.

Out of the corner of her eye, the glass doors of the gas station opened again, and Marty came out, carrying a map. He caught sight of her and waved it in the air for her to see that he'd successfully gotten it.

She quickly excused herself from the call and walked over to him—hopeful. "Any information?"

"More than just any. The clerk in there apparently doubles as an underage bar guide or something. He showed me every single spot without even having to pay him." He flipped the map down so she could see what he was talking about. It was an ordinary-looking map, nearly identical to the one she'd left in Derek's car—except for the red circles that marked about twelve different spots on different streets and corners. "Just like I said, they're all around the university."

Becca exhaled slowly, and for a moment she thought she might cry in relief. She could feel it. They had to be *so* close.

"Let's go." She didn't need to be convinced.

They left the gas station and headed out to the nearest dot. And then the next, then the next.

The first bar was closed. The second one, Becca immediately knew he wouldn't be at. She walked in and the place was nicer, cleaner—a more upscale place for the privileged out-of-state students. She didn't try to look too much into a place like that.

But the next few were more in tune with where Derek might choose to hang out. They were cheaper, greasier, easier to spend your last cent in. Just the type of place a runaway would go. But he wasn't at five of those. Two more were already closed, and their options were running low with each bar they checked and the nearing last call.

What if she had been wrong?

What if Derek wasn't in Madison at all? It was possible

he'd gone somewhere else, maybe Chicago, or even as far as California, though she doubted he would make it with the little cash she knew he had. What if she didn't know him as well as she thought, and they were looking in all the wrong places?

While Marty followed the street signs and map markings, her eyes remained peeled for the boy she knew so well and the car she'd ridden in a million times. Her hands began to wring together again, and she bit her lip, as her eyes scanned every face on the street, as if one of them would be his. Once, there was someone with hair like his—long, curly, and dirty blond. She nearly jumped out of the car as it was moving, but when they passed by, her shoulders slumped when she saw a stranger's face. She bit her lip and held back desperate tears.

Marty pulled into a narrow parking lot, right next to another bar, and Becca looked around the area. It was slightly more secluded than the others, with neon lights over the door. It was also darker where they parked, as there were fewer streetlamps than the other places they went.

That's why she almost missed it, because it was in the far back corner, sitting in nearly black shadows that made the dark metal blend in—a Monte Carlo. The license plate confirmed everything she needed to know.

Marty was saying something, but Becca heard nothing. Her ears were filled with white noise as he put the car into park, a loud ringing making it impossible to hear anything other than her heart.

She jumped out the second the doors unlocked and ran up the dirty sidewalk and through the black doors of the bar, into the smoke-filled room. It took a moment for the haze to clear, but if anyone were to ask in the future about this moment, she knew exactly what she would tell them.

She always told Derek that she could find him in a crowded room without trying. No matter what, she was drawn to him the second they were within proximity of one another.

And just like that, despite the smoke and the bodies and the music and stumbling of last-minute drunks, her eyes landed on him the second her feet were on the stained floor.

She didn't need some ray of angelic light to guide her way. He was there, clearer than anything she had seen since he left.

What she wouldn't tell them was the way he leaned over the counter, his head buried in one hand, with a glass buried in the other. His usually perfectly styled curls now stringy and flat against his head. He wore the same outfit he'd been wearing the last day she saw him. Leather jacket, white shirt, and a pair of now-stained jeans.

She froze from taking a step closer to him.

She'd almost forgotten—he hated her.

She'd put him in this position, made him resort to this state. He'd told her he never wanted to see her again.

In her mind, she had pictured some grand reunion between them, with misty eyes and hugs and apologies and forgiveness. But what if that didn't happen?

What if Derek Stokes truly wanted her gone forever?

"What are you doing?" Marty appeared at her side, leaning close to yell into her ear over the loud music.

She didn't want to admit it. "I'm scared."

"Why?"

"He won't want to see me." Her voice choked up before she could stop it. "He hates me."

Marty placed a hand on her shoulder, turning her so she was no longer looking at Derek, but at Marty's serious face. "Now I may not like the asshole, but even I know that he does not hate you. Anyone with eyes can see that prick cares more about you than anything else. I think if you hadn't come now, he would have crawled back, eventually, just to see you."

Becca looked back toward Derek as he lifted his glass to his lips. Hate her or not, it wouldn't change the fact that she made a promise to Derek long ago.

The walk to Derek was slow and calculated. But she made it to his side without him noticing. Her mouth opened once, twice, three times before she could get a single word out.

"Derek."

His drink froze halfway to his lips, and for what felt like ages, neither of them moved. Slowly, oh, so slowly, his head turned, and his eyes settled on her face.

She knew the phases of his eyes in any state. She had seen them drunk before—when they glassed over and became distant. They were like that now, barely registering her standing in front of him. He was so far gone in the alcohol, he couldn't even tell she was there.

Her heart ached so badly, she wanted to cry. But she kept her tears in and tried again. "Derek."

A light flickered behind the blue, and he set the drink down on the bar, turning his whole body to face her.

"God. Looks so real." His words were so slurred she could barely make them out. But his hand rose and settled on the side of her cheek against her skin. It was cold and damp from where the glass had left its mark.

Becca brought her hand up instinctually and wrapped it around his fingers.

"You came." He still didn't seem to think she was real.

"Of course, I came."

"Go away."

Like a bucket of ice water had been poured over her head, Becca's body locked up. He started to pull his hand away but she desperately held it in place.

"I'm not going anywhere without you." she said. "Let's go home."

"Home." He scoffed at the word with the same amount of affection he had for dirt and looked at the ground—sticky with crumbs and alcohol.

"You're drunk. You don't know what you're saying. Come with me."

"I said I never wanted to see you again." His voice was clearer as the interaction began to sober him up.

"You didn't mean that." Becca tried to sound confident, but it came out quiet, unsure.

He managed to rip his hand from her grasp, and he grabbed

the drink and tossed back the rest of it in a single go. Her confidence was waning, her hold on him loosening.

"I meant every damn word I said." He slammed the glass on the counter, drawing the attention of a few college students nearby, including Marty who pushed forward to be at her side.

Derek's misty eyes rose to lazily catch Marty's, and he swayed in his spot. "Oh look, you brought your pretty boyfriend." He chuckled, his words slurring more.

"Okay, big guy, time to get up." Marty wasn't as impacted by the severity of Derek's tone as Becca was.

Marty grabbed Derek by the shoulders and hoisted him off the stool he sat on.

"Get the fuck off me," Derek said, brushing Marty off with enough force that Derek stumbled a step to the side. He caught himself before Becca could and glared when he saw her reaching out for him.

He took a step forward, until his face was a few inches away from hers, the bitter alcohol on his breath hard to ignore. Becca blinked, and tears finally rose to her eyes, unable to keep them back anymore.

He softened. His hard eyes lightened, and he leaned into her slightly, like he couldn't resist. The anger was gone, replaced entirely by the broken boy she had seen many times. He didn't have the energy to fight anymore.

"Please."

She felt his fingers wrap around hers.

"Just let me live in peace."

Then his head was on her shoulder, his body going limp.

She barely caught him as he started to fall, and thank god for Marty, because without him, Derek would have been on the floor. She knew from experience that he was not easy to carry alone.

They shifted him out of the bar together and into the heavy wind. Groups of drunk college students didn't even notice them passing by. After some awkward shuffling and adjusting, they worked together to get his heavy body situated in the back seat of Marty's car.

Becca reached into his pockets, making sure all of his possessions were accounted for. A thinning wallet and his keys were all he had.

"What about his car?" Becca looked over to Derek's prized possession, hesitant to leave it behind. "Maybe I should take him in there instead."

"No way. I'm not letting you drive back alone." He took the keys out of her fingers and pocketed them. "Have someone come get it later or something. We'll figure it out."

Becca sighed but nodded, putting Derek's wallet into her own pants pocket. Truthfully, even though she knew how to drive, she didn't trust herself all the way to Highburg from here. It was already past three a.m., and neither of them had gotten any sleep. It would be better to take it on together and take turns if needed.

Marty opened the driver's door and stepped in, but rather than taking the passenger side, Becca opened the back door and squeezed herself into the back seat where Derek was passed out cold. Marty didn't say anything as he watched in the rearview mirror while she adjusted Derek's head to lay on her lap, running her fingers habitually through his hair.

"You know you owe me big time for this, right?"

Becca was glad that, despite everything, Marty could still make her smile, even if it was a halfhearted one. "As soon as we get back to Highburg, I'll even be your personal maid if you want it."

He smirked and backed out of the parking spot to pull away from the bar lot and into the city in the direction of their home.

JANUARY 1985

Before

The first day back to school after the winter break was the first refreshing sense of normalcy in a while.

Marty met her outside her place with his car, ready to drive her to the school as usual, and ready to tell her all about his week in Oahu and how warm it was. He chattered on happily, talking about the fish, how he got stung by a jellyfish and "apparently peeing on it helps," as well as a bunch of other cool stuff Becca would love to experience one day. Maybe in Hawaii, or California. "How was your break?"

She knew he would ask eventually, and she was wondering what she would say. The very first thing that came to her mind was the curly-haired boy she was apparently friends with now. But then she remembered that Marty didn't have the best opinion of Derek, since he'd moved here and stolen all female attention away from Marty. Maybe now wasn't a great time to tell him about their strangely intimate encounters.

"Oh, you know, Mom came home for Christmas, a little bit on New Year's, and of course, I spent most of the time raiding the video store like usual."

He looked over at the arm that still had the same bandage Derek had wrapped around it. Just another reminder. "What about that?"

She lifted her arm up. "Slipped on some ice. Nothing too bad."

He leaned his head back dramatically and sighed. "I leave you for two weeks, and this is what I come back to. I can't even let

57

you out of my sight."

"How about we get a movie this weekend? I was planning on renting *Footloose*."

"Didn't we watch that already?"

"Yeah, so? I like it."

He groaned, but he was smiling. "Fine."

Their conversation came to a natural pause as he pulled into the school parking lot and straightened between the lines of an empty spot.

A shaking rev of an engine made them both turn to look out her window as another car pulled right into the space next to Marty's ten-year-old BMW.

"What is this asshole doing here so early?" Marty mumbled, shaking his head as Derek's window lined up directly with Becca's.

She and Marty were always early to school. She much preferred to be the first person in the classroom rather than the last, where she was at risk of a great deal of attention on her. Because of that, she had never actually witnessed Derek arrive at school, since he infamously took his time waltzing into the hallways three minutes after the bell. Unlike her, he clearly liked a certain degree of attention.

She had heard all about his arrivals, though. It was easy to tell when Derek Stokes was at school, because girls would chatter excitedly about him.

But there he was. Thirty minutes before the first bell and parked right next to them.

He shifted the car into park and looked out his window at her, like he already knew she was there. He smirked when he saw her watching him.

"Let's go," Marty said, annoyance dripping from his mouth as he grabbed his bag from the back seat and opened his door to get out. His movement motivated her to follow along, opening her door and stepping out.

She crossed behind to the other side of the car, standing next to Marty as he tried to unbury his gym bag from the trunk.

One of Derek's car doors opened and out stepped Mal, much to Becca's surprise.

She didn't know that Derek drove Mal to school, but maybe if she had seen him arrive at the school before, she would have seen it for herself. Mal slammed the car door behind her, a steady frown on her face until she rounded his car and saw Marty and Becca there.

The girl's face brightened a bit, and she waved. "Hey, Becca."

The other car door opened, and out of the corner of her eye, Becca saw Derek step out of the Monte Carlo.

"You better be on time today, or else I'm leaving you," he called to his stepsister.

Mal rolled her eyes with no acknowledgment of his threat and walked away, leaving the three of them by the cars.

Marty shut his trunk and threw the gym bag over his shoulder. He glared at Derek, who was leaning against his door, cupping his hands around his face as he lit a cigarette.

Becca held her breath.

Marty would never admit it. He claimed that his hatred of Derek stemmed from how cocky he was. He'd once said that Derek's ego was "the size of the Soviet Union." But, really, Becca could tell that it had more to do with the fact that Derek showed up, and suddenly no one was interested in Marty anymore, because there was a shinier model available. That and the fact that he'd befriended the guy who stole Marty's girlfriend. It was a laundry list of reasons.

"Morning, Parr." Derek smirked, and a stream of cigarette smoke rose up with a puff into the cold winter air. His eyes slid over to Becca casually, but he didn't acknowledge her.

Marty just scowled, not bothering to respond to Derek's greeting, and turned to walk toward the school. Becca followed him. She chanced a glance over her shoulder, to where Derek still stood against the car, cigarette in hand. He didn't look in a hurry to move, but his gaze followed as she and Marty walked side by side—a small, knowing smirk on his face the entire time.

She looked away.

"What a prick," Marty mumbled, still glowering at the mere thought of Derek.

She swallowed, worried how she would ever be able to tell Marty about her friendship with Derek.

They entered the school, now filling up with incoming students looking forward to seeing their friends after weeks away. Some bursting with far too much energy, others dragging, trying to get back into the early morning swing after a long vacation.

Marty waved to a few girls, flashing a charming smile at new or old classmates. Some waved back, some rolled their eyes. None of it discouraged him. If he was anything, it was determined to redeem his title of ladies' man. He seemed particularly taken with Jenna Marcus at the moment, the brunette-gone-blond since before break.

Becca rolled her eyes. "Are you going to keep ogling her, or are you going to go put your stuff away?"

He smiled sheepishly. "I'll see you at lunch?"

"Go, go." She waved him away, and he made a beeline toward Jenna. Becca chuckled under her breath and continued to her locker at the end of the hallway.

Break hadn't really been a break, because she had been given multiple assignments to do over the two weeks. She was more than glad to unlock her locker and unload the unnecessary weight of the textbooks onto the shelves.

"I didn't realize you had a boyfriend." The voice in her ear caught her off guard, and she jumped in surprise.

Derek chuckled, hooded eyes bright with delight. He leaned back against the locker next to her. The cigarette had been replaced with a piece of gum that he chewed on.

"Jesus, can't you say hello first?"

He ignored her question. "How does Parr feel about us being friends?"

A few curious heads turned to glance at the unusual interaction. Then again, everyone was far too interested in what Derek Stokes did.

Becca shook her head perhaps too violently. "First of all, Marty is not my boyfriend. He's just a friend. And second of all, I haven't told him yet."

"Ooh." His eyebrow raised with piqued interest. "So I'm your dirty little secret?"

"It's hardly dirty."

He leaned forward, his face closing in on Becca's. His gum was mint, and the scent of it washed over her face as he exhaled, a hint of cigarette smoke still left behind. She leaned back and out of reach. "But it could be."

She scoffed and rolled her eyes, stepping away from him to focus on grabbing the materials she needed for her first class. "Do you flirt with all your *friends* like this?"

"Only the pretty ones."

She was ashamed to admit that her face heated. Of course, she knew that Derek was kidding, and that he was just trying to get a reaction. She saw him flirt with just about every girl he encountered—it was his instinct.

But she had never been called pretty by anyone other than her mother. Certainly not by any attractive guys.

She made sure Derek couldn't see her face by bending a tad too far into her locker, pretending to be interested in some notes in one of her notebooks. When it was just the two of them, he had never been very flirty. Maybe it was just something he *had* to do when others were around. Maybe, just like he liked to walk into class late, he liked the attention that he was getting from the groups of people intrigued by why Derek Stokes was leaning in so close to Becca Lewis.

"Everyone is looking," she mumbled, and he finally looked away to take in the observing eyes.

"What? You don't like that?"

"I'd rather not have rumors flying around about me. Not really my thing."

Derek went from a foot away, to six feet away, instantly putting distance between them. The flirty smirk was replaced by something softer. "Better?"

She nodded and shut her locker door.

"Stokes." A new voice entered the conversation from behind, and they both turned to see where it came from. Brent Duggan and his girlfriend—Marty's ex-girlfriend—April Perry approached them, his arm thrown casually over her shoulder, while April's eyes shifted to Becca with a brow raised. "Where the hell you been, man? You missed the party last weekend."

Derek's relaxed stance next to Becca stiffened enough for her to sense. She glanced at him through the corner of her eye to see if he looked upset, but he still had that cocky smile on his face. "I had better things to do."

Brent noticed Becca then, Derek's words seeming to have struck some baseless assumptions into his head. Becca cringed internally and frowned. "What's going on here?" There was a tease in Brent's voice, and April laughed, but her eyes were judgmental as they ran over Becca.

Derek noticed it too. He kept his feet planted, the whole six feet away from her, but his stance shifted to turn their burning attention back to him and away from her. "What? I can't chat with a classmate?"

Brent had been Marty's friend once upon a time, when high school first started, and by association, sometimes Becca's. April came along a year later, and fit her way into that dynamic a little too easily. Becca had never liked them; they'd never liked her.

"I don't know. Becca isn't exactly the type I'd imagine you going for." Brent spoke as if Becca wasn't standing right there. He even went as far as to lean in like he was sharing a secret with Derek, pretending to whisper, even though his words were loud and clear. "Take it from me, man, she's not very fun."

Becca bit her tongue as hard as she could without drawing blood. "I'll see you later," she said, her dismissal to no one in particular.

She never did get to see how Derek reacted to what Brent said, because she turned and walked away from April's irritating laugh. They lived for a reaction, and the best way to deal with people like Brent and April was to give them nothing.

She'd only interacted with Derek a total of four times now, and in that limited amount of time, she had seen more depth under all the fire and smoke than both Brent and April combined.

She just couldn't tell why he hid it.

***

Derek watched Becca walk away, while April and Brent sniggered next to him.

It had taken him months to have enough courage to face her straight on. After Halloween, he was too embarrassed to believe she might actually mean what she wrote on that paper. Instead, he hid and watched her quietly when she wasn't looking.

Including learning her name, and when her classes were, and who she hung out with. He wasn't pleased to learn it was Parr, but that didn't change the fact that he couldn't stop thinking about *her*.

After that night, when he'd been too drunk to drive and too beaten to stay home, he'd had nowhere else to go. The only reason he had enough courage to show up at her house was because he was too out of it to convince himself otherwise. Honestly, she had been the first person to even cross his mind.

For so long, he had been scared she would turn him away when it came down to it, but when he stumbled to her door and she opened it for him, she didn't hesitate a moment. She brought him in and cared for him until he was sober and gave him a bed he could sleep in without worrying his father would be there in the morning.

He'd never slept so well, and when he wasn't sleeping, he was so grateful he could have cried.

He guessed he could thank Mallory for the chance to really face Rebecca, though he would never say it aloud. He was less of a pussy now in front of her, and he'd had enough time to go over their short interactions to believe that she was one of the best people he had ever known.

It was worth the embarrassment. And the prying questions

63

from Mallory, who was confused why someone like Becca would be friends with Derek.

Something he wasn't sure of either, but selfishly did not want to throw away.

"God, she is such a priss." April's shrill voice pulled him away from the constant thoughts of her and pushed him straight into a net of annoyance.

He looked away from Becca's retreating form and turned toward his so-called "friends."

"I can't stand her."

Derek smirked at her, irritation simmering behind the well-maintained mask of composure, "Do you ever shut the fuck up? Your voice gives me a headache."

April squeaked in surprise, her attention successfully off Becca and onto him.

"What the hell, man?" Brent stepped up, frowning at Derek. "What did she do to you?"

Derek pushed off from the lockers and walked away, tuning out their outraged calls after him. They gave him headaches most days. He didn't want one today too. They would forget this entire thing later, and they'd be right back to him in hopes of drowning in the popularity that followed him.

Whatever. He couldn't care less.

He had much better things to think about.

SEPTEMBER 1985

After

The drive back was smoother than before. Probably because she knew Derek was safe now, lying in her lap as Marty drove through the dark.

Outside of Madison, Marty announced that he needed to stop for gas. Derek didn't stir as Marty pulled off an exit and stopped next to a gas pump.

"You have any cash I could use?" Marty asked, pulling what cash he had out of his wallet. "I don't have a whole lot left."

She carefully grabbed Winston's twenty dollars out of her jacket pocket next to Derek's head.

Marty took it and walked into the station, leaving her and a still unconscious Derek in the quiet of the back seat.

She took the moment alone to brush her fingers against his head, picking up a stray curl that was stuck to his temple and pushing it aside.

When Derek was awake, he spent so much of his energy trying to hide everything inside of him. His face was always calm, always angry, or always empty. On the nights when he showed up at her door, he preferred for the lights to be off so she couldn't see his red eyes or the way everything shone through them. She never said anything when she saw a tear fall against his best efforts. She just let him lay his head down on her lap like now until he fell asleep.

This position had become a comfort for them both.

And it was the only time he couldn't turn his face away from her, so she used the opportunity to observe every line on his skin.

It'd only been a few days since he disappeared, but they hadn't been apart for more than a day since January. She missed his eyes, his nose, his hair, his smell.

Her finger swiped over his cheekbone, and a small contented breath loosed from his lips like he knew exactly where he was.

She glanced up, broken from her trance, to see if Marty had come out yet. He hadn't, and for a moment she worried he didn't have enough cash. She dropped her hand from Derek's face and reached into her other pocket for his wallet.

Derek's wallet was usually bulky with cash and other things he liked to carry around. Now it wasn't as full. The cash was low, only a little bit left. In one pouch, there were a couple condoms, some gift cards and a credit card in another, but in one sleeve it looked like there wasn't anything at all.

Just to be sure, Becca reached her finger in and pulled out a single piece of paper.

She didn't recognize it until she unfolded it, and her heart clenched painfully in her chest at the familiar handwriting across the piece.

Call if you need anything. I can sit quietly and listen or laugh with you. Whatever you need.

He still had it.

She'd assumed that he'd thrown it away long before, but here it was. The pen scratch was faded a bit, and the folds in the paper were thin and worn like they had been opened over and over again.

A knock on her window startled her from the paper. Marty opened her door to hand her a plastic bag.

She slipped the paper back into Derek's wallet.

"I got some water and an extra bag, in case he pukes. The last thing I want to do is clean up after him too."

Becca accepted the bag and set it down on the ground in front of her feet. "Thanks."

He nodded and paused, taking in the sight of Derek resting against her lap as he inserted the gas pump it into the tank.

Becca's friendship with Derek had been kept entirely separate from Marty, so he never saw them when they were like this. It might look weird to him now, but he might think it was even stranger if he realized that this position was normal for them.

"He doing okay?"

She shrugged. "As far as I can tell."

"Uh-huh."

A moment of silence settled between them, luckily interrupted by the sound of the gas pump snapping off.

"Do you need me to drive?" she asked while he began putting the hose back up.

He shook his head. "Just make sure he doesn't make a mess in my car."

Becca nodded and they were off. She tried to stay awake on the highway but found it difficult to keep her eyes open anymore. For the past days it had been impossible to get any sleep as she worried about Derek. Now that he was here and safe, the relief became a relaxing pill, and she found herself dozing against the cool window several times.

She awoke fully at a particular turn into Highburg that was familiar enough to make her sense home nearby. Blue and pink twilight had snuck up on her while she was asleep.

Marty caught her eye in the rearview mirror when he saw her sit up and rub her palm against her face.

"I'm assuming that we're going straight to your place," he mumbled, like he was conforming to some sense of reverence after she had just woken up.

She yawned, looking out the window at the familiar streets that marked the way back to her house. "Yeah, he can't go home."

The turn onto her street was slow, steady. It was good that Marty drove. He always was the better driver. On her lap, she adjusted Derek's head, trying to get some feeling back into her thighs, which had fallen asleep. He shifted, exhaling, but he still didn't open his eyes.

"Is your mom home?"

"She's supposed to be gone until next week." Becca looked ahead as they approached her house. In the driveway was a car, black and unfamiliar. She frowned, an unsteady pitch settled in the pit of her stomach. The closer they got, the worse she felt, until she couldn't handle it anymore. "Wait, slow down. Stop here."

"What's wrong?" Marty asked but did as he was told. He pulled his car to the curb a few houses down from hers, far enough away to be subtle.

She slipped Derek's head off of her lap and opened her door.

"Whoa. Wait a minute, where are you going?" Marty turned in his seat to watch her get out of the car.

"I need to check something. Just stay here until I'm back, okay?"

She shut the door against Marty's protests, but he stayed inside the car, even turning it off to wait for her.

She wrapped her arms around herself and walked toward the house. It took her a minute to get there, and she studied the black car as she approached. Now that she was closer, she realized she *had* seen it before. Several times, in fact, parked in front of the Stokes' home right by Derek's.

Ice filled her veins, and her feet stopped moving.

She could turn and run now. Maybe if she was quick enough, he wouldn't even know she was there. Then again, if he did come around and saw her running way, it could make things worse.

Becca took a deep breath, trying to calm the terror in her chest and the stiffness of her shoulders. Forcing her body to relax, she walked around the car and to the walkway that led to the front door.

Mark Stokes stood on the front porch. He didn't hear her approach. He had his hands cupped around his eyes and was looking in through the front window in search of *something*.

She swallowed the lump in her throat and exhaled. "Mr. Stokes?"

If there was any true struggle, it was trying to keep her face straight and relaxed when facing someone like Mark Stokes.

He turned around, dropping his hands and running them over the bottom of his jacket. When he saw her standing there, the hard set of his brow relaxed into a purposeful, calm expression.

"Good morning, Rebecca." His voice was nonchalant, unbothered that he had just been caught snooping around her house before dawn. The upward turn of his lips fell short of his eyes. It had been a long time since his greetings and grins lost their fake sincerity on her. He still pretended though.

She nodded, and carefully stepped up the stairs to stand in front of him. "Can I help you?"

"I figured you might be the best person to come to for answers."

"What about?" She gave him a polite smile, hoping it was more convincing than his. At her sides, she consciously held her hands still, even though she wanted to wring them together.

He slipped his own hands into his pockets and took a step closer. Becca bit her tongue and resisted the urge to flinch away.

"Derek hasn't been home for a few days, maybe you know where he could be?" He didn't sound worried that his son was missing. Instead, he sounded accusing.

Becca frowned, knitting her brow in faux confusion. "I haven't seen him in a while. I thought he was at home."

Several seconds passed, with Mark watching her carefully. She knew he didn't believe her. Not with the minuscule lift in the right corner of his lips. But she had to keep her cool, because if he did try and dig around, he might find Derek in the back seat of a car three houses down. She didn't want to think about it.

"Huh."

"Is there anything else you need?" She kept her voice sweet, rushed to get him off her porch and as far away from Derek as she could. He paused for a moment, clearly thinking long about her offer.

She waited for him to say no and to leave, but instead he

motioned toward the front door. "You know, I could use a cup of coffee, if you don't mind."

The taste of metal bloomed in her mouth as she bit down too hard on the inside of her bottom lip.

"I'm sorry, now is not a good time." Becca smiled politely, then pulled the house key from her jacket pocket and unlocked the front door.

Mark Stokes's presence behind her sent alarm bells ringing in every survival instinct she had. Her hair stood on end, her ears rang, her muscles tensed.

But she ignored them, keeping her cool as she opened the door and rushed aside. As she closed the door, something stopped it.

Mark's fingers grasped the edge, preventing it from shutting.

Becca stopped breathing, giving Mark the opportunity to push it open and force her backward.

He didn't seem to care that he barged his way into the home of a seventeen-year-old girl. He just smiled and shook his head, shutting the door behind him. "That's no way to treat a guest. Didn't your parents teach you that?"

He briefly took in the entryway and walked past her into the living room.

She'd been in the Stokes' house a few times before, and both Mal and Derek had been in hers. But Mark? If it weren't for Mark, she would have gone to Derek's more. Now he was in her home. Her space, her surroundings. Everything felt tainted.

Her voice stuck in her throat, as trapped as she felt. She prayed that Marty wouldn't come looking for her and that Derek stayed asleep.

Mark sat down on the couch, spreading his legs wide, arms flinging on the back of the cushions like he was the one living there. He stared at her, challenging. "Now how about that coffee?"

11
JANUARY 1985

Before

Leave it to Mrs. Bernard to assign a partner project right when all the students are still recovering from a two-week break. On top of it, the teacher wasted no time increasing the disappointment by *assigning* partners rather than letting them pick their own.

If Becca had had a choice, she would have chosen the valedictorian, Tracy Urion. Not only was she a reliable partner, she was a guaranteed A grade.

Instead, she was stuck with Elaine Renfield—a not so guaranteed A. And if what Becca assumed was correct, it would be hard to even get her to meet up.

"How about four o'clock?" Becca asked the brunette as she packed up her bag post bell ring. "I'll come to your place, if that's easier."

Elaine sighed, annoyed she even had to do that project. "I can't do four. I have someone coming over."

"Okay. Five then?"

"If I say yes, will it make this end quicker?"

Becca nodded, and Elaine sighed again. "Fine, you can come to my house at five. But you better make sure it won't take long."

Becca was on the doorstep five minutes early. She wanted to get it over with as soon as possible too. It wasn't like spending an evening with Elaine Renfield was her ideal activity either.

She raised a fist and knocked on the door.

After ten seconds and zero movement, she did it again.

Nothing.

Shit.

If Elaine wasn't home, it was going to be a pain and a half trying to find another time that worked for her. If Becca couldn't find a time at all, well, there went any chance of even a B grade.

She gave it one last knock for good measure, banging on the wood harder than she meant to.

She might have felt bad, but it did the trick.

Within a few seconds, she could hear the rhythmic thump of footsteps on the other side, followed by a pause, and then a click as the door unlocked and opened.

Elaine stood in the doorway with her eyebrows drawn together. "Oh, hi?"

Great. She forgot. "We're supposed to work on the project together."

Elaine's lips formed an "O" shape. "Shit." She peeked over her shoulder then turned back. "I forgot."

"It's fine, it won't take long."

Elaine sighed the same way she had in class and opened the door wider, stepping to the side to allow Becca access. "The living room is to the right. We can work in there. Just give me a second. I need to go freshen up."

Becca looked her over. Only then did she notice that Elaine wasn't wearing any pants and only an overly large shirt covered up her bottom half. Her hair was mussed up, her face a bit flushed, and on her neck was a fresh bruise the size of someone's mouth.

Oh. My. God.

Becca's face heated, and she turned away from Elaine and toward the living room. She had interrupted something unholy. Jesus. There was no coming back from it, so the only thing she could do was pretend not to notice as Elaine walked up a set of stairs and said something to someone who had a distinctly masculine voice.

Jesus Christ, he was still here.

Becca looked at the clock. 4:57 p.m.

This was her own damn fault for always arriving early to things.

She distracted her mind by laying out her supplies, paying more attention to lining up her pencils and finding the assigned textbook pages than she normally would.

When Elaine came back down the stairs, Becca panicked and started explaining the study plan before the girl had even walked into her line of sight.

"So, I was thinking we could split the work in half. I could take chapters one through three and you could take four through six, then we reconvene, put our notes together, and get this whole thing done tonight. I bet it wouldn't take more than an hour." She was so busy flipping through the marked pages, she didn't realize Elaine hadn't joined her on the couch. "What do you—"

Her words caught in surprise when she looked up at where Elaine stood in the entrance of the living room. Except Elaine wasn't there at all.

Derek was, though, and he was grinning like a fool.

Even more mortifying was that he wore the same shirt Elaine had been wearing just a few minutes ago.

"As much as I'd love to take notes next to you for an hour, I doubt I'd be any help." His amusement was palpable.

Becca's cheeks were most definitely red.

"Where's Elaine?" Her voice was weak, drowned by mortification.

He jerked his head to motion to the stairs. "She's showering."

Of course, she was. Because that now meant that Becca was alone with Derek Stokes in some random classmate's home, right after they…did stuff.

He walked into the room, until he was close enough to settle onto the floral couch next to Becca. The cushions dipped as he sunk into the empty spot. She averted her eyes and pretended to focus on some random page in the textbook.

"Elaine did mention something about some dumb project she had to do with some chick in her class." She could feel his eyes on her face, even though she avoided them. "I didn't realize it was you."

"It's not like I chose to be her partner," she mumbled, and Derek chuckled.

"No, I wouldn't choose her either."

Becca rolled her eyes. "Sure you wouldn't."

"Ooh, she's got a bite," he teased.

Becca might have teased back, but the mortification from right now, and a lingering sense of humiliation from the morning encounter with Brent and April, set her mood with Derek.

"Aren't you leaving?" Her voice had more snap than she meant, which part of her wanted to take back. The other part wanted Derek to leave so he couldn't see how embarrassed she really was. They barely knew each other anyway. Why was she so worked up?

He was silent for a moment, and neither of them moved. His teasing smirk dropped.

After what felt like an hour, he opened his mouth like he was going to say something, but was interrupted by the heavy steps of Elaine descending the stairs. Becca looked up from her book as Elaine rounded the corner and spotted the two of them sitting on the couch.

A frown twisted Elaine's face. "Derek, what are you still doing here?"

Like it had never changed, the smirk was back on his face, and he rose from his spot. "Just saying goodbye."

Becca kept her face neutral as Elaine came up to him, not hesitating to throw herself into his chest, and giving him one last—disgusting—kiss on the lips. Becca averted her eyes, unsure how she would be able to get through the next hour after this. Out of the corner of her eye, she saw Derek's hand settle on Elaine's shoulder, putting a stop to the PDA.

Elaine didn't notice, though, and looked up at Derek with hooded eyes and a seductive smile. "Call me later."

"You got it," Derek said and walked away without any more

goodbyes. The sound of the front door opening and closing marked his departure.

Elaine shot Becca a weird look. "Are you friends with Derek?"

Becca didn't have the mental capacity for an interrogation from some jealous fling.

She gave a noncommittal shrug before she opened the page again and pretended that she didn't want to be swallowed whole by the couch.

***

As expected, Elaine was a terrible partner. She was too busy picking at her copper nails to focus on the reading. After an hour of trying to get her to concentrate on her assigned chapters and dodging prying questions, Becca was exhausted.

Elaine was more than happy to end the whole thing by agreeing to do her own part on her own time by next week.

Becca really doubted that would happen, but right now she just wanted out, and Elaine wasn't going to say no to that. They exchanged polite goodbyes, and Elaine closed the door on Becca the moment she was out of the house.

By then, the sun was down, and the winter air pinched the tips of her exposed ears. Hats weren't her thing, but she should have at least worn her hair down to create some sort of barrier between the breeze and her skin.

Rather than worrying about that, she bundled her thick coat closer to herself and pulled on the straps of her heavy backpack to make her way down the driveway and toward her house.

Bright headlights flickered on, making her wince and cover her eyes. She couldn't see the car they were coming from, but it was right on the corner of the sidewalk in front of Elaine's house.

A car door opened, and a shadowed figure rose from behind the lights, barely visible until she'd passed their intensity. Derek stood there, watching her approach.

She blinked in surprise. "You're still here?"

"I didn't see a car anywhere. Figured you'd need a ride." Like always, his lips pinched at the last inch of a cigarette.

"You waited out here the whole time?"

He shrugged and flicked the red-ended stick into the snow. "My stepmom's probably making dinner. I'd rather not sit through that." He motioned to the other side of the car. "Get in. It's freezing out here."

Becca opened her mouth to object, but he was already slamming the car door and settling back into his seat. It would be rude to walk away, so she walked to the other side and got into his car, slipping her bag off her shoulders and resting it on her lap.

Derek waited until she was settled in before he sped away from the curb.

"You got a hankering for frostbite or something?"

"Huh?"

He tilted his head to look at her. "You seem to like walking around in hellish temperatures."

"I don't have a car, so it's a bit hard to get around otherwise."

He nodded, one hand relaxed on the top of the wheel and the other settled on the middle console between them. "What about Parr? He drives you around, doesn't he?"

"He's got a date tonight."

"Ditching you for some chick?"

"I wouldn't go that far."

He clicked his tongue in disapproval. "If I was him, I'd make sure you never had to walk in the cold."

Becca rolled her eyes—she'd been doing a lot of that lately—and frowned. "I doubt you'd like to waste your time on me. Haven't you heard? I'm not very fun."

As soon as the words left her lips, she wished she could take them back. She didn't like to let others see the things that upset her. If she told someone her insecurities and worries and fears, she feared they would see them, too, and would never look at her the same afterward.

What Brent had said that morning had been weighing on her

the same way a plastic bag would wrap around a face. She knew she wasn't the most exciting person in the world, but Derek had wanted to be her friend anyway. Now that Brent had said that out loud to Derek, she was just waiting for it to click in his head that Brent was right.

Derek pursed his lips, his eyes squinted as he thought hard about something. Becca waited for him to kick her out of the car, but he didn't.

"Did you know that Brent passes out after, like, two beers?"

Becca blinked. "What?"

"And April whines about literally everything. God, she is so annoying."

Becca wasn't quite sure what to say to that. She wasn't sure why it would matter, or why he even brought it up. He seemed to sense her loss of direction and took his eyes off the road to meet hers.

"Neither of them would go to a party dressed like a whole-ass bunny rabbit or approach a beat-up stranger on the side of the road or walk a little girl home after destroying her skateboard."

"That was an accident."

"Brent doesn't know what the hell he's talking about." His words were firm. He was serious. His usually playful eyes didn't hold a hint of mockery in them. "Trust me, if I didn't think you were worth my time, you would know it."

The car slowed, turning into the driveway in front of her house. She hadn't even noticed they were there.

She wanted to ask why he found her after everything. Why, after she saw him so vulnerable and weak, did he not avoid her and keep his distance like he had at the beginning? Why now?

But she just asked, "Do you want something to eat?"

His eyebrow raised, and his lips turned upward. "You're offering me food?"

"I was planning on making spaghetti tonight, and I prefer to eat with someone else."

She knew quite a bit about Derek now. She'd tended to his wounds more than once, she'd seen him weak, she knew a little about where those bruises came from. But she hadn't said much about herself until now.

Maybe it was the closest to admitting to anyone how lonely she felt in that house alone.

He turned off the engine and pulled out the key. "Anything is better than sitting at a table with my old man, and I happen to like spaghetti."

JANUARY 1985

Before

"I heard something weird."

Becca looked up from her notebook and left her finger on the page to keep track of where she was at in her book. When Marty had picked her up in the morning, he'd been a little off. His greeting was forced, his hands a little tight on the steering wheel, his posture a bit stiff.

At the time, Becca thought maybe his date had gone bad the night before. It wouldn't be the first time that had happened.

"Oh yeah?" She smiled, eager to tap into any gossip. The project from Mrs. Bernard had destroyed her week and kept her on her toes with Elaine. She was desperate for relief. "Good weird, I hope."

He didn't match her energy. In fact, he looked annoyed. "Someone said they saw you with Stokes the other day."

Oh. Marty's off-kilter energy was toward *her*. Her smile fell. She wasn't ready to delve into that subject with Marty yet. Just yesterday he was complaining that Derek had knocked him off his feet in gym class, and he had assured her it was on purpose.

She swallowed and tried to stay calm. "In case you haven't noticed, Derek and I happen to go to the same school." She tried to joke about it, but the look he shot her shut it down. It wasn't that Becca was trying to hide this weird budding friendship from Marty, she wanted to ease into it. She wasn't sure how, but that had been the plan.

Okay, so maybe she *was* hiding it a bit.

"They said they saw him walking into your house."

She's screwed. "It's not as bad as it sounds."

He threw his head back, laughing humorlessly. He then stared at the road ahead of them. "You've got to be kidding me." A hand came up to run through his hair. "You're screwing Stokes."

"Whoa, what?" Becca blanched, caught off guard at the sudden jump in assumptions. Here she was trying to figure out how to explain this whole thing to Marty, and meanwhile, he's come to the conclusion that going into the same house together meant screwing. Granted, that was a very reasonable assumption in regard to Derek Stokes. "I am not screwing him."

"Then why the hell did he go into your house?"

"I—" God, it sounded so silly. "I invited him in for spaghetti."

His eyes looked like they were going to pop out of his head. "You made dinner for that prick?"

"He gave me a ride home because it was cold. It was the least I could do."

"Where the hell were you coming from with him?"

Now he was starting to piss her off. Sure, rumors floated around Derek like hungry little fish—greedy for their next bite. That's why she'd wanted to keep her distance from him at school in the first place, to prevent that sort of attention. Despite that, Marty was sounding awfully accusatory.

"Excuse me for not wanting to walk a mile home in below-freezing temperatures. And since when does a boy going into my house mean I'm screwing him? Need I remind you that you've been in my home hundreds of times and not once have we done anything."

Marty's face dropped, and he stuttered in surprise. "I didn't—it's just—he's—"

They arrived at school at the perfect time, pulling slowly into the parking lot.

"I get you hate each other," Becca continued. "I get that you don't like me being friends with him, I get it. But you don't get to go around accusing me of stuff like that. It's messed up."

She opened the door as soon as the car stopped in his spot

and slammed it behind her, leaving him alone in the car that wasn't even in park yet.

There was a war inside of her. Part of her hated herself for being friends with someone Marty considered an enemy. The other part of her couldn't forget those images of Derek in the dark, needing someone to turn to. Or the way he took her side against Brent—something that had taken Marty years to do when he was in that circle of friends.

No, Derek wasn't perfect, but he wasn't horrible either.

Unfortunately for her, others had heard the rumor too. The attention wasn't more than just a few side eyes or whispers until she got to Mrs. Bernard's class and had to deal with Elaine's cold shoulder. There went any chance of getting her help. The entirety of the project now lay on Becca alone.

After that, she was inclined to just skip out the rest of the day. An internal debate about that happened in the open door of her locker as she switched her history books for science.

"Trouble in paradise?" Derek leaned his back against her neighbor's locker. This was the closest encounter they had had in public since that day with Brent and April. She'd made it very clear to him, while slurping up spaghetti, that she preferred to not have attention on her. He didn't understand the sentiment, but he respected it and agreed they'd keep it low-key.

Now that their friendship was compromised, he didn't care about pretending anymore.

"Not my best day."

"You should've seen Parr in gym." He whistled low and tilted his head. "Off his game. Whatever you said to him before storming out of his shit-box of a car must have struck a nerve."

His words hit a soft chord in her heart and filled her with regret. She'd been harsh with Marty, and even though he wasn't the best either, she couldn't blame all his assumptions.

"Please tell me you didn't make it worse."

"Relax, I didn't even say anything to him. I even let him make a few baskets." He smirked.

She sighed in relief. "Just leave him alone, will you? I know you guys don't get along, but believe it or not, he's my best friend."

He sighed and rolled his eyes. "Fine. But know I rarely make exceptions."

"Well, then, thanks for making one for me." The bell rang, and Becca groaned. "God, I'm sick of this day already."

Derek smirked and leaned forward, a stray curl fell into his face. "Why don't we get out of here then? I'm thinking you're gonna need a ride anyway." His head jerked to the side, motioning toward the nearest exit.

Oh, now *that* was tempting. He dangled the idea in front of her by pulling out his keys and swinging them for her to see.

"What about Mal?"

He laughed. "She is more than capable of walking home." He drew closer, his voice lowering to a murmur as the last of the students filed into their classes. "Come on. You know you want to."

He was a terrible influence. And one she would have to resist for now. "No."

He groaned but pocketed his keys.

"It isn't fair to Mal, and now I'm late for class. Besides, I want to talk to Marty."

"You care too much about his feelings."

"I'm sure he would say the same thing about you." She shut her locker. "I'll see you later."

"I'll wait, in case you need a ride," he called after her, turning a few heads, but she ignored him and went into her classroom.

***

Once Ms. O'Malley started lecturing, Becca wished she had taken Derek up on his offer. The rest of the day went by so slowly, she wanted to jump out a window. But she made it, and when the final bell rang, she rushed out of the room to get out to the parking lot.

The time not spent paying attention to boring presentations

had been spent planning what she would say to Marty. The first part of her plan revolved on getting to him before he could leave her and make her lose her chance.

When she was out to the lot, she was relieved to see that his car was still there, but he was nowhere in sight.

Derek's car was still there, too, parked in the middle of the gravel. He stood against the hood, with his hands leaning back on it. She wasn't oblivious to the fact that his eyes were already on her as she walked across the drop-off area to Marty's car.

She nodded her head toward Marty's car to let Derek know she would still be going ahead with her plan and mending things with her friend. He responded by getting in his car. She half expected him to drive away, but he didn't. The Monte Carlo didn't even roar to life as he sat inside.

Unlike Derek, she couldn't get into Marty's car unless he unlocked it for her, so she would have to wait. She stood next to the passenger door a few more minutes before he made an appearance.

His steps faltered when he saw her there, but he kept coming anyway. They said nothing as he unlocked his door, and for a horrible and embarrassing second, she thought he wasn't going to let her in.

But then her lock clicked, and when she tried the handle, it opened. She hesitated, worried that her trying to mend things might make them worse.

"Can you hurry up? You're letting all the cold air in."

His words got her to move, and she slid into the seat like she had a thousand times. The engine turned on, and Marty started fiddling nervously with the air settings, making sure the dial was turned all the way to hot. He looked over his shoulder, back at where Derek's car was parked. "I thought you were going to ride with him."

Becca followed his gaze to where Derek sat in his car, watching them over the top of his steering wheel. "Why would you think that?"

"Someone heard him tell you to ride with him."

"And I told him I didn't need a ride because I was going to talk to you."

He went silent but backed out of his spot. He passed Derek's car on the way out, and Becca somehow resisted the urge to catch Derek's eye out the window.

Now was the perfect time for the dozens of lines she'd rehearsed in her head. Taking a deep breath, she willed all her strength and started, "Marty, I'm—"

"Why didn't you tell me?"

His interruption caught her off guard, but she quickly recovered and changed tactics. "I was going to, but I know you hate him, and I wasn't sure *how* to tell you."

"Yeah, I hate him. But you know what I kind of hate more? The fact that I had to hear my best friend is messing with the worst prick in school from Brent fucking Duggan."

God, Brent again? That kid was always getting her in business and causing her more trouble than he was worth. "I'm not *messing* with him."

"And that's just another thing I can't figure out." He shook his head. "Why? Why the hell would you even be *around* him. I mean, when did this start?"

She closed her eyes. She'd promised herself she would be honest to Marty about this, but man, she wasn't ready for the reaction. Her voice was hesitant as she spoke. "The first time we really met was after the Halloween party at Ruby's."

Marty's head moved in slow motion toward her, disbelief contorting his face. She winced.

"For what it's worth, we only talked, like, twice before last week."

"Yeah, it's not worth much right now." He sighed, running another hand over his head. It was messed up enough that it seemed he'd been doing that a lot throughout the day. "But I also didn't want to let an asshole like Stokes ruin things between us. I refuse to."

Becca blinked and turned to watch him focus too hard on the road in front of him.

"I'm sorry for what I said. I was upset and confused, but it doesn't excuse anything I said. I don't like the idea of you being friends with him, but I realize it's not my place to dictate who you can and cannot…associate with."

Becca's jaw dropped. This was really not the direction she had expected the conversation to go. She had gotten into Marty's car, fully anticipating dropping to her knees—as well as she could in this cramped thing—and begging for forgiveness. Instead, Marty came right out with these lines that sounded extremely… scripted.

Becca pursed her lips to hide the amused smile that was threatening to rise. "Marty?"

He finally looked at her, his eyes wide like a puppy.

"Who the hell told you to say *that*?"

He blinked and sheepishly bit his lip. "I may have asked Jenna for some advice."

A laugh burst from Becca, unable to stay hidden any longer, and she slapped a hand over her mouth.

Marty grew defensive. "So the words aren't *entirely* mine, but the sentiment is there. Be friends with him, don't be friends with him. Whatever." He threw his hands up in exasperation. "Just don't expect me to have any part in that. Alright? I'd rather keep my distance from him as much as possible and let you live your life, as long as he isn't an asshole to you too."

Becca couldn't stop laughing, but she still nodded. Even Marty bit back a smile when he looked over and saw her with her head thrown back in amusement.

"I'll accept that," Becca finally said. "I'd rather you not try and kill each other in front of me anyway."

Marty muttered something under his breath, but Becca couldn't hear it. He let her calm down, smiling softly to himself.

As her laughter slowed, Becca turned to her friend again and mustered up the main thing she had come here to say. "I'm really sorry, Marty. Not for being friends with Derek, but for hiding it from you. I should have told you the first time I met him."

He nodded. "You can make up for it by getting the movie and snacks for this weekend. And I don't want to watch *Footloose* again, so I get to choose."

Becca sighed in mock disappointment, but, a heavy weight was lifted off her shoulders. She would let Marty pick the movie every time if he wanted to. "Fine, you win."

13
SEPTEMBER 1985
After

Becca moved robotically in the kitchen under Mark's watchful gaze until she was hidden behind the wall.

He made no sound, but that didn't necessarily mean he wasn't doing something. He could be looking around, looking at pictures of her, her mother. He might see more of her than she wanted him to. He might be listening to hear if she tried to call for help on the phone on the other side of the room. Afraid of what he might do if she did, she remained in place next to the stewing coffee pot.

"Are your parents not home?" he asked from the living room.

His sudden question made her jump and nearly drop the mug in her hand. She put a hand over her chest and took a deep breath before answering. Good thing he couldn't see her.

"My mom's away for work." The coffee was hot enough now. She poured it into the mug and stepped back into his line of sight.

Mark hadn't left the couch, thankfully, but his eyes were settled on the pictures hung on the wall. All of them either of her, her mom, or the two of them standing side by side.

He only looked away when she reached the mug out. Without a thank you, he accepted and sipped at the steaming liquid without waiting for it to cool.

She wasn't sure what to do. It felt weird to sit down and settle in his presence, but it would be weirder to him if she stood there, carefully watching every move he made, and trying not to flinch if he shifted too quickly.

She chose the leather recliner furthest from him.

"What about your dad?"

Becca's arms crossed over her chest, creating as inconspicuous a barrier as she could between herself and Mark, and her hand grabbed a fistful of her shirt and squeezed. She forced a painfully calm smile. "He's gone."

She didn't want to get into ten years of trauma with this man. If he was looking for a reaction, he'd be disappointed she'd managed to bottle up anything about her invisible father.

He smiled and shook his head. "That's a shame. It must be hard to grow up without a real strong male figure to teach you how to show proper respect." He shrugged, faking pity. "That is a father's role after all. I've, unfortunately, seen too many kids led astray without it. They start acting wild, disobeying. Start getting into business that isn't their own." He took another sip, but his eyes locked to hers the whole time.

She couldn't bring herself to look away, no matter how much she wanted to, because the tone in his voice made her hair raise. His words hit her, cracking through the armor she'd built around the sensitive topic. He wasn't the first to say something like this. Her breathing was getting heavy, and the pit in her stomach grew rapidly by the second.

He smacked his lips, taking his time to set the mug down on the coffee table. Becca's nails dug into her arm as the silence grew suffocating. He was waiting for her to say something.

"It wasn't easy," she finally choked out, her heart aching at the admission.

"No, I bet it wasn't." He studied her, and she felt the pieces of her strength slipping through her fingers. "Say, we had some uninvited guests the other day in our home. Nothing too important, but certainly quite annoying. You wouldn't happen to know anything about that, would you?"

Her entire body sagged.

He knew. Oh god, *he knew*.

He wasn't asking, he was testing, seeing how much she

would admit. Seeing how much she could hide. He'd come here knowing that. He'd come here and asked about her mom when he already knew she was gone. He'd come here asking about her dad when he could see by the pictures that he was absent.

He knew she was the one who'd called those people, and he knew she knew where Derek was.

"I don't know," she said. Becca was not good at this. She had never been good at this, and it was going to cost her.

He smiled, nodding. "I'm sure you don't." He stood up, leaving the half-empty coffee mug on the table. A dark ring formed on the wood where he'd spilled some. He didn't wait to be shown out, and Becca was forced to follow behind him as he made his way to exit.

He paused, right before he opened the door, to turn to her.

In a moment that would sicken her for weeks, his hand came down on her shoulder in a heavy grab, disguised as support.

The same hand that had made Derek bleed, the same hand that had put bruises on Mal—that same hand patted her firmly on the shoulder.

She was going to be sick.

"If you see Derek, feel free to reach out."

Then he was gone, walking out the door and closing it before she could respond. She didn't move until she heard the car start and the crunch of gravel as it pulled from her driveway and away from the house in the opposite direction of where Marty was parked.

She collapsed into a crouch, her hands holding her balance against the ground as bile rose in her throat. She blinked away heavy tears, choked back aching sobs.

Ten *minutes* alone in the same room with that man had rendered her into this state.

She couldn't imagine the lifetime Derek had lived.

JANUARY 1985

Before

Marty wanted to watch *Star Trek*, and as much as Becca groaned and hissed about it, she went with him to rent it for their weekend movie.

Despite the film being his pick, he seemed far from interested in it. Ultimately, she watched it more than he did, since he was too busy whispering questions to her throughout the first half hour.

"How did you meet him again? Other than school, I mean." He pretended to have his eyes on the TV, but she could see the way he observed her from the corner of them.

Becca groaned. There had been a small hope he would try not to dig, but it was long gone.

"It was after the Halloween party that *you* left me at. He gave me a ride." It was the truth, but it left out so much between seeing him and actually getting the ride.

But the answer wasn't enough. Why did she get a ride from him? What happened afterward?

How *could* she explain what happened afterward? That she gave him her number with the offer of him reaching out whenever he needed her. Marty would jump to the same conclusions he had before.

Part of Becca felt bad that she had to hide such big details. Not only did it make it harder for Marty to understand, but it kept him in the dark of the full extent of their association. No matter what she chose to do, it would hurt one or the other. But it would hurt Derek more, she was sure, so she kept it quiet.

When Marty asked about the second meeting, that was harder to work around. She ended up telling him a full-fledged lie that skipped over the second meeting entirely and pretended it had never happened, leaving only the time she met Mal and broke her board.

"And I've never heard about any of this?" Marty wasn't even pretending to watch anymore. He took over the entire couch, draping himself over the cushions dramatically and rubbing his face in exasperation with each new revelation she shared with him.

Becca sat on the ground, shaking her head and throwing a kernel of popcorn into her mouth. "I knew it would be weird, okay? And to be fair, you reacted exactly how I thought you would, so I think my reservations were reasonable." She threw a piece of popcorn at his face. He tried to catch it in his mouth and failed. "Now watch the movie, or else I'm shutting it off."

More questions might have come anyway, if he hadn't been interrupted by a knock on the front door. He sat up, and both of them looked at the hallway that led out of the living room.

"It's probably Winston." she got up, brushing off crumbs from her lap. "I'll be right back."

The blue glow of the television was the only light leading her through the dark of the room and hallway. They preferred their movie nights to be as dark as possible. Another knock sounded on the door, and she reached it right as the last one slammed against the wood.

She blinked, swallowing her surprise at the uninvited guest.

No. He *was* invited.

Derek stood there. Even in the dark, she could see the red mark on his cheek, and the red rings around his eyes.

"It happened again?" Her voice was quiet and conscious of Marty's presence in the other room.

Derek nodded, carefully waiting for a reaction, not saying anything.

Becca pursed her lips and leaned in to get a better look at the damage. It wasn't as bad as what she had seen earlier, but from the look on his face, it went deeper than what she could see.

"Hurry up! You're going to miss the best part." Marty's voice rang down the hallway.

Derek's shoulders tensed, and he took a step away from her as he looked toward the source of both the only light in the hallway and Marty's voice.

"I didn't know he was going to be here." His voice was rough, but he didn't sound mad. Regret dripped from the phrase like he had interrupted, uninvited to an intimate moment.

"One second," Becca yelled over her shoulder, hoping to buy herself time to consider her options. She couldn't turn Derek away, not in this condition. But how would she explain his sudden arrival to Marty?

Derek shook his head, backing away. "Don't worry about it."

Her hand shot out, fingers closing gently around his arm to stop him. She stepped out the door, getting close to his face to survey the damage again. Her fingers rose and touched lightly at the reddened skin. He flinched, but his eyes studied her as intently as she studied him. She couldn't leave him alone. "Come in, let's get you cleaned up."

An internal debate ran through his eyes, weighing his options much as she had.

"What's going on?"

Becca jumped at the sound of Marty approaching from behind, his words cautious. She turned to him, not letting go of Derek in case he slipped away while she was distracted. Now Marty saw the whole scene, his gaze catching onto Derek and focusing immediately onto the marks on his face. "What the hell happened to you?"

"Marty, I'll be back in a minute." She shooed him away with her hand, well aware that Derek was shrinking away from them and tilting his face to hide even further into the shadows.

Marty's brows knit together.

"Don't worry about me. Go finish your movie," Derek cut in, pulling his arm out of her grasp and stepping far enough away that she couldn't reach him. His shadowed blue eyes, which, to her had, been gentle, were now hard set. His lips twisted into a sour expression as he met Marty's confused stare.

After a moment, he turned back to her and dropped his voice until it was soft and husky. His lips even rose slightly at the corners, a false reassurance, while keeping himself at a distance. "It's not that bad. I'll see you later."

She couldn't stop him even if she tried. Derek turned and walked from the porch, not looking back at the two who watched him walk to his car.

"What the hell was that?" Marty stood directly behind her shoulder.

She turned and pushed him back inside, closing the door behind them to prevent Marty from staring any longer.

"Did he just *smile* at you? What's up with his face? Why did he come here?"

The questions kept coming, even as she walked back to the movie and sat down, pretending to be interested in some lost storyline and her bowl of kernels. Just when she had gotten him off her back, his outraged curiosity was back.

She brushed all his questions off, not able to explain them without exposing Derek.

Derek.

Where would he go now? Would he go right back home to where he had come from? What would happen if he did?

The guilt ate away at her until Marty finally stopped asking because she'd stopped responding, even though his attention returned to her every three seconds. She should have stopped Derek, made him come in. She could have invited him to watch the movie with them—though that might have not gone over well. It was probably better than sending him back to the place he leaves with bruises.

She should call him. See if he made it home. See if he didn't.

A cold stone hit the bottom of her stomach as she realized she wouldn't be able to. She didn't have Derek's number. The rest of the night was spoiled for her—she had no idea how to check on

Derek.

All she could do was hope that he would come back.

***

He didn't come back.

Becca stayed up hours after Marty left, hoping there would be a knock on her door and a certain curly-haired boy standing there. But he never came, and a sick knot built in her chest.

It was still there in the morning and in the afternoon. The weekends were usually a time when she got to relax, but she found herself on edge most of the day—sitting by the phone, hoping he would call. Feeling even worse when she realized she couldn't call him.

Winston stopped by in the afternoon to check on her before heading to work and got her hopes up when he knocked on the door.

By early evening, it became overwhelming, and she knew she had to do something. So she threw on her boots and her coat, and started the trek from her house to Derek's.

She had only ever seen the place the one time Derek had dropped Mal off there. It wasn't much to go off, but she did her best to follow the faint memory of the route until she found herself on a mildly familiar street. She exhaled a steamy breath into the air when she saw the small symmetrical house up a short hill.

Any hesitance was muddled by the urgency to make sure Derek was okay, and she walked up to knock on the front door.

It took a moment for anyone to come. Finally, she heard the soft scuffle of footsteps behind the wood, and it opened to reveal a simply dressed brunette woman. It must have been Derek's stepmother, Mal's mother, but she looked very little like Mal. Aside from the same dark hazel eyes, both her skin and hair were lighter. Becca, with her tan skin and darker hair, looked more like Mal than her own mother did.

Mal must have gotten her looks from her real father, just like

Becca got them from her mother.

The woman was caught off guard, clearly not expecting any guests to appear at her door.

"Hello." The woman was soft-spoken. "Can I help you?"

"Hi, yes, I'm looking for Derek."

Mal's mother's eyebrows rose until they were covered by her bangs. "Derek?" She looked over her shoulder, down the hallway, like she was checking to see if he was there. "He's not here right now."

"Oh." Of course, he wasn't. "Do you happen to know when he'll be back?"

Her eyes drifted over Becca from head to toe. A bout of self-consciousness came over Becca, and her hand smoothed over the front of her crumpled shirt under her unzipped coat. It wasn't like she was wearing anything messy, but she wasn't exactly dressed up for a nice occasion. Didn't matter though, Derek's stepmother just looked curious about the girl on her doorstep.

Maybe she wasn't used to having people show up looking for him. Which would be a surprise, considering how many girls spent the night with him in the rumors.

"Dinner should be ready in about half an hour. He should be home around then."

Becca deflated. She still wasn't sure if he was okay, and she'd have to wait a while longer, it seemed.

Smiling, she nodded and hid her disappointment. "I'll come back later. Thank you." She waved softly and turned to walk away.

"Hold on."

Becca paused and faced the woman again. This time she was smiling gently.

"Are you Derek's friend?"

"Yes."

"Why don't you come in and wait for him. Do you like meatloaf? We'd love to have you stay for dinner."

Becca blinked, taken aback by the sudden offer. Truth be told, she loved meatloaf. Second truth be told, she didn't want to sit in the cold to wait for Derek, and she wasn't going to leave until she saw him. "I wouldn't want to impose."

"You're not imposing if I'm inviting. Please, come in."

Becca didn't object and gave the woman a smile as she stepped through the open door and into the small entryway.

"I'm Jennifer, Derek's stepmother."

Becca smiled. She wasn't sure what she had expected to find in this house. When Derek showed up on her doorway all beat up, she'd assumed she would find something terrible inside the house he lived in. Instead, she was met by a sweet lady and a tidy home that smelled faintly like the smoke she had come to associate with Derek.

"I'm Rebecca. Derek and I go to school together."

Jennifer motioned her in, leading her into the living room. "I've never met any of Derek's friends before. He prefers to spend time with them outside." She pointed to a couch off to the side. "Please, take a seat. I'll be in the kitchen finishing up. Derek should be home soon."

"Thank you." Becca followed Jennifer's direction and sat on the floral couch, taking a moment to examine decorations in the room.

Her own mother loved to put pictures of them throughout their place. She always said it made it feel more like a home when you could see the lives that were spent there.

But in the Stokes' living room, there were no pictures. Only a few *Car Craft* magazines set out on a heavy coffee table and an ashtray half filled with ash and stubs of cigarettes.

A door opened from the hallway, and Becca stood, expecting it to be Derek walking into the house. Instead, Mal entered the living room and stopped in her tracks when she saw Becca next to the couch.

"Becca?" She looked even more shocked than her mother had. But unlike her mother, she looked far less thrilled to have a guest in the home. "What are you doing here?"

Becca's hands came together in front of each other, sensing

Mal's uneasiness. "I was looking for Derek. He isn't here, so your mom invited me in for dinner to wait."

"Oh." She leaned against the back of an equally floral lounge chair. "Okay."

Becca looked to the spot where Jennifer had disappeared, and stepped closer to Mal. With her voice low, she did her best to keep her next words out of Jennifer's earshot. "Is Derek okay?"

"What do you mean?"

"He came to my place last night—"

"Last night?" There was a tone of understanding in her voice, mixed with shock that Becca would know anything about it. Mal also looked toward the kitchen and leaned in closer, keeping her voice barely above a whisper. "He left last night and hasn't been back since. Sometimes he doesn't come back for a while after…" She didn't need to finish her sentence.

Becca's heart dropped. "What if he doesn't come home tonight?"

Mal shook her head. "He will. Mark told him he had to. If not…" She drifted off again.

"Mark?"

"My stepdad."

Their house was nice and tidy, Jennifer was sweet. Then Becca remembered why there were no pictures on the wall. Could it really be a home when Derek left it with bruises and marks on him? And Mark was the one who did it to him. The one who put the marks on his face last night, who made Derek show up at her house in the first place.

And that meant this was Mark's home too. And he would be there for dinner.

Speak of the devil, and he shall appear.

Walking in the front door, still in his work uniform, Mark appeared. He didn't look how Becca had expected. His hair was close-cropped, unlike Derek's long, well-maintained curls. Across his lip was a solid graying mustache.

His eyes went immediately to her when he entered the living room, widening slightly. "I didn't know we were expecting guests."

Jennifer, having heard her husband's arrival, came back in the room. "Welcome home, dear. This is Rebecca. One of Derek's friends." Jennifer was focused solely on her husband, checking his reaction with eager-to-please written all over her face.

Mark looked Becca over, his gaze an intimidating evaluation of the person claiming to be his son's friend. He must've never met any of Derek's friends either. He reached out a hand. Becca ignored the instinct to flinch and took it. His grasp was firm as he shook.

"I haven't heard about you before, Rebecca."

"We've only recently met."

"Hmm." He nodded and let go of her hand.

She hid a small fist behind the bulk of her coat, and clenched and unclenched a few times in an attempt to get rid of the feeling of his skin on hers.

"Are you staying for dinner?"

Becca bit the inside of her cheek and swallowed. He wasn't as inviting as Jennifer had been. Even the simple question made her feel unwelcome. "I wanted to see if Derek was home. I don't want to intrude—"

"Nonsense." He cut her off, his lips raising slightly into a small smile that didn't reach his eyes. "You may as well stay. Jennifer is about finished."

Behind Mark's back, Mal stared at Becca. Her frown was deep and her gaze unsteady, like she was trying to send a message without making any sudden movements. Becca was no fool, the warning was loud and clear, even without words, but she was already here. She had already accepted the invitation once. It might lead to more attention if she backed out and left entirely.

And Derek. If no one had seen him, then no one knew if he was okay. She'd come here to check on him, and she would stay until she could.

"Thank you, I'd love to stay."

***

The smoke burned the back of Derek's throat, soothing the anxiety that always hit him when he pulled up to his house. Especially now that he was already late for dinner and hadn't been home since his dad smacked him across the face in another drunken fit of rage last night, while throwing out his favorite slurs and curses in Derek's face.

It also helped ease the ache in his joints from sleeping in the back seat of his car. He didn't have it in him to show up on Becca's doorstep again after he'd found Parr there last night.

He already felt guilty turning to her at his worst, and he felt even worse showing up and ruining her night. Leaving had been the only way to make it up to her.

Based on the quickly approaching dark, he was even later to dinner than he had been before, and the moment he walked into the house, he knew he'd hear all about it. He took one more deep drag of the cigarette before crushing it under his boot and walking up to the house.

The smell of Jennifer's cooking hit him as soon as he stepped through the door, followed shortly by the silence. A quick glance at the clock confirmed his tardiness—fifteen minutes after the time his father had told him they would eat.

In a normal household, he would hear chatter, or silverware clinking against porcelain plates, but at his, there was nothing. His father was strict. No eating until everyone was sitting at the table. Even if it meant waiting an hour for Derek to show up.

He took a deep breath and walked into the room, steadying his face and brushing at his hair to look somewhat presentable.

All eyes turned to him when he walked into the room. All three pairs.

Three.

One of them had dark brown eyes that stared at him from inside his head even when she was not there.

He blinked—once, twice—not fully comprehending what he was seeing. She shouldn't be here. The anxiety he had worked to quell grew tenfold, and his entire body froze, his mind playing catch-up.

All the while, his dad watched him carefully from his seat at the head of the table, analyzing his son's every breath.

"What's going on here?" Derek's voice came out hoarse, and he internally winced at how shocked he sounded.

Becca watched him, her eyes searching him up and down. He wasn't blind to the way they lingered on the marks on his face, or the clothes that were the same as the night before. Her back was stick straight, her hands fiddling nervously in her lap.

His father was the one to answer. "Your friend stopped by to see you. We figured she might as well join us while she was here."

A test. A sick, twisted test. He could hear it in the intonation of his father's voice and the clicking of his fingers tap, tap, tapping on the table.

A test he was quickly failing.

Derek's hands curled into fists, his jaw tightened so hard it clicked. Self-control was quickly being lost the longer he looked at Becca, who stared at him with her worried eyes.

He had already infiltrated her world with this bullshit, but he was terrified for her to see it this close up. He wasn't ready. He didn't think he ever would be.

"I don't think she's hungry." Test be damned, he couldn't drag her down. He stepped up to her seat, grabbing onto her hand, and urged her to stand. "Come on, I'll take you home."

A loud bang rang through the small dining area and shook the table. Derek winced as Becca jumped, her wide expression turning to his father.

Mark had replaced his tapping fingers with heavy fists. His testing stare shifted to show his fiery outrage at Derek's disobedience. "Sit. Down."

Derek wanted to be brave, he wanted to walk away and show Becca he was strong. But he was just the cowering pussy his father told him he was, and he didn't have it in himself to fight back. "Yes, sir."

He didn't want to let go of her hand. He wanted to pull it

to him, to bring her closer when he felt the slight tremble in her fingers. This was all his fault. His father's eyes watched everything he did, so Derek let go of her and sat in his chair beside her.

His father let the tension build up at the table, leaving them to stir and worry what would happen next. From the corner of his eye, Becca's head bent down toward her plate.

She didn't deserve this.

She deserved someone who had the courage to save her from this situation. And it wasn't him. He couldn't even save himself.

Mark clapped, and Derek bit his cheek to hide the scowl and hatred he felt toward the man. "Dig in." He finally announced, clearly unbothered by the tension everyone else felt.

Derek followed his father's lead, arranging his plate in the exact way his father did, careful to avoid any other comments. He ate when Mark ate, he paused when Mark paused. In the bitter situation, the food was tasteless.

Nothing was left on his plate by the end, just like his father. Becca had served herself very little, but her plate was clear as well.

None of them dared rise from the table until Mark excused himself.

The second he was out of the room, Derek rose and grabbed Becca's hand again. By some mercy, it had stopped shaking.

Mal and Jennifer stayed quiet as Derek led Becca from the room and out the door without another word. Becca didn't fight him. Her fingers wrapped tight around his, grasping him as hard as he wanted to hold onto her.

He didn't even turn on the stereo, not in the mood to try and pretend everything was okay as he sped away from the curb—away from Mark—as fast as he could.

Becca shifted in her seat, her eyes traveling to him every few seconds. He couldn't relax. Not until she was home safe. His jaw ached from the painful tension as he ground his teeth together.

"Derek." Her gentle voice felt like a dagger. He couldn't face her. She had now seen the inside of his world. She'd seen the results before, but now she'd seen what lay inside, and he couldn't stand it.

"No." He cut her off before she could offer any comfort or ask any questions. He was too weak to take it. "No talking."

He would never understand how he could be so lucky, in his entirely unlucky life, to find Becca. She said nothing else. There was no pushing, there was no prodding.

In the corner of his eye, she nodded, and that was that.

She'd written him that note months ago, the one tucked away in his wallet, with the offer of silence or laughter. Now he needed silence, and she gave him exactly what he needed.

SEPTEMBER 1985

After

Derek was heavy. His body was full of hard-earned muscle after hours spent working on his car, and while it might look nice, it made it extremely difficult to get him up the stairs of Becca's home. Even with her and Marty on either side, groaning as they made their way up the stairs.

It didn't matter though. The effort and struggle was a grateful distraction from the ten minutes she had spent sobbing on the floor after Mark Stokes's threat, disguised as a friendly visit.

Hopefully, it also distracted Marty, who had been so worried when she came back to the car with puffed red eyes. She told him it was Mark. He knew enough now to know that Derek's father was not someone who should be taken lightly, and his concern about what had happened in the ten minutes she was with the man was valid. She told him that, physically, she was fine, but they needed to get Derek into the house *now*. In case Mark decided to make another round in search of his son.

They both sighed in relief when they got to the top of the stairs and down the short hallway to the guest room.

Becca opened the door and led them the rest of the way to carefully place Derek on the plush bed.

It was amazing what he had slept through. She could imagine that the combination of alcohol and exhaustion and finally being someplace safe had taken a toll on him, and he would be sleeping for a while longer.

She pulled Derek's legs onto the bed, and worked his boots off his feet as Marty groaned and stretched his arms.

"God, he is heavy."

She shared the sentiment. "Can you open the closet and grab some pants and a shirt?"

Cocking a brow, Marty turned toward the small closet. He walked over, pulled the door open, and scoffed. "What the hell? He has his own closet? Exactly how often does he stay here?"

Becca mentally smacked herself for not warning Marty about that. Truth was, Derek was there so much, it was practically a second home, and this was his second bedroom. She kept a few easy pieces of sweatpants and shirts that were too large for her for these exact scenarios. This was one situation that certainly needed a new change of clothes. There were stains Becca didn't recognize all over his shirt. She wouldn't allow him to continue living in those. She didn't want to explain all that right now though.

"Grab me the gray sweats and one of the shirts."

Marty shook his head but threw the clothes at her and closed the closet door. Becca got to work on unbuckling Derek's belt and undoing his buttons.

"Whoa. What are you doing?"

Becca sighed. "Does he look like he's going to change himself?"

"So you're going to strip him?"

"Well, are you going to do it?"

Marty hesitated and cringed but stepped forward. "God, I think I'm going crazy. Give me that." He gently pushed a surprised Becca aside. "Turn around."

She blinked and turned at his command. A few minutes passed, filled with some curses and rustling, before Marty gave her the okay, and she turned to see Derek, not only changed into the clean clothes, but tucked under the comforter on his side.

He looked peaceful, his breathing deepening against the pillowcase. She sighed and let the heavy weight in her body float to the ground. He was safe. He was here, and he was safe.

Quietly, Becca led Marty out of the room, and they walked to the living room before settling onto the couch.

Marty leaned his head back against the cushions, exhausted.

"You should get home. Get some rest," Becca said quietly, rubbing her own exhausted eyes. They were still sore from the torrent of tears after Mark's visit.

Marty sat up. "No, no way. I'm staying right here."

"Marty—" she tried to object, but he had other ideas and cut her off.

"Clearly, that asshole's dad is bad enough that someone like him would want to run away, and I just saw him leave your house. I'm staying here until Stokes wakes up—*at least*."

Honestly, she was afraid he *would* leave. She didn't tell him the full extent of her and Mark Stokes's interaction. Like the fact that he now knew she was the one who had called CPS and that he suspected she knew where Derek was. If Mark were to find out that Derek was right there in her home, she doesn't have any idea how he would react.

She was scared. So scared. So she was glad to have Marty there for now.

"I'll bring you some blankets."

Once she got Marty settled on the couch in the living room with pillows and blankets, she told him goodnight before returning up the stairs. One peek into Derek's room assured her he was still safe and sleeping soundly, so she walked across to her own room and closed herself inside.

The exhaustion wore her down into dust, spread across her bed, and sunk into the thick covers. She wished she could be blown away in the wind.

However, for now, she'd stay there in place and face what was to come when her eyes opened again.

FEBRUARY 1985

Before

School had always been Derek's favorite time of the day. Not because he enjoyed classes or learning—that, he hated. No, it was because, for most of the day, he could get away from that house and that room and that man.

At school, he was a king. He was everyone's idol. He was a dream and a model of the perfect person.

But things were different now.

Now, Derek's favorite time of day was *after* school, because it was the time he got to spend with Rebecca.

In the dark, after hell, he got to experience a little piece of heaven.

He had long ago forgotten how nice it felt to be cared for, and she knew how to care for him so well. But he made sure to be there in the good times too. He didn't want to be someone she just associated with the darkness, so he often showed up in the evenings without any cuts or bruises.

He loved to drive. It's why he kept his car in such immaculate condition. Driving around was the best way for him to clear his head, and he found an even better way to enjoy his rides was to pick her up, and together they would drive and talk.

They did a lot of that. Talking. About this, about that.

Becca liked to laugh about the newest rumors.

She had told him she'd prefer if they kept their friendship between themselves, to avoid the attention it would bring in school, but their peers were far from blind.

Even though she claimed to hate the attention, she found it funny the conclusions people came to.

"Tracy was the third person to ask me if we are dating." She laughed, shaking her head. "*Just today.*"

"It comes with the territory, sweetheart. I'm a hot commodity," he joked, blowing a stream of smoke out the cracked window. They passed a worn-down barn off beside the country road they drove down doing eighty miles per hour. He had been happy to learn that she liked it when he drove fast.

"Tell me about it. None of them believe me when I say we're just friends."

He didn't blame people for that, and he knew she didn't either. They'd been spotted together outside of school many times by now. The past couple weeks, rumors had floated around about them being seen in the car, going into Becca's house, and once going to a diner late at night.

Of course, those people didn't know all the details. For example, if they'd been dating, Derek would have seen the inside of her bedroom by now. He'd seen the rooms of dozens of girls, but never Becca's. She'd never seen his either. She would also have his phone number, which is something he wasn't willing to give at the risk of *someone* other than him answering the phone.

Those people also never sat with them in the dark while she taped up cuts and dabbed at blood with wet rags. Or as they sat in silence on her couch, before she led him to the guest room, where he could be alone.

They only saw the little pieces, and they made up their own stories. They didn't know that their story was not a love story— it was something much, much more.

It had bits and pieces that couldn't always be mentioned. Like the times that Derek couldn't bring himself to explain the full extent of what his father did to him.

The most he had ever explained to Becca was, "My father is an asshole," and that was it. He wasn't eager to ruin it, and she wasn't eager to push harder than he was willing to give.

Derek was happy in the little world they had built in the past few weeks. The good and the bad, in the light and in the dark. And he now knew he would do anything for this girl.

***

Becca had worked hard to get Derek's phone number. He avoided sharing it with her for weeks. He never said why, but she could tell. He didn't want to chance her calling and his father answering.

She understood it, but she also would have felt much better if there was a way to contact him quickly if needed. So, she had secretly obtained it a week earlier from Mal, who was less concerned about sharing their number than Derek was.

She hadn't told him she got it. She didn't want to spoil it unless needed, so she kept it as her own little secret.

Until the night she got the call.

When the phone rang, she expected Marty or Winston on the other end. Her mother was likely on her shift in Connecticut and didn't have time to call, and Derek rarely gave a heads up before he showed up at her house.

But the voice wasn't either.

"Rebecca?" It was a woman's voice, an unfamiliar one. Whoever it was sounded around her mother's age, but with a voice hoarse from years of smoking.

"Yes? Who is this?"

There was a short beat of silence, followed by a shaky breath. "I'm your aunt, Shelby."

As far as Becca knew, her mother was an only child of dead parents. The only family Becca even knew of was dead or disappeared. "My aunt?"

"I'm your father's sister. Richard is my brother."

Richard. She hadn't heard that name since she was seven years old. The last memory she even had of her father was of him walking away. She couldn't recall his face, only the back of his head. As for his family, she never even heard of them.

A lump grew in her throat, which made it difficult for her to swallow comfortably before she answered the woman. "I don't have a father."

"He wanted me to call you."

Becca had long ago accepted that her father would never return, and she'd stopped waiting. Now, she was just angry. A spark lit in her, and she couldn't help lighting a fire on this woman she had never heard of before.

"He had ten years to call me himself. I'm not interested in hearing anything now. Goodbye." Becca pulled the phone away from her ear, intent on slamming it down on the receiver.

"Wait! Please wait."

The desperation in the woman's voice stopped her, and a war between the seven-year-old and the seventeen-year-old made it hard to hang up and pretend she had never gotten a call.

She pulled the phone back to her ear hesitantly. She didn't want her father back, but maybe it wouldn't hurt to hear a little from him. What changed so suddenly for him to want to talk to her?

"What?"

"He wanted me to call you and tell you he misses and loves you. He's very sorry."

Tears welled in her eyes, hot and angry. "He couldn't tell me himself?"

Shelby was quiet, and Becca waited patiently for her father's excuse to come from this woman's mouth. "I'm sorry for having to be the one to tell you this. Richard passed away the other day. This was just the last thing he wanted me to do."

Static replaced the sound of the phone, and filled Becca's entire body from head to toe. One minute she was tethered to the phone, the next she was floating. Barely registering the rest of what Shelby was saying.

From what she could hear, it was all excuses. Excuse after excuse after excuse.

Her father was dead. But it wasn't for ten years, or five, or one. It was for a couple days.

"I'm so sorry," Shelby said, and Becca could finally picture her dad's face. She had gotten her eyes from her dad, and his smile.

But that was all memory. Distorted by the crushing weight of time.

The dad in her mind was not the man Shelby was calling about. *That* man had died ten years ago—this was just time catching up with her memory.

"Whether he loved me or not, he should have told me himself. He had ten years to do it."

Becca slammed the phone down and cut off anything else Shelby might try to say—if she even tried responding. Becca didn't care.

The phone sat silent on the receiver. She half expected Shelby to try and call back, but it stayed still and silent. Shelby had done what she was asked and nothing more. Now it was Becca's turn to deal with the consequences and she had no idea what to do.

What was the appropriate reaction to finding out the father you hadn't seen in ten years was dead? That he loved you enough to tell you *after he was dead* but not enough to do it while he was alive?

She wasn't sure. But she picked up the phone anyway, and dialed the number her mom had given her for her boarding house. She tried that number five times. None of them went through and the sky was starting to crush her.

Only one other person popped into her head, and she dialed the newest number she'd memorized.

It rang twice before it was answered, an older man's voice. "Hello?"

Not Jennifer, not Mal, not Derek. Mark.

If she didn't feel so numb, she might have been afraid.

"May I speak to Derek?"

"Who's this?"

"This is Rebecca."

"Ah, Rebecca." He recognized her. "I'll get Derek."

There were a few moments of quiet, some shuffling, some

muffled words, and then a new voice. Relief washed over her when she heard the familiar bass, and she closed her eyes to bask in it.

"Becca?" Derek sounded upset. "How the hell did you get my number?"

"Mal." She didn't mean to tattle, but she wasn't thinking straight.

"That little shit—"

"Please come over." Her voice broke, and Derek stopped. She could practically hear his thoughts—or maybe lack of thoughts—flying through the phone.

"Are you okay?" The annoyance was gone. His voice was on guard—worried.

The care in his tone was so tender and gentle, it was the final strike to the dam that was built over a decade. Her knees gave out, and Becca broke down. Falling against the wall as she sobbed, she faintly heard Derek's sharp intake of breath.

"I need you." It's all she could manage.

The line went dead, leaving the long-winded tone in place of Derek's voice.

She didn't have enough strength to get on her feet and hang up the phone, so the beep became a background noise, as she dropped the phone and let it hang. She pulled her knees to her chest and tucked her head in between them.

She wasn't sure how long she sat there, crying to herself, but it felt like hours.

If Derek knocked, she didn't hear him. But she felt him the second he was in the room with her, his presence a warm bud in the cold.

She looked up at him and blinked away the sting of the light on her tender eyes. He was on his knees, panting like he had run, and his hands came up to her face.

Slowly, softly, he grabbed her cheeks.

She leaned into his touch, basking in the feel of his rough thumb brushing against her cheekbone to wipe away the tears.

He looked frantic as both hands held onto her. His lips were drawn tight, and his eyes were wide as they searched her face.

"Please stop. Please stop," he murmured, while his fingers brushed gently under her eyes at the never-ending water. "Look at me. Tell me what's wrong." His voice was a murmur she could barely hear over her sobs.

This was far out of Derek's element. Yet he came when she called and fell to his knees to do his very best for her.

"I'm sorry. I didn't know who else to call."

"Don't you dare be sorry." He frowned. "Talk to me, sweetheart. I'm here." His right hand lifted off her cheek and brushed against her forehead to clear away the hair that had come down to cover her eyes. He pushed it back behind her ear.

She told him everything. It flowed from her like a river that she couldn't stop with just her lips.

About the call, about the anger, the betrayal, the desertion, and everything she had chosen to forget.

She told him that she should be sad that her father was dead, but she was just so angry that her father could have believed he loved her, just to ignore her forever, and then try to come back after he was dead.

She did not miss him. She *hated* him.

She *did* miss him. She hated that, somewhere inside her, was a little girl who wanted her father back and now it would be impossible.

She panted between cries, and Derek never looked away from her. His hands never left her—whether it was wiping her tears or running over her hair, they were the rock holding her to the ground.

He stayed there and listened to it all. And he looked at her like he understood every word she said. Like he *heard* her.

When her tears slowed and her breaths evened out, her body was weak. She closed her eyes and leaned her head back against the wall to take a deep breath.

She became weightless, held together by solid arms, as Derek scooped her off the ground and against his body like she was a child. She wrapped her arms around his neck and buried her face into him without objection, letting him take her from the room.

He walked her up the stairs and into her bedroom, laying her on the bed. She pulled herself together enough to settle under the covers herself and laid back against the pillow. Derek tried to walk away, but there was no way she would let him go now.

Her hand shot out and caught his wrist. He looked from where they were touching, then to her, evaluating what it was she wanted.

"Can you lay with me please?" Her voice was quiet and weak.

Derek didn't care, though, and he nodded.

Becca drew the covers back, and Derek crawled in next to her, laying on his side so they were facing each other. How was it possible for a single person to make her feel so safe?

Derek Stokes of all people.

She had a hard time believing it could not be fate, to be brought together in such a way.

Eyes heavy, Becca let them close, while shifting so her body was closer to Derek, so she could feel his warmth.

He reached up a hand, and settled it on her shoulder, a gentle touch. "My mom left me," he said, quiet as a secret.

Becca opened her eyes enough to see Derek still watching her.

"When I was eight. She grabbed her bags and snuck out while I was asleep, because she couldn't handle my dad anymore. So, she left me with him and never came back." His hand left her shoulder and came back to her face, brushing along her hairline. "I hate her."

Becca nodded. "I hate him."

"We get to hate them. It's our fucking right."

He was right. Seven and eight. Too young to understand. Not too young to wonder why they weren't good enough.

Her head ached, her eyes stung. She squeezed them shut, trying to hold back more tears.

She owed nothing to the man who left her behind. Not her forgiveness, not her love.

Dead or alive, he was a stranger.

But Derek wasn't, not anymore. In five minutes, Derek had shown her more comfort and love and protection than she had received from her father in seventeen years.

His hand on her shoulder pulled her to sleep, and when the tears dried and the dreams came through, she had a realization.

Derek Stokes, from that moment on, was the most important person to her.

17

SEPTEMBER 1985

After

Derek's head pounded, and he thought he might be sick. When he opened his eyes, the heart-racing sensation of not knowing where he was hit him hard enough to send him bolting upright to take in the surroundings.

He'd woken the same way in the back seat of his Monte Carlo for the past few days, but this wasn't his car. It wasn't even a car. It was a bed. One that felt and smelled familiar.

A few days ago, the sight of the well-decorated room would have sent a wave of comfort and safety through him, but now it made his stomach drop.

The scent of lavender covered him, and a strong bile rose in his throat. He'd once craved that scent.

Part of him still did, but it was buried under the gut-wrenching betrayal he felt now when he smelled it. He swallowed the feeling down and got to his feet, swaying slightly.

Clenching his eyes shut, he pressed a fist to his forehead and willed the memories of the night to come back.

The last thing he remembered, he was walking into that dirty pub he'd frequented for two days in Madison. He didn't remember anything else. Not how he got back to Highburg, or how his clothes had been changed. Whatever it was he couldn't remember, he knew *she* had to be part of it.

Somehow.

And if that was true, he needed to leave. He couldn't risk seeing her.

He stumbled from the room and into the hallway, down the stairs, with his eyes focused on the door that would get him far away from here.

A hand pressed down on his shoulder and pushed him back, making him nearly trip over his already unsteady feet. He glared and turned to the perpetrator.

Marty Fucking Parr.

"Whoa, whoa. Slow down there, big guy. You can't leave." Parr looked like he also had just woken up. His hair was messed up, and on the couch behind him, riddled with ruffled blankets, was evidence of his slumber. He might have used that to his advantage, but really, Derek was the one at a disadvantage—with the ringing onset of a migraine and the incoherency of his hangover.

"What the fuck are you doing here?"

"Helping you, that's what. Now, why don't you come sit down. You don't look too great."

"No shit." Derek wasn't amused, and he shifted his shoulder to lose Marty's hand. He should have expected that the guy wouldn't give up so easily. "I'm so not in the mood for your shit right now." His voice raised, and his teeth ground together to hold on to his self-control.

Marty pushed back again and blocked the exit with his body. What Derek had over him in muscle, Parr earned it back in height. "You're not going anywhere."

Derek scoffed and rolled his eyes before getting up in Marty's face. "Get out of my way, Parr. There is very little keeping me from busting your face in right now."

"No." Marty didn't look scared or even threatened, and that pissed Derek off. More so when his attention flicked off of him and toward the stairs over his shoulder. "He's trying to leave."

The moment Derek realized there was someone else in the room, he knew he had missed his chance to escape.

He wished he hadn't looked.

Rebecca stood at the top of the stairs, watching them from above in her pajamas. Her skin was pale and sunken, like she had lost weight since the last time he saw her. Her hair was ratted from sleep.

A gasp stuck in the back of Derek's throat that would have given away the effect seeing her had on him if he'd let it go, so he swallowed it, even though it hurt.

He wanted to run away far, far away from here. Even standing near Becca made the resolve he'd built for himself crumble in seconds. He was still a spineless fool that wanted to wipe the exhaustion from her eyes and bring the color back to her face.

But he couldn't do that. *She'd* hurt him. He couldn't forget that, so he would just have to find another way to avoid the sick longing inside of him.

He clenched his jaw and bit his cheek, hoping the pain would distract from the ache in his chest as he turned back to Marty, who held his hands out to block Derek from moving past.

"I'm not staying here."

Even though he said it to Marty's face, it was directed at Becca. The words were sharper, more impatient.

"You can't leave." Marty was the one who answered anyway.

"Watch me," he hissed and lashed out against Marty's chest, sending him back into the front door with a wince. He bared his teeth and let the scared animal snap out as he grabbed onto Parr's collar, raising his fist over his head.

"Your dad came here." Becca's voice wrapped an invisible cord around his hand and pulled it still. "He's looking for you, and he isn't happy."

He'd been scared that hearing her voice would push him over the edge, but it did the opposite. It reminded him why he couldn't face her and why he ran away in the first place.

His dad was looking for him, and he wasn't happy. She was the reason for that. He ran away because she *betrayed* him and threw him into the line of fire. And she brought him right back to where he didn't want to be.

Once again, she thought she was helping, when all it did was ruin him.

Outside of his subconscious, her light footsteps alerted

her approach. "Just stay here. No one will know. We'll figure everything out."

How could he have deserved this? It didn't help him. It never helped him. No amount of desertion or beatings or betrayal would ever help him. It only made the bitterness grow.

He did look at her then, and the outrage hid the pain as he stepped up until he was close enough to feel her breath shudder over his face. That lavender smell overtook him. "This is your fault," he said between clenched teeth. "I was gone. I finally got away. I was safe from this mess, and you *brought me back*. Why? Why would you do that?" His voice cracked and the desperate need for real answers shined through.

Becca's mouth opened, then closed. Her silence hurt his ears.

He stepped back and looked at the front door. "I don't even want to look at you." He closed his eyes and fought away the image his mind created of her hurt expression.

She was so, so silent.

He would go anywhere, just to get away from her and the hurricane of uncontrollable emotions that she ignited in him and the hell that awaited him if his father found him.

Once again, he was alone.

***

Her fault. Her fault. Her fault.

Every word Derek had said was right. It was her fault.

Derek's home was never safe, and it was her fault that it was worse.

Derek had left to escape, and it was her fault he was back where he could be found.

Everything Derek said made her realize that her reasons for finding him had been selfish.

She wanted Derek here. And now he was, but he was gone.

Once again, she was alone.

10

FEBRUARY 1985

Before

Halfway between reality and a dream, Becca heard a door open and a soft intake of breath. But it wasn't either of those that made her squirm from her blissful sleep. No, it was the audibly female voice instead.

Becca's eyes opened and blinked against the early morning light.

"What the—"

Her head snapped to the side, and her consciousness caught up to her right after her body reacted by shooting upward.

Wide-eyed and slack-jawed, Becca's mother stood at the doorway with a tray of food.

"You're home?" Becca said, and it took her a moment to fully register the look on her mother's face. Or the fact that she wasn't looking at Becca but at something next to her.

Derek stirred in that moment, and Becca looked down at him and gasped.

Apparently, sobbing yourself to sleep makes it easy to forget things about the night before, until you're quite literally staring it in the face. Like the fact that she fell asleep right next to Derek and that his arm was slung lazily over her stomach.

Oh my god.

Derek's eyes opened and immediately rose to hers. He didn't look at all surprised by their position, and his arm didn't move. He blinked his hooded eyes slowly at her and raised a brow at her expression. His situational awareness was lacking.

"Uh."

The moment it clicked in Derek's head that the voice was not Becca's, his head spun around. Becca was frozen in place, her eyes rapidly darting between Derek and her mother.

Derek's arm stayed put.

"Oh." Obviously, her expression and the situation were finally catching up to him.

Becca wasn't sure if she should be surprised or not that he wasn't as alarmed as she was.

"I'll be downstairs," Becca's mother said the words so fast that, by the time Becca could interpret them, she was already gone from the room and the door closed.

The bang of it shutting snapped Becca out of her stupor and she fell back against the pillows, her hands rising to cover her face. "Oh my god." Mortification flooded her blood like lava.

Snickering made her eyes shoot up and land on Derek, whose lips curled up into an amused smirk, his damn hand still wrapped around her.

She glared and shoved him off, and he finally sat up all the way.

"How the hell are you laughing right now?" she snapped at him.

That only amused him more. "Oh, sweetheart, I've been walked in on doing much, much worse than this."

Becca shook her head and grimaced at the sudden images running through her mind. "That's disgusting."

He chuckled and stood up, stretching his arms over his head and making his shirt raise slightly to reveal the sun-tanned skin underneath. Her eyes remained purposefully on his face as he spoke. "Why are you so freaked out anyway?" He stepped forward and leaned in, his eyes scanning from her forehead down to her chin. "Your face is really fucking red."

Instinctively, her hands rose again to her cheeks, and she rested the cool backs of her knuckles against the heat, hoping to help with the rosiness. "You may be used to this sort of thing, but I am not. She probably thinks we were—" She stopped before she could go further, because, from the look on Derek's face and the giddiness in his eyes, he wouldn't let it go if she finished that sentence. She exhaled sharply. "Whatever. I'm going to go do damage control. You stay here for five minutes before you come down. Got it?"

The right side of his lips rose higher than the other, and he gave a single nod. "Yes, ma'am."

Taking one deep breath for courage, Becca steeled herself and left Derek in her room alone.

The house smelled amazing. Bacon, eggs, and toast. One of the best things to wake up to in the morning, and one that was rare for her.

Just as rare as the sound of her mother doing dishes. Her mother stood at the sink with her back turned. She knew her mom had heard her arrival, because her shoulders tensed up as she scrubbed away at a single cup for much longer than was needed.

"Smells good, Mom." It was the best sentence she could pick to ease into the situation. And it worked, because her mother shut off the water and turned to Becca with a smile on her face.

"Thank you, B." She dried her hands on a towel and walked over to the tray she had been carrying when she walked into the bedroom.

"I didn't realize you were coming home," Becca said, wincing at how awkward it sounded. She might as well scream *If I had known you were going to be home I would have made sure a boy wasn't in my room.*

"It's Valentine's Day."

Becca's lips formed an "O" as it all made sense. That was why she didn't pick up the phone. Her mother set the tray down in front of her on the table and Becca saw the heart-shaped eggs and toast right next to four slices of bacon.

Despite her mother's travel and constant absence, she never missed Valentine's Day. More than any other holiday, Valentine's Day was her favorite, so she made more of an effort to be home for it than even Christmas. And every year her mother "surprised" her with a love-themed breakfast in bed.

Clearly, that plan had been foiled this year.

There was a nervous spark in her mom's eyes as she gauged Becca's reaction. "But I figured you must already know it's Valentine's Day since—"

"No!" Becca yelled it much louder than she meant to. "No, Mom. God, no. It's not like that."

"Uh, huh." Her mom nodded but didn't look remotely convinced.

Becca slid a hand over her cheek. "Really. We're just friends. We were just sleeping. I promise, nothing else. Just sleeping."

She hummed and studied Becca closely. "You sleep in the same bed as your friend?"

"I…" How did one explain the situation? Derek showed up to comfort her and then carried her to her room, then she asked him to stay so he did. She wasn't sure if that made it sound better. "We're just really close friends."

"Do you sleep in the same bed as Marty too?"

"Mom."

"Fine, fine. But for being such a close friend, I don't even know his name."

"Derek. His name is Derek."

"Derek." her mom tried it and nodded. "Well, he *is* very handsome."

"God, Mom. Please act normal, okay? He's going to come down here, and I don't want to weird him out."

"He didn't look very weirded out earlier."

That she really didn't want to explain. "He's just very resilient. Now can we pretend nothing happened and when you see him you act like it's the first time you've ever met him?"

Her mom smirked and shook her head. "It is the first time I've ever met him." She chuckled, and walked to the pantry to grab a plate, dishing more of the bubbling eggs off the pan and onto the dish.

On cue, the heavy beat of Derek's footsteps came down the stairs, and Becca shot her mom a loud look before Derek walked into the kitchen.

Unlike Becca, he was all charming smiles and relaxed shoulders from the moment he entered the room. "Good morning," he greeted, crossing to stand next to Becca.

Her mother smiled at him and walked over to the table. "Hello, Derek, is it? It's nice to meet you. I'm Amanda, Rebecca's mother." She stuck out her hand, which Derek took easily and clasped between both of his. His face morphed easily into faux surprise.

"Mother?" He gasped. "I thought you were going to say sister."

Becca's jaw dropped, and her eyes rolled so hard she thought they might get stuck at the back of her head. Damn insufferable.

Her mom chuckled and let go of Derek's hand. "You're too sweet." She placed the newly filled plate on the table in front of Becca's neighboring seat. "You showed up on a great day. I made my Valentine's Day breakfast special."

That seemed to catch him off guard a bit. "Valentine's Day?" He shot Becca a look, and she shrugged. Clearly, neither of them had remembered. "I didn't realize that was today."

"Well, it is. Normally, Rebecca would take her breakfast in bed today. Maybe you'd both prefer that?"

Becca felt like she might as well jump out a window. Her mom knew exactly what she was doing, per the tiniest smirk on her face.

Derek laughed out loud, his eyes sparkling with delight.

Oh, she is so glad they were getting along.

"Mom."

"That's very thoughtful, but I think she's embarrassed enough." He didn't have the guts to meet her eyes, and Becca could only get her annoyance across with a glare at the brief glance he gave her from the corner of his eye.

"Thanks, guys. I'm *really* feeling the love today." Becca pulled out her chair and threw herself down into it. She picked up a piece of heart toast and bit into it. It rewarded her with a satisfying crunch that did little to quell her annoyance at becoming the butt of their joke.

Derek followed her lead and sat down in his chair. However, instead of taking in the food, he leaned over to her. "Okay, okay. I'll back off now." In her periphery, she saw him tilt his head. "Happy now?"

She rolled her eyes and dipped a piece of her bread into the golden yoke of her over easy egg. "Whatever."

Derek's otherworldly charm worked as well on her as it did everyone else. She forgot quickly about their egregious teasing and settled easily into the exchanged conversation.

She hadn't seen her mother in weeks, and she certainly hadn't expected her to meet Derek this way, but she was glad they had met.

After the meal, Derek rose from his seat and told them he needed to go. She offered to ride with him to school, but he said he had some stuff to do beforehand and that he would see her later.

The sink was already running as her mother finished the last of the breakfast dishes under the running water.

"Sorry I teased you so much, B," she said, and Becca sighed.

"It's fine. I knew you were joking."

"Yeah, but I'm not joking about being surprised seeing you in bed with a boy. Not exactly what I was expecting from a girl who barely even has crushes on anyone—even if that clearly isn't the case here."

Becca frowned, her mood dimming at the remark. "I've had plenty of crushes."

Her mom looked over her shoulder, her eyebrow raised. "Have you? Why haven't I heard about any?"

Becca blinked, staying quiet for a moment, as she wondered if her mom was serious in asking that. To her, the answer was obvious. When her mother waited for her response, Becca gave in. "You're barely here. When would I even have a chance to talk about these things with you?"

Her scrubbing movements froze, and her mother turned her face away from Becca's sight. Regret pinched in her, and she nearly backpedaled. She always felt bad for bothering her busy mom with her own issues, afraid it would stress her out. It's why she never mentioned anything over the phone other than progress with school and a few extracurriculars or if she'd completed her chores. It's hard when they're so far apart.

Mom spoke before she could take it back, and changed the subject. "Why was he in your bed anyway? If you weren't doing anything."

Becca's mind rewound to the night before. She hadn't forgotten about the phone call, and the devastating news, or the words Derek had said to her. But the pain of the night had been hidden by the brighter energy of the morning. Which was now clouded by her mother's question.

Becca averted her eyes and focused on a small chip in the linoleum on the countertop. "I needed to talk to someone after I heard about Dad, and so I called Derek. He stayed to help me."

Silence settled the room into an uncomfortable stillness. It lingered so long that Becca couldn't resist her mother's eyes anymore. When she met them, her stomach sank at the confusion on her mom's face.

"What about your father?"

She didn't know.

Oh god.

She didn't know he was dead.

Her mother and father had not spoken since the day he walked away. Becca knew her mom had tried, but as far as she knew, she was never successful. Other than that, she never spoke of him.

Maybe it shouldn't be a surprise that her mom hadn't heard first, but it was jarring that, now, Becca had to repeat the words out loud to deliver the news to her own mother.

What a cruel situation. Becca sat back down and closed her eyes, finding the right way to start in her mind. Her mother's focus remained a spotlight on her.

In that moment, she wished she could go back to the night before, with Derek's hand on her shoulder and his words calming her bitterness.

Maybe if he was still here, this all would be so much easier.

***

Becca got to drive herself to school. It'd been a while, but while her mom was on her short vacations at home, Becca could drive their only car.

She'd be a lot more excited about it if she hadn't been the one who'd delivered news of her father's death.

Her mom, unsurprisingly, was worried about Becca. Even after Becca kept telling her that she was okay, her mother kept asking over and over.

She left for school late, because her mother had insisted she stay home instead, and it took too much time to convince her otherwise. It was funny that now her mom wanted to have an active role or even talk about her dad. Where was that eagerness the past ten years?

That was the last thing she wanted. To stay home while her mom babied her and gave her too many opportunities to think about it all. School was a better distraction.

When she pulled into the parking lot and found a spot, most of the place was already filled.

Inside, the school was just another reminder of the love-infused holiday her mother so loved. Pink, red, and white had taken over the hallways overnight, and students walked around with flowers and candy. There was even more giggling than usual in the hallways on Valentine's Day.

Marty was just as wrapped up in the festivities, and when he found her by her locker, his hands held onto a heart-shaped box of chocolates.

Becca eyed it as she pulled out her books for the first two classes of the day. "Are you giving or receiving this year?"

He shook it, and the chocolates inside made a rattling noise. "A little bit of both."

"Who gave you that?"

"Samantha Crowley."

Becca's eyebrow raised. Marty had been going down his list of potential valentines just the week before, and Samantha had been at the very top since Jenna dropped off. Maybe he was finally getting his groove back. "I thought you were going to give her stuff."

"I did." He pointed at the box. "And she gave it right back."

An amused snicker slipped out at her friend's expense. She covered her mouth with a free hand and laughed silently into her palm.

Marty rolled his eyes at her reaction. "Yeah, yeah, laugh all you want. At least I have chocolate I can eat. What do you have?" He made a show of looking at her arms, which were filled with books and void of any sweet treats from a secret admirer. "Looks like another year of lonely valentines for you."

It was Becca's turn to roll her eyes. She could shut him up right here, right now. All she would need to say was that she woke up in bed next to Derek Stokes, and Marty probably wouldn't be able to speak for a week.

If she did that, however, she would have to deal with the fallout of Marty thinking that she and Derek had something going on. Unless he counted sobbing into Derek's shoulder as "something going on," then it wouldn't exactly be fair to herself or Derek to spread those sorts of stories. Besides, she didn't think of him in any way that would be remotely appropriate for being each other's valentines, and she was sure he would say the same.

"Ha, ha. Hilarious. It's just as funny as the first five times you said it. At least we can wallow in our loneliness together this year. How does it feel? Finally getting a taste of nothing for a change." She smirked as she said it, the cringe on his face amusing her to no end.

"It's just a short hiccup. One day, Samantha is going to come crawling back to me. Jenna and Josie too."

"Wait a second. How many—"

A metallic bang rang through the hallway, followed by a mix of murmurs and startled yelps. Becca and Marty glanced toward the sound, and from where she was, it was hard to see much above the growing crowd in the area. Based on the energy of the bodies, whatever they were looking at was exciting.

She stepped on her tiptoes, trying to get a better glance without much luck. Her line of sight was blocked by a group of boys in letterman jackets, who were oohing and chanting at something.

"What is it?" She had to ask louder than normal just for Marty to hear her. Like her, he was trying to get a look past the assembly. His eyes widened and his mouth dropped open.

"Oh, shit." He shook his head. "Looks like you're gonna need to start reeling in that asshole of yours."

Becca's head shot back in the direction of the commotion, and she stopped trying to look over shoulders and heads. The best way to get in and see if Marty was serious was by shoving through the wall of letterman jackets and denim to get to the front lines.

And, what a sight it was.

Brent Duggan was flat-backed against a row of lockers with a certain curly haired boy in his face. Derek had his hands wrapped in the collar of Brent's shirt, and at first glance, it looked like a mild altercation. No bruises or welts as far as she could tell.

Both of Brent's hands raised over his head in a defensive surrender, and his expression was both pained and a little afraid. When she saw Derek's face, she couldn't blame Brent for being scared.

His teeth were bared, and his face was red.

Becca's heart shuddered. She had never seen him like this. Never this…angry.

"It was just a joke, man," Brent said, doing his best to melt back into the lockers and out of Derek's grasp. Physics held him in place, though, and as long as Derek had a grasp, he wasn't going anywhere. You didn't need to be a genius to see that Brent's lean arms couldn't hold up against Derek.

After a few more seconds, Brent's pleading must have been

enough, because Derek dropped him, and took a step back—brushing his palms together to get rid of invisible filth—and turned to storm away from the group.

Becca's feet were moving before her mind caught up with her body, but she didn't resist it. Instinctively, she followed Derek across the open area in a semi-circle of students, and even though she knew that dozens of pairs of eyes were now looking between her and Derek, it didn't bother her the way it once did.

Not when Derek was *this* upset about something.

Brent noticed her, too, while he popped his collar and straightened out the wrinkles Derek had left behind. Brent never was very bright, but his worst moments were the ones when he couldn't keep his damn mouth shut.

"What the hell did you do to him, Lewis?" he yelled after her, and the sound of her last name grated against her nerves.

She shot him a glare out the corner of her eye but didn't stop walking. She didn't notice that Derek had frozen in place, right on the edge of the crowd.

But Brent wasn't finished. "Did finally opening your legs do you some good?"

Brent was all bark, looking for a fight wherever he could get one. Becca was used to those games, and she knew them inside and out by now. The best way to piss him off was to just keep walking and ignore him.

But those fighting words weren't for her.

Derek spun around and whipped past Becca before she could stop him—leaving her in a wake of his scent.

Derek was on Brent again, but this time his hands didn't bother grabbing his shirt. They flew fist-first into his nose, sending Brent back into the lockers, leaving him groaning in pain as blood poured from under his cupped hands.

Chaos erupted, and Becca froze as April screamed.

OCTOBER 1985

After

The fact of the matter was that Derek couldn't go home. But he wouldn't stay at Becca's either. The only other option was a reluctant offer from Marty, and when backed into a tough corner, Derek had no choice but to accept.

Becca tried her hardest to not be hurt by his choice. He and Marty hated each other, but now Derek would rather be stuck in the same home as his enemy than be with her.

What else could she do when he wouldn't dare meet her eye. She hadn't seen him for three days, not since he left in Marty's car, leaving her behind.

Could she blame him? No.

Did it hurt? Like hell.

To watch someone who had naturally become your other half choose anyone other than you—who wouldn't want to curl up and sob?

That wasn't a choice though.

Derek might hate her now, but she wasn't going to give up until he was safe.

As nice as Marty's house was—the perfect place for a teenage boy to hide—her nerves would be on edge until something was done about Mark. It had already proven unsuccessful the first time, and things weren't looking great the second.

When Becca wasn't dazed in her classes, she was at home on the phone.

Marty answered when he wasn't working at the shopping mall

theater, and his response was the same every time. "He's barely eating anything, He locks himself in the room all day, and my parents come home at the end of the week from the Bahamas."

She could imagine a frustrated hand running over his face.

"I don't know what I'm going to tell them."

She nodded and bit her lip. There was nothing she could say to Derek that would help—if he would even hear her. There was little she could do to make any of this easier. The only win was that Derek hadn't disappeared yet. She wondered why he hadn't tried to run while Marty was gone, and the best explanation was that he was scared. Now that he was back, now that he knew his dad was looking for him, he might be nervous that, if he left the stronghold of the Parr household, he would be found.

"Thank you, Marty." She sighed.

Winston was next, and the conversation was short.

Derek was in Highburg. No, he wasn't home. Had anything useful been found about Mark Stokes? No. Nothing at all.

Once again, helpless disappointment.

Follow-up calls with the same CPS operator led to the same dead end. They'd found nothing suspicious, and therefore, were not considering it a high priority. In less than ninety days, the case would be closed, if they decided it wasn't worth pursuing.

Of course, they hadn't found anything suspicious when they visited. By the time they decided to show up, Derek was long gone, and any evidence of what Mark did gone with him.

Would it have been better to not tell Derek about it in the first place?

The entire situation did nothing for her grades, and that was something she found very difficult to care about. She looked down at the returned test from Wednesday, which she had not studied for: C–.

Three weeks ago, that would have made her cry. Now, she was numb, and crumbled the page into a ball before dropping it into the closest garbage bin.

A flash of braided black hair caught her attention, and her head shot up in time to catch sight of Mal walking on the other end of the hallway with a pair of headphones hanging around her neck.

Becca's heart stilled the closer the girl got. Dark patches of tired bags polluted the unusually pale skin under her eyes, and a long-sleeved jacket was pulled down to her hands, which were stuffed into her pockets. To anyone who didn't know the girl, she might have looked normal for a teenager. To Becca, who saw her as a sister, she was a mere shell of herself.

"Mal," she called out.

Immediately, Mal's lowered gaze rose to her, and her pace halted on the side of the hallway. The empty look in her eyes exploded with a scowl so hard that Becca could feel the heat from yards away.

Without greeting her back, the girl turned and walked quickly in the opposite direction.

Becca moved, pushing past a group of chatting girls to get to Mal.

She reached out as she closed in and grabbed onto her jacket sleeve. The action did its part, and Mal spun around to yank her arm away from Becca.

"Can't you leave me alone?"

Derek liked to say that he and Mal were nothing alike, but Becca had always thought otherwise. They might not be blood related, but they had the same scowl and the same bite to their words. They both knew the best things to say to scare someone away. They both now looked at her with the exact same mix of hatred and betrayal.

"I know you're mad at me."

"Mad?" Mal scoffed a humorless laugh and rolled her eyes. "That's the understatement of the century."

"I just want to make sure you're okay."

Mal shook her head. "Until Derek is home, I don't want to talk to you."

Becca's hand hung in the empty air as Mal pulled away and disappeared with the crowd of students moving to their classes and lunch.

***

Helpless was the only word Becca could think to describe how she felt—but it didn't feel strong enough.

She couldn't get to Derek, she couldn't get to Mal. She couldn't do anything for either of them.

Maybe that was her problem though. She so badly wanted to help, when everything she did made everything worse.

She sat in silence at the empty kitchen table and poked half-heartedly at a half-cold meal that had been sitting in the freezer for months. When she cut a piece of the mysterious meat and stuck it in her mouth, there was no taste.

The house was quieter than usual, and it was always quiet.

She jumped midbite at the sound of a door opening, followed by the shuffling of bags. If she wasn't so used to the sound by now, she might assume an intruder. She rose from her unfinished meal and walked into the entryway to greet the arrival.

Maybe her mother had mentioned something about coming home on their call the other night, maybe not. If she had said something, Becca must not have been paying attention, because she was a little surprised to see her mom walking in with her travel bags in tow behind her.

Her mother's eyes brightened when she saw Becca standing there, and she dropped her luggage to open her arms in invitation. "Hey, B."

Becca walked into her mother's embrace and closed her eyes as soft arms wrapped around her. Inhaling through her nose, she was surrounded by the familiar scent of antiseptic hidden under a rose perfume. It was so her mother, the scent she grew up with.

But it didn't ease her worries the way it usually did. Not on this level.

The thoughts must have been written on her face clear as day, because her mom frowned as she pulled away from Becca. Instead of letting go, her hands came to Becca's shoulders and rubbed gently.

"Rebecca, honey?" The frown overtook her face. "What's wrong?"

She hadn't told her mom anything. She hadn't told her why Derek came over all the time, often late at night. She hadn't told her that she called CPS and that she made Derek run away. Her mom didn't know anything about anything that was going on. Not that she ever asked on their calls.

The smile Becca pulled on was far from believable, but she tried anyway. "Nothing. No, nothing. Just tired from school. You know how it is this time of year."

Maybe it was because she was her mother, but her mom wasn't convinced in the slightest. "Don't you dare try to lie to me. Come on, tell me."

Annoyance prickled in the back of Becca's throat. Having her mom try and get involved with her life during the fleeting moments she was home grated against her ridged nerves. "How long are you home for?"

"Changing the subject isn't going to make me move on. Come on, B, talk to me. I'm right here."

Right here. Yeah, she was right here—for now. In a couple days, she'd be somewhere else and they wouldn't talk for a while, and then she'd come home and play mom again.

The weight of everything crumpled on Becca too quickly, and she pulled out of her mother's hold. "Why do you care? You're never here. Why the hell do you care right now?" Becca snapped.

Her mother's face always showed exactly what she felt, so Becca could see the shock at her outburst. Was it really a surprise though? She's practically lived alone since she'd started high school, and saw her mother a total of four months in an entire year, broken apart into bits and pieces.

"Rebecca."

Becca almost felt bad at the hurt in her mother's voice, but she swallowed it down and let everything she had packed deep inside her flow out. "What gives you the right to come home and care about me before you run off to the next place? We barely talk. What makes you think I want to tell you things when you're practically a stranger to me?"

Her mother's brow furrowed, and Becca saw her defenses rising right before her eyes. "B, come on. That's not fair. You know I need to work so we can live."

"Are there not jobs for nurses anywhere closer than Michigan or Florida, or wherever the hell you're going next? I mean, come on." She threw her arms up in the air. She knew she shouldn't be talking to her mom like this. She knew she worked hard to give Becca opportunities other single mothers couldn't, but at what cost? "Do you remember when dad died?"

From the widening of her mother's eyes, she remembered.

"You weren't there to tell me my dad died. You didn't even know. I had to be the first to know. *I* was the one who had to hear that my dad had died, and then you know what I had to do? *I* had to be the one to tell *you*. I shouldn't have to do that." Frustrated tears welled in her eyes. She wiped angrily at them, hoping to stop their barrage, but they kept coming, no matter how much she tried. "That's what a mother is supposed to do. You should have been the one to tell me and not the other way around. Maybe you think it's unfair, but that's how it's supposed to work. It's a parent's duty to take the weight of a child's burden, not leave me alone to bear it on my own all the time. I…I…"

Becca broke down, finally letting the tears fall freely. She hung her head and pushed the heels of her hands into her eyes as a loose sob released. "I never had a dad, and I barely feel like I have a mom."

Her mother sucked in a gasp, and now that Becca had let everything out at her mother's expense, the guilt started to rack up.

If her mom walked away right now, Becca wouldn't be surprised. After everything she did for her, Becca was acting like an ungrateful brat—she was aware of that.

But her mom didn't leave—she stepped closer. The space between them was filled with understanding and forgiveness and apologies as her arms wrapped around Becca, pulling her in.

Becca lifted her face from her hands and buried it into the solace of her mother's grasp. It felt like forever since the last time she had been held like this—like a child in need of a mother.

She sobbed into her mother's shoulder as she rubbed gently against the back of Becca's head and hushed her softly.

"I'm sorry, Mom," Becca hiccupped between sobs.

"No, honey. I'm sorry. I'm sorry I haven't been around." She pulled away to meet Becca's eyes. "I never knew how you felt, and I figured, since you didn't say anything, you were okay. I'm sorry I haven't been around to see you struggling."

Becca had never felt like she could tell her mom things. She was constantly afraid that telling her mother about her life or normal teenage problems would distract her from her work, so she kept it to herself. Now that she had started, though, she wanted to tell her mother everything. About Derek, about his dad, about Mal. About every little thing, even if it made Mom lecture her about her choices.

"It's not an excuse, I know it, but I'm going through a really, *really* hard time…" Becca paused, playing with her bottom lip as she gauged her mom's reaction. She didn't wave her away or tell her to talk about it later. Her mother's kind smile welcomed anything Becca needed to say.

"Talk to me, B."

So she did, and she didn't stop until she'd said every last piece.

***

Her mom left after the weekend to return to her next assignment, but not before promising that, after this job, she would find somewhere local to go work—permanently.

"One month, B," she said, with her bags in hand. They were lighter than they normally were, since she had opted to leave some of her things behind to make the transition from traveling to being stationary easier. "One month, and then I'll be back for good. I'll call you."

Thus ended two days that could have been considered some of the best and some of the worst days of Becca's life.

When they weren't spending much needed mother-daughter time together at the mall or watching a movie, Becca was making calls to Marty's house or casually stopping at the theater during his shift.

She wasn't sure what she expected.

Maybe she was hopeful that he would say Derek wanted to see her now, or that he wasn't hiding away in his room and refusing most of the food offered to him.

But that wasn't the case. Each time she hung up the phone, she felt a little bit worse.

She even borrowed her mom's car for the afternoon, to drop by Marty's house.

She only tried the doorbell twice.

Once, to signal her arrival to Derek, who—according to Marty—was the only one home until his parents got back from their trip on Sunday.

Twice, when she saw the curtain shift in the upstairs bedroom window like a ghost. He *had* practically become a ghost to the busybodies of Highburg, who had noticed his absence in the school and town.

She wanted to keep ringing until he was annoyed enough to answer the door and face her, but she couldn't bring herself to do it. Not when she remembered what his face had looked like the last time he looked at her. The hatred she saw—she wasn't quite sure why she so badly wanted to see it again.

If she had to guess, she just wanted to see *him* again, even if it meant being hated.

Even the great moments with her mother couldn't prevent the late-night tossing and turning in an effort to get Derek's face out of her mind. His smile, his frown, in the dark, in the sun. Every moment they'd ever spent together skipped like a record in her head.

She wasn't sure if she wanted to grasp onto it or throw it away.

Her mom was a wonderful distraction over the weekend, and now she was gone again—even if it was for only one month.

One month was too long to worry about what was going to happen next.

She didn't have to wait long though.

The knock on the door pulled her away from the TV. It was hard, and heavy-fisted. Who knew a couple draws on a door could hold such a serious tone and spark such nervous energy in her.

She swallowed and rose from her seat to cross the living room to the window. Hooking her finger against the curtain, she pulled it slowly just enough so one eye could peek out the front window to see who was waiting for her. The familiar worn truck answered her question, and she dropped the curtain to rush to the front door.

Winston stood on the steps, fully decked out in his police uniform. He was probably stopping by to make sure she was doing okay for the week.

Becca opened her mouth, but her smile and greeting faltered at his expression. His lips were downturned, his eyes serious. Her heart dropped to the level of her feet. Heavier than a stone and racing away from her at the same time.

"What happened?"

Winston took a deep inhale and gestured into the house, silently asking for permission to enter. Becca stepped aside and shut the door as he passed over the threshold.

He sighed again and turned to look at her. "Derek Stokes's parents reported him missing."

Missing. Derek had been missing for a week now. Mark was looking for him, which she was well aware of, but she didn't expect him to go to the authorities about it. Especially considering the allegations and eyes that were on him.

"You knew he was gone, I told you that. He's fine now."

Winston pulled his hat off his head and ran a hand over his thinning hair. "I didn't have to do anything, because there was no official report made. People weren't paying attention, so we could ignore it for you and him. Until a family makes a report, nothing needs to be shared with the public."

"So, what now? People are going to be looking for him?" Becca could feel a slow panic rising in her chest. If Derek were to be found and sent back home, things could get worse for him. A sickness boiled in her—Mark wasn't looking for Derek to make sure he was safe—he was looking for Derek to keep him under his guard.

Winston shook his head. "The Parrs arrived home from a trip this afternoon and found Derek staying in their guest room."

Becca stopped breathing, and the slow panic erupted at full force.

The lines between Winston's eyes deepened. "Sorry, kid. There's little I could do. They took him home before I had a solid case against Mark Stokes."

20

FEBRUARY 1985

Before

Excitement rushed through the hallway, and more people gathered to get an eye-full of Derek Stokes beating down Brent Duggan. It wasn't anything new—Derek picking a fight—but never like this.

It lasted until a teacher came running into the area.

The crowd broke apart and left before any of them were singled out by the other teachers coming into the commotion to deal with the situation.

Unlike the rest of them, Derek didn't stop until he was physically ripped away from Brent by the arms—putting up enough struggle that another teacher had to assist in keeping him away.

Becca didn't move from the same spot she was in when it started. Not even when they pulled him away from Brent, who was grasping his bleeding nose and howling in pain.

Derek said nothing and let them pull him away quietly, but Brent made a show of proclaiming his innocence.

"I didn't do anything! He just attacked me for no reason."

Mrs. Bernard shook her head in disappointment as she walked him behind the others.

He removed his hands from his nose to show the smear of blood covering his skin. "Look at my face. Look what he did to my face!"

April sobbed as she shuffled along next to him, with her hands hovering by his side like she wanted to help but wasn't sure what to do. Not that Becca was any more help.

All she could do was watch Derek walk away, wondering what had triggered his violence against Brent. Sure, Brent was annoying and thrived off creating tension, but it wasn't like Derek was new to this.

They'd been friends since the day he walked into school for the first time.

She didn't want to admit it, but it felt like it had something to do with her—if Brent's last comment had anything to do with it.

That thought got her moving, and she followed with some distance as they led the group toward the school office. She stopped next to a wall when they were all shuffled into a room and the door shut, creating a barrier she couldn't get past. Several other students lingered long in the area, and those who missed out on the action asked around trying to figure out what happened.

One of the teachers paused at the front desk to whisper something to the secretary, Mrs. Simon, who shook her head and picked up her phone.

The first bell rang, and the hallway slowly cleared, growing quiet while Mrs. Simon said something into her phone. Becca pushed away from the wall and walked toward the desk, her ears working hard to catch a piece of what she was saying.

"Yes, sir. That's right." Mrs. Simon held up a single finger as Becca approached.

Becca's toes tapped on the ground as she waited.

"Whenever you have a chance. … Uh, huh. That's great. … We'll see you here soon."

The phone clattered as she placed it back onto his hook. Her eyes sparkled kindly as she finally glanced up to Becca, "What can I help you with, dear?"

Becca opened her mouth, then paused. That was a very good question. She wasn't quite sure why she'd followed, or why she came to the secretary. What exactly was she expecting from all this?

"Oh, uh. I was just wondering how long they're going to be in there?" She pointed at the office door.

"Probably a while. Why? Do you need something?"

"I was just wondering." Becca bit on her bottom lip, looking through the window toward where they were in the presence of the school principal and counselor. She wished she could see in, maybe get a better idea of what was happening.

Mrs. Simon raised her eyebrows above the thin rims of her glasses. "Well, get to class then. You're going to be late." The second bell proved her right and Becca jumped.

"Thank you." She pushed away from the desk, with one final glance at the closed room, before making it to her first class of the day.

Not that it mattered, because it was difficult to focus on anything other than what trouble Derek might be getting into.

She watched the clock closer than whatever her teacher wrote on the board and thought too much about Derek getting into trouble because of Brent's comments about her. The more she thought about it, the more she wanted to rush out and make sure he was okay.

Last night, Derek had stayed with her and brushed away her tears. Today, he might have broken Brent's nose because of what he said about her.

Any doubts she had about Derek Stokes were long gone.

Becca was a little scared of how much she had come to appreciate Derek in just a few months, and after what he'd done for her, she wanted to give it right back.

Her hand shot up, catching her teacher's eye and causing her to pause in the middle of her lecture. She pointed at Becca.

"Yes, Miss Lewis."

"May I use the restroom?"

She sighed, clearly disappointed it wasn't some interesting question about whatever historical war she was teaching, and motioned her hand. "Don't forget the hall pass."

Becca rose from her chair and grabbed the hall pass from where it hung on the wall of the classroom.

There were three restrooms closer to her than the one she

walked to. But none of those passed in front of the school office.

She walked quicker than she normally would through the hallways, speeding just enough to be fast, but not enough to be running. Because of that, her reaction was delayed as she turned the corner and saw the two men standing outside the office in the empty hallway. She slid to a stop when she saw both familiar faces standing in front of the empty front desk.

One younger with his face downturned, avoiding the eyes of the older man, who had one hand grabbing onto the boy's collar.

She wasn't close enough to hear what he said, but she could see Derek's face and the finger that Mark stuck into it, wagging it like he was chastising a small child. Becca's heart pounded at the look on Mark's face. The tension in his jaw, the slight reddening.

He was angry—trying to hide it behind a casual expression—but he was angry, and he was losing his cool in a school hallway.

Becca stayed in place as Mark said something, and Derek's hung head slowly rose until his chin raised. His eyes connected with his father's.

Becca saw his fists clench. From where she stood, she could make out the scabbing red on Derek's knuckles from where his barrage on Brent had broken the skin.

She swallowed, unsure if she should continue forward or back up. The last time she saw an interaction between Derek and his father, Derek shut down and grew quiet. Would it be better if he didn't know she saw the way his eyes reddened slightly, or the way his breathing quickened when his dad pulled him roughly by his collar until their faces were right in front of one another?

The choice was snatched away from her when a classroom door opened somewhere in a hallway behind, and Mark's head snapped in her direction. It took him a few moments to register that he and Derek were not alone.

Becca held her breath, her grip on the hall pass tightening until the edges of the wooden stick dug into her palm.

Mark smiled, and Derek followed his father's diverted

attention. His eyes widened slightly when they saw her standing there. A heavy shame washed over her at the same moment it appeared in his face.

The grip that Mark had on Derek loosened, and he patted his son's shoulder in a way anyone else might interpret as a fatherly comfort before stepping away and letting go.

He mumbled one last thing to his son, who did not react to his words before the man turned and left.

Becca stayed in place, listening intently as Mark's footsteps faded down the hallway and the front door of the school clicked open.

She moved when they were alone. He didn't avoid looking at her. This time he stared with every step until she was right in front of him.

His eyes weren't just red, they were rimmed with the shine of tears.

"Are you alright?" Her hand skimmed over his face, over his neck, and down his arm to his injured knuckles. His hand was hot to the touch, and she had to gently pull the tension out of his clenched fingers until he relaxed in her grasp. Brushing the uninjured skin around his knuckles, she pulled them to her lips and blew onto the bloody marks.

He flinched as if the air hurt him and nodded.

Becca exhaled.

There were a million things she wanted to say to him. She could tell him he shouldn't have done it. That giving in to what Brent said was playing into his game. That by defending her, he was hurting himself.

But who did that help?

Her arms flew up and circled around his neck, pulling him against her into a hug.

He froze up under her embrace and grunted in surprise as she closed her eyes and buried her face into his shoulder.

"Thank you, Derek."

A few seconds passed where Becca wasn't sure how he would react, but then he relaxed, like the words were the only thing he'd needed to hear. His arms slid around her waist, pulling her in close. His face came down and settled into her neck. He sighed into her hair.

Becca could have stayed like that all day, wrapped in Derek Stokes's arms. It didn't even matter to her that they were standing in the middle of the school hallway. All she could think about was that she never realized how wonderful Derek's hugs would be.

Before

When you really care about someone, it's crazy how little you mind what others say anymore.

In such a short time, they had become inseparable, and she no longer stressed what rumors floated around about them.

Marty wasn't as thrilled about her newfound friendship, and he didn't understand why she felt so connected to Derek, but she couldn't blame him. She also couldn't explain it, so he just accepted her lame reasoning, which left out just about every real detail.

Her time with Marty remained simple: watching movies and playing games and doing the same stuff they'd always done since they were kids. She loved their relationship and how simple and dedicated they were to one another. Out of everything in her life, Marty was the most consistent.

Derek though—it lacked simplicity and it became depth. It went from nothing to emotional, lovely, fun, and often scary to let someone see her the way he had. She knew it scared him too.

Marty was the surface, and Derek was everything underneath.

There was no overlap. Marty wanted nothing to do with Derek, and Derek wanted nothing to do with Marty. It wouldn't be fair to either to force it, so she let the two different paths take their course and went with the flow.

Except when it came to parties. She didn't like parties, but they were the one thing that Marty and Derek had in common.

She let them have those to themselves. They both loved the

girls, they both loved the attention. Especially Derek. He never missed a party, and he was the life of them. People loved him. They wanted to *be* him, to *have* him. If they couldn't do that, they just wanted to be next to him.

One reason she hated parties so much was because, half the time, Marty ended up disappearing for a while with someone else, and she sat alone in a random corner until he showed up again.

Clearly, that had stalled for Marty during his dating "dry spell," but Becca assumed that the experience would be similar with Derek—who got about twice the amount of women that Marty ever did. She preferred not to get ditched by both, so she stayed out of it all together.

Whenever she convinced one of them to not make her go, the other would come running up from behind to have their try.

She'd talked her way out of five different parties, twice each.

Until the last Friday of March.

Marty had already tried, and she'd turned him down. It worked out in the end, because he ended up having other plans, so he gave up the pestering. Derek tried, too, and she turned him down on Monday. Then again on Tuesday, Wednesday, and Thursday. By Friday, her wits were close to cracking. Derek had never asked more than twice, or pushed when she said no—he was surprisingly great at not testing her limits.

It took her until Friday to realize that this must not be just a normal party for him.

"So what is it?" She leaned against the hood of Derek's car and crossed her arms. It was warm enough outside she only needed one layer instead of the two she'd worn all winter.

"What's what?"

"What's so great about this party that you want me to go so bad?"

It was a sunny day, so Derek had his sunglasses on and flicked ash off the bottom of his cigarette. All she could see was her own curious expression in the reflection over the slight upturn of the corners of his lips.

"I just want to hang out with my friend. Is that so bad?"

"We hang out all the time. Don't you have other friends that will be there?"

"None that I care about."

Becca sighed and shook her head. "If I say no, you're not going to give up, are you?"

He smiled for real then, showing all his teeth. "Not a chance, sweetheart," he said, and smoke floated from his mouth as he spoke.

She groaned and threw her head back. "Ugh, fine. But you owe me one. And you better not ditch me. I hate that."

He shook his head, still grinning. "I'll be by your side the whole night. I promise."

***

Becca felt ridiculous. She'd curled her hair and teased it higher than she should have—even slapped on a decent amount of makeup. Maybe this was another reason she hated parties.

She hated feeling like dressing up was a necessity, but she did it anyway.

Derek was there at exactly seven o'clock, knocking at her front door, just like he said he would be. Becca cringed as she caught sight of herself in the mirror in the hallway. Maybe she should have just worn the same outfit she wore to school. At least then she wouldn't look like she tried so hard.

Too late now.

She opened the door to Derek standing there. He wore his leather jacket, with a button-up shirt unbuttoned all the way down and hands tucked into his pockets—perfectly on-brand.

Brow raising, Derek took her in from head to toe, and Becca's face flushed. "Damn."

Becca winced and shook her head with a warning. "Not. A. Word."

Derek smiled so hard that his only attempt at hiding it was biting his bottom lip—a piss-poor attempt if you asked her.

He made a zipping motion over the grin to comply with her request.

God, that smile was infectious. She couldn't help the unavoidable upturn of her lips as she rolled her eyes. "Let's just go."

Sure it was warmer than most of the winter, but it was not nearly warm enough for the number of people that were jumping into Greg's pool.

"Jesus, I don't understand why you like these things."

"Come on, lighten up, sweetheart," Derek said, bumping her shoulder with his.

Somehow—in the two minutes since they walked in the door—he'd managed to get his hands on two cups of some random liquid that Becca had little interest in drinking. Holding one of the cups out to her, she accepted it and grasped it in both of her hands.

He winked. "This will help."

She didn't want to get drunk, but a little buzz wouldn't hurt the experience. She sipped at the bitter liquid and scrunched her eyes in distaste. Derek chuckled, and brought his own drink to his lips, chugging it down without reaction.

Like Becca expected, about a dozen people approached them as soon as they were noticed. Or, more accurately, they approached Derek.

Guys from his classes patted him on the back and pressured him to try to do a keg stand, girls leaned on his shoulder and giggled at whatever he said—joke or not.

Across the room, Becca's eyes paused their skimming when she spotted Brent and April leaning into one another, glaring in their direction and whispering.

After Valentine's Day, when Derek actually *had* broken Brent's nose, the loose friendship between the two was over quicker than it had started. Derek had two weeks of detention and showed up a couple nights in a row at Becca's house, since his dad wouldn't let Derek forget how upset he was about the embarrassment he'd caused him.

"You're supposed to ignore them."

Becca jumped, as Derek's breath touched her ear. Inches away from her face, Derek followed her eyes toward Brent and April. The uppity couple perked up once they realized that they had Derek's attention too.

Derek smirked and turned back to Becca. "That's what you told me, remember? They're not worth it."

Becca crossed her arms. "And I stand by that." Her gaze went over his shoulder, toward a group of girls who glared at just her. A second ago, they'd been batting their eyelashes at Derek, and they weren't happy that he'd been drawn away by someone else. "You've got a line building behind you."

"Fuck 'em." He put his hand on the small of her back and led her away from the scowling girls without a glance back. "You've got all my attention for the night."

So maybe there were some fun things about parties. Like the drinking games she'd never tried—until Derek offered to down her alcohol whenever she lost. Or the dancing she'd never done—until Derek was next to her and laughing along to all the stupid moves she spun.

There were multiple instances of girl after girl after girl coming up to flirt, but Derek would just smirk and give short answers before turning to Becca and ignoring anything else they said.

It gave her an inexplicable satisfaction every time Derek gave her more attention than them. Parties were so much fun with him—he really was the life of the party.

But he surprised her, nonetheless.

She'd expected to spend their entire night there, maybe leave early in the morning. But they were only there for two hours before Derek put his hand on her shoulder and paused her swaying to the loud music.

He leaned in, his mouth parallel to her ear so she could hear his voice over the music. "Let's go somewhere else."

Becca furrowed her brows. "Already?"

He nodded. "I want to go somewhere with you." His fingers

wrapped gently around her wrist, pulling her away from the bass of the stereo and crowd.

"It's not even nine-thirty yet."

He peeked over his shoulder, grinning. "They close at ten."

She wasn't sure who "they" were, but her interest was successfully piqued. "Fine, but I'm driving."

They stepped into the cool night, and Becca wrapped one arm over her chest while the other reached out toward Derek for the keys.

He shook his head. "Hell no. No one drives my baby but me." His keys jingled as he pulled them out of his pocket and walked to the driver's side of the car.

"You're drunk, Derek. I think it's in your '*baby's*' best interest if I do the driving." She bent her fingers inwards and motioned for him to place the keys in her hand.

He paused, looking between his keys and her hand, then he sighed and gave in without a fight. The keys flew right into her awaiting palm, and he switched spots with her, so she could enter in the driver's side and he the passenger's.

"Wait."

Her hand froze right above the handle of the door, waiting for him to finish his thought.

"Consider this a privilege. You're the only person who has ever driven her except me."

"Her?" Becca teased.

He winked and lowered himself into the passenger seat.

There was no hint about where he was guiding her. He could have just told her where, but all he did was give her the directions right before every turn. They arrived downtown a quarter-to-ten, and he told her to pull over to the side of the road in front of a small ice cream parlor with flashing neon lights.

"This is it?" Becca put the car into park and took in the small place. It wasn't even a real building, just a small hut that you had to walk up to to order.

Derek answered by getting out of the car, and she followed his lead.

"You left a party for some ice cream?"

He ignored her question and walked up to the window, Becca on his heel. The girl behind the counter looked up and perked up when she saw Derek there. Most of the time, bored part-time employees would be annoyed by customers showing up ten minutes before close, but she grinned at Derek and leaned both elbows on the counter to get closer. "Hi there. What can I get for you?"

The menu was huge, full of thirty or so different flavors—some of which sounded absolutely bizarre.

"What do you want?" Derek wasn't looking at the board. He was looking at Becca as she observed the insane amount of options. "My treat."

Two sets of eyes were on her, waiting for her to answer. After a few more moments of rushing to decide, she settled on something familiar and easy. "I'll have chocolate."

"Two chocolates—with the waffle cone." He pulled a bill out of his wallet and pushed it across the counter.

The girl beamed up at him and scooped their orders before handing them both to Derek. Becca rolled her eyes at the way the girl's fingers lingered over his in the transaction. She reached into the register, but Derek shook his head and winked. "Keep the change."

Ice cream wasn't exactly the first treat Becca would pick on a chilly night at the end of March, but she accepted when Derek ignored the girl's coquettish grin and placed the cone into her hand. She licked at the sides of the treat, catching parts that were melting faster than she could keep up with.

They could have sat on the circular tables stationed outside the ice cream hut, but the heat of the car sounded much better. Becca took her spot in the driver's seat, while Derek slipped into the passenger's again, and they sat in the comfort of the locked and heated car, licking at their dessert. In the background, Derek nodded along to the Metallica playing through his stereo.

While Becca couldn't bear the thought of biting directly into the freezing treat, Derek ate like he was starving. She cringed.

"How can you do that? Doesn't it hurt?" She shivered thinking about the way the ice felt on her teeth.

He shrugged, already nearing the top of the waffle cone. It crunched as he took a bite. "It tastes too amazing to care." He leaned his head back against the headrest and sighed, content.

Shaking her head, Becca moved slower. The ice cream was melting too fast, coating her hands in sticky chocolate. "Dammit. It's getting everywhere." Becca leaned over the middle console trying to search for some napkins. The motion made her hair settle on the top of her cone, and she winced. "It's in my hair."

Derek paused his eating and placed his cone in a cup holder to hold it while he took over Becca's job and rummaged through the console. She licked at her cone and hands and waited. When he looked up, there were no napkins in his hand, only a light blue hair tie.

"What are you doing with that?"

"Hold still," he instructed, bringing his right hand up, brushing away the hair in her face until it was back behind her ears.

Becca stopped moving, becoming acutely aware of the gentle brush of his hands as he guided all of her hair over her shoulders and turned her so she was facing away from him. Behind her back, Derek's hands moved quickly and pulled her hair up into a tight ponytail, twisting the hair tie until almost all the strands of her hair were secured away from her ice cream.

Becca's hand came up and touched the ponytail with a few clean, tentative fingers. She laughed. "Did you just use another girl's hair tie to put my hair up?"

"It's Mal's." He scanned his work, before nodding in approval, and picked up the remainder of his cone.

"Well, thanks." She licked at the stickiness on her fingers, now confident enough not to worry about her styled hair getting in the way.

Derek chuckled, shaking his head in amusement. He'd sobered up a bit, she could tell.

He was relaxed, his sighs deep and his eyes clearer. Becca

leaned her seat back, too, wanting to feel as content as he looked.

He closed his eyes, and for a moment, Becca thought he might be falling asleep. Sleeping sure sounded nice right now, and Derek's comfortable car seats practically called to the lingering sedative qualities of the alcohol, but she still had a tiny bit more of her cone left.

"I have a confession to make." Voice low, it sounded like he was about to share a deep secret.

Becca paused from finishing the last of her ice cream to look at him. His smile was so slight she almost couldn't see it in the dark car.

"What is it?" Becca matched his volume and tone in reverence.

He released a deep sigh. "It's my birthday today."

Ice cream forgotten, Becca shot upward and nearly lost her grip on the cone. "Derek! What the hell?"

"What?"

"Why didn't you tell me? I would have gotten you something."

He shook his head. "I don't want anything. No, actually I did. *This* is exactly what I wanted for my seventeenth birthday." He gestured at the general space between them.

"Sitting in your car?"

"No, ice cream." He pointed at her cone. "I just wanted to go to a party and then get some ice cream with you."

"That's it?"

"Yeah, that's it." He paused and turned away from her to look out the window. The night was clear, so the stars were bright and easy to see. He didn't answer her right away. He took his time and let the quiet sit in the car with them. "It's what I used to do with my mom."

Becca blinked. Derek hadn't mentioned his mom since the night she found out her father died, and she knew it wasn't something he liked to talk about. The history of their parents was a sore topic for them both. "Every year until she left, she took me to this ice cream place, just like this one. Right on my favorite beach outside LA. She'd let me pick whatever flavor I wanted and let me get three scoops." He laughed and closed his eyes.

Becca wondered what he must see in his mind's eye. What did the beach look like? What did his mother look like? Was he as happy right now as he was back then?

"Those were the only times I cared about my birthday."

The story had been short, and Becca was positive there was more to it than just that, but from the smile on Derek's face it was sweet how it was and she didn't want to ruin that.

"Except this year," he added.

"What changed?"

He looked back at her. "I thought that was obvious."

Becca furrowed her brow.

"I have something else to confess."

"Oh, great." His confessions, like the first one, always packed a punch.

"I planned on leaving Highburg soon. I was gonna get as far away from this place as I could. Go back to California and never step foot near here or my dad again. I've been planning it since he dragged me here."

Becca stared at Derek, inhaling deeply with her mouth open, unsure of how to respond to that.

A painful crack formed in her chest, and a lump grew in her throat that made it difficult to swallow the ice cream in her mouth. She no longer cared about the chocolate cone, or the fact that her hair was sticky, or anything else. The thought of Derek leaving Highburg made the world around her stand still and shatter all at once.

"You're running away?" She hated how weak her voice sounded.

He shook his head. "Not anymore."

Relief flooded over her so quickly she might have collapsed had she been standing. She wanted to throw her arms around Derek and pull him closer to her, but she held still and resisted. "What changed?"

"I thought that was obvious too." He laughed in disbelief and shook his head. "*Sweetheart*, you're the only thing in this hellhole of a town that keeps me sane. I'm not ready to give that up yet."

22
OCTOBER 1985

After

Handcuffs were unnecessary. He was a runaway, not a criminal.

The two officers had thought it was necessary in case he tried to get away while they picked him up and took him to the last place he wanted to be. The light metal chain holding his wrists within inches of each other jingled as he rubbed at his heavy eyes, swollen from lack of sleep.

It wasn't like he could run even if he wanted to. Derek was locked in the back seat like a child, and a pane of glass separated him from them. He was as good as an animal stuck in a zoo.

Trees moved past the car window in a blur, and the dread in Derek's gut grew the closer they got to his house.

He knew exactly what awaited him there. Or rather, who.

And he was terrified.

His leg shook, tapping anxiously at the floor of the car.

The officer in the passenger side, glared at him in the corner of his eye. "Knock it off, kid. You're shaking the whole car."

Derek barely heard him over the ringing in his ears. All of his focus was on steadying his breathing—deep inhale through his nose, and out through his mouth.

The police car slowed and pulled around the corner leading down the last stretch of road.

Derek clenched his eyes, ignoring the pain. In, out. In, out.

It hauled to a stop.

"Alright. Home, sweet home." The officer crawled out of his

seat and opened Derek's door. "Get out."

Derek opened his eyes and let himself be pulled by his arm out of the car. While his cuffs were unlocked, he picked the officer's name badge to stare at—Robertson. He hadn't realized how tight the metal handcuffs were until they were loosened and pulled away. He rubbed at the reddened skin on his wrist.

"Come on. Let's go."

Even though he was untied, the cop's grip stayed on his upper arm and forced him to follow them.

Derek stared at the car parked in front of the house. He hated seeing it there.

There had once been a lot of fight in him—when he felt strong enough to stand up against his dad. To talk back and hold his ground. But the fight was long gone, and he knew once he entered that door, he would completely resign himself to whatever was behind it.

The other officer knocked on the heavy wood, then they stepped aside, mumbling some normal conversation between them that Derek didn't care about.

The door opened up.

Mark stood there, a worried expression on his face.

"Son."

Derek tensed as Mark's arms wrapped around him. To the officers watching, he looked like a father welcoming home his prodigal son, but his arms squeezed hard around Derek's shoulders, tighter than was comfortable or loving.

"Found him camping out at the Parrs' house."

Mark let go of Derek and reached out to grab Robertson's hand and shake. "Thank you, officer. I really appreciate you finding him."

Robertson puffed his chest out. "Just doing my duty, sir." He tipped the brim on his hat and said goodbye.

Mark gave them a wave and shut the door.

Derek turned to escape down the hallway and to his room but was forced to stop by a heavy hand on his shoulder.

"Hold on."

Derek met Mark's eye and watched the false gratitude melt away. His father's face grew hard, his brows folded together into a look Derek was disgustingly familiar with—his stomach sank.

A loud lock clicked into place, followed by Mark crossing the living room and pulling the blinds closed so no one could see into the house.

Derek's hands started to shake where he held them helplessly to his sides.

"Derek." There was an unsteady calm to his father's tone, and he motioned for his son to approach. "Let's have a talk."

JULY 1985

Before

Sandals swinging from one hand, the summer pavement burned at the soles of Becca's feet as she used the wet path to guide her way to an open chair on the other side of the pool. She'd barely had time to visit the community pool since their junior year ended. Between summer assignments, researching colleges, and starting her new job with Marty at the theater, she didn't have a ton of free time during the week.

Since the manager at the theater didn't let her study while working slow shifts, it was great that she and Marty were able to make a new friend, a girl named Nicole, who rotated between ushering and concessions with Becca and Marty. Come to find out, she was in some of Becca's classes in their coming senior year. Marty especially enjoyed the arrangement—a new pretty girl was nothing to object about. But when Becca was able to get away from her obligations, she was lucky to have a little empty time.

Left with a rare free day, Becca had a few options to fill it, but on a hot day like today, the pool never sounded better. Seeing Derek while he patrolled the pool as a lifeguard was an added bonus. They didn't get to see each other as much as she would have liked—between both of their jobs and chosen extracurriculars, their only times together were often late at night.

Children screamed and giggled as they splashed in the water, and Becca laid her school bag on the chair to remove the shawl she wore over her single-piece bathing suit.

God, the sun felt amazing. She spent too much time indoors during the summer.

Maybe she should have given in to Derek's attempts at persuading her to take the job as a lifeguard with him, even if she didn't know how to swim.

Becca laid her towel over her chair and sat down, leaning back to bask in the heat of the sunlight bearing down on her. Based on his usual work schedule, Derek's shift would start in about five minutes, so she shut her eyes and waited.

It was the long trill of the whistle that told her he was about to come out. The stationed lifeguards all moved to switch, and Derek emerged with a few others for his shift in his red swim trunks, white top, and sunglasses.

He didn't notice her right away; his eyes were devoutly scanning the water where kids splashed and screamed playfully. It was fun watching him take his job so seriously. He enjoyed working there. He loved the sun, even though he couldn't often take his shirt off, with all the bruises it was hiding, and he once said he liked having the security of his own income to distract from home.

Becca waited, amused, for Derek to notice her as he walked to his post, and when he did, she could pinpoint it to the second.

Even with his dark glasses covering his face, the change in his expression was noticeable from where she sat. His nonchalance grew into a beam, and he lowered his shades slightly so he could catch her eye above the rim of them. He sidetracked from his path to his post to approach her, and she sat up as he did, smiling up at him in greeting.

"I thought you were busy today." Derek took his sunglasses off, so she could see his eyes clearly. They sparkled in the bright light.

"I was, and then I wasn't. The new summer advisor at the school canceled my college application meeting at the last minute, so I figured I'd come and visit my favorite lifeguard, work on my tan, do a few laps perhaps."

"Your favorite, huh?" He pursed his lips, hiding a grin. "Just try and stay in the kiddie section. I don't feel like having to keep you from drowning on top of all these other little brats I have to watch."

In the corner of her eye, two of those "little brats" were roughhousing behind Derek's back—taking advantage of the brief unwatched moment. Becca laughed. "Speaking of which, you're slacking on the job."

She nodded in the kids' direction, and Derek spun to see what she was talking about. He groaned and lifted the red whistle that was hanging against his chest to his lips, filling the air with its high-pitched ring.

A few people around them paused, then moved on when they realized Derek wasn't whistling at them. The little boys both froze and sheepishly bowed their heads as Derek instructed them to never do that again if they wanted to swim there anymore.

With one final shake of his head and a wave at Becca, Derek situated his sunglasses back at the bridge of his nose and finished the short walk to his lifeguard post.

Even if Becca wasn't at the school today to figure out what she wanted to do for her future, she still had other things she had to do—like summer assignments for her literature class. Just one of the curses of choosing advanced placement for her senior year.

Reaching over the side of her chair, Becca opened her bag and pulled out the assigned reading she had been given a month earlier when school was let out. At least this way, she was doing something productive on her day off and getting a tan at the same time.

A pool might not have been the best place to complete schoolwork, but the background noise of laughter and Derek's whistle didn't bother her at all. Combined with the hot summer air, reading a book could be more enjoyable in a place like this.

For about thirty minutes of reading, Becca did her best to get enthralled with the written word, making sure to annotate her thoughts as per the instructions of the assignment. She got about five chapters in and would have gone further if a shadow hadn't blocked out the sunlight she had been using to write down a note in the margin of the page.

She paused midsentence and looked up at the source of the interruption. For a split second, she thought it might be Derek coming over in the middle of his rounds, but the person standing there didn't have his long, curly hair or blue eyes.

He had slick dark hair, tanned skin, and dark eyes, and this might have been the first time she'd ever seen him wearing something other than his basketball jersey.

Becca barely knew Chance. They'd never spoken before, and the only interactions they'd had might have been when she went to watch Derek occasionally play football or basketball after school. And calling that an interaction might be too generous when she was only cheering for Chance as much as she cheered for any other member of Derek's team.

That's why it didn't make a whole lot of sense *why* he was standing by her.

"Aren't you worried about that getting ruined?"

"What?" Becca raised a single brow, confused.

He gestured at her hands. "The book."

She looked down at the pages she had been working on, expecting something to be wrong with them. But they looked exactly as they had before he'd distracted her—perfectly fine.

"Wouldn't it get ruined if you get it wet?"

Oh, that's what he was talking about. "Oh, no. Not really. People don't usually splash this far away." She nodded toward the bone-dry ground around her to make her point.

She thought that would be it, but to her surprise, he wasn't on the same wavelength. The chair next to her, which had been occupied by some kid a minute ago, was now empty, and Chance settled into it sideways so he was facing her rather than lounging back like it was meant for.

Becca watched him, the book still open in her hands, intrigued by his sudden approach. For a second, her eyes flicked over his shoulder to the lifeguard post, where Derek lounged back, to check if he had even noticed Chance's random approach.

He had.

In fact, all of his attention was focused directly on her and Chance. His sunglasses were off again, clutched between his fingers as he held the tip of them between downturned lips.

Becca raised her brow higher. She thought that Derek would have been amused to see her awkwardly singled out by one of his teammates, but now she couldn't read his expression. His lips were halfway between neutral and a frown, but his eyes were entirely unreadable. She'd never seen his face like that.

"Why are you reading it so early? The assignment isn't even due until September."

Becca forced her attention away from Derek and back to Chance. He was leaning over to get a better look at the cover of it, and she held it up. "How did you know I'm reading this for school?"

"I have the same one collecting dust in my backpack. Mrs. Johnson, right? I've got her for fifth period next semester." He shrugged and leaned his hands back against the seat of the chair, making himself at home next to her. "Couldn't imagine anyone would willingly choose to read it."

Now she couldn't decide if she was more surprised by the fact that Chance was talking to her or that he was also taking an advanced placement course. Maybe it was her own case of prejudice that led to the assumption that a basketball player would never be in an AP class. He wasn't wrong, though. This book was nothing like what she would normally choose.

"I have her for third," she said.

His friendly smile dropped a bit, disappointed. "Too bad. We could have partnered up for any projects. I hear they're brutal."

Becca laughed, closing her book and setting it down next to her. Maybe Chance wasn't so bad. He was also reasonably attractive.

"Why aren't you swimming? It's a hot day, doesn't the water look better than whatever is in that book?" He stood up and looked toward the pool.

Becca followed his gaze. He was right, again, the water did look much nicer than anything in some book with hidden meanings she needed to decipher for a class.

"She can't swim."

Chance jumped in surprise at the abrupt voice next to him.

Becca was so focused on Chance, she didn't notice that Derek had come down off his tower and crossed the pool. His glasses were back on, hiding his unreadable expression.

Becca frowned and rolled her eyes. "Thank you, Derek. How would I have ever been able to say that myself?" The sarcasm was thick. Unlike him, she didn't have sunglasses to hide her annoyance.

"Oh, hey, Stokes." Chance was oblivious to the silent passing of words between them, and his acknowledgment of his teammate was brief. Then he turned back to Becca. "You can't swim? I don't mind helping you out. Maybe show you a few things. I actually taught my younger brother to swim, so I guess I have some experience. We could—"

"Sorry, man. She's scheduled for lessons with me today."

Blanching, Becca shook her head in confusion. "Derek."

"Oh, okay." Chance stepped down, his friendly smile faltered, and his eyes shifted back and forth between them. Becca could read body language enough to note his shifting feet as he grew uneasy in Derek's presence. "I guess I'll see you around."

Becca deflated in disappointment. A cute boy showed a little interest, and Derek just had to come in and ruin it. "See you."

Chance gave her one final close-mouthed smile before leaving.

Becca spun on Derek in frustration. "What the hell?"

"What?"

She scoffed. "Jesus, I know you're not blind. I was talking to him."

"He was *flirting* with you."

"So?"

"So, he wants to get into your pants."

"So?" Becca leaned forward, waiting for him to give a better reason.

He paused, his frown deeper than before. "What do you mean, so?"

How could he be so oblivious? "So, what if I wanted to get into his pants too?" She wasn't serious, of course, but Chance was cute. Hot even. She didn't mind flirting with a hot guy and seeing where things went. She didn't get to do that kind of thing very often. "Believe it or not, you're not the only one who likes that kind of stuff."

Derek's expression was an enigma. She wasn't sure what to expect him to do next—laugh, or yell, or walk away. He didn't do any of that.

His hand reached out and closed around hers, face unchanging. Then he was pulling her behind him straight toward the water of the pool. "What are you doing?

"Swimming lessons."

"Wha…? I thought you were kidding."

The back of his hair swung back and forth as he shook his head. "I've never been more serious."

Becca tried to pull her hand from his, but his grip was solid and unrelenting. "What about your shift?"

Derek stopped for a moment, looking toward the pool house, where a few off duty guards chatted. "Robby," he called out, and a kid with blond hair looked in his direction.

"I'm taking my break." He didn't wait for Robby's response, but kept pulling Becca toward the shallow end of the pool.

She stopped resisting as he helped her walk down the stairs into the refreshing water. She sighed as they walked a little deeper until it reached up to her chest. He made a show of ordering people to clear an area for them, and Becca cringed at the attention it brought to them.

"Do we really need to do this right now? People are watching."

"Yes." He didn't hesitate, and then, lower than before, almost too low to hear above the splashing of water, he added, "He needs to see."

Becca stared at him. He moved on before she could question him, and she let it drop to follow his instructions.

"You can't swim if you can't float, so let's float." One of his hands came to her back. "Lay back."

Becca sighed but did as she was told. Derek had done this a lot for dozens of kids, and the words were rehearsed. Step by step, he guided her into the necessary movements needed to float on water.

"Put your arms out, like a starfish."

Becca giggled, amused by the childish description. He splashed some water onto her face, forcing her to shoot up and wipe it from her eyes.

"No laughing." He acted serious, but Becca could see the amusement hidden there. "Now lay back again, tilt your head until your ears are covered and close your eyes. It's easier to focus if they're closed."

She lowered herself back again, and covered her hair until it hung suspended in the water around her head. Arms and legs spread out, she willed herself to float. It wasn't as easy as he made it sound.

Her upper half stayed above, but her legs kept sinking, no matter how much she kicked at the water.

A finger caught her under her chin, and pushed up until her head went further into the water.

"All the way back, sweetheart. Close those eyes."

With her head bent back all the way, and her face parallel to the sky, she closed her eyes.

He continued his explanation. His voice was muffled by the water, but the touch of his hands moving her to his will was not.

"When your head is back, your hips will follow it." His touch, which had been at the small of her back, slid to her waist, down to her hip, and guided it up to the surface. In the cool water, his hand was hot on her bare skin. "Arch your back."

As he had one hand on her hip and the other on her back, Becca inhaled sharply as her entire body floated and her heart pounded in her ears.

It wasn't like she and Derek had never touched before. Hands, shoulders, backs. She'd touched his face the same day they met, and they were no strangers to one another.

However, his gentle hands correcting her positions and holding her above water were an entirely different experience. One that made her feel like she was both floating above the water and sinking to the bottom.

"Steady your breathing." It was amazing she could even hear him, because his next words were covered by the loud pounding of her heart echoing in the water in her ears. If someone else had been under there, they'd have heard it too.

She tried her best to take in a deep breath and let it out slowly, but it was shaky and uncertain. No doubt, the speed with which her blood pumped made it more difficult than it should be.

Like ice, the hot spots created by his hands were washed away as he removed them.

Seconds passed. Her mind raced. It raced so fast to catch up with what her body was feeling that it took a moment to realize she was floating on her own. Once she did, her body sprung the rest of the way, and she shot up.

She snapped out of it. The second her ears were out of the water and her eyes opened, the world came back into focus and the heat in her body cooled down. The confusion did not.

Embarrassment? Fear?

One of the two was the reason it took her too long to look at Derek again. What if he could tell how his hands had lit her body on fire?

"Not bad, sweetheart."

Derek looked proud, while she try to play it cool. "Thanks."

She needed to get out. Out of the water, out of the area. Just anywhere away from Derek for a moment.

"I think we should call it good for now," Becca said. She started wading to the side of the pool.

Derek stopped her with his hand on her arm. "We just barely started."

She pointed at the glaring lifeguard staring at them, "You're supposed to be working, and Robby doesn't look too happy to be covering for you." She was grateful for the excuse.

He followed her gaze to Robby, who tapped an invisible watch on his wrist to show time was up. "He's fine."

"Just go back to work. I have stuff to do anyway," she lied and pulled herself up onto the side of the pool, managing to slip away.

"I thought you were free today."

"I just remembered." God, she was terrible at lying, and he was great at reading her. She could tell right away that he didn't believe her, but mercifully, he didn't push.

"You owe me," he called out, and Becca paused her escape. Derek stayed in the water, his arms folded over the side of the pool, as he looked at her from below. "For the free lesson."

"What do you want?"

He tilted his head, and looked away for a moment to contemplate. "I'll think about it."

Becca scoffed at his antics. "Whatever. Just tell me what it is, and I'll do it."

"Promise?"

"I promise."

Before

Becca poked at the newest bruise on Derek's back, gently testing how much damage had occurred. He winced, air hissing as he sucked it in through his teeth.

Becca flinched away like she'd been burned.

It wasn't even the worst one, but it was the newest. Just another colorful splotch on his back that had shades from yellow to blue to green to purple to fresh red littered on it.

"Derek," Becca reached for the warm damp rag sitting next to her. She bit her lip, anxious to say what she wanted to. She'd been thinking about saying it for a while now, but with how things were going, she decided now was the best time. "Have you considered talking to anyone?"

He lay on his stomach, with his head turned away from her, but the defined muscles on his back tensed up. She couldn't tell if it was from the rag touching his skin, or from the suggestion.

"About what?"

So now he wanted to play stupid.

"It's the fourth time this week."

He didn't respond for a while, and Becca thought he might not respond at all. That had been one of the many possible outcomes she expected when she planned this conversation.

"I told *you*, didn't I?"

"You know I don't really count." She moved her attention from his back to his arms. She used the rag to clean around the new bruises there.

"Why not?"

She thought that was obvious. "Because I can't do anything."

"You're doing something right now."

She sighed and dipped the rag back into the bowl of warm water to rinse it off. "You know what I mean."

Minutes passed without any sound other than the fan running in the guest room, and the wet towel brushing against Derek's bruises. If he didn't respond in the next few moments, she would consider the conversation dead and let it be for now.

These topics were delicate with Derek. Sometimes, they wouldn't speak at all. Becca was lucky he didn't clam up entirely after the week he had. His dad was "stressed from work" and spent more time at the bars than usual. Just about every little thing Derek had done this week triggered him, and Becca saw the aftermath of that under her fingers right now.

She wouldn't be surprised if this triggered the start of a silent session. She was pushing her luck.

Derek stirred and flipped onto his back, forcing Becca to pull away as he hid away the bruises. He winced but raised an arm behind his head to support him against the pillow. Becca put her towel in the bowl while she wasn't using it.

"If he finds out that I tried to talk to *anyone*, it will only make it worse." He watched her closely, observing her reaction.

She knew that. He had never said it outright, but Derek was more afraid of his father than anything else, and he avoided upsetting him however possible. Mark was already a loose screw, and if someone was told and nothing was done, it could put Derek in a difficult position.

But it could also help.

"There's got to be some way to get help without him knowing. It could really benefit you and Mal, and—"

"No." His voice raised, not much, but enough to catch Becca off guard. "Drop it. It's not happening."

His expression grew hard, guarded in a way she wasn't used to around her. He was never entirely open, but in times like this, in the dim lighting of her home, she saw bits and pieces he would never show in daylight.

Averting her gaze, she shifted on the bed. "Okay. I'm sorry, I'll drop it."

She felt him watch her. His eyes left a tingle on her skin she knew to be his stare. The tension in the room was thick enough to breathe. She needed to get out, give them both some space.

She stood from the bed and reached for the bowl.

Gently, Derek's hand reached over and rested on hers on the bowl, pausing her escape.

"Promise me something." His voice was low, not as harsh but still serious. "You can't *ever* tell anyone."

Becca looked from his hand to him. The guarded expression was gone, and instead, she saw desperation. Her heart clenched at the sight. She couldn't stand to see him like this. "I won't."

"Promise?" His grip on her hand squeezed, silently begging for an answer.

She smiled at him and nodded. In all she knew in that moment, she meant every word. "I promise."

OCTOBER 1985

After

She thought she would never be at this home again.

Yet there she was, standing on the street, looking up at the house she'd run from a month ago. All the blinds were shut closed, and no cars were parked in the driveway.

She wouldn't have gone through with this if there were—she couldn't be anywhere near this house if Mark was home.

Releasing a shaky breath, Becca gripped the side of her jeans and walked up the steps and onto the front porch. This plan was a reach—even if someone opened the door, they would probably turn her away. It was wishful thinking, but she had to try—for him.

Her three knocks on the door were weak, but audible, and her wait was short before Jennifer opened the door to reveal her brown hair in disarray.

All the times that Becca had come before, Jennifer had been smiling—whether out of kindness or politeness. Today, she frowned. New lines had formed on her forehead that Becca hadn't noticed before. But Jennifer didn't look upset to see her there—she looked nervous. Her eyes shifted to where Mark's car was normally parked and then over her shoulder down the hallway.

"You shouldn't be here." Jennifer's voice was hushed.

She'd come this far, and she didn't want to leave now. Not when she didn't know how Derek was. She'd beg if she needed to. "I know. I know, but please I just need to see him. I'll be quick."

"Rebecca—"

"Please, Jennifer." Becca stepped forward, feeling desperate now. "Five minutes and I'll be gone."

Jennifer looked over her shoulder again, conflict on her face. It didn't take long for pity to win. Jennifer sighed and stepped out of the doorway to create an entrance for Becca. "Five minutes"

Becca didn't push her luck, on the off chance she would miss her opening, and rushed into the house, making her way down the hallway to Derek's room. She hesitated before the door, her hand hovering over the knob.

He wouldn't want to see her. He'd tell her to leave. She knew that already.

She also knew that whatever she saw on the other side of his door would break her heart. But she couldn't leave him on his own—not again.

The door creaked as she opened it.

His curtains were drawn, and lights were off, bathing the area in darkness, even at midday. A purple candle lay on its side on the ground.

Derek sat sideways on his bed with his back facing her. He didn't turn to see who entered, but maybe he already knew.

Becca cut off the only light in the room by shutting the door behind her.

Opening her mouth, she tried to say something, but the words died on her tongue.

"How many times do I need to say something to be heard by you?" His voice was deep, slightly hoarse. Weak. "I told you to stay away from me."

"You know I'm not going to do that."

"Then what the fuck are you going to do?" His voice rose slightly. "Because I see you trying to do a whole hell of a lot, and it doesn't really look like it's helping. Does it?"

Swallowing took effort, but she managed it and tried to steady her breathing and keep her focus. "Look at me."

He didn't. He remained facing away from her, his back slouched forward.

"Derek. Look at me." Her voice got higher and more demanding—for the first time since entering the room, she moved, walking around his bed until she stood right next to him.

Any feature of his face was hidden in the shadows as he turned to avoid her eyes, and frustration and desperation bubbled in the pit of Becca's stomach. Her hand shot out, reaching around his cheek to pull him toward her so she could see everything he was hiding.

Just like Becca thought it would, her heart shattered, and a bitter bile rose to the back of her throat.

His blue eyes looked up at her, tears streaming down over his cheeks to his chin. Sadness was not his reigning emotion, though. It was anger. His brows drew together to create a sharp line between, and his jaw trembled under the pressure of his gritted teeth. His hands—hung by his side—clenched into fists.

But it was barely *his* face. One eye was swollen to the point of closing. His nose was blue on the bridge and a cut crossed over his cheek the length of a finger. She'd become so good at seeing him in the dark, but that was also a curse, because every small blemish stood out like a blinding light. More bruises and broken skin littered under the collar of his shirt. Nausea rose in Becca's gut as she imagined all that could be hidden beneath it.

A gasp snuck from her throat even though she tried to catch it, and it cut the tension between them like a knife.

Derek didn't try to hide anymore. Now that she could see all of him and the damage done, he rose from his spot and stepped closer—towering over her and forcing her to crane her head back to see him. She couldn't look away.

"You try so fucking hard, don't you?" he hissed, his mouth just inches away from her. "Well, here you go. Have a look." He lifted his chin, his eyes wild. "Jesus Christ, you can't listen, can you? I *told* you not to tell anyone. I *told* you to stay away. I told you *everything*, and you didn't *fucking* listen."

Tears welled in the corner of her eyes. "You stayed in Highburg because of me. I couldn't watch it get worse the longer you were here." Her voice was weak and trembled on the emotion stuck in her throat.

Derek smiled until all his teeth were bared in a cruel, amused sneer. "Ironic, isn't it? Now I can't *leave* because of you." He stepped away and spun in a slow circle while he barked a humorless laugh. "It was all manageable before. I could handle it for a while until we graduated. Then we'd go to California or Madison or wherever the hell you decided. But this—" he motioned to his face, and Becca held back silent sobs, "—*this* is worse. *This* is because of you."

Becca broke. Every word he said was right. *This was her fault.* No matter what her intentions, Derek was *here*, and he was hurt. Because of her.

The tears and cries and whimpers she had been trying so hard to prevent surfaced in one big wave, a choking sob that cleared her lips. Tears fell faster than she could wipe them away, so she clenched her eyes shut to hold them back.

The air of the room settled as Derek stopped moving, his stare burning into her face.

Since the night she'd met Derek until now, all she'd wanted was to help him. After all those nights, all those secrets, and all those moments, all she'd ended up doing was hurting him.

Derek stirred again, stepping forward until he was in front of her—slower than before.

Becca opened her eyes. Unable to meet his, she couldn't lift her gaze above the red split in the corner of his lips.

Derek leaned forward so the side of his face ran parallel to hers, their cheeks close enough to touch if she moved. "You said it yourself." His breath moved against the hair settled near her ear. The anger was gone and all that was left of his voice was fatigue. "You can't do anything to fix this. So *stop trying*."

Before

"You think she'll like it?" Becca ran her hand over the textured surface of the skateboard, while her fingers fiddled with the ribbon bow she'd brought along to pretty it up a bit before gifting it.

"I already told you, she's gonna love it." Derek's fingers tapped rhythmically on the steering wheel along to "Sign of the Wolf" by Pentagram playing from the tape he'd put into the stereo. He had his window down to let the warm, late-evening breeze brush through the car and mess with his hair. "Better than that piece-of-shit one someone lent her."

Since she'd broken Mal's board at the beginning of the year, Becca had wanted to make it up to her. Mal had replaced it with an old one that her elderly neighbor's son had left behind when he went to college, but after sitting in a garage for years, it was far from par quality.

Once Becca found out Mal's birthday was today, she convinced Derek—with some bribery—to drive her around town after school, to a few different shops, until she found one that fit perfectly with Mal's personality.

"Why can't I just take it to her myself?" Derek shook his head and huffed. It had taken even more bribery to get him to agree to take her to see Mal at home so she could drop off her gift in person.

The big fat elephant in the room was Mark. Derek didn't need to mention that his father was going to be home for Becca to know that was exactly why he resisted her pleas. If they were lucky, Mark would have already wound down for the night and retired to his room, making any chance of crossing paths with him slim. Worst case scenario, she would end up having to exchange greetings with him before she gave Mal her gift and left.

It wasn't ideal, but in order for her to get Mal her gift before her birthday was over, it was necessary.

"I want to see her reaction." Becca rolled her eyes, exasperated from having to explain herself. Again. "And I don't want you taking all the credit for it."

"She's not even gonna believe it's from the both of us, much less just me."

The closer they got to the house, the less relaxed Derek became. He lit a cigarette about halfway there, and Becca rolled down her window to help him clear his head. His rhythmic fingers slowed down, until both hands clutched the sides of the wheel, and his cigarette dangled from the side of his mouth.

When the house was in sight, Becca pretended not to notice the visible smoky exhale of relief he gave at the absence of any other cars parked on the street. They were lucky and got the best-case scenario.

Mark wasn't even home.

Derek was much more compliant as he parked and flicked the butt to the ground. They both exited the car. He led the way up the stairs and into the house.

Becca clutched onto the skateboard and grinned as excitement fizzed in her. She couldn't wait to see the look on Mal's face.

"Mal," Derek called, padding down the hallway toward her closed door. She didn't respond right away. "Mal, get out here." He pounded a closed fist on her door—loud, but not aggressive.

"I'm coming." Mal's exasperation was muffled behind her doorway, and after a few halting steps, her door opened. She glared up at Derek. "What the hell do you want, asshole?"

"Mallory!" Jennifer's voice spoke up from the kitchen, chastising her daughter's choice of words. "Language."

Mal huffed but conceded. "What do you want?"

Derek turned to shake his head at Becca, who Mal hadn't noticed standing off to the side. "I don't really think she needs a birthday gift." The teasing jeer on his face said otherwise.

Mal perked up upon seeing Becca standing there, and then her eyes widened when they slid down to the gift-tied board in Becca's arms. "Is that for me?"

Grinning and giddy, Becca held out the board, presenting it with cheery theatrics. "Happy Birthday, Mal!"

"Oh my god." Mal beamed, passing Derek to walk forward and look closer at it. She inhaled a long, elated gasp and accepted it from Becca, turning it over in her hands to look at the bottom design. "This is so cool." She fiddled with the bits and bobbles on the board—spinning the wheels, brushing the sides. Her face was lit up the entire time, and Becca's heart jumped in satisfaction. This was well worth making Derek bring her here.

"Derek chipped in too. It's from both of us."

Derek observed from the side, leaning against the wall. He wasn't exactly smiling, but Becca could tell he was pleased by Mal's reaction.

Mal turned to him, raising a brow and trying to see if Becca was being serious. Whatever she saw on Derek's face must have convinced her she was. "Thanks." Surprisingly, there was no sarcasm in her words.

Derek only nodded in response, but his lips turned up.

"I just wanted to bring that by myself, but I've got to go now," Becca said.

"Okay," Mal said. She pursed her lips and paused. After a brief moment of contemplating, she set down her new board and wrapped her arms around Becca in a tight hug. Becca froze in surprise. She'd never taken Mal for the physically affectionate type, but this was nice. She returned the hug.

Mal nodded, pleased. "Thank you, Becca. I love it."

Over his stepsister's shoulder, Becca caught Derek's eye and mouthed the words *I told you so.*

She grinned, and for a simple moment everything was just

right.

She and Mal let go of each other, and Mal picked up her board to look at it again.

"I'll drive you home," Derek said, walking past them.

Before he could reach the door, though, it swung open. They all jumped, and Becca knew she wasn't the only one whose heart sank when she saw Mark standing there.

He scanned the area, seeing all of them, but focusing on Derek. Particularly on the keys in his hands. It wasn't too late, not much later than eight, but it was dark outside.

"Where the hell are you going?"

Derek didn't answer Mark's question right away, but took a moment to evaluate the man who stood in the entrance. Whatever he saw had him backtracking.

He turned to Becca and lowered his head and voice, "Go outside and wait for me, alright?"

She nodded, searching his eyes, before stepping around him without question.

Becca might as well have been a gust of wind to Mark Stokes. He didn't blink when she passed, but she caught the strong whiff of alcohol surrounding him. From close up, she saw the tell-tale signs of intoxication—flushed face and bloodshot eyes. Scared to catch his attention, Becca held her breath until she exited the door and closed it behind her.

Derek's Monte Carlo was locked, and he had the keys. She leaned against her door and looked at the house, wishing he would hurry and get out of there. From the little Derek had shared about the type of person his father was, Becca knew there were few redeeming qualities, and a lot of alcohol. This was the first time she'd seen Derek's horror stories with her own eyes.

She didn't want to see it play out any more than it already had, so she pinched the skin on her knuckles anxiously and counted the seconds down. She made a mental promise that, if Derek didn't come out by the time she reached three hundred, she would go back in and find him.

The window blinds were drawn, so she couldn't see if anything was happening inside, but the lights were still on, as they had been when she left.

He'll be here. She repeated the mantra in her mind. *He told you to wait.*

And she tried. She really did try.

She tried for a whole 137 seconds before she heard the crash. Her hands halted their counting. She didn't move a muscle, but strained her ears. It could have been her wild imagination, expecting the worst. 138, 139, 140—

There it was again.

This time louder. This time followed by a deep yell.

She really did try.

The adrenaline coursed through her blood and numbed the terror that shot her blood cold. She wasn't sure if that yell had been Derek or Mark. On the off chance it was Derek, she wouldn't sit here and wait for him to emerge different than he was three minutes ago.

Her footsteps pounded up the steps and then the porch, and the front door slammed against the wall as she shoved her way in—throwing caution to the wind.

There was no winning for her. She could have stayed by that car and dealt with whatever happened later—the guilt, the anger, the sadness. Or she could have done what she did and stood shocked in the open doorway as Mark pounded on Derek, who was backed against the wall, hands covering his face to block the blows—an image that would haunt Becca forever.

It was Mark who had yelled. Who *still* yelled.

With every strike, he screamed another word, as if it would brand the message right into Derek's skin.

"Do not disrespect me in my home." *Thrash.* "You will obey me when I order you." *Thrash.*

Becca choked on the horror that stuck in her throat, a gargled sound somewhere between a gasp and a scream.

Mal was gone—thank god—locked behind her closed door. Jennifer stood at the end of the hallway, averting her eyes from the beating, but not interfering.

Mark, unused to being interrupted, clocked the noise immediately and turned.

His attention was off Derek, who sagged against the wall as the assault stopped.

But Becca was inexperienced, unprepared, and underestimating what would happen when the cutting rage in Mark's inebriated leer turned its focus to her.

She wasn't a harmless wind to him anymore. She was a threatening fire he needed to put out.

"Who the hell do you think you are to walk into my house?" He straightened and let go of Derek. His body turned toward her, and his long-gated steps closed the distance between them.

Her breath hitched in shock. Her back pressed against the closed door. This is when fight or flight should kick in.

It didn't.

She froze, flinching and waiting for the inevitable.

Jennifer, who had been a statue a moment before, made her move, grabbing onto her husband's arm and pulling him away. "Mark, no. No, you can't. She's someone else's child."

His advances decelerated to a stop, but his face was still fuming.

Jennifer sighed in relief, and hugged Mark's arm closer to her.

Becca felt sick.

These were the parents that Derek had been given. One long gone. One a danger. One who only stopped Mark, not to protect Becca, but to protect him from the consequences of what he sought to do.

Becca wasn't just "someone else's child." She was the child of someone who would *actually* report him and get him arrested.

Derek would never be safe. Not as long as he was under the same roof as these people.

The harsh truth, the painful reality, was easy to diminish when she only saw the effect. But when she was standing right in the middle of the cause, she couldn't remain blissfully blind.

Mark pulled from Jennifer's grip and approached Becca with

less aggression, but enough to make her cower against the door.

He opened it and grabbed her arm, before pushing her out, stumbling onto the front porch.

He leaned toward her, his teeth bared like an animal. "Keep your mouth shut, bitch, or I'll make sure you regret it."

The door slammed inches from her face, and she was left in the nighttime air, with the smell of cigarettes, autumn leaves, and alcohol on her face.

***

Derek didn't come to school, and Becca didn't have it in her to search for him for three days.

She was officially a point of interest to Mark, enough that he'd threatened her and scared her away. And it worked. She was scared. She left her bedroom light on at night, and she checked the locks on the doors several times before curling up in her bed.

Her mom was hundreds of miles away, while Becca hid with the lights on afraid of the monster that might come for her. Like a little child, she wanted her mother home to check under the bed and tell her she was safe.

She became a hermit in her own home, secluded for the weekend and scared that, at any moment, she would get a knock on the door. She never did.

Not from Mark, not from anybody.

The image of Derek was burned into her mind, replaying over and over again.

While she was here in her home, Derek was constantly in the range of fire.

She understood now why he tried to keep her blind to that part of his world. Why he never wanted to be seen in the light. He was afraid when she saw it she would never look at him the same. And now that she had actually seen it, she feared he was right.

Derek had looked different to her then. He'd looked fragile, and stuck, and at risk of losing.

She couldn't lose him. The fear of losing Derek was what made her pick up the phone and risk everything else.

Winston listened. He gave her everything else—the names and the numbers. Child Protective Services, he said they were called.

She spent a day wondering if she should do it. Mark's threat and her promise to Derek were what held her back. She was fearful of what might happen to her.

But the fear *for* Derek was what made her pick up that phone and dial that number.

After

She couldn't get Derek's words out of her head: *Stop trying.*

The image of his bruises as he glared and cursed her blinded her to everything else in the passing period between the first and second classes.

Groups huddled together, chattering on about something Becca didn't care to try and hear. Whatever had stimulated this rise in gossip mattered little to her, and she pulled on her headphones to play the music from her Walkman and drown out the crash of chatter.

Nothing fazed her anymore. Over the past week, she'd become a shell, mindlessly following schedules and overly focused on school assignments. It was the only thing that could successfully distract her from *other stuff.*

Since everyone was so caught up in the hallway, she was the first into the classroom, with four minutes to spare. She chose to stare at the back of the teacher's head as he scribbled his poorly written chalk instructions on the board and zoned out to the beat of the Bowie song playing in her ears.

A poke to her shoulder startled her, causing her to jump, and she covered her heart as it sped up. Even more surprising was the boy sitting in the unassigned desk next to her.

"Hey, Rebecca." Chance smiled at her, the same way he had at the pool over the summer—which was the last time he'd spoken to her at all. He was oblivious to her reaction. "How are you?"

They'd been in the same class since school started over a

month ago, and he just now felt the obligation to say something? Apparently, she'd transformed into a cynic in a single week—that had to be a record.

"What do you need?" It was rude, she knew it, but she'd rather get this awkward moment—plus whatever his ulterior motives were—over with.

Chance at least had the decency to look sheepish as he skipped over the pleasantries. "Where was Derek at for the past week?"

Becca didn't give him the answer he wanted. Not because she didn't want to, but because she couldn't.

Stop trying.

"Not sure."

"Really? I thought you, of all people, would know."

"Well, I don't."

His face set into an unsatisfied frown. "Did you guys break up?"

She made a face at Chance, unable to hold back. "We weren't dating."

Unsure if he'd been joking or not, she evaluated his astonishment. It looked genuine. "Sorry, I just kind of assumed."

"Class is about to start." She pointed at the clock, and to the students who were finally starting to fill up the seats.

"Right. I'll just ask Derek about it later in gym today."

He'd just said the first thing that really interested her.

Back straightening, her hand shot out and grabbed his arm, stopping him from moving to his own seat. "Derek's here?"

"Yeah." He raised a brow. "You didn't know?"

No.

She didn't know.

She hadn't seen him since that day in his bedroom. Part of her thought she would never see him again after everything he said. All of her knew she deserved that.

But he was here, in these hallways. His class was just four doors down from hers.

If Chance said something, she didn't hear it. She heard nothing at all past the ringing in her ears.

***

"I've heard three people so far say he was following AC/DC around the country on their tour. Four people said he got involved in some underground fighting ring. And my personal favorite, coming in at a whopping twelve people—'Derek ran away to hide from his stalker, Rebecca Lewis.'" Nicole had made a list of every rumor she'd heard passed around about Derek's return and read them off to Becca as she nibbled at the ends of her crust. "Thoughts?"

Good thing Nicole had been paying attention to what was being said, because Becca hadn't heard much of anything after finding out Derek was back at school. At that point, her main focus was avoiding any route she knew he was likely to take—going so far as to eat on the outside bleachers, just so she didn't have to see him at lunch. Nicole didn't object, and Marty was too busy with something else to join them.

The rumors about Derek had always been bad, but these were just outlandish. Half of them attributed his sudden and lengthy disappearance as something to do with her.

They weren't far off about that—it just wasn't as simple as they imagined.

"Hello?" Nicole waved a hand in front of her eyes.

Becca pulled away from the same small section of sandwich she'd been working on for the past five minutes. "What?"

"Thoughts on these theories? Or, perhaps, some insider knowledge." Nicole tapped her notepad, where she'd scribbled down theories, with tick marks next to them for each time she'd heard them repeated.

"I'm not really sure."

Nicole threw her head back and groaned. "Bullshit."

"Nicole."

"No, bullshit. Bullshit on this, bullshit on that." She slapped her pad onto the metal bleacher, and it echoed in the air. Her joking, prying smile was gone now. "I *know* you know. I *know*

Marty knows too. You both know stuff, and I feel like some squeaky third wheel trying to play catch-up in this little secret you've all got going on. I mean, come on! How can Marty share a secret with Derek Stokes and not tell me? I'm dying over here."

"It's really not a big deal," Becca lied.

"I'm not stupid, Lewis. I speak three languages, okay? Four if you count how fucking good I am at reading body language." Nicole held up her fingers, putting down one each time she listed off something. "Translation one: Stokes goes missing and, coincidentally, you and Marty both start acting like you're hiding something. Translation two: Stokes shows up a week and a half later and you—the one person he can't get enough of—avoids him like the plague. Translation three: Stokes won't tell *anyone* where he was, and if anyone even mentions your name, he tells them to go fuck themselves."

"He what?"

"Oh, translation four: you didn't know *that* either."

Becca sighed and gave up on her lunch. Nicole accepted the barely-touched sandwich without question and took a bite. "Please, Nicole. I-I can't do anything else about it, and I'd rather just try to forget everything."

Nicole's expression went from offended odd-man-out, to protective friend. She leaned forward. "Did Stokes do something to you?"

"God, no." Becca cringed at the thought of anyone thinking he'd done something wrong. "No. It…It was me. I did something I said I wouldn't and ruined everything. That's about it."

Nicole put her hand on Becca's shoulder. "That's heavy."

"Yeah, I guess that's one way to describe it."

The bleachers were supposed to be a quiet spot where Becca could get away from the gossip and, most importantly, Derek. Wishful thinking on her end.

A rush of chanting from inside the cafeteria drew their attention.

"What the hell is going on?" Nicole muttered, her interest growing when it got louder and moved from inside the cafeteria to the outdoor area where they were.

The chant gradually became clear—"fight, fight, fight."

Nicole rose from her spot and walked to the top bleacher to look over at the action below. Becca didn't care much until Nicole mumbled a quiet, "Oh, shit," under her breath.

Interest piqued, Becca got up, too, and stood next to Nicole to lean over the edge and look down over the area.

In the crowd, it didn't look like anything more than a typical fight. A couple of guys sending punches at one another, until one of them emerged at the top and got the upper hand. Something Becca never cared about.

But once she saw who was fighting, Becca cared. She cared more than she should.

Derek grabbed the kid by his collar, saying something into his face before tossing him to the ground. A couple of the guys followed Derek around, cheering him on by calling his name and patting him on the back. He didn't eat up the attention like he used to. He just frowned and walked away from the crowd back inside, ignoring the people who urged him to continue.

Becca didn't realize her hands were gripping tight onto the railing until they ached. This was the first time she'd seen Derek in a week. His eye which had been swollen closed before looked normal now, and all the bruises were gone—at least that she could see from her perch as he disappeared into the building.

Nicole's attention was on Becca, waiting for something specific to happen.

Whatever Nicole expected her to do, Becca was sorry to disappoint. She turned and walked down the bleachers, opposite where the fight took place. She'd apologize to Nicole later about ignoring her calls, or maybe she would just pretend she never heard them.

She just needed to get far away from Derek and avoid getting involved with anything that pulled her to him.

Stop trying.

Yeah. For him, she'd stop trying.

After

Ms. Roylance put a bowl of wrapped, hard candy on the small coffee table between them and sat down. "Third time you've been in here this week, Derek."

Derek hid his discomfort behind as charming a smile as he could and leaned casually against the arm of his chair. "What can I say? I can't get enough of you, Regina." He smacked at the mint gum in his mouth and gave the guidance counselor a coy grin. "You don't mind if I call you Regina, right?"

Having a new, young counselor helped a lot with getting away with the shit he'd been doing lately. All he had to do was throw in a few flirtatious comments, wink, and give her a smile. and she'd hang up the phone before she dialed his dad.

It'd been working like a charm.

She chuckled at his antics, shaking her head. "Call me whatever you want, but I still would like to talk about your behavior."

Derek slouched back into his seat, oozing nonchalance. "They were all assholes. They had it coming."

Ms. Roylance pursed her lips, and her forehead wrinkled in worry. "How are you doing?"

Derek shrugged and tried to ignore the turn of his stomach at the question. If he really thought about it, his answer would just lead to more inquiries aimed at prying into his deepest emotions. He'd managed to flirt his way out of a lot, but this time, Ms. Roylance seemed determined not to let him get away without a deeper dive into the reason he'd been forced into her office three times in a single week. "I'm doing just fine."

She pointed down at something. "That doesn't look too good."

He followed her finger to the reopened scabs on his right knuckles. Normally, they would be well on their way to fully healed by now, but he'd delayed the process by sending his fist into another classmate's face for getting a bit too courageous with his theories on Derek's disappearance.

He opened and closed his fingers, stretching out the skin around the wounds to create a shooting sting up his nerves. "I barely noticed it," he said, chuckling to ease the serious tone.

Ms. Roylance smiled, but it lacked the genuine sparkle she'd had the last two times. "I'm going to have to call your father, Derek."

His smile slipped, and a heat rose at the top of his shirt collar. She might be able to see the cuts on his knuckles, but she couldn't see the fading bruises over his back and ribs that hadn't healed, even after two weeks. His fingernails dug into his palm, and the skin around his knuckle split slightly, making a bead of blood form over the thin scab.

Metal bloomed in his mouth—the only sign that he'd bitten his tongue as he clenched his jaw.

"I don't see why it's necessary to involve him." He could barely hear his own voice, much less whether it gave away how uneasy he felt.

"This escalation in your behavior will need to be reported to him. One small tussle isn't a big deal, but this is the third time this week *alone*. Not counting last week." She shook her head, at a loss. "If you're not willing to talk to me, I have to assume this is something that needs to be communicated at home and not here."

Her voice rattled in his ear, sending a jolt through his body. "No." His hair brushed his cheek as he shook his head violently. Desperation melted the cool composure he'd worn like a mask since he'd come back. He didn't want to beg. "No, please don't."

Ms. Roylance tilted her head, sympathetically, and sat on

his words. Derek imagined she was used to kids begging for another chance in these situations. "Talking about these things can really help you figure out where this behavior is coming from. Do you have someone else you can talk to?"

"No." He didn't need to discover the root of his issues—he was well aware of where they came from.

"What about Rebecca Lewis?"

Derek wasn't sure if his heart rate slowed or rapidly increased at the sound of her name, but the change in his composure was probably noticeable. Ms. Roylance tightened her brow. He hated that name as much as he craved to hear it—his body recoiled.

Putting on a steady face was useless now, but he was grasping at straws in front of his lone audience. "Why would I want to talk to *her*?" he asked, spitting the words.

Caught off guard, Ms. Roylance's lips formed a surprised "O" and her brows rose. "I apologize, I was under the impression you two were in a relationship. It seemed like you liked her." Her sentence trailed off. Derek could hear the hidden meaning behind it, like she was screaming into his ear: *I can see right through you—and I'm probably not the only one.*

Exposed. Vulnerable. Weak.

You're a fucking pussy.

There was nothing else to say. Less than half an hour, and she'd completely stripped him bare.

Fool.

Sighing, Ms. Roylance laced her fingers together around her knee. "I won't talk to your dad—for now. If this keeps up, I'll have no choice." It was a blessing and a warning wrapped in one.

He swallowed, not feeling better at all. "Sure." He stood up before she dismissed him, and turned to the door, rushed to escape.

"You know, my consultations are not only for when you're in trouble, you're welcome here whenever you want." Her words followed him out the door, cut short as he closed it behind him harder than he meant to.

He wished the door closing would be the end of it, but it was just a gateway into another problem.

Becca walked down the hallway, directly toward him. The only mercy being that she was looking down at the floor, not even aware that he stood straight ahead.

Derek's chest burned—whether from holding his breath or something else, he wasn't sure, but he didn't want to look further into it and risk her raising her gaze. If she did, she would see him standing pale-faced in front of the counselor's door.

The dumb choice would be to leave the school and risk getting caught—furthering the trouble he was already in. Dumb choices were his specialty now, so he did what he did best and turned away from the office to the front doors before she noticed.

He let go of the breath that was burning in his lungs, but even after a deep inhale, the pain lingered like a steady flame.

JULY 1985

Before

He remembered the exact day *it* hit him.

It was Becca's seventeenth birthday—July 15th.

Hot, humid, sunny mid-July, and Derek was far, far away from the cool water of the community pool—unlike where he'd told everyone he would be. Hanging out at the mall was for little girls with pigtails and airheads like Marty Parr. But he wasn't going from store to store to "hang out"—he was there on a very specific mission, and one he wanted to complete successfully on his own.

Becca had told him repeatedly not to worry about getting her a gift. She didn't think it was fair, when she hadn't known about his birthday until it was too late.

Derek disagreed. He thought she deserved every little thing she could get, and he wanted to be the one to give at least some of it to her.

However, the problem was that he had no idea how to pick out gifts, much less ones that could make a girl hug him in gratitude. So, he figured the best way to find the perfect thing was to go to a place that had everything—the mall. There had to be something somewhere.

And it took a *long* time.

Shirts didn't have much of an impact. Plush bears were too cliché. A small little silver ring looked cute, and he could imagine he'd love how it would look on her, but it wasn't her style.

Nothing connected to him the way it should to be worthy of her.

The last place he would have willingly gone into was the small candle shop tucked away in the corner. He paused outside the entrance and glanced between the store and the rest of his options—all behind him and all duds.

He sighed and rubbed his face.

The things he would do.

With a sigh, he reminded himself he wasn't going into a place like this for himself. He was going for Becca, and that was all that mattered.

He stepped into the shop and walked through the short aisles lined with candles. The girl at the counter glanced up from her newspaper crossword, clearly bored by the lack of foot traffic the shop got. She raised a brow when she saw who it was.

Derek internally cringed when he recognized her. Cammy or Sammy or something from his math class.

She didn't greet him, but her eyes followed him through the candles as he browsed, pretending she wasn't staring.

He'd start hearing about it soon.

Derek Stokes buys himself candles. What could that possibly mean?

People would be asking him about it at his next shift, and maybe the rumors would still be going around at the start of the school year.

Whatever. There were too many candles to smell, and he'd promised he would pick up Becca and go for a drive in two hours. At this rate, he'd be late.

He wasn't aware that candles had so many possible scents. Lemon, rose, pumpkin, and, strangely, linen.

None of them stood out to him, and after about twenty different scents, they started to meld together into a single unidentifiable concoction that was distinctly candle and nothing else.

Maybe this was another dead end, too many candles and none worth pursuing.

One more. He would try one more and leave.

He picked a pastel purple one, and read the name written across it—Lavender.

Twisting the lid off, he inhaled.

He'd smelled this before.

Waking in the mornings, driving in his car, late in the middle of the night, eating ice cream.

It was her. It was the scent he had smelled in any situation that Rebecca was a part of and that he had long since come to associate with the memories and moments of her.

He didn't know it had a name.

It was perfect. Clearly, she loved this scent, because it followed her everywhere. Silly, but this was the perfect gift for her.

He took his findings and checked out with Candice—according to her nametag—placing two of the candles on the counter. She looked from him to the candles, then back at him, a single eyebrow raised.

He leaned against the surface and crooked a corner of his mouth up at her. "Put them in two different bags for me."

She enjoyed the attention and tucked a piece of hair behind her. "Sure thing, Derek."

He left the store satisfied with himself. Becca would be happy with anything he gifted her—she was that type of person—but the effort he'd put into finding her something she'd actually like would make it even better.

He leaned against the escalator railing, holding up his purchase, and took another look at the two bags, grinning in delight. He couldn't wait to see her smile when she opened this. Of course, he would only be giving her one bag.

The other candle was for him. Silly, sure, but the thought of having something that smelled like her all the time in his room made him—

His grin fell, and halfway down the escalator, Derek was hit with the realization…like he was opening his eyes for the first time.

He loved her.

First it had been gratitude he felt. That quickly morphed into trust, then turned into an unfamiliar longing and nervousness, and all it took was a mall candle for him to realize he was madly, fantastically in love with this girl. Even if it was just her scent, he wanted to imagine she was with him, even when she wasn't. He wanted it to wrap around him, to give him the comfort he had when she was there, the tenderness, the happiness.

God, he *loved* her. So much, it ached when she was away. So much, he saw her in the tiniest things around him. So much that, if there was a single person to have for the rest of his life, he would pick her without hesitation.

"Fuck."

After

Picking up her old job at the theater was Marty's idea. She'd quit after the summer, thinking that her time would be taken up with classes, studying, college applications, exams, and…other things.

Unfortunately, the main thing she had counted on filling all her free time was gone now, and she had a glaring vacancy for a much-needed diversion.

It took her all of five minutes to get the job back—being the valuable and reliable employee she was—and then she'd been in the theater after school three days a week and on the weekend for the past week. Scooping popcorn and filling sodas was never her ideal way of earning money, but it was easier having Nicole and Marty there to help distract her. They made everything else bearable.

"Let's get something to eat." Marty leaned against the counter as Becca wiped down the greasy outside of the popcorn machine to give her hands something to do during an early stall in customers.

She paused and shot him a disappointed look. "We just got here."

"I haven't eaten today."

"Go grab a corn dog or something."

"We're obligated to take a lunch break. Come with me."

She rolled her eyes and threw the dirty rag at him. He grimaced as it hit his uniform and fell to the ground. "And leave

Nicole all alone?"

"First of all, that was disgusting," he told her. "Second of all, it's so slow she probably won't get a single customer by the time we're done. She'll never know."

The swinging door between the back room and the front counter opened to reveal Nicole glaring daggers at Marty. He jumped. "If you were any louder, Burger King might hear you and start on the whopper I'm sure you're going to order."

Shooting a quick, communicative "oh shit" look to Becca, he gave Nicole a sheepish smile. "Hey, Nicole. Whatcha doing?"

Becca scoffed and shook her head at him as she walked around the corner to make a show of picking up the rag he'd left on the ground.

"Oh, you know, just listening to my friend betray me behind my back."

"I was going to grab you something too."

"Mmhmm. I'm sure you were." She didn't sound sure. Nicole turned to Becca, who raised a brow at her look. "Make sure he pays for *everything*. I want a large combo, with Coke."

Becca grinned and shifted into her customer service persona, her voice theatrically higher pitched. "Of course, ma'am."

Becca grabbed Marty by the arm and pulled him along, not giving him time to process the sudden change. He didn't resist, though, and she brought him after her toward the food court.

"You're an idiot." Becca laughed, still with her arm wrapped around his.

He frowned. "I swear she has super hearing."

"Maybe whisper next time."

He grumbled under his breath, and though she couldn't hear what he said, she giggled as they turned the corner.

She didn't see the security guard where he stood in a blind spot around a large pillar until she ran smack dab into the front of his uniform.

The collision caught her off guard and she stumbled back. If she hadn't been holding onto Marty's arm, she would have landed flat on her ass. Marty let out a collection of "whoas" and steadied her with a hand on her back.

An apology slipped out of her mouth before she completely reoriented. "I'm so sorry, I didn't see you—"

The words stalled when she finally met the security guard's eyes, and she froze. His gaze was familiar blue, with that graying mustache and hard-set stare. Marty wasn't as quick to realize who it was, but eventually he did, which Becca could tell by the tensing of his biceps under her hand, where she squeezed him for steadiness.

A static interrupted her mind, and fear raised the hairs on the back of her neck and down her arms.

"Rebecca. I thought that was you." Mark Stokes scanned her, pausing at the name tag attached to the deep red uniform. His words sounded conversational, friendly even, but the smile didn't reach his cold eyes. "Do you work here?"

Anytime it came to Mark Stokes, she was frozen in her tracks. She had a hundred different escape routes in the shopping mall, yet it felt like she remained constrained to a box only large enough to stand in. "Yes."

"I just got transferred here for security. I guess we'll be seeing each other more often," Mark said.

Becca's blood ran cold. He watched her like a bug under a microscope, waiting for a reaction. She could see the way he focused on her face, searching for *something*. She held her breath and gave him nothing.

After a few seconds, his lips drooped slightly, as he finally acknowledged she wasn't alone. Marty stood still, observing the uncomfortable interaction. Maybe a breath or a blink had caught Mark's attention, because his eyes flicked to Marty. He looked over him the way he had Becca, starting at Becca's hand holding onto Marty for support, then going to his nametag.

Mark's eyebrow raised. "You're the Parr boy, right?"

Marty nodded but didn't say anything.

A spark lit in Mark's eye, and Becca could have sworn she saw them flick to her before going back to Marty. "I hear you're friends with my son, Derek."

Becca felt the tingle of Marty turning to her in question, but she was too afraid to look away from Mark.

"We're just classmates."

"Just classmates, huh?"

Becca couldn't explain how Mark's triangular eye movements brought such terror over her. First to Marty, then to her hand on his arm, then finishing his focus on her. She connected the dots as quickly as he did.

"Interesting."

She couldn't feel Marty. She couldn't feel the floor under her feet. She could barely see Mark. Her mind had shut down into a static, glaring red, warning sign. Nausea twisted in her stomach.

Derek had been found hiding at Marty's house. And now here *she* was, clutching Marty like her life depended on it. That was no coincidence, and Mark now knew it. She had everything to do with what happened that week.

"I'll let you kids get back to work." He addressed it to both of them, but only looked at Becca. His heavy hand came up, landing on her shoulder the same way it had when he'd showed up to her house searching for Derek. He squeezed firmly, enough to be uncomfortable but not painful. Bile rose in her throat. "I'll tell Derek you said hi, Rebecca."

He left them there and continued on with his patrol.

Marty watched her, clearly unsure what to make of the entire interaction. She didn't blame him. He knew only the surface of the story. He didn't know what Mark Stokes did and what he had now confirmed for himself.

"Hey, you okay?" Marty said, but his voice was muffled by the ringing in her ears.

She dropped her hand and walked toward the closest restroom, waving him on weakly. "You go ahead and grab food. I'm not very hungry."

"Becks," he called, but she waved him off again and increased her pace as her stomach churned.

He couldn't follow her into the restroom, and the heavy door slammed behind her.

Rushing into an open stall, Becca locked it and emptied her empty stomach into the toilet.

***

"What the hell, Derek?" Elaine Renfield hurried to tame her tousled hair as she clumsily followed Derek down the stairs of her house. His sudden departure left her fumbling to keep up. "You're leaving?"

"I've got to get home." A weak excuse, he knew, but he couldn't drag it on any later. He glanced at the clock on the wall—an hour later than his father told him to be home. Good.

"We didn't even do anything," Elaine said, reaching out to catch his arm.

He paused as she pulled him to a stop on the stairs, and looked at her fingers sliding seductively over his skin.

Derek wasn't fazed by the action, even though he so badly wanted to be. "I'm not in the mood."

Her hand dropped once she realized it brought no reaction, and she glared at him. "Oh, okay. So you're not in the mood to screw me, but you're in the mood to beat the shit out of Scotty." She rolled her eyes, the intense sarcasm as thick as honey. Her arms crossed over her chest. "What the hell is going on with you? You're acting like a freak."

Derek rolled his eyes and opened the front door. "And you're acting like a bitch."

He left through the front door in the wave of Elaine's outraged protests, followed by a wake of curses and insults that flew right over his head.

He *wished* they would affect him. Make him mad, make him sad, make him *something*. Like the last few times he'd done this with some random girl, or when he fought Scotty and a few other nosy bastards—he felt nothing. Completely numb.

He'd been so afraid at first, so fucking angry. And then… nothing.

His dad beat the shit out of him the day he returned, and

then nothing. Like it never even existed. Derek had spent his entire life walking on eggshells around his father, worried how he would react to the smallest things, and now—because of the men Sheriff Wade had driving by the house multiple times a day—nothing.

Right when he *wanted* to feel something, there was nothing to make him feel *anything*. Even his asshole father.

It only made him want to provoke Mark more—to get any reaction from the man. If that happened, then he could be upset at *her* for putting him in this situation. This home was as stable as a pane of glass. It was only a matter of time before it shattered and cut him bloody. The longer it lasted, the worse the fallout would be.

He slammed the car door shut as he slipped into the front seat. Sheriff Wade was the one who'd managed to get it back from Madison for him—another thing Rebecca had probably arranged.

He shook his head and lit a cigarette, trying his best to not think about her. The smoke cleared his mind, and he peeled away from the curb toward his house.

He blasted AC/DC and tapped at the steering wheel up until the moment he shut off his car in front of the house, announcing his arrival as best he could to the entire neighborhood. The more people he pissed off, the better.

The front door brushed against the floor as he opened into the lit home. The smell of whatever Jennifer had made for dinner lingered in the air. There wasn't any sign of her or Mal, but the television in the living room played sports coverage.

Derek walked down the hallway and paused to look at his dad, leaning back on the couch with a cigarette smoking in one hand and a beer can in the other. Mark wasn't watching the TV.

"You missed dinner," Mark said.

"I had plans."

Mark scoffed, and took a sip of the beer, not excusing Derek yet. "You always have plans, don't you?"

Derek shrugged, something he would have never dared do

before, and made to head down the hallway.

"I saw that friend of yours. Rebecca. I didn't know she worked at the mall too," Mark called after him, and Derek's retreat halted.

His heart jumped and he hissed under his breath.

"Guess I'll be seeing her more often."

When he turned, Mark didn't look a bit upset, but Derek knew better. He grinned, like this was all a game to him. Derek's jaw clenched, and his nails dug into his palm. He hated just the thought of Becca being anywhere near his father—much less on a regular basis.

Mark wasn't done. "I also met that boy, Marty Parr. The one whose home you hid in. Turns out they're quite cozy with one another." Marks eyes studied Derek over the rim of his can as he gulped down the last of its contents and chased it with a drag of the cigarette. "Small world, isn't it?"

Derek felt queazy. Mark had his attention on Becca now.

He wished he could just forget all about it, but when his dad brought her up of his own accord, Derek's progress regressed several steps and made it difficult to pretend she didn't exist. It also made it a pain to swallow.

He forced an unnatural smirk on his face, feigning nonchalance, while he panicked internally. "I've got no interest in what she's doing."

Mark hummed, and observed Derek carefully as he set down his empty can and snubbed out the rest of his cigarette in the ashtray on the table. He shut off the television and stood up, leaving them in unbearable silence. Derek flinched as his father raised a hand.

But there was no blow. Instead, Mark's hand came down onto his shoulder and patted. "Good. You've got no use for useless, meddling bitches like her."

There was no possible way Mark did not feel Derek tense at the use of the words *bitch*. *Useless*.

Both words made it impossible for him to stifle the cacophony of feelings that errupted in his chest. He couldn't even place which was which anymore.

Derek stared at the satisfied smirk on his father's face as he let go and walked down the hallway, leaving Derek rooted in place and stirring in everything that disturbed him.

How was it impossible to feel *anything* until it came to her— then *everything*? A mere mention sent his heart into overdrive, but an insult—it sent him into a rage.

Derek pounded to his room, slamming the door behind him, and grabbed the closest thing to him. An empty glass cup. He put every ounce of anger and sadness and longing and grief into the pitch and hurled it against the wall. It crashed into a million pieces, and Derek stood to watch as they scattered to the floor.

Before

Becca tapped the tip off her ballpoint pen against the top of her notebook, syncing it to the rhythm of Cyndi Lauper singing "She Bop" from the tape Derek had picked from her assortment and put into her player. Lying stomach-down on her bedspread, she kicked her legs up in the air behind her.

"This is shit music." He cut the song short and ejected the tape and continued to rummage through everything she had.

"Excuse me." Becca rolled her eyes and dropped her pen. "I happen to love that song."

"That's the problem, sweetheart. You could do so much better. Let me go grab something better from my car."

She held up a hand. "Don't you dare. If I have to listen to Metallica, I won't be able to focus on this. And I *need* to focus."

Derek pushed the tape back in and continued the song he'd just claimed was shit, his attention successfully diverted from messing around with the stereo. He came forward, stopping to peek at the papers scattered on the bed in front of her. "What are you doing anyway?"

She gestured dramatically at the extensive lists and scribbled notes in front of her, particularly at the bold letters at the top of every page: the names of universities around the country.

"College applications." Only the same thing she'd been prepping for at the library while Derek was working at the pool all summer. The lists of requirements and addresses had all been provided by Ms. Roylance in one of their meetings, when they'd narrowed Becca's choices to a few select schools to study nursing like her mom. The notes on each school, written in Becca's chicken scratch, were all her doing. "Most of the deadlines are in December, so I want to be early."

He raised a brow, looking both impressed and overwhelmed by the extensive information in front of him. "Four months early?"

"I'm just starting on the essays. Then I'll have to get letters of recommendation, maybe do some interviews. It just depends on the school." Becca frowned. "When are you going to do yours?"

He pulled away and laid down on the ground. He tilted his head backward so he could look up at the ceiling. "Not sure I am."

"What?" Becca slid her papers to the side and leaned forward so she could see him. "Why not?"

He shrugged. "Never thought about it."

"Well think about it now. We could go somewhere together. I hear college is easier when you already have friends there. You don't even have to go to school if you would rather work."

That piqued his interest, and his head lolled to the side to meet her eyes. "Where are you going?"

"I've got a few that I'm interested in." She took a moment to slide around the papers on her comforter, searching for the master list of her options in the unorganized pile. She found it and pulled it out, turning it for him to read.

His eyes scanned the list, pausing halfway down. "You've got some in California."

"Some of the best schools are in California." She smiled. Seeing him intrigued at the idea made her heart warm, and maybe she was getting ahead of herself, but she loved the idea of Derek being with her. Truth was, she wanted to go to school somewhere new and different, but the inevitability of leaving her comfortable little town scared her. If Derek could be there with her, everything would be perfect. "I know you wanted to go back to California."

He nodded and read them off. "Madison, Boston, New York, Seattle. They're all over the country."

Becca pursed her lips. "I wasn't sure if you'd like those places."

He pushed the papers down, and Becca let them settle on the bed. Derek smirked, his eyes sparkling, and Becca's heart fluttered, "Go wherever you want, sweetheart, I'm sure I'll like it too."

After

There were only a few days in a year that Derek remembered as significant: His birthday, Mal's birthday, Becca's birthday, and Halloween.

He didn't care for Halloween in particular, but it was an event that took place on Halloween night that meant the world to him. Well, it used to.

It was on Halloween—one year ago—that he met her.

And that's why he wanted to forget it.

Parties were his escape on the regular, but now they were a necessity. Ruby's fucking Halloween party was the best place to go to get cheap alcohol and hazy memories—everything he needed.

Apparently, he had other responsibilities first, though—like getting his stepsister to her friend's house so she could go trick-or-treating.

He wouldn't do it when his dad asked, but when Mal asked him herself, he couldn't say no. He could count it as a distraction.

Mal was grateful for the ride, even if she didn't say it. Her way of showing appreciation was sitting in the passenger seat and *not* moping—a new record. They'd gotten better in the past months, but they weren't the perfect brother or sister by any means.

When she asked for a ride, he didn't expect a conversation, so he played his music at top volume, just shy of being painful. A favor was a favor, whether they spoke or not. But the side glances from Mal had him second-guessing that thought. He might have been able to brush it off the first few times, but after five minutes, it was digging into his skin and running over his nerves.

"What?" he asked, the question overly accusatory and abrupt.

Mal didn't flinch, though she leaned back like she had finally gotten what she was working toward—a reaction.

"You're acting weird," she said, not having the decency to ease into it. She never did. If there was one thing she was good for, it was saying exactly what she thought.

"Fuck you." She would only be about the fiftieth person to make that observation. Mal was the first, however, to not blink at his venomous outburst. Maybe a year ago she would have shrunk back into her seat, terrified of what he would do next— but she wasn't scared of him anymore. Something he was both grateful for and weirded out by.

"Is this about Becca?"

Her name had become a chemical reaction. Anytime it was mentioned to him, he bristled and exploded like potassium metal in contact with water.

His hand slammed against the steering wheel to release his pent-up frustration. Mal leaned away with an eyebrow raised and scoffed, annoyed.

"It is so *painfully* obvious how attached you are to her and now you don't even look at her."

He might have been able to throw some sarcastic remarks at anyone else, and they would scurry away without a fight, but with Mal—his little sister—lying would only make him shine with dishonesty.

So he didn't answer at all, instead, making the strategic choice to keep his mouth shut.

Mal wasn't finished though. "I'm mad at her, too, in case you're wondering."

Derek's hand tightened around the steering wheel. For some reason, he felt he had some otherworldly claim to his anger toward Becca. Only *he* could be upset at her, no one else.

Therefore, he turned and set his hardened glare on Mal, who looked like she'd expected it. "Why the hell are you mad at her?"

She scoffed. "I know you live in your own little bubble all the time, but maybe if you paid a little more attention, you'd notice certain things—like the fact that you weren't the only one who got the bad end of your dad's..." She paused, but Derek already knew what was coming. He prayed silently for her to never finish the sentence. "Episodes."

That was a kind way to put it—episodes. It made it sound temporary, short term. As if Derek hadn't been dealing with it every day for his entire life, waiting for the bomb to explode.

But it wasn't just Derek now. Not based on what Mal said.

He searched for the lie behind her hazel eyes. There wasn't one.

She averted her gaze to stare at the dashboard. His focus peaked where her hand rubbed at her clean, bare wrist. Derek's eyes homed in on the movement.

He'd probably done the same thing thousands of times.

The skin on her wrist looked the same as always, but those sorts of mannerisms didn't appear out of thin air. They hadn't for him.

"When you left, Mark was...upset. He wasn't sure what to do about those people coming in, and he was frustrated, so he needed another target and..." Her sentence died off before it was done.

She didn't need to finish, because Derek felt it. He felt those hands on his wrists, the pull of his skin, the burn of the tug. That was just the beginning for him. His wrist tingled as if the past injuries had risen up to the surface—an invisible reminder.

He'd never been at a loss for words before, but now, everything about him was as blank as the skin on Mal's wrist. Hidden, secret, but not unfounded.

"Mal—" It was between a warning and a plea. She never did listen.

"I went to Becca, you know? I think I'm part of the reason she tried so hard to bring you back—I practically threatened her if she didn't."

Derek blanched, shocked by his sister's words. Mal wasn't lying. He could see it in her eyes when she met his, the overly serious challenge she held in them—it was the truth. Not just some lie she'd created to protect the girl she saw as an older sister.

"Why the hell are you telling me this?"

She shrugged, her hand holding her wrist gently. "Just thought you would want to know."

He didn't. He didn't want to know.

The longer he went on avoiding Becca in the school halls and drawing his father's attention from her to him, the harder it became to keep away. As much as he tried not to focus on her, it only made him think about her more. He'd managed, purely high on the power of hatred he felt from her betrayal, but he wished he could feel nothing toward her…the way he felt nothing toward everything else.

Hatred was so easy to manipulate with the right tools—simple things, like Mal's words, cut through the anger and gave way to crumbs of the love he wanted to forget.

Dammit.

"It's her fault we're in this situation," he said, his hands tightening to the wheel.

"I dunno. By that logic, I guess it's also her fault he hasn't done anything in a month."

Mal didn't *know* anything. Maybe she was hopeful that this was the start to a brighter era, but Derek knew better. Nothing good would come from Mark bottling it up.

Nothing good ever came from bottling those intense feelings up.

"You don't know what the fuck you're talking about," he ground the words out through his teeth. Luckily, he wouldn't have to sit in silence with her, as he pulled to the curb outside her friend's house and gave her a pointed look to get out.

She rolled her eyes at his tone, but didn't waste any time freeing herself from the stuffy air of his car. "Just think about it, okay? I don't think this is easy for her either."

"Get out."

She slammed the door and rushed up the grass as Derek peeled away from her.

Think about it?

He barked a maniacal laugh and slammed his palm against the wheel.

No. He won't think about it. Not her, not his dad, not anything.

If there was one thing he wanted to do tonight, it was forget. That's all he intended on doing.

***

Becca missed how exciting Halloween used to be when she was younger, up until her mom told her she had to hand out candy to trick-or-treaters rather than be one herself.

Last year, she'd tried to bring back that spooky excitement at one of Ruby's infamous parties, courtesy of Marty's invite, and that had almost ended in walking home alone, ditched by her friend. Somehow, it became one of the most significant nights of her entire life, all to be ruined not even a year later.

Stop trying.

There were no more reasons to try and fix something that didn't want to be—like Halloween. At least for her.

Clearly, some people still enjoyed it—like Marty, who was back at Ruby's house for the fifth year in a row. And others.

Others she wanted to avoid.

In its place, homework would be taking precedence over the rabid night, just like it had the regular nights.

She found she focused better at the kitchen table, with the TV playing some random show in the background to fill the silence that had expanded the past month. Her mom would be back soon, permanently. Until then, she'd have to make do.

She'd always been a good student but had transformed into a *great* student, who worked on assignments late into the night. Even reports like the one in front of her—an extra credit assignment she'd begged Mrs. Bernard for.

"An academic monster," Marty and Nicole called her now. Suddenly, she had no time for anything but school and the rare shift she took at the mall she now avoided like the plague. Of course, the school part wasn't all academic. It included swimming in the school pool after hours thanks to Derek's lessons through the summer. Through Marty and his connection to the swimming team coach, she was able to get into the facilities easily.

It gave her something to do when her hand was too sore to write and her brain too fried.

She sighed and set down her pencil to stretch—craning her neck and shaking her sore wrists. Swimming sure sounded great right now. She'd give anything to dunk her head under the water and silence the world.

Especially the irritating ring of the telephone on the wall. It was probably her mom, checking in to see what she had done that week. As much as she loved her mother, she really didn't feel like chatting with anyone today.

The ring went silent, and Becca sighed in relief. Maybe she'd gotten the hint. It was late anyway—Becca could just pretend she was asleep.

But when it rang again, Becca turned to look at the receiver rattling in place. There were a few moments of internal debate, but she gave in finally and rose to answer.

"Hello?"

The first thing she noticed was the noise, loud and rhythmic with music. Certainly not a hospital or her mother's rental apartment. "You're gonna need to get over here ASAP."

"Marty?" She wasn't expecting a call from him tonight, and based on the coherency of his words, he wasn't drunk like she thought he would be by this time. "Aren't you at Ruby's right now?"

"Yes, and so is Stokes—who's going psycho, by the way."
Stop trying.
"I'm not interested in getting involved with—"

"He won't listen to anyone else, and he's going to hurt himself at this point."

Becca paused. Her lies were useless on Marty—who knew her too well. He knew when she was hiding things, and he knew that she wouldn't stand by and let Derek get hurt.

She sighed and closed her eyes. She'd have to go against Derek's wishes again, just this time.

"I'll be there in a bit. Keep an eye on him until I'm there."

Hanging up the phone, she rushed to grab her jacket and pulled it on as she went out to the side of the house for her bike. It'd been a while since she'd ridden it, but walking would take too long, so she hopped on and peddled toward Ruby's house.

It took about fifteen minutes to get there—by working her legs into overdrive. She passed dozens of trick-or-treaters dressed up, but barely paid attention to them besides dodging them as they crossed the residential roads.

All the windows at Ruby's house were lit, and Becca could see people drinking, both outside and inside, as she approached. She dropped her bike on the grass and ran to the front door.

People were leaving as she walked in. She caught some of the words they said—*Stokes. Crazy. Sucks.*

The entryway reeked of alcohol and cigarette smoke, and she was wildly underdressed in an oversized t-shirt with a bun on her head.

Didn't matter though—the looks she got weren't even a worry as she pushed through bodies, her eyes searching frantically for any sign of either Marty or Derek.

"Thank god you're here." Nicole appeared from within a group and grabbed Becca's arm. "Marty was trying to deescalate the situation, but who knows how much help that will be."

"What's going on?"

A chorus of yells guided Becca's attention right to where it needed to be.

Over the music playing in the living room, it was difficult to focus on any one conversation that might help her find what she was looking for, so she focused on their eyes instead. The stares and pointing fingers lit up a path that Nicole led her down, pushing past people to reach the opening in a semi-circle of kids.

Ruby stood to the side, sobbing about how much trouble she was going to be in, while her friends patted her shoulder. Marty ran an exasperated hand through his hair not far from her, but the main attraction took place dead center.

Derek stood next to an empty table that clearly hadn't always been empty. From the look of it, it's where all the alcohol had been.

Now it was scattered over the floor—red punch staining a rug, glasses and the punch bowl shattered around his feet. Derek didn't look like he cared. With one hand, he chugged a can of beer, and in the other, a smoking cigarette. His eyes were bloodshot as he leaned his head back to spout a stream of beer into the air over him. Some people cheered, some left— annoyed that the alcohol had been ruined.

Still oblivious to Becca's presence, Derek tossed the can over his shoulder and slipped the cigarette into his mouth. Ruby continued to sob off to the side, unwilling to step in and stop him, but Greg Wolski looked much more eager to put an end to it. He rushed up from behind an unsteady Derek, turning him by his shoulder to make sure he had a clean shot to Derek's face.

Becca's covered her mouth and yelped into her fingers as Derek stumbled backward.

He was never easily fazed by a punch, so he caught his balance against the table and retaliated with a strike of his own. The crowd oohed and ahed, but Becca flinched as another hit crashed into Derek's jaw.

"Fuck you, Stokes," Greg said, grabbing Derek by his collar.

Derek's lip was split, and a drop of blood slid from the corner of his mouth. He laughed straight into Greg's face, eyes crazed with intoxication. "You wish, Wolski."

Becca's stomach churned, but she finally found the courage to move out of Nicole's grasp, so she could push her way through the bodies to throw herself in the midst of the tussle.

It was a stupid choice, sure, but she couldn't stand by and watch Derek get beaten any more.

Marty appeared on the other side and grabbed Greg from behind as Becca reached Derek and pulled him from the other boy's grasp. Unlike Greg, Derek didn't resist being pulled away, still laughing at Greg's angry face.

"Leave it be, Derek," she said, from behind, her hands holding onto his arm and tugging him with her.

His grin stalled and his resistance against her slowed as her voice caught up to his impaired mind. His expression cleared, like someone had dumped a sobering bucket of ice water over his head.

She didn't stop towing him toward the front door, taking advantage of his stunned confusion. He tried, with little effort, to escape her hold.

He could have done it easily if he wanted, but when they emerged into the fresh air, she still had a strong grip on him.

"What the hell are you doing here?" His words were slurred, but clear.

"Do you even need to ask?"

He frowned, but it was really more of a pout. "I had it covered."

"Clearly," she said, scoffing.

He dug his heels into the ground and forced her to stop too. "I'm not going anywhere with you."

It would have stung more if she weren't so upset with him. "Sorry, but that choice is automatically void when you aren't sober enough to drive yourself home."

She reached into his jacket pockets, searching for his keys. He protested lamely with a few cuss words, but in the end, gave in as she wrapped her fingers around his car keys. She dragged him to his Monte Carlo, opened the passenger side door, and shoved him carefully into the car, taking care to make sure his head didn't hit the roof.

God, what was she doing? He didn't want her here. He'd avoid her even more the next time she saw him at school.

She shook her head and walked to the driver's side.

As long as she went into this knowing that nothing would change, she wouldn't be as heartbroken in the morning when he was gone.

The engine roared, and loud music blared over the speaker, making Derek wince. She glanced at him out of the corner of her eye and turned it down.

He wasn't trying to get out, which was good, but she locked his door to ensure he wouldn't change his mind halfway to her house, before pulling away from the stalled party.

Most of the trick-or-treaters were done for the night, and the rest of Ruby's neighborhood had shut down their lights to bring an end to Halloween. It was better that way. She could drive faster to her place, without worrying if am eight-year-old Hulk Hogan would jump in front of the Monte Carlo.

She couldn't tell if Derek's eyes were open, but his forehead rested on the cool of the window—a small cloud of fog forming on the glass every time he exhaled.

Silently, she hoped he was asleep as she turned onto a familiar dark road. She would take another route if she could, just to avoid the path that had been the scene of their first meeting. Everything she wanted to avoid tonight was clinging to her like a sweet nightmare.

It was a long road, unfortunately, and her hands gripped tighter on the wheel as they reached the midway point, where, exactly a year ago, Derek Stokes had sat on the side of the street.

"Pull over."

Becca startled at his voice. He was in the same position as before, but he wasn't asleep like she'd hoped he would be.

"No."

"I'm going to puke."

Becca slammed on the brakes and pulled to the side—only feet from where this very car was parked a year ago. If he made a mess in the car, it would give him another reason to be mad at her.

He clumsily unlocked the door and stepped out, before stumbling away from the road and to the same tree she'd seen him at then. She watched out the window, waiting for him to get sick, but he never did. He just crouched down to sit and leaned back against it, tilting his head to look up at the sky.

A potent rush of déjà vu splashed over Becca, and suddenly she was one year younger. Standing on the side of the road in a bunny costume and looking at a beat-up boy sitting alone against a tree.

Once again, they were two strangers meeting on the side of the road, but everything had changed.

Becca swallowed and shut off the engine. The area went dark without the headlights on. The car door opening permeated the still, chilly air, and she crossed in front of the car and stepped down to the tree and Derek. He didn't rustle at her approach or jump when she sat down next to him and leaned on the adjacent side of the trunk.

She sighed into the air. Her breath formed in front of her and floated up into nothing. She didn't want to fight anymore. She just wanted to surrender and deal with the heartbreak now—let herself heal with time.

They sat in silence for minutes, both staring at the sky.

Derek was the first to move, reaching into his pants pocket and pulling out the leather wallet. She glanced over to watch his fingers dig through the pouches and pull out the familiar, faded piece of paper.

Becca held her breath as he opened it and read over the words.

"I still look at this thing every fucking day," he said, his voice hushed. The moon was bright enough to make her handwriting visible in the dark. "I couldn't believe that someone was willing to actually do something for me. Some random girl in the shittiest costume I've ever seen and suddenly I can't keep away."

Heart jumping, Becca went lightheaded watching him closely as his finger slid over her note. She felt like an intruder in the moment—his words held the weight of a private thought that she wasn't supposed to hear, yet here she was. Watching them leave his mouth in a wisp of breath, then float around her.

"She stayed by me all the time. I was never alone. I thought

I didn't want to be pitied, but it turned that being pitied and cared for was the best feeling in the world." He laughed, living in the memory. "I wish I could go live that again. Over and over and over again."

The desire to intrude on the moment became a need, and she spoke out—desperate to know. "What about right now?"

His carefree, intoxicated smile dropped into a frown and his mouth snapped shut.

No. No.

This wasn't what she wanted. As much as she tried to give in to his wishes, she didn't want to stop trying. She didn't want to keep her distance. She wanted it all to be okay. She wanted her Derek back.

Her hands shot out, grabbing his fingers, and his eyes finally met hers for the first time in a very long time. Blue and bright and hurt—he could see her. He could really see her.

"I'm still here. I'll be right here whether you like it or not. All you need to do is ask, Derek."

An electricity crackled through the air, sending her hair on a pleasant edge as he stared at her. His gaze flicked between her eyes and then landed on her lips.

Becca froze.

There was no time to register the change in position—one second she held onto him, waiting for a response. Where Becca's hand held his, his grip tightened and pulled her forward.

The next second she was against his chest—Derek holding her at the nape of her neck and tilting her lips to fit perfectly against his.

Becca gasped into his mouth, eyes wide. A dizziness fogged her head, like the misty effects of alcohol setting in, even though she hadn't touched a drop, and a burn grew in her chest.

Without realizing it, her free hand rose and connected with his chest, as her eyes slid shut. She *melted* into Derek Stokes.

She was malleable in his touch. Moving from her neck to under her chin, he slanted her mouth, as his lips moved against hers in a rhythm she couldn't deny.

He was desperate—a man searching for water in a desert, and she was an oasis, giving him all he needed—all he wanted.

Never in her life would she have imagined herself in this position, longing and grabbing at him like she couldn't get enough. She couldn't pull away.

His insistent mouth parted her lips, and she opened them eagerly as tremors wracked her body—originating at every point Derek's body touched her. His hand, his chest, his fingers, his *lips*.

Everything he felt radiated into his kiss—the passion and the anger and the hurt and the desire. She soaked it up through her pores, and gave back twice as much, sighing into his mouth and breathing him in.

She needed Derek Stokes as much as he needed her, and she *wanted* him even more.

This moment—she could stay in it forever. Forever clinging to him and kissing him and letting his mouth work on her like it was created to be right there.

But this moment wasn't real.

Her eyes opened.

Derek was drunk. He wasn't thinking straight. She didn't want to be an moment of oversight he regretted when he woke in the morning and reality set in.

She let go, falling back against the dead leaves behind her and gasped—the dizziness snapping from her mind and clarity filling her with regret. Not that she kissed Derek, but that it would never happen again.

Derek opened his eyes, and Becca's mouth dropped in shock when she saw the tears in them. "You broke my heart." His voice cracked.

"Derek—"

He stood, turning away from her. She jumped to her feet, but still unable to reach him from her spot a foot away.

Even if she reached out and touched him, she knew they would be miles away from one another.

"Take me home," he said, and Becca made a sound somewhere

between a cry and an inhale.

She couldn't take him home. Not like this. Not with Mark there. "I can't."

"Take me home. He won't touch me. He's noticed all the eyes you have circling, and he doesn't dare. Just take me home." He didn't wait for a response before he walked to the car and climbed in, leaving her alone at the tree, with her heart skipping and breath racing.

***

Words failed her as she drove in the direction of Derek's house. He leaned against the window like he had when they left Ruby's house, his slow breaths fogging the window. The moment on the side of the road barely existed anymore, a mere pause in the inevitable path they were bound to take. And there was nothing she could do.

"I'll probably forget all this tomorrow," Derek said, and Becca's hands lost their grip on the wheel for a millisecond. "You should too."

She didn't reply. There was nothing she could think to say. So she turned the final corner onto Derek's street and pulled to a stop. It wasn't her car, so she turned it off and put the keys where Derek could reach them—afraid her fingers would touch his if she handed them to him directly.

She walked home that night and wiped at every tear that fell from her eyes before it could drop further than her cheek. Forget? No. That was impossible.

It had been impossible before, and it was even more impossible now.

NOVEMBER 1985

After

The harder she tried to forget, the more it stuck to her mind like glue. Two weeks passed, and the memory sat as raw as the moment it happened.

He seemed okay, though—must have forgotten, like he said he would. He acted normal in the halls and continued on like the world just kept on spinning, while, for her, it was stuck on that night.

Becca had always felt an empty spot in her life—something missing. When Derek had appeared, that spot slowly filled somewhere along the way, and she hadn't even noticed.

But now he was gone, and the spot had grown into a blaring, blackened hole.

With it came the confusion. Blinding, unrecognizable confusion.

It left her restless.

She hadn't realized that that hole was flammable. Halloween night and Derek's kiss had set fire to it, and it burned harder than a normal absence would.

She found the best way to tame the flame was in the water.

Her time in the school pool tripled, and she spent every free moment swimming laps or floating in the middle of the room alone, with her ears covered and eyes closed. Sometimes she had to keep her eyes open, just to get the tingling feeling off her lips.

She'd spent a summer learning how to swim. Floating was

the easy part, but all she wanted to do now was sink to the bottom until her head went dizzy from the pressure and her lungs burned.

She didn't hear the pool door open, or the echo it made as it slammed shut. She could have easily remained oblivious to the additional presence in the room if water hadn't splashed onto her face.

She shot upward, treading as she spat out the few drops that had landed in her mouth.

Marty crouched at the side of the pool, laughing at her glare.

"How did you know I was here?" Becca asked.

"When are you not here?" he said, slipping his sneakers and socks off.

Becca paddled slowly to the edge of the pool and held onto the cement as he sat down and lowered his feet into the water.

"It's impossible to see you nowadays. You haven't been to work all week."

Becca sighed and leaned her head back into the water so her hair floated around her face. That was on purpose. "I'm busy."

"Uh, huh." He wasn't convinced. "So busy that you've been in a pool all alone for hours, multiple times a week. Sounds *really* busy."

Becca frowned at him but didn't respond.

He exhaled deeply and kicked some water to the side. "I've given you tons of space these last couple weeks. I didn't even try to get answers when Derek was living in my house for a few days, but you're acting weirder than usual." He motioned to the pool water. "I didn't even know you could swim until you wanted me to get you access to the pool. We could have had pool parties at my house during the summer."

That was kind of her fault for never mentioning it before. Even though she could swim now, it still made her nervous. Only with Derek was she safe under the water. Maybe this was her way of convincing herself she could live without him.

"We can still do that."

"What's going on with you?" He didn't beat around the bush.

"I'm doing just fine, thank you very much."

"What aren't you telling me? You promised you would be honest, remember?"

How honest could she be for it to be enough? Her mind jumped back to the kiss—again—and she shook her head. Marty hadn't reacted well when she first told him about Derek, and he was worried Derek would try to make a move on her. She wasn't sure if this counted as "making a move" or not, but Marty might not take it well.

"Tell me."

Honesty. He was there for her; he always was. He deserved some honesty.

She shut her eyes and braced herself. "Derek kissed me."

A pause, then softly, almost in a whisper, Marty said, "Took him long enough."

Becca's eyes shot open, and she looked up at him in surprise. "What?"

"I get it now."

"Get what?" This wasn't even close to the reaction she'd expected. A grin was not a part of the list of expectations, and she blinked.

"You're lovesick."

Becca paused, tilting her head to the side, and tried to translate the words in her head. "Lovesick?" It felt foreign on her tongue.

"You're moping around all the time because you're in love with Stokes."

What?

What?

"What are you talking about?" Becca said, her voice breathless. Her treading kicks slowed.

Marty lifted his hand. "Let me guess." He ticked off a finger every time he said something. "You can't sleep—often because you're worried about him—and when you can sleep, you always dream about him. You don't have the same motivation you did before. You keep thinking about how you could have done this or that differently. Especially the kiss—you just keep thinking about it over and over again. And it hurts. So. Fucking. Bad." His eyebrows raised, and his gaze searched her eyes, looking expectantly for a reaction.

She felt stripped bare—of everything that had been bothering her for the past two weeks, maybe even the last few months—perfectly worded in a way she'd been unable to do herself until right now.

Her chest ached. Her mouth dropping open and her eyes going wide gave Marty the reaction he needed to confirm everything he'd said.

Leaning back, he smiled, pleased with himself. "See, I knew it," he said. "Trust me. I was the exact same way when April cheated on me. It took, like, a year to feel the same."

A year.

Becca couldn't imagine feeling like this for weeks, much less an entire year. She might go completely insane if she couldn't be with Derek—

"Oh my god," she said.

Marty was right.

"Why so surprised, Lewis? If there's one thing I know, it's heartbreak." He didn't need to sound so cocky about something so devastating.

Great. Fantastic. Just wonderful.

She loved Derek.

Not just loved him, but was *in* love with him.

And what made it even worse is that she had no idea how he felt about her. A kiss in the heat of the moment was one thing. But love?

It hurt too much to hope.

∗∗∗

Derek was a liar.

Halloween night he'd been drunk, but when he kissed Becca, he was stone-cold sober.

You don't forget easily when you're sober—unfortunately. Every detail haunted him—the soft touch of her lips, the taste of her mouth, the fact that she'd kissed him back.

He'd imagined kissing her thousands of times. Lying in bed, he'd wonder what it would be like to have her against him, to *feel* her.

Now that he'd had a taste, he would never get enough. The betrayal was effortless to swallow when he closed his eyes, and all he could see were her gorgeous eyes, wide in surprise, and her delicious lips red and plump from his.

He'd cursed himself to an eternal struggle between wanting her *gone* forever and wanting *her* forever. He was *exhausted.* Too exhausted to try not to want her anymore.

It was torturous to see her every day at school, pretending to be blind at the same time. A cocktail of embarrassment and returning to his old habits.

Never going inside that night after she dropped him off, he'd walked to Becca's house, instead, in the middle of the night. There, he just stood outside, smoking a cigarette or two.

The hardest part was finding the courage to face her head-on again.

He leaned his head forward and let the shower water run over his hair, curtaining around his face and secluding him in his own world. A thin veil, because right on the other side was the muffled noise of his classmates joking and washing off their gym sweat.

They had noticed his strange behavior. Even though most people moved on from the scene at Ruby's house, no one was as eager to approach him as he slouched forward and shut them out. It was obvious to everyone that Derek Stokes hadn't been the same since he came back post-disappearance.

Water droplets flowed down his eyelashes, as he waited for the sound of rowdy boys to quiet. The majority exited the locker room and left to go home for their vacations. He didn't have the same eagerness they did to be stuck at home for a week.

"Hey, Stokes."

Opening his eyes at the sound of his name, Derek looked over through the water to where Greg stood at the edge of the communal shower, already dressed, with his gym bag slung over his shoulder.

"Party at my place on Tuesday. See you there?"

Greg had clearly forgotten the drunken brawl at Ruby's, or was just acting like it never happened. Truth be told, it was a bit fuzzy to Derek, too, and even if it had been memorable, he didn't care. Derek had better things to worry about.

"Sure." Derek wasn't sure if that was true.

"Cool, man." Greg nodded his chin in approval, then lifted a hand in farewell. "Later."

The door clicked shut behind Greg, and Derek finally twisted the spray off, allowing goose bumps to rise as cold air replaced the hot water.

He ran his hands over his face and wiped the drops from his eyes so he could see clearly. Locker rooms were exceptionally quiet once the echo of screeching sneakers and towel whips subsided.

His towel hung where he'd left it above a bench, and he pulled it off to wrap around his waist, crossing the rows of lockers to where his was. It would have been nice to be completely alone, but that was asking for too much.

Marty Parr sat on the bench, in the middle of tying his shoe. He looked up, spotting Derek, who held in a sigh.

They weren't exactly on speaking terms, but Derek didn't feel like smashing his face in all the time—an improvement between them, to say the least. Even though he technically knew Parr before he ever met Becca, Marty was just another bitter reminder of the girl he couldn't forget. He also happened to be a person who was with her when Derek was not, which put Derek in a tempting situation, standing on the edge of a cliff.

"Hey, man," Parr greeted him.

Derek nodded but kept the question he wanted to ask to himself. If he opened his mouth, he was afraid he wouldn't be able to get it to close.

He dragged out his process of dressing, taking his time with his pants, then his shirt. He shook the water out of his hair and was acutely aware of the fact that Parr was still behind him, seemingly unmoving, on the bench.

A quick peek behind might give away how conscious Derek was of his presence. He shifted a bit and caught sight of Parr in the locker mirror. Huge mistake because their stares connected. Damn.

"Go ahead and ask, Stokes," Parr said.

Derek paused, his hand tangled in the curls he'd been working through. He averted his eyes away and pretended to focus on his hair. "What the hell are you talking about?"

"Even you don't stare in the mirror that much. Spit it out. I don't have all day."

The facade dropped with Derek's hands, and he hesitated, staring at himself. His brows were furrowed, his lips pursed as he chewed unconsciously on the inside of his cheek. A tempting situation, and he was throwing himself to it with the barest of fights.

"How is she?"

There wasn't a need to clarify who "she" was. He felt Marty shift behind him and flicked his gaze to see him in the mirror.

Marty stood from the bench and crossed his arms over his chest. "Why don't you ask her yourself?"

Derek cut off the eye contact by shutting his locker, the bang echoing off the concrete walls of the locker room. Turning, he looked directly at Parr. "Not possible," he lied.

"But kissing her is?"

Shit.

So he knew *that* much. Derek bit his tongue, his jaw tensing as he dug his teeth into the flesh. "I was drunk."

"Don't they say the truth comes out when you're drunk?" Parr said, shrugging.

"Just answer the damn question. Stop wasting my time."

Parr rolled his eyes. "She is in the pool for hours a week. She's doing so much homework her fingers have calluses on them. She just quit her job at the mall again because of your dad, and I know that she misses you like hell." Parr's eyes bore into him, studying his reaction. "But I guess she's doing fine."

Derek didn't answer. He couldn't. His throat blocked up, holding back enough emotion to choke him. He imagined her doing all that. Swimming and writing and quitting and *missing him*. If he closed his eyes, he'd bet he could see it, clear as day. It was a relief to hear something about her, and it was a stab in the heart to know that not all of it was good.

"I never liked the idea of you two being friends. I didn't trust you, Stokes. Still don't, just to be clear." He had every right to say that because Derek wouldn't trust himself either. "But, for what it's worth, I can tell you love her."

Derek blanched, his eyes widening and mouth opening in surprise.

Love her.

He'd never heard it out loud. Never said it out loud. Maybe he never thought he would.

And it made him vulnerable. It made him weak. It sent tremors up his body, that gave way to indignation and fear.

"What do I do?"

"I'm not quite sure how I ended up becoming a love doctor for you two, since we all know that I'm about the least qualified person right now, but my best advice to you is do something about it."

"That's shit advice, Parr."

"Just ask her yourself." Marty slung his gym bag on. He stepped to Derek, and patted him supportively on the shoulder, "Have a good break, Stokes."

AUGUST 1985

Before

If Derek ever admitted how much he enjoyed this cheesy mermaid romance film, Becca would never let him forget it.

Avoiding her eyes was the best way to prevent her from seeing how he bit his lip at some overly cheesy line or leaned back to shake off a budding laugh.

When he finally let himself glance her way, his heart stuttered. He'd been so focused on the movie, he'd been missing out on the best part of the night.

Becca's head lolled to the side, bobbing as she attempted to stay awake.

A silent huff of air came from Derek as he snorted a laugh— the movie had been her idea, and she couldn't even keep herself upright. He watched her, caught in a cycle of will-she or won't-she fall over.

The answer was: she will. Her head fell toward him, and her body followed suit. Luckily, Derek was quick and scooted next to her fast enough to catch her shoulders and halt the fall into the couch. He lowered her slowly onto his thighs as the movie played on. He was careful, gentle, worried that if he moved too fast, she would snap awake and out of his hands. The background noise was far less interesting than the girl breathing softly onto his leg.

It wasn't often they were in this position—her head on *his* lap. He was always the one lying on hers, while her hands either cleaned up wounds or played with his curls. It wasn't that Derek didn't want to do the same for her.

He'd *love* to be in this position every single day. The difficulty was having the same courage she had in offering herself as a human pillow. She was much more forward in pulling him onto her, even when he protested, and by now, it became natural. He, on the other hand, still wasn't entirely sure how to approach these situations that made his heart thunder in his chest so loud he was sure she would hear it so close to his chest.

Ever since his "revelation" in July, things hadn't been quite the same—for him, at least.

For her, the world continued on as normal. He, on the other hand, was acutely aware of how every little thing she did sent him into a spiral of unrequited longing. His love for her was a pile of stones, and she threw a boulder with every word and blink.

Love.

Love.

He couldn't say it aloud, but even thinking about it left a bittersweet aftertaste on his tongue.

Love. The way her eyes moved under closed eyelids.

Love. The stray hair that blew upward every time she exhaled.

Love. The hand that unconsciously held the fabric of his jeans.

Love. The flowery scent surrounding her, which now sat on his bedside table.

Love. The seconds that let him take in all of her without worrying about what she might see in return.

He might not be able to say it, but he sure as hell could think it.

I love you. I love you.

35

NOVEMBER 1985

After

Derek quietly stuck a chair back under his unlockable doorknob, then turned his attention to the window, slowly pushing it open. He readied himself and paused only to look over his shoulder at the glowing red numbers on his bedside clock: 11:57 p.m.

Everyone would be well taken with their dreams by now, not worried whether Derek was in his room or not. He slipped through the window and into the dark night, sliding it not quite closed, so he could get back in before the sun was up. It was clockwork to him now, a new habit formed on the foundation of an old one.

He started his car—parked a little further from the house than usual, to make sure he didn't wake his dad when he started the engine—and followed the familiar route to Becca's house.

He used to park in the driveway, but even that felt too close now. He was here purely out of his inability to stay away, nothing else. He wouldn't go to her door. He wouldn't even step on the grass that was yellowing in the cold weather. He'd stay here, parked along the curb, and lean against the car door with a lit cigarette.

He never believed his father's description of him as much as he did in these moments: weak. He hated himself for being weak. Unable to go against his heart and listen to his head. As stubborn as he'd been his entire life, his heart beat him at his own game.

Denying it did nothing now, not when it came to Rebecca. He could resist as much as he liked; it was futile.

She was a weakness he couldn't shake.

Maybe she made him weak, maybe she made him a fool, but goddamn, if he didn't want to be with her right now.

He longed for her as much as he longed to be in the sanctuary she'd proven herself to be. He wouldn't dare go to her door, but he knew that what lay inside was the only place he ever felt truly safe. Now, he was left in the open without the security of the safe haven he'd clung to months ago.

No matter how much he yelled and hit and cursed, it couldn't keep him away once the sun went down and his father's words got to him. Even if it was just along the borders of her yard.

He inhaled against the butt of his cigarette, sucking the thick smoke into his lungs and holding it, begging it to brush and sooth the pain in his chest. Once he could not hold it anymore, he released with his head tilted back, straight into the night sky, where it dispersed into nothing.

"Derek?" a soft, timid voice broke through the cold air.

He hadn't heard the door opening, or the light steps coming around the house and pausing when they noticed him standing against his car. Snapping his head up, it took a few seconds for his eyes to adjust to the figure ten feet away from him with her arms crossed over her chest to hold the remaining heat against her.

Derek's grasp on the cigarette slipped, and the stick fell next to his foot, snuffing out slowly on the dark asphalt of the road.

A ghost, manifested by his yearning mind, Becca's head tilted to the side, and the longer he stared, the better he could see the draw of her brows and pull of her lips.

Seeing her standing in front of him, their eyes meeting in the dark, split him in two halves. The half that wanted to call her all sorts of names, and the half that wanted to lay with her and feel her hands run through his hair.

"What's wrong? Are you all right?" She took a step forward.

The question pulled him back to his body and he straightened his back and deepened his frown. "I guess you're always expecting there to be something wrong."

She didn't respond right away. Her mouth opened and closed several times before anything came out. "Do you want to come inside?"

"I'm sure your mom wouldn't be too happy."

"You know she's home?"

Know. Knew. He'd known for a long time that her mom had transferred full-time to a local hospital a couple towns over. He guessed she wanted to be closer to her daughter. The rumor mill was easy to follow, especially when you have a vested interest in certain pieces of news. Not that he would tell her that. He didn't want to tell her anything, so he turned to his car and pulled open the door to make his escape.

"Can I tag along?" The request made him pause. He glanced back at her to take in the fact that she wore a thin coat over pajama bottoms and a pair of running shoes. "I was going for a walk, but a ride sounds better."

A silence settled over their heads, waiting for his answer. He didn't know what to say, but he knew what he wanted to say. The dark made it so much easier.

"Get in."

Becca pattered quickly to the passenger side of his car, climbing in before he could change his mind. He sighed, breath forming a cloud in front of him, before he took his own seat and started the engine.

He turned on his music and let it fill the awkwardness. There were a million things he wanted to say—half of them questions. But he wasn't going to do that. He'd keep it simple, just to fill the silence.

"Why the late walk?"

Her head turned toward him, and he felt her gaze land on him, but resisted the temptation to meet it. "I couldn't sleep."

He nodded, understanding that. He was here for the same reason, among others—not that he would tell her.

Becca shifted in her seat, adjusting uncomfortably. "How are you doing?" It was her turn to ask questions.

He scoffed and shook his head. "That's a loaded question."

"It's a simple question that only needs a simple answer. Good, bad, so-so. I'll take a single word."

How could he possibly describe how he felt in a single word? Did he want to tell her?

Yes. The answer was always yes. He wanted to tell her everything.

Derek sighed and gave in. "Tired." He turned to her, meeting those eyes that studied him with trepidation and something else.

She nodded but didn't smile. "Me too."

***

The drive was short. No more than ten minutes before he connected the loop in front of her house, stopping right on the curb instead of entering the driveway. She lingered in her seat, wanting to bask in the first moments she'd had with him in what felt like forever. He made no rush to push her out, but he didn't pull her closer.

How the hell did they end up here? This strange limbo of when and if and what and but.

She wasn't sure. She wasn't sure about a thousand things anymore, but there was one thing that was clear to her now. As if a piece of the sun fell to her feet and lit the answer that had been hidden in the dark the entire time.

She loved him.

Ten minutes was all the confirmation she needed that his presence sent her heart into a place it had never been before. Crushes were one thing. Crushes were simple and sweet, like sugar melting on your tongue.

A first love was another. It was the rattling and shaking of all common sense. It was the constant, unrelenting ache in your chest when you looked at their face. It was every possible emotion rolled into one impossibly small ball and thrown at your head—knocking you off your feet.

Now that she knew that, it was hard to accept that she might be the only one who felt it.

"Goodnight, Derek."

Her hand trembled as she grabbed the door handle and pushed outward, the cold air a thankful numbing sensation against her flushed skin.

"'Night, sweetheart."

It was a habit, she was sure, but her heart still leapt at the nickname as she climbed out into the dark and shut the door before he could hear it.

He drove away, and Becca stayed to watch the taillights go down the road and disappear.

NOVEMBER 1985

Derek grunted as he lifted the last tire off the studs and set it aside. He wiped the sweat from his brow with the back of his hand. A routine tune-up and cleaning of his car kept his head steady on the weekends, but he needed it more during the weeklong break from school.

Staying inside that house was the opposite of his ideal vacation, but he could use the time that Mark was working the pre-holiday rush at the mall to relax. Jennifer and Mal had left a couple hours before to grab whatever else she needed to put together her Thanksgiving dinner. He'd be forced to spend the entire day inside with all of them tomorrow, so for now, he would take all the time he could get alone and make the most of it by keeping his car in pristine condition.

He'd already changed out the serpentine belt, and after checking the oil level he would rotate the tires, switch out the overdue filters, then finish up by scrubbing her down inside and out until she shined like she was supposed to. It would take hours to finish, and he planned to, because this hobby was his solace.

His stereo blasted Def Leppard and bounced off the inside of the hood as he bent in to twist the cap off the oil to peek inside, followed by the dipstick and—

"Hello?"

Derek hadn't heard anyone approach, or noticed the little red Aries parked across the street. He stepped around the hood and found the unexpected visitor.

She was a middle-aged woman, dressed in a gray blazer and skirt, her hair tied up so high and tight her eyebrows peaked on her forehead when she saw Derek standing there in his shorts and tank top and wiping grease off his hands with a stained rag.

"Derek?"

He raised a confused brow. "Yeah?"

She smiled and held out her hand. "I missed you last time I was here. Your father said you were visiting some relatives out of town. I'm Margaret Fremont with Child Protective Services."

Caught off guard, Derek's brows shot up and he nearly dropped his rag. He had two seconds to react before she would notice the tension in his back or clench of his jaw.

Pasting on his most charming smile, he relaxed his stance and reached out with his cleanest hand to accept Margaret Fremont's shake.

"Ms. Fremont, of course. To what do I owe this pleasure?"

"Oh, a routine checkup. Nothing serious, just protocol." She used her free hand to point past Derek's shoulder at the house. "Do you mind if I come in and talk to your parents?"

He shifted subconsciously, blocking her prying eyes. He knew everything looked fine—Jennifer always kept it in pristine condition inside and out to hide any blemishes that might raise concern to an outsider—but a fear that something had been missed unsettled him. He didn't let it show on his face, though, staying mindful of even the smallest movements his eyes made. "That would be lovely, but unfortunately, neither of them are home at the moment. My dad is working and my stepmother went off to the store with my little sister."

"Oh, that's no problem. I don't mind waiting for her to get back. Plus, I just need to take a quick look around the place, nothing crazy."

Shit. He was caught in a heavy predicament. If he let her in, the overstretched rubber band around Mark would pull even tighter when he found out, but if he turned her away, it would raise eyebrows. He wasn't sure which would be worse.

He met her eyes, trying to understand what she was hoping to find—or not find. She gave nothing away. Either she was not concerned at all, or she was as skilled at masking her true feelings as Derek was.

He was slowly spiraling into a panic, teetering on the edge of a fence. No matter where he fell, the outcome was a loss.

"It'll only take a few moments," she clarified, and the choice was yanked away from him. There was no winning, so he would have to comply.

He smiled, trying to make it more relaxed than he felt. "Sure, come on in, Ms. Fremont."

"Call me Margaret, please," she said, and accepted his invitation.

Derek led her up the sidewalk and into the house, aware of the way she immediately began her evaluation of everything she could see from the entrance. He wasn't sure what to do with his hands, or his feet, for that matter. Should he follow her as she wandered the house, or stand still and wait for it to be over?

He chose the latter, and watched her disappear down the hallway, looking in through doors and opening closets. Logically, he knew that Mark wouldn't be home for a few more hours. Illogically, he feared his father would walk through the door at any moment.

"You're in school, right, Derek?" Margaret called from another room.

"Yes," he said, and swallowed the lump in his throat.

"How's that going for you?"

There was no way he could be honest right now. Everything he said needed to be perfect, just like the spotless walls and carpet that Jennifer maintained. One slip and he'd feel it.

"It's going great." He hoped his voice didn't sound as sickly chipper as it felt.

"You must have a lot of friends," she said, appearing back around the corner. She didn't look any different than when she'd disappeared—nothing had caught her interest.

He smiled and leaned against the closest wall. "Sure, it's not that hard to make friends here.”

“What about your little sister, Mallory? Does she seem like she's doing well?”

“I don't think I ever see her without friends. I think she does well in class. She loves it here.” His face started to hurt from the effort of smiling.

“That's really great to hear.” And she looked like she meant it.

This could be a success. He might actually pull this off without anyone knowing. He might actually get her out before Jennifer and Mal came home, and he could pretend it never happened.

A sudden jitteriness ran through him, eager to get her out as quickly as possible. His heart raced at the potential of preventing any fallout.

Then the front door rattled. His heart stilled.

Mal entered with her arms full of grocery bags, and Jennifer right behind her.

Unlike Derek, Mal recognized the woman the instant her eyes saw her, and Jennifer followed suit. Both of their mouths opened, startled.

Jennifer was the quickest to recover, rushing Mal into the house and closing the door behind them. She didn't miss a beat as she set down the bags on the ground and approached the caseworker with a bright smile.

“Margaret! Hello! I had no idea you were stopping by.” She took the woman's hand in hers, greeting her like an old friend.

“Hello, Jennifer. I'm sorry to barge in like this without notice. Just here for a quick routine follow-up from before.”

“Of course, of course.” Margaret might not be able to tell, but Jennifer was worried. Her high-pitched voice and quick words gave her away to Derek and Mal, who watched from the side. She turned to them, smiling too much to be comfortable. “Derek, please help Mal take the groceries into the kitchen.”

Nodding, Derek obeyed without resistance and picked up the bags that Jennifer had set down and followed Mal out of the living room. The women waited until the kids were gone, out of the room, before they continued the conversation.

It might be another room, but the walls were thin, and Derek and Mal were not going to pretend they were deaf. They set the grocery bags onto the counter, but the chore ended there, as they both held still and listened intently to the hushed conversation between Jennifer and Margaret.

"Is there something wrong? Was there another false report?" Jennifer asked.

Leaning against the countertop, Derek's hand tightened around the edge.

False report. Nothing about it was false. What was false was everything else in this palace—but Margaret didn't know that. How could she? Even Derek played a part in keeping the truth carefully concealed.

"Nothing to worry about. I just need to make at least one checkup within two months after the initial report. Lots of times, in real cases, we end up spending a lot of time with the kids and in home before we find anything. That's not necessary here. The good news is, you won't be getting any more visits like this from me, because, as far as I can tell, everything is fine here."

Derek's jaw clenched, and out of the corner of his eye, he saw Mal's head spin in his direction. He looked at her and saw the same emotions in her face that he felt writhing through him: anger, helplessness, fear.

Did he make the right choice? Was he doing the right thing by keeping silent?

He wasn't sure.

The woman in the other room was an unreachable line to safety, who might be able to help, but what if they tried to grab ahold and their hands slipped? What were the risks if they failed? She and the entire organization had already been told what was happening here, and all it had done was turn the entire home into a ticking time bomb with Mark at the fuse. These people claimed to be help, but they couldn't see what was right in front of them.

That was enough to reassure him that his silence was

necessary.

"That's great to hear," Jennifer said, breathing a genuine sigh of relief.

"Your case closes on December twentieth, and since everything looks good, you have nothing to worry about."

He wished that were true.

"Thank you for stopping by, Margaret. I'm sorry to waste your time."

"Not at all. We'd rather it be a waste of time than something else."

The friendly laugh that Jennifer let out grated against Derek's nerves, but he'd done the same thing. He'd played it cool. He'd pulled on his charm like a mask to hide what was really happening in the home, just like Jennifer. He was just as guilty, just as afraid of the consequences as she was.

He and Mal stayed in the kitchen until Margaret was gone, and a collective exhale of breath shook its walls. It did nothing to ease them.

Jennifer's quick pace slowed considerably, and the energetic friendliness faded by the time she walked into the kitchen where the kids waited. She was not smiling, and her posture slouched as she turned to them. In minutes, she'd aged ten years.

Her eyes went from Mal to Derek, who stood with his hand grabbing onto the counter corner so hard it dug into his palm.

"Let's not tell your dad about this, alright?"

His jaw clenched, but he nodded. It's all he could do.

Jennifer stepped forward and raised her hand, laying it gently on Derek's cheek in a way that might have been motherly in another life. Now, it was cold, clammy, and shaking. And there was no promise of protection in it.

Without another word, Jennifer turned and left the room, leaving the groceries untouched on the counter.

Mal spun her whole body toward Derek as soon as her mother's door closed. She wasn't as compliant as her mother. She hadn't been broken down like Derek—enough to understand why it was worth it to do as her mother said and pretend it never happened. "What do we do?"

Derek finally let go of the counter and took note of the indent it left in the skin of his palm. He wished he could give her a real answer, but there wasn't one. At least, not the one she wanted.

"We don't do anything."

NOVEMBER 1985

Three more to go. After months and endless hours of collecting everything she needed for these applications, she only had three more prompted essays to answer before she could seal them up with the rest and send them out in the morning, as soon as the post office opened.

Sure, she was still a week early from some of the deadlines, but she'd rather get it done now than risk being too late and missing it.

She scribbled on the lined paper, writing the words as they came to her head, as she bobbed along to Queen playing through her headphones. Honestly, she wasn't writing them as quickly as she could. She purposefully took her time, focusing closely on each one. Not because she couldn't go faster, but because once she finished these pages, part of the stress in her life would be gone, leaving a wide-open space for more to fill it in.

These applications had been a wonderful diversion throughout everything else, pretty soon it would be gone, and she'd be back to trying not to think about the things that her mind really wanted to.

Like a certain curly haired boy she hadn't seen in a few days. The same one she definitely *wasn't* checking for out her window several times a night, in case a dark Monte Carlo was parked out front.

She pretended not to be disappointed each time she peeked and it wasn't there. She didn't know what she was expecting.

She missed the knock on her door—the music was too loud in her ears—but the movement of it swinging open caught her eye, and she paused her writing to look up. She pulled the headphones down, and the sound disappeared to leave the quiet of her bedroom, with her mother obviously waiting for an answer to a question Becca hadn't heard.

"What?"

"I was asking if you want a piece of pie. We still have some left over."

Becca sat up and stretched her arms over her head, exhaling. "Sure. Pecan, please."

"Okay." Her mom smiled and shut the door, once again leaving her alone.

Her knuckles cracked as she bent them, and she massaged her hands to ease the ache of endless writing. She still wasn't entirely used to her mom being home so often. She still worked long shifts, and sometimes Becca wouldn't see her for a few days because of their opposing schedules, but it was more than she had in a long, long time.

It was nice though. She didn't feel so lonely. Which was really great during this time when she was still so confused about what she had and hadn't lost in the past couple months or so.

Especially after the other night.

Every time she was ready to accept that her friendship with Derek was forever compromised, something came up to corrupt the progress and send her into a disorienting whirlpool.

One minute, she was about ready to officially give him space, and then he kisses her, leading to the unexpected discovery that she was in love.

After that, she'd only tried to make sense of it all. Things felt…better. At least, she thought they did. He'd talked to her, sober, and for a little bit, she wondered if it would be possible for things to go back to the way they were.

Becca groaned and fell back onto her bed, studying the popcorn ceiling to search for some sort of answer in its patterns. This was exactly why those applications had been so important.

A few minutes away from them and she was stuck in a never-ending spiral.

She just wanted an answer. She just wanted to understand. She just wanted closure.

In this state, she wasn't sure she'd ever get it.

The door opened again, and Becca didn't bother to look up—her attention was too focused on the ceiling's abstract shapes.

"Just leave it on my dresser," she said. As much as she loved pie, she didn't particularly feel like eating right now.

Her mom didn't answer, and Becca waited for the clatter of the plate being set down. The door closed instead, and Becca could feel the air in the room shift around her mom's lingering presence. Becca closed her eyes in light irritation.

It was great that her mom took more interest in how Becca was feeling, now that she lived at home more often, and Becca was more than happy to share. But sometimes, like right now, she just needed to think to herself rather than discuss it with another person.

"I have to focus on these applications tonight, so I don't have a lot of time to talk."

"It won't take long."

Becca shot up, and her heart fluttered from her chest into the back of her throat. That voice was certainly not her mother's, and she certainly couldn't ignore it.

Derek stood still with his hands in the pockets of his leather jacket.

Her stomach filled with feathers, and a sweet, addictive bitterness settled on her tongue. It took her a second to collect her thoughts and form a response.

"I thought you were my mom," she said, and cringed at how stupid she sounded. Her hands rose, flattening her messy hair. She'd never cared about how she looked around Derek.

He stayed near the door, waiting for an invitation. They'd never cared about any of that before.

Becca hid the deep steadying breath she took while adjusting her position on the bed. She crossed her legs and sat so her back was straight. The last thing she wanted was for him to see how much his presence affected her—how lightheaded she got just from looking at him and how her fingers trembled slightly at the thought of touching him.

She wanted to touch him.

"This would be much easier if you just came in." She said.

Her stomach churned as he followed her directions, a mixture of elated delight and sinking dread forming as he took his spot on the edge of her bed. It'd been a long time since he was willingly in her home. She loved him here—she hated what it might mean.

Breathing was hard. It was even harder to hold it in, scared that a single exhale might disrupt the tension that settled between them and scare him away.

This was all much easier before. Before, he would walk into her room and lay next to her in the dark as he said everything he needed, or they would just lay in silence. Now, she didn't know what he needed, and the light on the ceiling felt like a spotlight on the interaction, making it harder to tell what he wanted.

Derek was her favorite book—the one she could quote from, the one she could predict. The times that he came and wanted silence were easy to read—his body would shift away, his eyes would avoid hers. She knew when he needed just her presence and nothing else.

But this wasn't one of those times.

He didn't turn away. He held her gaze with such intensity, she was the one tempted to avert her eyes. She didn't, though, because Derek didn't want silence now. He just wasn't willing to be the one to break it.

"Tell me what you need," she said, her voice gently laying the offering before him.

He took a deep breath. "They came to the house again. Child Protective Services."

Becca's hand clenched around her messy comforter, trying to control the trembling. This topic frightened her, because it originated with her. Derek made it clear that he didn't want her help, he didn't want her input, he didn't want anyone else involved. She saw how he reacted the last time, and a fear sparked inside her that this was just another order to stay away.

But he didn't continue. He waited, watching her for a response. In the past, she would have begged him to ask them for help. Now, she realized that was exactly what had gotten her into this mess. She swallowed. "What are you going to do?"

Finally, his eyes moved away, and his hands rose to cover his face. "There's nothing I *can* do."

Becca's heart dropped. It killed her to see him like this—it always had and it always would. In the light and in the dark, she wanted to take away his pain. She wanted to fix it all.

She knew now that she couldn't do that.

Her hand gripped harder onto the blankets, resisting the urge to wrap herself around him and hold him.

Her lips stung where her teeth bit into them, and tears pricked at the corners.

"If we do anything, *anything*, and my dad finds out…" He trailed off, lifting his eyes to reveal the red rings around them. The ones that she only ever saw in the dark. "You have no idea how it's been. He's holding it in—everything. It seems better, but he's going to get worse and worse and worse, and then he'll hear something like this, and it will all go to shit. I can't sleep, I can't chew, I can barely breathe there without worrying when he will explode."

Becca's mouth was full of ash, and a boulder dragged her down, down, down.

She did this. Derek was miserable because of her.

She may not be the one who beat him down or held such nuclear rage that could explode after just months of being contained, but Derek had asked her to stay quiet. She'd promised she would. He told her why, and she'd said she understood.

It turned out she didn't actually understand. She would never fully understand what it was like to live like Derek did.

If she had, she would never have tried to call for help, she would have never gone against what he wanted—what he needed. Just her silence for his peace.

"I'm sorry." Her voice broke, and Derek lifted his head.

The guilt on her face had to be as devastatingly obvious as the dread on his.

"Stop," he said, his hair bouncing as he shook his head.

"But I am. I'm so, so sorry. I should have listened to you when you told me. I should have kept my promise and trusted you." A tear escaped Becca's eyes, followed by more and more. "It was selfish. I wanted to save you."

"Save me?" Derek said, scoffing with painful sarcasm.

Becca flinched as he stood up from the bed, leaving her on the spot alone.

His eyes watered, but his brows drew together as he glared down at her until she withered under his gaze.

Becca tentatively rose, hoping that being closer to him would make this easier.

It didn't.

He still stood half a head taller than her, and she still had to look up at him. She still wanted to wipe away the tears that fell from his eyes. Her breath still caught.

"I never asked to be saved by you. I never wanted *anything* from you. Why can't you see that?" He stepped closer, and the space between them collapsed to only inches. She could smell him—cigarettes and leather and all.

She stood her ground, tilting her head back further as he towered over her. He could have yelled in her face, but he didn't. His voice lowered, his head sloped downward. Her exhale shuddered as his words slid gently over her face.

"All I wanted was you. Nothing else, just *you*."

She couldn't believe him. She shook her head, her words barely a whisper. "You hate me."

"Hate you?" He laughed, unbelieving. "I *tried* to hate you, I really did. Every day, I tried to forget you, but I can't. I think about you all the time. I can't *stand* to be away from you."

It couldn't possibly be real. She was in a dream, floating away from her body, which prickled where his chest nearly touched hers, where his fingers brushed her knuckles.

"I can barely hold myself back right now." He said it through clenched teeth, deep and raspy.

Becca snapped back into herself, and her eyes widened. Everything she wanted stood right in front of her, and the resistance she'd built snapped away like string.

Selfish. She was so *ready* to be selfish.

"Then don't."

There was a split second that Derek's eyes widened a fraction, and then the next she was taken.

His lips consumed hers, and she drowned.

The heavy wall that had been built between them crumbled into dust and was replaced by flames. Sucking, burning, eating flames that engulfed Becca over every inch of her body.

She was ready to be burned alive against him, to let it leave her as ash under his feet.

He didn't let her go. His hands came to her—one on her cheek and one on her waist—and he held her together.

Afraid she would fall, she wrapped her fingers into Derek's hair at the back of his neck and clung to him as he tilted her face up and opened her lips with his.

This was the second time, but it felt brand new. Like a secret never whispered before.

His touch was skilled, as his fingers brushed gently against her cheek, contrasting the hungry rhythm of his lips.

She never wanted it to end. She never thought it could get better.

Then his lips moved from hers, and she whined at the loss of them. But he didn't pull away.

He moved even closer, his mouth brushing along her cheek, to the edge of her ear and skimming at the bottom as he whispered something only she would ever hear. "You have no idea what you do to me."

A heat ran through her face and traveled through every inch of her body.

The fiery combination of lust and love consumed her, and she would become whatever Derek wanted, whatever he needed.

His mouth continued to move down, and instinctively, her head arched to the side, granting him access to the skin where her shoulder and neck connected. That was enough for him.

Becca gasped into the steamy air of her room as Derek's mouth opened against her bare skin, and in response, he groaned.

The sound sent chills down her arms and spine and sent her head backward in delight.

He stepped forward, and Becca followed in sync until the backs of her knees hit the edge of her mattress. Slowly, oh so slowly, Derek managed to control their fall onto the sheets, while his mouth continued to work steadily at her neck.

Becca panted, her hands grabbing clumsily at his shirt, desperate for more of him. She wanted to see him, wanted to feel him bare against her.

She grunted in disappointment as one of his hands engulfed hers and pulled it away, pinning her by the wrist against the bed. Opening her mouth, Becca prepared to beg.

A cold bucket of water showered over them as a knock sounded on the door.

They sprang and stared into each other with wide, darkened eyes. Becca remained on the bed and watched Derek as he stood frozen in the middle of her bedroom. His chest rose rapidly, meeting the same pace as hers.

Neither of them moved.

"I brought you guys some pie."

She loved her mother, but *god*, did she hate her right now.

Becca, somehow, was the first to recover. Her hands came up to her head and flattened against the frizz and tangles Derek's hands had inevitably left behind. Her movement seemed to snap him out of a trance, and he followed suit, both of them trying to straighten their clothes and feign normalcy.

Becca walked to the door and shifted the collar of her shirt upward just in time to cover the spot on her neck that still sent chills down her back.

Her mother stood outside with a plate of two pieces of pie.

Becca must have taken too long to respond, because her mother raised a brow and looked her over. "Everything okay?"

"Yeah," Becca's voice came out rasped, and she coughed to clear it. "Yeah, we're fine. Just chatting."

"Well, I brought pecan for you, and cherry for you, Derek." She handed the plates to Becca, who turned and set them on her desk.

"Thanks, Amanda," he said.

Becca glanced behind her.

Goddammit.

He was much better at this stuff than she was. He sat on her bed, leaning back with such believable nonchalance that even she wondered for a second if she had imagined everything that had just happened.

"Of course." Her mother smiled at Derek, then raised a brow at Becca, lowering her voice slightly. "Derek's room is available if he needs to use it tonight."

Becca flushed. There was no way she could handle Derek sleeping down the hallway from her tonight—so, so close. Not in this state.

"Thanks, Mom."

"I'm going to head to bed. You kids let me know if you need anything." She leaned forward and planted a kiss on Becca's head before turning and disappearing into her own room.

The door shut quietly, and Becca stayed put, with her hand on the knob, afraid to turn back around and see Derek sitting there.

The moment was over. She was well aware of that. She wanted to grasp hold of it, and keep it forever, but it was gone. She was afraid that, if she looked back around, everything would have disappeared, including him.

She closed her eyes. "What now?"

There was a rustle from behind her, the sound of the sheets moving and the weight on the mattress lifting. She could feel him getting closer, like there was an invisible string between them, and the tension relaxed the closer he got. She didn't expect the gentle touch on her arm that urged her to turn around.

She couldn't resist Derek, even if she tried. Her eyes moved up, meeting his. They stood like they had before, him towering over her. She bit her lip. His eyes tracked the movement, then flicked back to hold her gaze. She inhaled.

"I'm not mad anymore. Not at you. So please, come back to me," he said.

It was so straightforward. He made it sound so easy.

And it was so easy. So easy to get lost in those blue eyes, to love the way his gaze looked over her. It was so easy to love him.

Her lips turned upward and she nodded. His eyes softened.

"Okay," she said.

It was impossible to wish things could return to how they were before. It was impossible to imagine everything would right itself. But, maybe now, it would be easier to bear it as the world tilted on its axis.

DECEMBER 1985

Derek bit his lip and grinned into the rearview mirror, chuckling breathlessly to himself.

He'd tried to think of the right word to describe how he'd felt since last night, but nothing was strong enough to encapsulate the full extent. Happy? Elated? Euphoric?

All were correct, but didn't fill the corners of the full, fluttery feeling in his chest.

The gray edges of the world were vivid again, blinding him.

He sighed and tapped his fingers giddily on his steering wheel.

And it all centered on Becca—just like always.

"You're starting to freak me out."

Mal's voice rattled him, and it took him a moment to remember that she sat right next to him in the car. *She* hadn't forgotten, though, and her arms crossed over her chest as she raised a confused eyebrow.

"What?" He tried to play it cool, but the smile on his face gave him away. He didn't really care.

"You're smiling."

"What? I can't smile?"

"You haven't smiled in months." She looked him over with a weird expression. "Especially not like that."

He shrugged. He was high on the addictive feeling of being in love and knowing that it wasn't entirely one way.

She'd reciprocated his kiss—Becca had wanted him to some

extent. He'd take that. He'd take anything at this point.

"What happened? Did you and Becca suddenly make up?" she asked, and the high-pitched taunt in her voice told him she was kidding. Trying to get a rise out of him, like she loved to do. But she wasn't expecting him to look at her, allowing the smile on his face to grow as he bit his lip.

Mal's back straightened and her eyes grew into saucers. Her face lightened cautiously. "No way. You did."

He neither confirmed nor denied, but he might as well have screamed yes out the window with the way his head fell back against the headrest, as he chuckled.

"*Thank god.* I thought I was going to go crazy with your moping, on top of Mark's intensity. I swear he's getting worse."

If she was trying to kill his mood, she succeeded. His bright grin dimmed slightly at the reminder of his father. Mark was the last thing in the world he wanted to think about when *something* was starting to go right for him.

It made it even worse that Mal was right. Mark's intensity was becoming unbearable. They could feel it in the air in the house. It was like breathing in a flammable gas every second he was around.

Derek didn't want to think about this. He didn't want to deal with him even when he was out and away from the toxic cloud that was his father. One word about the visit from CPS would be like lighting a match in a gas canister—so they did as they'd agreed and kept silent.

"Just avoid him," he said.

"I already do."

He took a deep breath and turned onto the street to the sheriff's house where Mal would have a sleepover with her friend Jane. He'd been happy enough to say yes when she asked without a fight or attitude today.

"Thanks for the ride." Mal slid out of his car, pausing just long enough to give him a suggestive smile. "Give Becca my best." She puckered her lips and mockingly kissed the air before slamming the door and running away so he couldn't yell at her.

He flicked his middle finger up, but she missed it as she ran to the house.

The moment she reached the front porch, the door opened, and Sheriff Winston Wade let her in.

He would have driven down and out of the driveway immediately upon seeing the sheriff, but Wade raised his hand in greeting, and Derek hesitated with his hand on the gear and foot on the brake. He could easily leave, but he'd already got enough attention from the man lately. And clearly, Sheriff Wade was heading right toward him, walking down the dirt drive past his beaten-up truck toward Derek's car.

Instead of running, Derek rolled down his window and nodded politely at the older man as he approached his side of the Monte Carlo. They hadn't interacted much, and the few run-ins they'd had weren't anything to write home about—aside from Derek's brief runaway.

"How's it going, Derek?" The sheriff tilted his hat to shadow his face from the bright afternoon sun.

"Just fine, Sheriff." Derek smiled up at him.

"How's the old man?" There was a look in his face as he asked it, and Derek immediately knew it wasn't an innocent question. It was an investigation.

Derek's hand tightened slightly on the gear, but his face remained carefully careless. Wade's eyes were attentive.

He knew Wade knew, because the sheriff wouldn't have his men circling Derek's home every so often if Becca hadn't told him *something*. Still, Derek wasn't entirely certain of the full extent of what Wade knew about his home life.

"He just started working security at the mall."

"So I heard." Of course, he'd heard. It was his job to know what the people in Highburg did, especially those that had been noted to be something other than harmless.

Derek met Wade's stare for a moment, and he could sense him looking for something deeper than that meaning, but Derek kept his expression straight.

After a few seconds, the sheriff backed off and exhaled. "You give me a call if you need anything, alright?"

"Yes, sir."

Wade hit the top of the car, a signal that he was excusing Derek. "Drive safe."

Derek smiled, but it didn't reach his eyes. "Yes, sir."

His window rolled up at an agonizingly slow pace as he backed out of the drive and sped away down the street. This isn't what he'd wanted to do with his day.

The brief mention of his father plummeted his mood, but he brushed it aside and ignored the stone in his stomach. He didn't want to think about this. Not now, not when he was so happy.

He held onto that happiness as he drove away from the cabin and back into town. He begged for it to stay. He wanted the warmth in his stomach and chest to linger just a little longer before it was doused out.

There was one thing in this town that could bring the flame back to life…with just the smile on her face or a touch of her hand. He needed that—right now.

***

Those damn applications took her much, much longer than she anticipated.

And yet, she wasn't upset about it. She'd spent the rest of last night stuck in the unbelievable sensations Derek left in her body and head, even after his departure.

That was no state of mind to be writing college essays in.

The result was waking up later than she meant to and having to speed through the last of them before the post office closed for the rest of the weekend.

And yet, she *still* wasn't upset about it.

She had to pause every few minutes to bury her head in her pillow and giggle in school-girl excitement whenever a fresh memory popped into her head. The things he'd said to her that set her hair on delightful edge, the adept movement of his lips and fingers.

Even now, putting on her coat to leave the house, she spaced out for a few seconds to try and come to terms that the boy she was madly in love with had kissed her and told her how much he wanted her.

God. It couldn't be real.

God. She would *kill* to see him right now.

She slipped on her walking shoes and bundled herself up, with a folder containing each of her completed college applications wrapped protectively in her arms. She'd have to walk to the post office today, since her mom had taken the car to work earlier in the morning.

Not that she minded. It gave her more time to think about Derek.

She stepped out of the house and shut the door behind her, before walking down the sidewalk toward the driveway to make her way to the post office.

But the driveway wasn't empty. There shouldn't have been any cars there, but there was one.

There was *the* one—the exact one she wanted to see right now. Leaning against it was the person she was itching to see.

Derek sat on the edge of the hood of his car and smiled at her as she paused her walk.

Her heart thumped from her chest to her ears, and her breath quickened.

He looked radiant. He always looked good, even on his bad days. He was the most beautiful human being that ever existed in her opinion. Right now, though, she thought her knees might give out just from staring.

He wore a black shirt, unbuttoned halfway down to display his chest, even in this cold weather, and his jeans did wonders for his thighs. He wore a leather jacket, the same one as the night before, and Becca's nerves skyrocketed. She gulped down a lungful of air to calm herself.

"Don't they call this sort of thing déjà vu?" he asked, pushing off the car to walk toward her.

Her eyes followed him closely. Half of her expected him to

lean forward and kiss her lips like he did before, but he didn't.

In hindsight, that might have just been a wish.

Her face heated at the thought, and his smile curled up just a tiny bit more.

"Derek." She could barely manage to say his name. "Hi."

He raised an amused brow. "Hi." His gaze traveled down, taking in the coat and shoes she wore. "Where are you going?"

She looked down, following his gaze to the packet—bulky from dozens of papers. "The post office. I'm mailing off the last of my applications."

He nodded. "Let me drive you."

Sitting in an enclosed space with Derek Stokes—alone? Not a good idea right now.

"Oh, it's fine. I was—"

"Get in."

"Yeah, okay." Curse her heart, betraying her common sense in favor of Derek.

She stepped around him and walked straight to her side of the car, getting in before he was even to his door.

She wouldn't say the drive was awkward, per se, but she had no idea where to place her hands. She didn't know the best way to tilt her jaw so she looked pretty from his angle.

There was a very conscious need to look good when Derek looked her way, and he looked her way *a lot*.

She should have worn her hair down, instead of up. She should have worn that one red shirt that her mom said made her eyes pop.

The back of her hand came up to her face, and she pressed her knuckles to her cheek to test out how hot she was—very hot.

This was a terrible idea. Pretty soon, Derek would notice what a mistake he'd made and—

Warmth overtook her fingers, and the endless stream of thoughts and worries came to a shrieking halt as she looked down to find Derek's fingers covering hers. He moved them after a few seconds, and Becca stared, empty-headed, as he turned his palm toward hers and intertwined their fingers together.

"How long are you going to be uncomfortable around me?"

His words caught her off guard, and she looked up.

This was Derek.

This was *still* Derek. Her Derek. These were the same calloused hands she had touched dozens of times. It was different now, but this was Derek.

The slow rub of his thumb on her skin reminded her of that.

She exhaled and shook her head. "I'm not sure how to act." A weight she hadn't realized was holding her down disappeared as soon as she said it aloud to him.

His fingers squeezed around hers. "Just to be clear, I'm not either."

She chuckled and gave him a look of disbelief. "You liar."

"It's true."

"There is no way that you don't know how to act. You've been with, like, a hundred girls before." She swallowed the pinch of discomfort in her chest as she said it.

"I don't think you quite understand." He slowed the car down as they approached a red stop light. It was too perfect of timing, because it gave him the chance to take his eyes completely off the road and focus on her, leaning in slightly to lower his voice like they were in the dark. "I don't hold their hands, I don't agonize over them for months, and I don't lo—" He stopped, his eyes widening like he'd caught himself about to do something really bad.

Neither of them moved as Becca's breath deepened. Then the light turned green again, and he pulled away to focus back onto the road.

"My point is that this is *nothing* like those. Not by a long shot." He finished.

Becca's teeth picked at her lip and worried the skin to death. Whatever he was about to say, she had a feeling she would love it as much as she loved him.

But she didn't need to hear the rest to be assured. She trusted Derek. She knew him better than anyone. She believed every word that came out of his mouth—not just because she wanted it to be true.

Her fingers tightened around his, and she relaxed into the seat, smiling softly as he continued to drive.

They got to the post office half an hour before closing time, and she gave him brief instructions to stay in the car while she ran in.

After getting a bit of help from the representative to pick out an envelope for each of her applications and papers, she managed to get them all packed and ready to go in about ten minutes and paid for in fifteen. She was back out of the building right after.

She practically skipped back to the car and climbed into the passenger seat.

When she glanced at Derek, he wasn't looking at her. His attention was caught on something else outside the window. She followed his gaze to the man who stood right in front of the post office, staring straight back through Derek's windshield at the two of them together in the front seat.

Mark didn't feign any pleasantries. Not even a nod or fake smile like he usually did with Becca. He frowned at Derek through the glass.

A sickness grew in her stomach, churning and sucking away her joy.

She wasn't the only one. She caught onto the tightening of Derek's fingers around the steering wheel, and the tension clicking his jaw. The veins stood out in his neck.

Mark shook his head and gave a visible disapproving scoff that soured the scored lines of his face. Derek's face grew pale. Hers had to be the same.

Mark didn't stick around. He turned and walked away from them, heading to the black car she hadn't noticed parked a few spots over when they first arrived.

Derek sat statue still until Mark got into his vehicle and peeled out of the parking lot. Even from where she sat, even in a different car and far away from Mark, she could feel the dark, angry energy of him lingering around them.

Derek's shoulders slumped, and his chin fell forward to touch his chest. He sighed shakily.

She'd seen this before, seen the way that interacting with Mark sent Derek into a tumultuous spiral.

There were a million things she wanted to do to make him feel better, but she couldn't fix everything. He didn't want her to. Reaching across the console, she gently placed her fingers on the back of Derek's tense ones and peeled the digits off the steering wheel until they relaxed and settled against hers.

His dimmed eyes lifted. Becca did her best to hide her own fear and frustration with an easy smile.

"I need to go home," he said. He was trying to act okay, but she could see from the tense lines in his face that he wasn't. Try as he might, there was no hiding from her. "I wanted to go somewhere, but we'll have to do it another time."

Her fingers stroked his knuckles gently. "Will you be okay?"

"I'll be fine."

She wanted to argue and demand more information, but she let it go, and just continued to brush his hand with hers.

They held to each other that way the entire drive to her house. It wasn't as exciting or bashful or dreamy as before, but it wasn't nothing. She'd stay grateful for any Derek, in any form, now.

He pulled into her driveway, and Becca opened her door to leave and say goodbye. She paused, because goodbye wasn't enough for her with him. She didn't want to say goodbye anymore, not when she was so close to a goodbye before.

"I'll be here," she said, and spoke the rest with her eyes.

He saw it all, eating up the meaning from her pupils, and his lips lifted briefly. "I know."

***

Dragging it out wasn't worth it. In his weaker moments, Derek might have lingered outside longer than necessary to delay the inevitable, but these past days had given him a burst of courage that made him eager to face it.

The door brushed against the floor as he opened it, and the warm air of the inside entry hit his face. The TV was already playing in the living room, and Derek took a breath to steel himself before turning to enter the room.

Mark sat on a chair, facing the living room entrance. He wasn't focusing at all on the background noise of the television—instead, he was already observing Derek, who stared straight back.

"I see you're not listening again," Mark said, and stood from his chair to cross slowly until he stood right in front of Derek.

Derek held his father's gaze, carefully studying his moves and choosing to keep his mouth shut. Bear it. Just bear it. His teeth brushed at the inside of his cheek as Mark rubbed his nose.

Derek held in a cringe as Mark's bitter breath flooded his nostrils, rank with the prick of alcohol.

"What exactly did that whore do that's got you so desperate to be her bitch, huh? She suck your cock or something? Must be pretty damn good if she makes you go against your own father so easily."

A punch of anger and sickness bit painfully down on Derek's brain, and for a moment, he lost some of the strength to bear his father's taunting. "Don't talk about her like that."

In his mind, the words were forceful and strong, threatening even. Out loud, they were fragile, but they still got a reaction.

Mark's eyes widened a fraction, his brows shooting up in outraged shock. "What did you say to me?"

Derek was slowly losing the battle, and his eyes involuntarily averted to the wall over Mark's shoulder, unable to take the intensity of his glare.

An ache ran up his jaw as his father grabbed the sides of his face with his fingers and yanked so Derek was forced to look back at him. Derek winced. Mark's fingers dug into his cheeks and jaw.

Mark scoffed. "You're so weak, it's pathetic. No wonder your mother couldn't stand to stick around. Not with a pitiful fool of a son like you."

Mark spit the words into his face, and Derek blinked away the watery pain in his eyes. The imprint of Mark's fingers wouldn't be there in the morning, but they might as well be permanently etched under his skin.

"You're wrong." He didn't mean to say it. The words came from his mouth so quietly they were barely a breath, but Mark heard them, and that was enough.

"Wrong?" Mark's face grew red, his hand raising into the air. Derek flinched.

The blow flew past his ear, but it didn't come down on him—in fact, Mark's grasp on Derek disappeared entirely.

There was a loud crash, and Derek looked up to see his father's fist straight through the wall, leaving a gaping hole of white drywall and chipped paint.

Panting, Derek watched as Mark pulled his hand from the wall. He glared at Derek with furious intensity. He lifted a finger, and shoved it in Derek's face, as white dust fell from it and littered onto Derek's shirt. "Don't you *dare* leave your room tonight."

Then he was gone. And Derek stayed right where he was. On the ground, the debris of Mark's outrage scattered around his feet.

He breathed in, once, twice.

He wanted to be angry. He wanted to smash and cry and break things. The humiliated tears pricked pitifully at the corner of his eyes.

But he continued to breathe in and out as he walked to his room and closed the door behind him. He wanted to sneak out that window and go see her, but his dad would notice the sound now. It scared him that his father noticed her. It scared him that Mark saw Becca as a threat.

He didn't want to put her in harm's way. Not when Mark had made it clear he'd pay extra attention to anything Derek did.

He sat on his bed and stared at the door, his fingers clutching at the comforter. To his right, on his bedside table, sat the small purple lavender candle, right where it had been for the past half a year.

He pulled his lighter from his pocket, lit the wick, and let the calming scent surround him.

"Hi, Becca." Mal raised her hand in greeting, as Jane smiled next to her.

Becca looked between the two teens and raised her eyebrow. "What are you two doing here?" When she'd heard the knock on the door, her heart had jumped, and she'd rushed over, expecting to see Derek there. Instead, his little sister grinned mischievously at Becca.

It was both a relief, and a worry.

A no show was a good sign, right?

"Do you want to have a sleepover?"

Becca's brows knit together. "A sleepover?"

"We were going to have one at Jane's house but thought it might be fun to include you."

It sounded innocent enough, which is exactly why Becca questioned the girl's motives. Especially since they both looked suspiciously eager.

"Do your parents know you're here?"

"They know I'm having a sleepover with Jane."

Becca bit her lip. She'd seen that look on Mark's face when he noticed her in Derek's car outside the post office; she knew he didn't trust her. There's no way he'd be okay with Mal staying at her house.

Mal, sensing Becca's hesitation, brought her hands up and clamped them together, pouting her lips theatrically. "Please," she begged.

Becca scoffed, but laughed at the girls' antics. Her weak spot for Mal was almost as strong as the one for her older brother. "Fine. Make yourselves at home, I guess."

They didn't need to be told twice. They made their way in, with a bag of clothes each, before plopping themselves onto the couch and getting comfortable.

Becca followed them in.

"Let's play a game," Mal announced, pulling her legs onto the cushions of the couch to get comfortable.

"That was quick," Becca said. She planted herself onto the floor next to the couch, and raised a single brow at the suspicious question.

Mal shrugged like it wasn't that big of a deal, but the smirk sitting on her face gave her away. "I'm just eager to get started."

Jane giggled and shared a look with Mal.

Oh shit. Just what sort of trick had she allowed these girls to pull on her?

"Becca, truth or dare."

"Oh, no. No way." Becca shook her head. "I'm not playing this game."

"Come on! It'll be so fun." Mal leaned forward. "Truth or dare?"

Becca blinked, and bit her lip. She was going to regret this, she could already tell. "Truth." She didn't want to take the chance of whatever these girls might come up with for a dare.

Mal grinned, and both girls simultaneously got closer to Becca as Mal asked the question, "Have you and Derek kissed?"

Jane cackled, finally letting out the laugh she'd been holding since she came in the door.

Becca blanched in surprise. She bit her lip and tried to act calm. "Why would you ask that?"

"You have to answer."

"I don't want to answer."

Mal grinned, her entire face lit up. "Oh my god. You totally did." She turned to Jane and grabbed the other girl's hand in excitement. "I told you! I knew it as soon as he giggled like a little boy earlier." She clapped her hands in triumph.

Becca inhaled sharply. "He did what?"

"He was totally grinning and laughing to himself the entire way to Jane's house. Seriously, it was kind of freaky."

Becca's chest grew light, and a fluttering settled into her stomach. She herself had been all sorts of giddy after their interaction last night, but to imagine Derek that way—her heart soared.

"Is he your boyfriend?" Jane chimed in, leaning her elbows onto her knees.

Becca shot up, caught off guard by the question. "What? No." Right? They were friends. Friends who just happened to have kissed—twice. He was her best friend—who she just happened to be in love with. That's it.

Jane frowned at her response. "You kissed him and he's not your boyfriend?"

"I didn't say we kissed."

Jane stared at Becca a moment, while Mal laughed so hard, she clutched her stomach.

"Mal." Jane's attention turned back to her friend, who stopped cackling long enough to look up. "Truth or dare?"

Mal sat up, her eyes shining with entertained delight. "Dare."

Jane looked just as mischievous as Mal. "I dare you to call Derek and ask him if they kissed."

Mal was already on her feet, walking across the room, laughing once again. "Oh my god. He's so going to kill me." If she actually believed that, it didn't deter her enough to not do the dare. In fact, she seemed to be enjoying it too much.

Silently, Becca panicked and froze in her spot. It was still embarrassing for her. To know that she loved him, that they had reached a level they'd never be able to come back from, and not knowing if the extent to which she loved was matched. She worried something simple would add cracks to what already felt like a delicate step forward.

"No. Mal."

But she was already on the phone, and it was already ringing.

Becca covered her face with her hands, hiding the redness that was surely swelling.

She couldn't hear much more than a mumble from the other room, and then, less than a minute later, it was over and Mal was back in the room.

Jane's eyes were huge, expectantly watching Mal cross the room, and Becca lowered just one of her fingers to try and evaluate Mal's expression. But she wasn't eagerly throwing "Ha, ha. You two kissed" into Becca's face.

"What did he say?" Jane finally asked.

Mal fell back on the couch, and slouched into it, looking disappointed. "I didn't talk to him. Apparently, he's in his room and can't come out right now."

Becca's embarrassment faded, and she dropped her hands into her lap. She would have rather Mal came in and never let her live it down. Instead, she had to silently wonder what "can't come out right now" meant. Her fingers curled into her palm, and she dug her nails into the skin, trying to distract herself.

As much as she wanted to, there was nothing she could do that would make it easier for him. Whatever *it* was.

She took a deep breath and put a smile on her face. A distraction was needed. "Jane. Truth or dare?"

Jane sat up straight, her mouth forming a surprised "O" shape. "Truth."

"Have you had your first kiss?"

Mal laughed and turned to Jane, waiting for an answer, while Jane looked bashfully down at her hands.

Meanwhile, Becca's fingers scraped against the inside of her hand, and tried to calm her nerves. This was all she could do—until he came to her first.

***

Derek laid on his bed with an arm tucked under his head. The sun had risen an hour ago, and he'd only left the room momentarily to get a glass of water, but had promptly returned to his seclusion after seeing that the hole Mark smashed in the wall was gone. The dust was gone, the ground was clean, and all that was left was a picture of flowers in a vase hanging right where the hole should have been. Like it never even existed.

Jennifer had done her job of "peacemaker" in the home. That's what she liked to say anyway.

Derek flicked his thumb over his lighter's trigger, and a small flame came to life. He brought it right to his face, then blew out the fire. Then he did it again and again. He wouldn't leave this room until it was safe.

He knew Becca. He knew she would be waiting for him. He'd seen it when he dropped her off at her house—the way her brows crinkled and her nose wrinkled in concern. He'd seen it a million times.

But Mark was watching, he was waiting for Derek to slip up with Becca, and he couldn't let that happen.

Around seven a.m., Mark left his room and shuffled around the kitchen. The scent of coffee sifted through the crack under Derek's door and mixed with the scent of lighter fluid. The lavender lingered on his pillow, even though the candle flame had long since been blown out.

Around eight, there was the click of the front door opening and closing, then the start of the engine.

Derek didn't relax until 8:30, when he knew Mark would be on shift, and the chances of him coming home at all were none. He stopped flicking the lighter, finally setting it down on the table. He rose from his spot to go to the mirror on the wall. His curled hair was frizzier than usual, and he hadn't rested well. The area under his eyes was dark and his skin sallow. His hand rubbed against his cheek, trying to help the blood flow through his face better.

Quite frankly, he looked like shit.

It was time for him to shower and clean up. He wanted to see her today. No, he *needed* to see her today.

But he didn't want her to see him like this—she'd ask questions.

With the house clear, he left his room and slumped into the

bathroom to wash off. He turned the shower knob to the left. Undressing, he stepped into the tub and hissed as the water came down in bullets, hitting his skin with a painful sting as steam rose around him.

He was back in his room in minutes, pulling on a pair of jeans and a black t-shirt.

There was a familiar click, and Derek froze. The front door creaked open, and a pair of quick steps stalked down the hallway.

For a brief moment, panic ran over Derek, and intrusive thoughts mellowed his eagerness to leave.

Somehow, his dad had found out his plans. Somehow, he knew Derek was going to see Becca and was coming to punish him. Somehow, he was going to punish her too.

A loud knock rattled his bedroom door, and Derek jumped.

"Derek! Wake up."

The panic subsided at the young, feminine voice. It wasn't his dad. They were okay.

He cleared his throat. "I'm busy, Mal," he said.

She never did take no for an answer. The knob rattled, and before Derek could stop her, she pushed it open. He sighed and crossed his arms.

She raised a brow, taking in the outfit he wore and his freshly showered hair. "Are you going somewhere?"

He rolled his eyes and grabbed the side of the door, attempting to force it shut. Mal wedged her foot between the floor and door, effectively stopping him.

"Whatever you want to say right now, I'm not interested."

"Even if it has to do with Becca?" she asked.

The pushing stopped, and Mal grinned in triumph when Derek's expression gave way to interest. Derek let go of the wood and crossed his arms over his chest. He tried to keep his face straight, but he knew that his eyebrows peaked slightly higher than they would when relaxed. "What do you want?"

She stepped into the room and mirrored his stance. Her head tilted to the side, studying him. He frowned, feeling like a bug under a microscope. What the hell was this about?

"Did you kiss Becca, or did she kiss you?"

His mouth opened, so caught off guard he didn't even try to hide it. "What are you talking about?"

"Oh, don't even try." She laughed, excitement scrawled into that mischievous smile. "I slept over at her house last night, and she said you guys kissed."

Derek blinked. "She did?"

"Well—" she shrugged, "—pretty much."

Oh god. A burn rose from his neck and swelled over his face.

He caught Mal off guard and gave her a little shove, strong enough to get her to step out of the doorway before shutting the wood in her face. Expecting her to try and barge her way in again, he leaned against the door and used his body weight to prevent that from happening.

Like he expected, she tried to push it open a few times, yelling that she didn't know he'd be so embarrassed by a little kiss, and chuckling when he told her to fuck off. After a minute of relentless teasing, she just kicked the bottom of the door. It sent a small shock through the wood, but she backed off, and Derek thought she had given up and left to go to her room.

But she always had to have the last word. "By the way. She's waiting for you outside."

By the time he got his bedroom door open, Mal was already running into her own room and closing the door behind her. He could hear her laughing.

"You little shit."

Derek didn't stay in the house long enough to hear her response.

DECEMBER 1985

Quite frankly, Becca was too afraid to go inside the house and get Derek for herself. Mark's car wasn't around, luckily, but even being near the place made her shake her leg in nervous anticipation.

It didn't help that Mal had gone inside nearly five minutes ago to get Derek for her, and there was still no sign of him.

God, where was he?

If something was wrong, Mal would come and tell her… right?

She leaned forward across the passenger seat of her mom's car, trying to get a better look at the front door and the windows of the house. As far as she could see, there wasn't any movement.

She hadn't really accounted for her next move if Derek never came out. There wasn't really a reason for him to not see her right now, as far as she knew. He wouldn't be avoiding her, right?

She debated between driving away and going up to the house herself. Neither option appealed to her.

Luckily, she didn't need to make a choice.

After minutes of nonstop worrying, the front door opened, and Becca exhaled.

Partially, because she was glad to see Derek with a soft crooked smile on his face—unharmed. And partially because he looked really, *really* good.

It was amazing the things he could do to his appearance with so little effort, and Becca had weak knees and shaky hands just looking at him as he walked down the sidewalk to her car.

His hair was wet, clearly fresh out of the shower, and something that shouldn't be so confusingly sexy was. The curls stuck to his skin and hung into his shining blue eyes, giving his look the perfect combination of tousled and strategic. A loose black shirt tucked into tight denim jeans had Becca biting her lips to keep herself sane.

God.

Three light taps on her window shocked her out of her stupor just in time to feel her face flush when she realized that Derek was *right there*. The smirk on his face as he leaned down to look at her through the glass made her question whether he had heard every thought in her head.

Clearing her throat, she steadied herself and rolled down the window.

"You just couldn't stay away from me, could you, sweetheart?"

She sucked in her lips. Derek noticed—there was no way he wouldn't—and his smirk grew into a delighted grin as his gaze swept over her face.

Was there even a point to playing it cool?

Her pride told her yes.

"I was just dropping Mal off. Thought I might as well say hi while I'm here," she said. She shrugged, trying to add a believable element of nonchalance.

She knew he didn't believe her, but if, by chance, he did, he sure wanted to change her mind. He leaned forward, folding his arms over one another and resting them right on her windowsill. His head was in the car now, and Becca had to lean back to put some much needed—unwanted—space between them.

"So that's where she heard about our kiss," he said, and his voice oozed a disgusting amount of glee.

Becca's back straightened, and her hands slapped the steering wheel. "I didn't tell her that."

He tilted his head. "No? But you told Parr about Halloween, right?"

Becca blinked.

Where the hell did he find that out?

"I just needed his advice." Her voice was higher pitched than she meant, and it gave her away.

He chuckled and leaned in closer. She didn't back away this time. "And what did you learn?"

Oh, she had learned a lot. Maybe too much. Maybe just enough. But a *lot*.

I learned that I love you.

She wasn't going to say that, even when his eyes encouraged an answer. Derek was still Derek, and in what she'd seen in his interactions with other girls, that meant love didn't work the same way. She didn't want to give him the satisfaction of knowing she was just like all the other girls—completely enchanted by him.

"What was it you wanted to do yesterday?" she asked, not caring that it was a sloppy distraction.

"Changing the subject?" He raised a brow and laughed. "Fine. I'll bite. I wanted to take you on a date."

And just when she thought she had the upper hand. "A date?"

Derek had been on dozens of dates during his time in Highburg. For sure, he was experienced in all it entailed. The problem was, she had no idea what his idea of dating was.

Long ago, she'd decided she just wanted to remain in the dark about what Derek did with other girls, but now she wished she had a better idea.

"Dinner, a movie—whatever you'd like, sweetheart. I hear they've got a nice ice skating rink set up in Richmond. You like skating?"

Becca's mouth opened slightly. This was certainly not what she'd expected. "I've never been."

"We'll learn together then." Derek grinned, and she admired the way his eyes seemed to lighten. "Let's go after school tomorrow, okay?"

"Isn't that a little late in the day? Richmond is over an hour away."

"Better than staying here in Highburg."

She almost missed it—the worried tone in his voice. When she did catch it, she wasn't quite sure what it meant. Still, she smiled, because she couldn't for the life of her resist when he looked down at her like that. "Okay."

He nodded and straightened so he no longer leaning in through her window, but he stayed next to the side of her car. "Dress warm. I'll see you tomorrow." And that was that.

He raised a hand, and Becca rolled up the window as quickly as she could—worried that the longer she left it down, the more he'd be able to sense how badly she wanted to giggle and kick her feet in excitement.

A date. With Derek. Not just as friends.

As…something else. Something she wasn't quite sure of, but something she really, *really* wanted to be.

Her eyes followed him away from the car as her heart soared. As soon as he was out of sight, she really would squeal.

She raised a brow when he paused, halting his retreat into his house and turning back around. He caught her eye through the windshield, and she couldn't read his expression quick enough to decipher before his grin returned, and he jogged back to her window.

Confused, she rolled it down again.

He didn't rest on the sill as he did before, but he did lean his hand on the door frame right above the window. He leaned in so he was right in front of her face again. She held her breath.

"You can tell Parr all about this, too, if you'd like." And then his lips were on hers.

Two seconds, a quick peck—but long enough to steal the air from her entire body and leave her lungs gasping for more. She didn't even have a chance to close her eyes from the surprise.

His lips still felt exactly how she remembered, soft but confident, until the moment they pulled away.

He smirked, enjoying whatever face she was making, because he chuckled, then turned away, returning to his house for real this time.

Before, watching him walk away in those jeans was an *option,* but now it was a necessity. She couldn't tear her eyes away, even after he was inside the house and the door was closed.

The dopey smile remained on her mouth the entire drive home.

***

Becca tried her best to be discreet. It was like last January, and she was worried all over again about the rumors that would rise when people spotted her by Derek's car right after school.

She wasn't worried so much about people associating her with Derek as she was about the rumors that would come from the sudden, drastic change in dynamics. One minute they were avoiding each other in the hallways, the next they couldn't keep off each other.

Okay. So that was an exaggeration—an irrational fear that everyone could look at her and just tell how much she wanted him. How much she thought about his kisses, or how her eyes followed him.

So maybe it was pointless, but she was careful nonetheless—hiding near the outdoor cafeteria door after school and waiting for Derek to make his appearance.

"What are you doing here?"

Becca jumped in surprise and turned to see Nicole standing there with a pile of books in her arms.

"Aren't you leaving?"

Becca had failed to mention to Nicole earlier that she was going on a date with Derek.

Actually, she'd failed to mention *anything* to Nicole. From the kiss to the fact that they'd kind of made up. She hadn't told her a single thing—nor Marty.

Even though Derek had jokingly told her she could tell Marty about him kissing her again, she hadn't even known what to tell either of them. They would be supportive—that wasn't the worry. The worry was that it all felt far too good to be true. She was scared that, if she said it aloud, it would slip through her fingers again and that really would be it.

She blinked. Nicole blinked and then raised a brow. Becca's mouth opened, but nothing came out. Nicole's other brow lifted.

It was both a blessing and curse to have an observant friend.

"What is it?" She stepped closer. "You're not telling me something."

Becca was a deer in the headlights, completely giving herself away. "I—"

Right then her eyes were drawn to the curly haired boy who walked out of the school doors, putting a cigarette to his lips. He was like a magnet, and even when she tried to look away, his mere presence drew her attention to him and only him.

Like a magnet, both sides drew together equally, and his eyes snapped to hers immediately. Her eyes widened, and he grinned.

In her own little world, she forgot about the single audience member watching her face carefully. Nicole turned and followed the invisible line Becca had painted between herself and Derek.

"Holy fuck. You're waiting for Stokes."

Over Nicole's shoulder, Derek motioned his head toward his car, and Becca nodded in understanding, before sheepishly looking back to Nicole, who'd watched the entire interaction with an open mouth.

"What happened last week?"

God. Nicole was asking for a quick sentence-long explanation, but that wasn't possible. It would take hours to tell her the full story.

A familiar BMW entered from stage left, and Becca used it as a distraction.

"Oh, look, your ride is here."

Marty pulled to a stop and rolled down the passenger window to look at them.

Nicole groaned. "Of course, he's on time today. Does he know?" Nicole asked. Becca shook her head. He watched them with furrowed brows. "Yes! Okay. Tell me later. Don't you dare tell Marty until I know. I want to rub it in his face that I knew something first."

Becca neither confirmed nor denied Nicole's request—no, *command*—as her friend ran and jumped into the passenger seat of Marty's car. Becca followed and peeked into the window as Nicole closed the door.

Marty looked at her, and Nicole pursed her lips. "Do you need a ride home?" he asked, clearly noticing that she didn't have her mom's car.

Nicole shook her head aggressively. "No, no. She's fine. She's staying after to get some extra credit." Nicole gave Becca a knowing wink, clearly satisfied with her lie.

Becca raised her brows. "Uh, yeah."

Marty shook his head. "You need to let loose a little. Take a break and go out to do something fun for once."

Becca smiled genuinely. "I'll call you when I'm ready to do that."

"It better be soon." He put the car into drive, and Becca stepped away from the window. Marty gave her one final wave. "Bye, Becks."

She waved and watched the car leave, ignoring the way Nicole wiggled her eyebrows. She'd be lucky if Nicole didn't burst and tell Marty about it herself.

Derek was in his car by the time she started to cross the parking lot, but she felt him watch her the entire way over. Frankly, she was surprised he wasn't out and walking to her himself.

He was always one to make a scene. But it wouldn't be much of a scene when only a handful of students lingered by their cars. Most of the student body had already disappeared to their homes and activities away from school.

Still, her mind got carried away. She imagined him leaving his seat, crossing the parking lot and hugging her, pushing his lips against hers where everyone else could see.

Her eyes widened, and her thoughts screeched to a halt.

Was that something Derek would do, or was that just what she *wanted* him to do? Maybe a bit of both.

But it didn't matter, because it didn't happen. She reached his car and opened the door and slid into the passenger seat.

She lifted her hand and gently pressed the back of her fingers to the warmth on her face, avoiding Derek's hawk-like gaze. She pretended to pay attention to the handful of people eyeing them through the windshield.

His grin burned into the side of her face.

"I guess you haven't told your friends about our date yet?" He leaned a little closer, studying where her fingers pressed against her cheek. The tease dripped from his voice like caramel. "What's wrong, sweetheart? You're looking a little red."

Oh, he knew what was wrong. She could see the understanding, right on top his teasing smirk. He knew exactly what he was doing to her just by simply existing.

"Oh, shut up." Try as she might, she couldn't fight the smile that fought its way to her mouth. "Let's go."

"As you wish." He gave her one more charming smile and then turned on the car and revved before running out of the parking lot.

This all felt normal. It felt perfect.

Like the last couple months had never happened and she was back with her other half, driving around Highburg like they loved to do. The only thing that was noticeably different was the route they took, heading east out of town toward Richmond. Derek still played his music on the stereo, he still tapped his fingers on the wheel in that way she loved, but their eyes would meet every few seconds, and her chest would flutter…a reminder that this wasn't normal.

Not for them.

This was a date. One that Derek had asked for explicitly, right before kissing her on the mouth for the third time.

That wasn't normal, and Becca wasn't sure how to act sitting next to him anymore.

It took some effort to keep her nervous hands still, but they fidgeted when she wasn't making a conscious effort. Her fingers played against each other, a comforting technique that gave her away. On top of biting her lips and staring intensely out the window to avoid Derek's glances, she was a picture-perfect example of an anxious girl going on a first date.

It wasn't actually her first date. She'd been on four other dates before, and she's had some mild flutters right before those, but nothing like *this*.

God. What was happening to her?

Derek never made her jumpy before. Was it the fact that it was a date? She'd naturally been somewhat comfortable around him since the day they met, and suddenly it was like a switch was flipped, and she couldn't control the churning in her stomach and the pounding in her chest.

Like a tether to reality, Derek's right hand dropped from the wheel and reached across the car to cover hers, snapping her out of her head. Her fidgeting froze as his fingers wrapped around hers. Eyes widening, Becca stared at their hands for a second before looking at him.

"It's me, sweetheart," he said. "It's just me."

His blue eyes softened, and his grasp tightened just enough to be comforting. There was no teasing. Just his sweet words soothed her nerves, and Becca relaxed into her seat as he continued down the highway.

Derek.

Of course. Whether they were dates or friends, or anything else, he was still her Derek. Whether they were kissing or holding hands or mending wounds, they were still the same.

She'd realized it last time they were in the car together, and she realized it even more now. No matter the circumstance—whether it was just a drive or an actual date—they were the same.

A loose breath left her lips, and this time, she weaved their fingers together and held onto him. His thumb brushed gently against her skin.

She smiled at him, and he returned it.

"It's you," she said.

The sun was setting earlier and earlier these days. Richmond was an hour away from Highburg, and by the time Becca saw the "Welcome to Richmond" sign, the sky showed only traces of the last remaining light blue streaks. Darker meant colder, and the two layers Becca wore were apparently not enough.

"I told you to dress warm."

"I didn't know the ice-skating rink was going to be *outside*." Becca crossed her arms over herself and watched the puff of air ride over her face as she sighed.

Derek clicked his tongue and walked to the trunk of the car. Becca stayed to the side, shivering, as he opened it up and rummaged through its contents.

"You're lucky I knew this was going to happen." The trunk thumped shut and Derek appeared in front of her, throwing something over her shoulders. It took her frozen mind a few seconds to thaw enough to comprehend what was happening, when Derek started helping her arms into the sleeves of one of his thicker jackets.

It was a dark leather jacket—the one he wore often—and the material covered more of her than it did Derek. The nice thing about a jacket a few sizes too big was that it could comfortably contain the two smaller layers she had stacked under it.

Not to mention that stomach-fluttering smell of Derek that lingered on it. If the warmth of the extra layer wasn't enough, the smell of him did the trick to stop her shivering.

He also brought out a smaller pair of gloves, pink, and clearly not his.

"Are these Mal's?" she asked as she accepted them and pulled them over her fingers.

"She won't even notice they're gone."

Unlike her, Derek was prepared for the cold. Becca took him in. Somehow, he made even a winter coat and leather gloves look good.

Derek held out one of his gloved hands toward Becca, which she gladly accepted as they walked toward the ice rink.

Thirty minutes later, she questioned whether ice skating was a good idea. She knew she wouldn't be good at it, but she didn't realize she'd be *this* bad. People always said it was similar to roller skating, but those people were liars.

She wobbled unsteadily and tried to take another step forward. It was only half successful, but at least she wasn't on the ground—like Derek.

That was the one consolation in all this. She wasn't nearly as horrible at ice skating as Derek was.

Maybe roller skating a lot when she was younger *did* make it easier to stay upright, but Derek—who always claimed that roller skating was too lame—was clinging to the siding of the rink desperately trying to straighten his legs.

Becca bit her lip as she approached him slowly and held in the laugh that bubbled in her chest. "How's it going there?" she asked.

His response was a well-timed misplacement of his feet that sent him scrambling backward and falling flat on his ass.

The laugh Becca was hiding burst out, and she grabbed onto the siding to keep her balance as Derek turned to glare at her.

Maybe this was why he wanted to come all the way to Richmond to skate. Better to make a fool of yourself in a place where no one knew you.

He wasn't as amused as she was and cursed under his breath as he grabbed back onto the railing to pull himself up.

Derek always held himself with such confidence and ease

that it was bizarre to see him so out of his element—she loved it.

It was just a part of him that only she would know about now, and that made it even better.

"Are you okay?" She finally managed to form the words she wanted to ask.

He glared at her, but it wasn't scathing. If she looked really close, she could see the way his lips struggled to remain frowning.

"I *really* hate ice skating."

Becca pushed off the rail and shifted so she was standing beside Derek on the ice. Carefully, she removed Mal's glove and slid it into the pocket of Derek's jacket before holding out her hand to him. "You said we'd learn together, right?"

He studied her hand, then looked into her eyes. He must have seen the sincerity in them, because he straightened and did the same as Becca—removing his own glove and putting his hand into hers so that their warm skin connected together.

"Catch me if I fall," he said, eyeing her as he pushed onto the ice.

She grinned. "I promise."

She kept that promise for the next hour. Every time he stumbled, Becca somehow found the right way to grab hold of him to keep him steady. Somehow, he did the same for her.

As bad as he was, Derek was a quicker learner, and pretty soon, he moved more smoothly than she did. His movement on the ice became fluid, like real skating, instead of stepping. Just like they said they would, they learned together. From falling every few seconds, to easily following the wave of people around the oval rink, hand in hand.

The cold air pushed her hair back as they rounded the corner, steadying each other. She giggled at the euphoric feeling.

Without having to constantly look at her feet, Becca's eyes scanned the people around them. Some went slower, some faster. Some of them were families with children, some were friends, and some—like Becca and Derek—held hands around the ice.

One thing stood out to her above any other—she didn't recognize a single person's face.

In this crowd of strangers, she and Derek blended in as just another pair of faces, one right next to the other.

In Highburg, eyes would be following them everywhere. The rumors would have already reached the edge of town, and by the morning, everyone would know that Becca Lewis and Derek Stokes were holding hands and ice skating.

Here, it didn't matter.

There was no backstory. They were a simple couple to the people who even looked twice. A couple on a date with nothing else ruining the story.

How nice that sounded. To be a blank slate with just two words: Becca and Derek. Nothing else.

A girl who loved a boy, and a boy who beamed at the girl with his gorgeous smile and beautiful eyes and messy hair.

She loved Derek. In moments like this, there was no ignoring it.

Once upon a time, they'd talked about going somewhere far away from Highburg. Derek said he'd go anywhere she wanted to go. Now she wanted that more than ever. She wanted Derek to be safe, in a place where they could go on dates without watchful eyes, without the rumors and history lingering on them.

She wanted to just love him, freely and completely.

When the snowflakes started to fall on them, covering Derek in soft white petals, her heart nearly busted from her chest.

It took every part of her willpower to keep herself from spewing out the words she wanted to say to him.

"Sweetheart."

"Huh?" The nickname snapped her out of her trance. His brow raised.

"How about some hot chocolate?" He pointed over at the edge of the rink, where a small concession stand had a line building outside of it. Thanks to the thickening snow, people were starting to exit the rink to head home.

Even if they were better at skating now, they weren't ready to face an inch of snow too, so Becca nodded and tilted her head up to look at him. "I'd love some."

Ten minutes later, they rushed across the large parking lot with their cups of cocoa in one hand as thick, heavy flakes of snow came down and rested on their eyelashes.

"You didn't mention anything about a snowstorm," Becca called over the roof of the Monte Carlo, before sliding into her seat. The car was cold, but more bearable than the assaulting snow and frozen breeze.

Derek didn't answer until he was in his seat as well, and the both of them shook the powder from their clothes and hair. "I didn't know until you did."

Becca observed the sudden storm outside her window. The entire world was a white noise of snow blanketing the car. They were the last vehicle in the parking lot, and soon enough, all the windows would be covered, and it would be like their own little snowed-in shelter.

But neither of them was in a rush to leave. They sat in the comfortable safety of each other's company, sipping cautiously at the sweet, hot liquid, trying not to burn their tongues by drinking too fast.

At this rate, they'd be home no earlier than ten or eleven. That was late for her on a school night, but it didn't matter, because the thought of Derek would keep her up until morning anyway.

She glanced over to Derek, who leaned his head back and watched with a contented smile on his face, as the rest of the windshield covered.

This was it. This is something she could have for the rest of her life. A warm drink clasped in her hands, and the man she loved sitting beside her. They were in their own little world, content, happy. Oblivious to anything else outside of this car.

"I love you." She didn't mean to say it. The words had been threatening to slip from her tongue the entire night, and before she even realized it…there they were. Floating from her to him and then lingering in the cold air of the car as she waited for a reaction.

He didn't move at first. His cup, halfway to his lips, paused in midair, and his eyes widened a fraction.

She wanted to avert her eyes, pretend she never said it, but she couldn't look away from him. He was all she could see. Every breath was agonizing, every movement an earthquake.

She dreaded and craved what he would say.

He shook his head, just enough for her to sense, and her heart dropped.

"Don't say that," he said, his words incredibly quiet. A whisper that felt like a gust of wind.

Her courage died in the back of her throat, and she choked on it. It took all the effort in the world to speak again. "Why?"

He put the cup of hot cocoa back in the cupholder and turned toward her. His hands came up and rested on her cheeks, with his thumbs brushing under her ears. "Because I was supposed to say it first."

Becca's breath hitched, and her thoughts lost their coherency. All she knew was that Derek looked at her like there was nothing else to see.

"I was going to tell you how much I love your voice, and the way you say my name. I love your hair and those lines in the corner of your eyes when you smile. I love that you take walks in the cold, and that you love to give gifts, and that you learned to swim at seventeen. I love your handwriting, and lavender, and seeing you in the sun and in the dark. I love your laugh, and your heart, and how much good you have in you. I love the good you bring out in me. I love you, Becca. More than I've loved anyone else…more than I've loved myself." He paused, and his eyes searched hers.

She saw it now. That look she could never place in his gaze, the one that had stumped her on more than one occasion. It had to be the same one he saw when she looked at him.

"You're everything to me. *Everything.*"

He loved her.

He loved her like she loved him.

Her heart soared, and all inhibitions disappeared with it.

She was so fucking ready to love him.

Becca leaned forward and closed the space between them across the console. Derek's reaction was slow, and by the time he blinked, her lips were already against his.

In that snow-covered car, alone in an empty parking lot, Becca kissed Derek Stokes.

And she knew, as a matter of fact, that it wouldn't be the last.

DECEMBER 1985

Derek exhaled into Becca's mouth and accepted her kiss like a habit. Their eyes closed, and Becca's hand came up to steady herself on his chest as she leaned into him.

He tasted like chocolate and cigarettes. He smelled like leather and ozone.

She was in heaven—floating so high that the ground became an afterthought.

She smiled into his mouth, and Derek's lips twisted against hers as he did the same. Her chest puffed to make up for the breath she couldn't catch. She was weightless, contained only by his hands as they pulled her in closer.

He flicked his tongue over her lips, and she opened them for him, granting permission that he took with enough passion to burn a hole through her skin. Yet, she was still too far from him.

Trying to lean across the console left a canyon of space between them. This damn car was too small and yet not small enough, and she wanted more, more, *more*.

She pulled away from Derek, and he whimpered—deep and airy. Her voice caught in her throat as the unfamiliar sound shot straight down and lit her insides.

His hands remained attached to her face, but his eyes softened. There was nothing else in this world she wanted more than all of him at this very moment.

A thought popped into her mind—scandalous and needy. There had to be a quarter of an inch of snow covering every window, blocking out any prying eyes from looking into the car.

It gave her enough courage to follow through with her idea and she moved.

Without a word or warning, she crawled—as swiftly as she could—across the middle console and slung a leg over Derek's lap, lowering herself until she pressed against him.

She'd never done anything like this.

When she imagined it in her head, she always thought she'd be nervous. Instead, lust gave her a confidence she didn't know she possessed.

He looked up at her, his hands and chest still, his mouth slightly open as he waited. Waited for her to make the first move. The intensity of his stare bore into her heart and core. She gave in.

Biting her lip, she tentatively ground her hips down and rested her hands on his chest.

Again, he let out that whimper. The one that collected in the pit of her stomach and swallowed her breath. His jaw dropped lower while his eyelids hooded but didn't close.

He didn't take his eyes off her for a second, and she did the same.

God. She could *feel* him. Right there. Just between layers of denim, he was right there, and she wanted *all* of it.

There was no blue left in his eyes. He radiated in the dark, but his irises were completely taken over by his black pupils, and his softened eyes looked up at her through thick lashes—and they *begged.*

Soft, desperate.

How could she deny him when he pleaded silently to her?

How could she deny herself?

One of his hands lowered to her hip and delicately pushed up the hem of her shirt to gain access to the skin right above her jeans. The tips of his fingers dug into the supple flesh on her love handles. His other hand brushed over her face, letting his thumb skim over her cheek.

His head leaned back against the headrest of his seat, and

his mouth hung open as he breathed shallow breaths. "You are stunning."

Hand cupped over her jaw, Derek pulled her in once again, so their mouths clashed together, continuing where they left off.

There was a hunger in his movement that hadn't been there before. It wasn't a gentle massage; it was starving.

Becca dug her fingers into his toned chest and leaned in. Her long hair cascaded around their faces and created a curtain that encircled the moment in its own cocoon.

She ground down against him, over and over again, shooting sparks of pleasure up her body. Her hair stood on end, and her toes curled in her boots.

His hand left her cheek to take over the empty spot on her other hip, and he pulled her down harder onto his lap.

She gasped, and threw her head back, panting into the air. The car, which had once been freezing cold, now fogged over as the air became hot and humid.

"Shit." He muttered in a gasping breath.

She loved that. She wanted to hear him say more, say everything and anything. She wanted to make him moan and whine and gasp.

She picked up the pace, twisting herself into him and reveling in all the sounds that fell from his lips. She couldn't avert her gaze, as his eyes squinted shut and he groaned.

Faster and faster and faster. His grip grew tighter, and his panting became louder.

She, herself, was losing control, seeing him so easily falling to pieces before her eyes.

And then his grip tightened, and his hands pulled her hips straight off him.

The space she'd tried hard to get rid of was between them once again.

She winced at the loss of friction, and he leaned forward so it was more difficult for her to get her spot back on his lap.

"Please, baby. Stop." His voice was high, almost pained.

Becca froze, and immediately pushed all her weight away

from him. She backed so far away that her spine bumped into the steering wheel.

Worry draped over her as she took in his wince. "What's wrong? Did I do something wrong?"

He shook his head and exhaled a deep breath, as a dopey smile settled on his face. "No. *God no.* You're perfect." His fingers on her hips rubbed gentle circles into the skin where her shirt had risen up. "But we can't do this. Not like this. Not here."

Becca's hands pulled away from his chest, and she rose up even higher, until there was more space between them. It was difficult, because all she wanted to do was touch him.

Their breathing slowed to a more natural pace.

He let go of her hips, and rose to brush the curtaining hair out of her face and behind her ears. His eyes flicked between hers, searching her expression. "As much as I want it—and I *fucking* do—you deserve something so much better than this."

The pooling between her legs didn't disappear right away, and one small glance downward would tell her the same about Derek, but as much as she wanted to object, she didn't. "Okay." She nodded and leaned forward. If Derek didn't want it like this, then neither did she. "Okay." She pressed one last lingering kiss to his lips, and then pulled away for good. The hot air between them was corrupted as she clumsily crawled back over the seats and adjusted back into her seat.

Derek's hand grabbed hers the moment she settled in, and Becca returned his easy grin with a smile of her own.

"Let's get you home, sweetheart."

***

Never in a million years did Derek think he could be this happy.

Even the discomfort of his constrained arousal was comfortable when he was so high on the cloud nine in his head. All he needed to do was repeat her words in his mind and anything was bearable.

He didn't even notice he'd made it all the way home on the slippery, snow-covered roads after dropping Becca off, and he hummed a song as he walked up the steps toward his house.

He was dreaming. That was it. He had to be dreaming.

She loved him.

Was that even possible? For someone as incredible as her to love someone like him?

Real life was never that lucky.

But then again, real life had brought her to him in the first place, and that was the luckiest he'd ever been—even after a year, he still had a hard time believing that.

He was so caught up in his giddy smile, wistful sighs, and disbelieving chuckles that he didn't notice the living room lights were on in the house.

He didn't notice Jennifer kneeling on the floor next to the coffee table until he heard his name.

"Derek."

His stepmother's voice cut through the clouds like a strike of lightning, and he blinked. The world came into focus around him, and he looked over to take in the scene in front of him.

She looked surprised to see him standing in the doorway, her eyes wide, like someone caught in the middle of doing something wrong. In her hands were broken pieces of glass— the rest of which were scattered over the carpeted floors, along with several other things that weren't supposed to be there.

The smile fell from his face as he took in the scene. It was like a storm had passed through and ravaged just their living room. An ashtray and magazines were scattered around, some thrown all the way to the opposite wall. One of the decorative pillows looked like it had been ripped apart, small pieces of white fluff coating the couch and ground near it.

"What happened here?"

"Oh." Jennifer's voice rose an octave, and her eyes turned toward the hallway, where her and Mark's bedroom sat at the end. She didn't realize how easily she gave things away sometimes. "Just a little accident."

An accident. The second little *accident* to happen in the home in the past couple days.

"Right." He didn't even bother to sound convinced. She would be a fool to think he believed her.

Jennifer bit her lip, and her brows drew together.

He couldn't stay here. The clouds in his head hadn't darkened completely, but the longer he stuck around, the higher the risk. He left Jennifer on the floor and went to his room.

He heard the sound of broken glass clinking together as he quietly closed his bedroom door.

He stood in place, staring at the wall.

He was living in two different worlds at once. The faux peace was starting to quickly evaporate from the home, like water in summer heat, and it rattled the barrier into the dreamlike euphoria he desperately grasped onto.

He clenched his fist. He would hold to it as long as possible.

He slid his chair under his doorknob and shed off his layers, leaving them on the bedroom floor near his bed. He nearly fumbled as he grabbed his lighter, then sat on his mattress next to the purple candle, which now only contained a quarter of the wax it once had.

He lit it, and leaned back against his pillow and closed his eyes. He pictured her face, her taste, those words.

I love you, she said.

For now, it was all he would think about. It was all he needed, so he sighed in the lavender.

Derek walked through the school hallway with a small smile on his face.

The stares following him barely fazed him—granted they never did—but now he enjoyed it a little more than usual. People were already talking about Becca getting into his car the night before and out of all the rumors spread this was the first time they were almost right.

In fact, he'd love to yell it out and make sure everyone at school knew how much he loved this girl. That would give them something to talk about.

But he couldn't do that. Not yet. Not while word might eventually get to his father somehow.

The likelihood of high school drama reaching his father was low, but not impossible.

His reason for going to Richmond for their date wasn't random. None of his choices with her were random anymore, but it was impossible to stay away, so he'd be careful.

Right now, it was all speculation to the students who murmured as they passed him, and he ignored it to focus on getting to his next class. They passed him in droves, and he kept his eyes ahead, a light smile on his face.

Out of the corner of his eye, coming from inside one of the offices, he spotted a familiar black braid and slowed his walk.

Mal didn't notice him as she looked up at the school counselor and nodded at something she said. Normally, Derek wouldn't go out of his way to talk to his sister at school, but seeing her with Ms. Roylance made him halt and watch the interaction.

Ms. Roylance had a reassuring smile on her face, but Mal was frowning deeply. After a second, they both waved goodbye, and Derek walked over to their direction.

Ms. Roylance spotted him first, and he saw the way a look of pity crossed her face. She waved at him in greeting and closed the door. Something wasn't right here.

"What was that about?" he asked, coming up from behind Mal and eyeing the office.

She jumped and turned around. "None of your business," she snapped, crossing her arms over her chest as she looked away.

Derek raised a brow at the moodiness. "Did you get in trouble or something?"

She scoffed. "Not everyone is as unhinged as you, you know." The sarcastic comment didn't have the same bite that she normally used.

He looked again at the door to Ms. Roylance's office. Sure, he'd been in there many times, and all because he'd been in trouble. The kids who went there for reasons other than being in trouble went willingly to talk about their problems or to figure out their academic plans, like Becca. Mal was still a little young to be picking out colleges. He frowned and looked back at Mal.

His eyes scanned her from head to toe. Her jacket was zipped all the way up, and her sleeves were pulled down and grasped by her fingers. Overall, she looked okay. Other than the angry expression on her face.

"Is something wrong?"

"I'm fine," she said, and rolled her eyes. "Since when did you become so pushy?"

Her shoulder bumped his as she walked past him and made her way down the hallway. He watched her pull her headphones over her ears and dig her hands into her pockets as she disappeared around the corner, leaving him alone in the hallway with the last lingering students.

Mal was always sassy, often in a mood, but this felt slightly different. Just the other day, she'd been smiley and teasing him about Becca. What the hell happened since then?

The final bell rang, and he was officially tardy to class. He shook his head, and continued on his way. All the while, the lingering sense that he was missing something followed him.

***

Derek pretended to pay attention to the snowy roads as he drove, going slower than usual, but he couldn't help that his attention continued to drift to Mal, who stared gloomily out the window.

"Did something happen?" He had considered dropping it earlier, like she told him to. But, still, it didn't sit right with him through the rest of his classes. The fact that Ms. Roylance was involved didn't help alleviate any of his concerns.

"You've been happy lately. I guess things are going well with Becca." She responded so quickly that he thought she might have been waiting for him to say something just so she could pull the distraction out. When she turned to him, her face wasn't as hard as before, but it wasn't the same childish smile she gave him when she usually teased him about Becca.

He frowned. "Don't change the subject."

She rolled her eyes. "I'm being serious. I heard you guys went somewhere yesterday."

Her lighter tone helped ease some of the anxiety in his chest. Maybe there really wasn't anything wrong and she was just in a mood?

"So, are you guys dating now?" She raised a brow and fiddled restlessly with the fabric around her wrists.

He shrugged his shoulders at the question. "Yeah?"

"Yeah?" Her back straightened. "You haven't asked her?"

"Asked her what?"

Mal scoffed. "To be your girlfriend. Obviously."

"Do I need to?" He turned onto their street and slowed to park the car along the road.

She unbuckled herself and opened her door. "Jesus. And here everyone thinks you're, like, the highest of the high when it comes to understanding women." She shook her head in disbelief and left.

Derek sat frozen in his spot, dumbfounded as Mal walked up to the house and went inside.

***

Girlfriend.

Everything with Becca had always moved naturally. They became friends, somewhat naturally. They drifted apart and then back together. Never did it cross his mind he might actually need to *ask* her to be his girlfriend.

He thought long and hard about it all night in his bedroom and came to the conclusion that Mal was right. He needed to officially ask Becca to be his girlfriend.

That's why he had explicitly asked her to do something with him after school. He'd stayed up late to plan it: They'd go for a ride, and somewhere along the way, he would ask her the question.

She would say yes, he was sure. She'd been the first to tell him she loved him, after all.

He was excited all day. So excited that he didn't notice Mal barely paying attention in the morning when he told her he wouldn't be able to take her home from school today because he had plans, so she needed to find a ride with someone else. So excited he didn't think much about catching a glimpse of Mal walking away from Ms. Roylance's office again after lunch.

He left his final class as soon as the bell rang and made his way to Becca's classroom just a few doors down. Leaning against the wall, he tapped his foot on the linoleum floor and waited patiently for her to appear.

She came out and jumped a little when she saw him there. His heart clenched. She was so cute when she was nervous. Always biting her lip in that way that drove him crazy. Her eyes shined against the slight pinkening in her face.

"Ready to go, sweetheart?" he asked, stepping up to her.

He'd said it was a date. Maybe not the same as holding hands while ice skating, but he wanted her to know going into this that it wasn't a normal hangout. There had to be a sense of romance when you ask someone to be your girlfriend.

"Yeah. Let me just get my stuff from my locker."

He followed her and tried not to smile too obviously when he looked at her. He wasn't nervous, but he didn't want to give himself away yet, so he bit down on the inside of his cheek and pursed his lips.

They passed by the front office, right as Ms. Roylance walked out of her room. Becca smiled at the counselor, and waved a greeting, but Ms. Roylance's focus homed in on Derek.

"Derek. Mind if I talk with you for a moment?"

Becca's smile faltered, and Derek looked between the two women as his brow knit. He hadn't done anything wrong. He'd taken exceptional care to make sure that Ms. Roylance never had a reason to call his father.

A familiar wave of unease hit him, and he recalled Mal coming out of there earlier that afternoon.

Derek frowned. "Sure." He turned to Becca. "Go get your stuff. I won't be long."

She nodded, confused, but did as he said and turned to walk to her locker in another hallway.

Ms. Roylance didn't say anything else but stepped aside and ushered him in with an inviting hand.

DECEMBER 1985

Ms. Roylance picked up the bowl of hard, strawberry candies and held it out to Derek. "Candy?"

He shook his head. "No thanks."

She set it back down. "It's been a while since we last talked."

Yes. It had. He'd been careful to not get caught after their last meeting. Clearly, she was starting to grow suspicious before, and getting into more trouble wasn't going to help. But this was the first time he'd sat in this office completely unscathed. There were no cuts on his knuckles from fights, and he didn't *need* to be here like he had before.

"I've missed our time together, Regina." He smirked and did his best to channel the same energy he'd used before. It was harder, though, because not only was he about to ask Becca to be his girlfriend, but Ms. Roylance wasn't receiving his compliments like she had before.

She smiled, politely at best, but her tone was still serious. "I wanted to ask, Derek. How are things at home?"

His hand clutched the arm of the chair he sat in. "Better than ever."

It was the truth, but it was also a bold-faced lie.

He wasn't being smacked around every second like before, but the nervous energy around the entire place got worse day by day. It nearly suffocated him, even though he reminded himself over and over that it was better than what it could be.

She nodded slowly, her lips set into a straight line. He couldn't read her. Her face gave nothing away.

"I've met your little sister recently, Mal."

"Yeah," he said. His grip on the chair tightened.

"She came in here a few times herself a little bit ago and told me some stuff." Her voice trailed off, but she didn't need to finish the thought for him to immediately catch on. That *stuff* was the same stuff he'd been trying to keep quiet.

His jaw clenched, and his mouth rose to an undeniably unconvincing smile. "She likes to make up stories," he lied.

"They sounded pretty realistic."

"She's creative."

She didn't respond, and they sat in silence. She stared at him, and the seconds bore down on him, one by one, the weight of each settling onto his shoulders.

His patience quickly drew to an end. "What do you want me to say?" he snapped.

She'd been expecting that. Ms. Roylance finally relaxed a bit and leaned forward. "I just want you to tell me what you need. These meetings are 100% confidential, Derek, but I'm not going to lie to you—if there is something harmful happening in your home, I have an obligation to report it. What Mal said leads me to believe that there is."

The sour taste of bile filled his mouth, and his right hand trembled just enough for him to feel it. He intertwined his fingers to hide the movement and swallowed. "I can handle it."

"Mal mentioned that Rebecca already told someone about these things?" She raised her brow and posed the sentence like a question.

He stared at her. How much had Mal told this woman?

She took his silence as a yes. "Is that why you were upset with her?"

Derek's temper was starting to rise, boiling on the fear that bubbled in his chest. Mal didn't know what she was doing. She might think she was making the best choice, but she didn't know what it would bring.

"It's why I know that reporting it isn't worth it. It's better for you to not waste your time and pretend Mal never told you anything. Trust me. I know my father better than anyone, and it *won't help*. Not the way you think it will. You want me to tell you what I need? Fine. I need you to not tell anyone. We can handle it," defensive anger spat through his words.

"Believe it or not, Derek, but you're both still so young. You should not have to handle it on your own."

"But we can."

She paused, her eyes searching his face. She had to see his desperation, had to see the fear. Maybe if she did, she'd keep quiet. After a minute, she shook her head. "I had to do my job."

Derek's entire body froze. His blood chilled, and he felt like a rug had been pulled out from under him, and he was falling into a deep, endless hole.

Had. Past tense. She already did.

He stood up so quickly that the chair he was on pushed back, wobbling. He pointed his finger at her. "You don't have to do *shit.*"

Ms. Roylance didn't say anything else as he turned and barged out the door.

He'd felt this way before—the crippling feeling, like the only way to survive was to run as fast and far away as he could. He could get into his car. He could drive until he ran out of gas. How far would a half tank take him? Madison? Chicago? Not far enough.

There was a pressure in his chest, wrapping around his heart and tightening by the second. His lungs weren't holding air the way they should, and his eyes blinked rapidly as he rushed from the room and down the hallway.

He had to escape.

"Derek."

The soft voice called out, and he froze mid-retreat. Immediately, a numbing sensation flooded his body, and dulled the thoughts of leaving.

He turned just as Becca's soft hand wrapped around his upper arm, and she moved to stand in front of him. Those gorgeous eyes were wide under a worried brow as she looked him over. Like him, she was panting after running to catch up with him.

Her frown hit him in the chest with a sting. She always worried about him. Ever since they met, she'd worried and gone out of her way to fix him up.

He didn't want to do that to her anymore. He didn't want to be the reason she cried or the reason her stomach dropped. He wanted to be the reason she smiled, and laughed, and did everything she wanted to do.

"What's wrong? Did something happen?" She searched him over.

He didn't want to drag her down with him.

He forced a calm smile and raised a hand to her hair, tucking stray pieces behind her ear. "Not at all, sweetheart. Ready to go?"

She stared at him, confused. "You sure?"

"Positive," he said, brushing a thumb over her cheek.

He was a man falling to his death, and there was nothing he could do about it. So he was going to embrace it, and enjoy all that life had to offer before hell boiled over.

He wasn't going to run anymore.

He was going to hurtle peacefully toward the inevitable.

***

Something was wrong.

Even though Derek smiled, and turned up his music as they drove, his hand held her a little tighter than usual.

She'd seen his face.

When he rushed out of Ms. Roylance's office, he didn't see her standing outside the room at first, and she caught the panic on his face.

She'd seen it before. When she told him in September about going to CPS, the dread that had contorted his beautiful features scared her to death.

When she reached him today in the hallway, he turned

around, and it was gone. Like it never existed. Like the whole thing was a figment of her imagination.

He acted fine as he drove her home after saying they would have to cancel their date until another day since something came up. In fact, he acted too fine. The world might as well be sunny and bright and cheery, when, in fact, the dark winter clouds dulled all color and the roads were icy.

Something was very, very wrong.

"You okay?"

He tilted his head toward her and grinned. "Never been better, sweetheart." He leaned over to pop a sweet peck on her lips. The flutter in her chest was mild compared to what it usually was since the confusion and uneasiness trampled it down.

He didn't wonder aloud why she was asking those questions or ask why she didn't return his smile.

She wanted so badly to believe him, but she didn't.

The eye of the storm was the most dangerous part. The winds subside and the world pulls to an unnatural still, putting people at ease and making them let down their guard. He'd been sitting in the eye for three months, and now he could finally see Armageddon looming over him, approaching, with nowhere to turn.

Weak.

He'd wait for it, sitting on his bed. He wouldn't run this time.

Fool.

He knew it was coming.

The red glow of the digital numbers on his alarm clock was the only light in his bedroom. 8:36 p.m.

There'd been no sign of Mark or Jennifer since he arrived home after dropping Becca off with his lame excuses for postponing the date. Mal was here. He could hear small movements from down the hallway every so often, but not once did she open her door or leave her room.

It was better that way. He didn't want to see her right now.

He was so angry at her. But what was the point in getting mad anymore? She didn't know that it wouldn't help. She didn't understand it.

He shouldn't waste his energy making her feel worse.

He was drained. The fight in him was long gone, so he would sit here and wait for his punishment.

It came at 9:13 p.m.

A chill ran down his spine as he heard the front door swing open and hit the inner wall. It shook the house, along with the pounding steps that came down the hallway. Behind them, smaller, trepidatious steps followed. In his mind's eye, Derek could see Jennifer with her head bowed, following obediently behind a furious Mark.

Derek held his breath and watched the warm line of light coming in from the hallway. Any second now, he would see the dark shadow of his father's feet stop in the entry, and the door would open, and he would stand, and he would take it all. Maybe it wouldn't be so bad now that he was prepared.

The shadows disrupted the light under the door, and Derek clenched his jaw, closing his eyes to brace himself.

But the door didn't swing open.

The shadows never stopped.

They kept moving.

The steps passed further down the hallway, and Derek's eyes opened as the pounding started on another door. Not his.

"Mallory," Mark's voice roared through the house. "Open this goddamn door."

Derek's body ran cold, and his heart dropped.

He thought he was prepared, but he wasn't.

Mal told him that Mark hurt her when Derek was gone. She said that it was because he had no one else to focus on. But now Derek was here, sitting on his bed, waiting for the punishment he was sure would come, and it walked right past him—straight to *her*.

And he didn't know what to do.

Five more bangs rattled the house, and Derek's door shook. His body stiffened.

Mal, unlike him, still had a lock on her door. It was her last line of defense against Mark, but Derek knew from experience that it wouldn't last long.

"Please, Mal. Just come talk to us, okay, honey?" Jennifer's softer voice was like a perfectly red apple hanging from the branch. The kind that lured you in, hiding the rot behind the beautiful skin.

And Mal loved her mother. She, as disobedient as she was, always did as Jennifer said.

Derek's mouth grew dry. He wasn't used to sitting behind the door, watching the storm pass him by like he was a sturdy tree.

This must be how Mal had felt all those nights when she locked herself in her room. Maybe now he understood the fear of opening the door and risking being caught in the crossfire.

There was a moment that the shaking slowed, and the house calmed, and Derek swallowed. The click of a lock echoed in his head, and Mal's door slowly creaked open.

Derek stood and took a tentative step, two steps.

A slap rang out in the hallway—familiar contact of palm and skin—and then the crash of something falling.

Derek's shaking hand wrapped around the knob, opened the door, and he stepped into the hallway.

He didn't know what he expected.

Everything he heard made sense. Everything was exactly as the sounds suggested it would be, but it was like his soul and mind disconnected from his body and he became a ghost, staring down at the scene. Numb.

Mal was slumped against the door with one hand on her cheek, and wide eyes gaping up at Mark, who towered over her.

Her wrists, no longer covered with sleeves, revealed dark bruises in the shape of fingers. Deep purple lines that couldn't have been made in the last few seconds, but, instead, in the last couple days. And Derek had never noticed.

A snapshot was taken in his mind. He'd never forget this scene. You don't forget the things you see for the first time, and yet he'd seen this all before.

And he's there all over again. Ten years ago, in a small kitchen in California, standing next to a table. Mark is there, and his mother is on the ground, holding her cheek.

Derek is reduced to being that eight-year-old boy, with no clue or strength or knowledge.

He just stood there—his feet rooted into the floor like a

tree—as Mark stepped closer to Mal. Even Jennifer, Mal's own mother, stood there and did nothing as her daughter looked up in terror.

"I guess I didn't teach you enough, Mallory. Your mother and I just spent two hours being grilled by officers because of you. Respect is all that is important in this world—maybe I didn't make it clear." He bent over, and Mal winced away. "Apologize."

Mal's mouth snapped shut. Her head shook in defiance.

Derek flinched.

The world slowed around him, and it took him only a millisecond to predict what would happen next. It was easy to predict when you'd seen it all before.

Weak.

His feet were moving across the hallway, and his mind snapped back to him. No one noticed him there.

Fool.

His hand reached out, just as Mark raised his open palm and swung. Derek lurched forward and pushed against Mark's chest, hard.

"Don't touch her."

Mark stumbled back, his mouth opening in surprise as he hit the wall. Jennifer jumped and yelped as her husband crashed next to her.

Derek always felt four feet tall in front of his father—scared and helpless.

Now he saw it. Not in his mother, but in Mal. The young girl recoiled, and tears ran down her face. She didn't deserve this. Neither of them did.

No one ever stepped in front of Derek. No one ever stopped the blows. And he'd wished and prayed for his entire life that someone would.

Mark straightened himself and reoriented his footing. Rage burned behind his eyes as he got into Derek's face and spat. "What the fuck do you think you're doing?"

Derek wasn't four feet tall anymore. He stood over his dad, looking down at him. Mal needed him now as much as he needed himself.

There was a soft shuffling, and Mal pulled herself off the ground and bolted from her room to the front door.

Derek didn't watch her leave.

He kept his eyes on Mark, whose face was red and eyes shimmering with hatred.

Jennifer sobbed and called after Mal, but the girl was gone, disappearing into the night that offered her more safety than these walls.

Derek turned, intending to follow Mal out, away from this storm, but Mark stopped his retreat by grabbing the collar of his shirt and slamming him back against the wall outside his bedroom.

"Look at me when I'm talking to you, you pussy." Mark slammed him against the wall again, and Derek's head hit. A ringing went through his ears, and he blinked rapidly as stars ran through his vision. "Did neither of you learn anything? I guess I have to make sure you do."

DECEMBER 1985

The numbers on the worksheet in front of Becca all blended together. She could barely tell the difference between a two and a five anymore in her hazy mind, not from lack of trying.

There were no more college applications to keep her distracted. She'd finished all her work in class today, leaving only this math, and nothing was working to avert her mind away from Derek.

Her pencil tapped onto the binding of the notebook, and her head rested in her hand, which grabbed, frustrated, at a fistful of hair.

He hadn't told her.

Something was wrong and he hadn't said a thing about it.

There was a chance that she was overthinking it, that nothing actually was wrong, but the look on his face lingered in her mind and convinced her she wasn't crazy.

But what could she do?

Calling or showing up at his house wasn't an option. Mark hated her.

Nothing. She should do nothing, because that was what Derek wanted. He made it clear before, and just because they were on much better terms did not change the fact that distance was put between them. She should forget it unless Derek specifically needed her help.

The phone on the wall started to ring, and Becca looked at it. She glanced at the clock: 9:27. Her mother was upstairs, enjoying a night off work.

Staring at the phone caused a sick feeling to pool in her stomach. Maybe it was her sixth sense, but she knew immediately that it was about Derek.

She pushed up from the table and pulled it from the receiver. "Hello?"

Small, out-of-breath pants echoed over the line. "Becca." Mal's voice was watery, and when she stopped speaking, her words were drowned by sobs. Becca's eyes widened, and nausea boiled in her.

"What's wrong?"

"Mark…he… something really bad is going to happen. I don't know what to do," Mal said. Her words were barely coherent, even as she managed the last part. "It's my fault."

Becca let out a shaky breath as panic grew in her chest. "Where's Derek?" It came out quiet, and she wondered if Mal even heard her at first. She clenched her eyes shut and bit her lip.

Mal let out a wailing sob in response, and Becca knew that was her answer. Her head fogged over and her stomach clenched. "Are you somewhere safe?" Her mouth was running on auto, her brain playing catch-up.

"I ran out. This was the closest phone booth."

Becca nodded, and her hand gripped the coiled phone cord so hard it dug into her skin. She took a breath, and collected her thoughts as best she could. She needed to think. "Stay there, okay? Uh…um, call Sheriff Wade right now and tell him—"

"I can't. If Mark finds out I did it again—" Another bout of weeping interrupted her sentence, but Becca already knew what it was. If Mark found out it would make things worse. That was what Derek was afraid of all this time too.

Becca could hear the paranoia and guilt in Mal's words. And she could understand it like she was listening to the version of herself from three months ago.

"You have to listen to me, Mal. Call Sheriff Wade. *Now.*"

She hung up the line and dashed away from the phone to the front door. The keys to her mother's car sat in a bowl next to the entrance, and she grabbed them. In the back of her mind, she heard her mother coming out of her room, but she didn't have the time to explain or chat. She slid on her shoes and ran from the house as her mom called her name, confused.

Becca always tried to drive safely, but it didn't matter anymore. She sped through stop signs and turned corners too fast all the way to Derek's street. The entire way, a silent plea fell from her lips.

Please, please, please be okay.

The house lights were on when she jumped out of her car. A basic look at the house wouldn't spark any interest to an average passerby. But then she heard a yelp.

She bolted up the sidewalk, onto the porch, and shoved her way into the house.

The world became a blur.

On the right, Jennifer sat on the living room couch, her head in her hands as she sobbed.

Down the hallway, loud banging and crashing came from inside Derek's bedroom. A terrified sob escaped her throat, and Becca ignored all the sirens and alarms in her head that warned her away.

She heard the blows before she saw them, and when she did, she froze. Becca's knees went weak, and she grew lightheaded at the sight in front of her.

Mark held Derek against the wall, and one by one, threw punches at his face.

But Derek wasn't blocking them. He wasn't even fighting it. Instead, he stared defiantly into his father's eyes—with blood running from a cut brow and lip—and screamed as loud as he could, cursing into Mark's face. "Fuck you."

Her body moved on autopilot, and she took an uneasy step toward them, unsure of what to do, but unable to just stand still and watch.

The subtle movement caught Derek's eyes as Mark retracted his fist.

His eyes widened, and the anger and defiance guarding them

shattered to reveal surprise.

The change in energy caught Mark's attention, and his head snapped to her, arm still held ready for a blow.

The rage in his eyes cut clean through her, and his grip on Derek let go. The sudden shift didn't give Derek a chance to catch his footing, and he stumbled to the ground, barely catching himself on his hands and knees.

Becca gasped.

Mark stepped toward Becca, distracted from Derek.

Derek had told her that, one day, Mark would snap, and it would all come out. That every bit of that anger and rage would crash to the world like a meteorite, and he knew he would be at the center of it all.

Now, here she was. Standing in the debris as the flames approached. She could run. She could hide.

But she couldn't, not when Derek was struggling to get back to his feet behind Mark. Not when Mal had called for help.

A hot rush of terror sent a burst of energy through Becca's veins, and she stepped backward. Her knuckles brushed against something cool and metal—Derek's lamp.

"You bitch," Mark spat, advancing toward her.

Her fingers wrapped around the lamp, and with a small cry, she picked it up and swung it in front of her.

There was a loud crash as the glass of the light bulb broke on impact with Mark's head. Mark grunted and grasped the side of his face, stumbling a step to the side.

She didn't know shit about fighting, but she knew enough to hurt someone.

Mark hissed as he straightened and looked at the red coating his hand. Becca held the lamp between them like a sword, creating a barrier and a threat to dissuade him from advancing.

"You're going to fucking regret that," he said, dropping his hand to charge at her.

She swung again, but this time he was ready. His left arm took the blow, enough to probably bruise him, but not enough to stop him. Her defense was too slow, and his right hand raised and came down on her face.

She couldn't tell if it was a slap or a punch, but it sent her flying into Derek's dresser with a crash.

A deafening ring and pain exploded in her ears and head. For several moments, her body couldn't move at all. When she managed to open her eyes, the world was dark around the edges, and white specs floated through the air in her vision.

Panic ate at her, and she tried to push herself up, while her hands searched for the fallen lamp, but Mark was faster.

He dragged her back to her unsteady feet, and she cried out as a flashing aftermath of pain rang out in her head. He shoved her against the wall behind her, and the corner of the windowsill dug into her lower back. She winced and tears fell down her face.

"Fucking useless whore." His tongue clicked with disapproval, like he was disciplining a small child.

Becca whimpered.

"I told you to mind your own fucking business."

She expected a second blow, maybe even a third. She shut her eyes and braced herself, but it never came.

There was a loud thunk from behind Mark. Immediately, his grasp loosened on her, and he crumpled to the floor.

Becca stared at Mark on the ground with wide eyes. He moaned and grabbed the back of his head, writhing from some blow she hadn't witnessed. Around him, dark ash scattered on the ground.

Derek stood on uneasy legs behind his father—in his hand was a thick glass ashtray.

He dropped it, and it thudded to the ground. He stared down, dazed.

Becca blinked through the dizziness and pushed away from the wall, reaching out to Derek and catching him by his shoulders.

God. His face was beaten so badly that large bruises already grew on his cheekbones and neck. But, somehow, he was still walking.

She wanted to wrap her arms around him. Tell him she loved him and that he didn't deserve any of this.

But he knew that, and she didn't have the time. Mark, though incapacitated for a moment, was still conscious and slowly pushing himself up off the ashy floor.

Desperately, Becca grabbed at Derek and pulled him as she made her way to the door. He continued to stare down. "Let's go. We have to go," she said.

He looked at her and blinked. A clearness filled his expression, and it was like it all clicked in his head. He followed her out, and away from his father.

***

Somewhere along the way, everything had started to feel unreal. Like his father wasn't actually pounding his face over and over again. He couldn't feel the pain. The adrenaline coursing through him was so potent that each blow only made it stronger.

And then Becca appeared, and it threw him off. He wasn't sure what to do.

When she got hit, his patience and mind snapped, and he suddenly had enough energy to plow through the pain and disorientation.

He'd never fought back against his father—until he rammed that heavy ashtray into his head as hard as he could and then left the room with Becca.

It all felt too easy. His body still buzzed with the adrenaline.

It *was* too easy.

He heard Mark's steps coming from behind and turned just as the man who was supposed to be his father tackled him.

Mark's hits were harder and faster than before.

Weakly, Derek's hands pushed up, trying to get his father off of him, but Mark weighed a thousand pounds, and each second crushed Derek further.

He couldn't see much, couldn't feel much, but he could hear

Becca yelling his name. It echoed in the back of his mind, like a beacon.

He opened his eyes.

The world cleared enough for him to make out Mark's rage. He saw the punches hitting his own face, his chest, his neck. Relentlessly.

But then there was a falter in movement, a slowing, and then a pause.

Mark's attention left him, and just for a moment, Becca was in view again. Her hands were on Mark, punching and scratching and pulling. Her mouth was open and screaming something Derek couldn't make out.

A hollow pain echoed in his chest, seeing her there, fighting for him.

She shouldn't be here. He'd wanted to keep her away from all this, and yet, she somehow was right back in the middle of it all.

Mark shoved, and then she was gone, falling out of Derek's view once again. Somewhere. He had no idea if she was okay or not.

Derek exploded. A fury sent strength back into his muscles, The next second, he gained enough momentum to take control and flip the man. Now he was on top, and he had the advantage.

He threw his fists down on his father, who tried to cover his face—but it did nothing.

After all that, Derek thought he may never think straight again. But he'd never been more lucid in his life.

He fought like he'd never fought in his life. Every blow he sent, a piece of him went with it. He was not a child. Not a fucking punching back. He wasn't anything his father said he was, and he was sick of believing he was.

"*You're* weak," he screamed in Mark's face, hitting him to punctuate the insult. With each strike, a chain around him broke.

"Freak."

"Pussy."

"Fool."

"Worthless."

"Disgusting."

He yelled it all. Every single word his father had ever said to him throughout his entire life.

He screamed like he'd never screamed before. He cried like he'd never had the chance to.

He wanted out of this prison he'd been held in for years.

Ages passed before anything came between them. A blur of fists and cut knuckles on bloody noses pulled to a stop by hands on his shoulders, which lifted him off of his father with ease.

He resisted, at first, but then his eyes caught sight of the people around them in that hallway.

Becca stared at him, her wide eyes silver with tears. He realized the hands holding him had faces and were speaking to him. Familiar, and wearing uniforms.

"Relax, kid." Sheriff Wade shook him a little and brought him back to the ground. "You've done all you need."

On the ground, Mark didn't move at all.

Derek exhaled as the words put a stop to his resistance, and his body slumped against the two officers holding him back. He leaned his head back and sighed up into the air.

He went light.

All the fear, and worry, and shame were gone. They evaporated around him as he smiled, eyes closed.

He was free.

DECEMBER 1985

She'd answered the same questions three times already.

The first time for the receptionist, the second time for an Deputy Brigby, and lastly for Winston.

It was easiest to tell Winston, because he already knew part of the story, but it still hurt to say it all.

What happened? they asked. *I got a call from Mal,* she said. She'd driven to Derek's house, and by the time she got there Derek was badly beaten.

Did Derek do this? they asked. *No, he was protecting himself,* she said. *Mark did this. Mark always did this.*

She learned some things from Winston, as well. Apparently, Mal ran after being hit in the face, similar to how Becca was, but Derek stopped it before it got worse for her. It wasn't the first time she'd been hurt by Mark just this week—a fact that rattled Becca more than she could say. Neither she nor Derek had noticed.

Derek was being held in custody, because when police arrived, he was the one on top and had hit Mark so hard it knocked him out and landed him in the hospital.

Jennifer was keeping quiet—she hadn't uttered a single word since being taken in. Her denial to take either side defaulted her to Mark's. For her negligence of the kids, custody was revoked from both of them.

Both Mal and Derek were okay. Bruised, cut, but okay.

Becca dropped her head and looked at her hands. There was

blood on her. She wasn't sure if it was Derek's or Mark's or hers, but it was there. Heavy tears pricked at the corner of her eyes, and she exhaled, relieved.

He was okay. Thank god, he was okay.

"Is he going to get in trouble?" She couldn't look up, and instead, stared at the small spots of red splattered over her skin.

Winston leaned back in his chair. "Not likely. In another circumstance, maybe. But I have a trail of unofficial reports for the past three months supporting his side—thanks to you."

That's right. How many times had she called him? Dozens of times, she was sure. A part of her wanted to be upset at Winston for waiting until so much damage had been done. She knew he cared, and that the little he could do, he did. But why did the stakes have to become so high?

Becca sighed. She didn't have enough energy to be mad. She would pick her battles carefully, and this one she chose to lay to rest.

"When can I see them?" She finally looked up.

Winston crossed his arms and shook his head. "Not for a while. They'll be going straight into CPS custody from here."

Becca furrowed her brows, and her chest constricted. She wanted to see them. Confirm for herself if Derek was actually okay. But this wasn't about her. She sighed. "Will they be safe?"

Please keep them safe.

"Safer than they probably ever have been."

Okay.

Okay.

She took a deep breath and held it in her lungs. Her head, while hurting, had cleared, and she knew that what was most important now was that they got what they needed. Even if her heart longed to be with Derek, it wasn't the time.

"Thank you, Winston."

He dismissed her, and Becca left his office.

Her mom sat in the waiting chairs outside the door and jumped to her feet when she saw Becca. She came over and gently laid her hand on Becca's shoulder. "Is everything okay?

How are you feeling? Look at me." She grabbed Becca's face, angling it so she could see into her eyes better. She scanned her for the fourth time tonight.

The paramedics had already looked her over and deemed her okay, with no lasting injuries. She'd made it out better than Mark, who would stay in the hospital until he was released to be taken into custody himself.

"I'm fine, Mom," she said, but let her mother worry about her. "Everything is fine."

Her eyes scanned the area, hoping to catch a glance of familiar dirty-blond curls or black braids, but she didn't. She wasn't sure how long "a while" meant, but she hoped it wasn't too long.

There was nothing else she could do there, and with the office becoming crowded, the secretary, Florence, rushed them out into the cold early morning as her mother mumbled about how hard she was going to press charges against Mark.

And that was that. The heavy weight on her shoulders since meeting Derek had gone. She breathed in the frigid air and exhaled it out.

Nothing had felt real since she got that call from Mal. Like she was walking through a nightmare, and now she was in a regular dream. A weird, discombobulated dream that didn't answer all her questions, but left her longing for more.

She slept sixteen straight hours and drifted into the real dreams all day and all night, until the next afternoon. She never knew she could be this exhausted. The emotional exhaustion from not only being worried about what was happening between them, but the longstanding anxiety about Derek's welfare at all hours had filled her with so much pent-up anxiety, she finally burst.

It wasn't her mother who woke her. It was the rambling and bickering of her two best friends barging into her bedroom.

Becca blinked groggily and turned over.

Marty and Nicole froze when they saw her stir on the bed, both staring at her with wide eyes.

"I told you to be quiet." Nicole's elbow came up and dug into

Marty's stomach, causing him to wince away from her.

"She's been asleep for sixteen hours. She needs to wake up." He flicked the light switch on and flooded the room in bright warm light.

Becca flinched and buried her face into the pillow. "Turn it off."

There was some pattering across the carpet, and then the side of her bed dipped down. Becca peeked to see Nicole sitting there.

In the blurriness, as she adjusted to the light, Nicole's hand came down and rested gently on her shoulder. "How are you feeling?"

"It would be better if you two would quiet down."

"Give us a break here. We had to find out through the grapevine that you attacked Mark Stokes and got Derek arrested," Marty said.

Becca was quickly wide awake. She popped up from her pillow and sent a burning glare at Marty. "He wasn't arrested. Not really."

She realized, after saying it, that he looked far too satisfied at getting a reaction from her. Of course, he knew that it wasn't true. Her attention caught onto the bouquet of flowers he held in his hand.

"But you did actually attack Mark Stokes?" he asked, walking over to the bedside table to lay the bouquet next to her alarm clock that she must have slept right through. "Or were you going to wait to tell me about that too?"

"Marty." Nicole sent him a warning glare. She looked at a confused Becca whose eyes bounced between the interactions. Maybe if her mind wasn't so sluggish, she would already understand what was going on.

"Sorry, sorry. A conversation for another day, I know." He sat down on the bed, too, and sighed.

"He overheard some people who saw you leaving with Derek the other day. I had to explain the situation to him." Nicole sounded far too proud to say that.

Becca's mouth formed an "O" shape as it clicked in her head. "I was going to tell you both everything, but honestly, I was still figuring it out for myself."

"You don't need to apologize. Right, Marty?" Nicole said.

He relented and leaned forward. The stubbornness left his face quicker than it had appeared. "I'm glad you're okay, Becks. You had me worried there for a while."

"I'm fine. Really. You guys don't need to worry."

"Oh, but we do." Nicole stood. "In fact, we don't plan on letting you out of our sight until we are absolutely sure that you are not going to run out and beat the ass of someone's dickhead father."

"That's not—"

"Get your ass downstairs and in front of the television. I brought thirteen movies, and we are going to watch every single one of them, starting right now." She held up her school bag, which must be where said thirteen movies were.

Becca blinked and looked between the pair. Marty looked just as determined as Nicole. "What about school?"

"Who the hell needs school?"

Both Becca and Nicole gave Marty a look.

"You are not helping our case here with your grades," Nicole snapped at him.

He glared at her.

She rolled her eyes and looked back to Becca. "School can wait, but you, my friend, need us right now. We are here to be your personal distractions from whatever is running through that little head of yours. We won't even require an explanation, or a story, or anything from you. Just your company will do."

Becca didn't know how she had been so lucky in life. A mother who loved her. Two best friends who cared for her at her lowest. And her Derek.

Derek, who was safe, even if she worried about him.

She wasn't used to that feeling. She wasn't used to the comfort of knowing that, wherever he was, he was okay. That he didn't need her help. That he was perfectly capable of fighting his own battles.

She could rest her mind. She could stay up all night with her friends and watch movies and no longer be scared that he would show up bruised and hurt. He was safe, and she could let herself be happily distracted for a little while.

"I love you guys."

"You're so lucky to have us." Nicole stole the words right out of her mind. "Now let's go. I've already got the first movie picked out."

Nicole rushed from the room, and Becca pulled the covers off to follow.

Marty, however, wasn't moving. He stood by the door Nicole had gone through, watching Becca carefully. His face was serious, and Becca stopped to observe him. He wanted to say something. She could tell.

"What?"

"Are you happy, Becks? Even with all this stuff? I don't know the whole story with Stokes, or what happened lately, but I'll accept it all without question if you're happy and okay."

Becca looked at him, her best friend since they were kids.

She'd put him through a lot, and he'd gone along with everything she said. He gave her the advice she needed to hear and did things for her that no one else would. He never pushed, he never forced, he always let her come to him on her own terms. He deserved only the truth from her.

She smiled and walked up to him. Her arms wrapped around him, encasing him in a hug.

"I'm happy," she said, the words muffled by his shirt. "I was so scared for so long and everything I was afraid of is gone now. I'm happy. And Derek makes me happy. So unbelievably happy."

She couldn't see his face, but she could feel him smile as he returned her hug. "Then I'm happy you're happy."

Becca pulled away, and they let go of each other. She didn't realize she could feel so at ease. Without another word, she made her way out of the room with Marty close behind, and the air in the house became an easy oasis.

Just as she was about to walk down the stairs, Becca paused as another thought popped into her head. Something she wanted to share with Marty. She turned to him, and he raised a brow in question.

"By the way, it's true," she said.

"What is?"

She bit her lip. "I did attack Mark Stokes. He was hurting Derek, so I hit him with a lamp."

Marty's eyes widened in amazement, and he laughed, taken aback by the confession. The rumors in this town were often exaggerated beyond belief, but they'd been right about that.

Marty reached forward and ruffled her hair with his hand. "I always knew my best friend was a badass," he said, raising his chin in pride. "Stokes is one lucky son of a bitch."

She didn't attend school the rest of the week, and two weeks of holiday break followed.

Marty and Nicole did as they said they would, and neither of them never left her alone for more than a few hours. One or the other of them—or both—fluttered over her worse than her mother did. Always prodding her head like she was a newborn baby, forcing her to drink lots of water, all the while making her comfortable and happy to have them around.

Never once did she feel suffocated. She was just grateful to have them in her life. Their distractions were vital during the period of silence.

Every day passed with a little less news than the last—no word from either Derek or Mal.

She called the person she'd talked to when she first reported everything to CPS, but the response she got was that, for the protection of the children, they couldn't share their information.

Becca wasn't worried about them. She'd been assured time and time again of their safety. But she longed to see Derek's face. Her heart ached more, the longer it went without seeing him. The last time she saw him, he barely looked like himself.

The best piece of news she received that next week was that Mark was officially being charged with an array of misdemeanors and a few felonies. He faced at least twenty years behind bars.

They asked her if she wanted to testify—she said yes.

Now all she had to do was wait for them to call her in, and she would go. She wasn't afraid of him anymore. He'd been reduced to a man in chains and a jumpsuit, and he could hate her guts for the rest of her life, for all she cared. She would do the same.

Christmas passed.

New Year's approached.

And she still waited.

She finally convinced her mother to return to work, and on her first day back, Becca sat on the couch and let an old television show drone on as she dozed off. Marty and Nicole finally deemed her well enough to be left alone for the day, while they made up missed shifts at the theater.

Sleep had nearly overtaken her when there was a knock on the door. Her head popped up, and she blinked to clear her foggy, tired mind.

Sluggishly, she rose and walked to the door, slapping her face to wake her up for an interaction. It wouldn't be the first time one of her friends had shown up unannounced with another movie to watch or a box of Chinese takeout.

She opened the door and froze.

Nothing had felt real for the past week, but this may have taken the cake. Maybe she was dreaming—a very, very good dream. One she didn't want to wake up from.

"Hey, sweetheart." His voice bloomed a warmth in her heart and sent a lightning strike through her whole body.

"Derek," she said, and his name was barely more than a breeze, but it solidified it for her. He was there. He was *actually there.*

He stood in his leather jacket with that curly hair and sweet smile. His face was mostly healed, though some small, bandaged scratches remained, but he was okay. He was *real.*

She blinked—once, twice.

And then she fell forward and threw herself around him.

Her arms circled around his neck, and she buried herself into him. He caught her, his arms holding her with such familiar strength and security that the tears began to fall.

The other half of her heart was found, and the emptiness filled. She hadn't believed it was possible to miss someone this much until he held her against him so tight she could melt into him.

She cried out, and he pulled her closer. His face buried into her neck and he inhaled. He lifted her, so only the very tips of her toes brushed the ground. She felt weightless.

Gently, he backed her up until they were inside the house and then kicked the door shut behind them with his foot.

She let go of his neck, and he released her enough that her feet were back on the ground, but he didn't let go of her. Shining tears flowed down as she blinked, and her hands rose to his face, pulling him down to her, capturing his lips with hers.

She kissed him again and again and again, murmuring between the movements. "I missed you. I love you."

The urgent pull of their lips slowed, and then, when it was barely a brush, they pulled away. He was glowing, his smile beaming and his eyes shining. There was a healthiness in his face she'd never seen before.

She held his cheek and cried. "I didn't know where you were," she said.

"I know. They put us somewhere safe. We couldn't go anywhere while things were being processed. Apparently, we'll be moved somewhere soon and who knows after that. They'll kick me out as soon as I'm eighteen, but Mal will be stuck wherever they put her."

When she'd first met Derek, he couldn't stand Mal. They were at each other's throats constantly, throwing names and insults around.

How could this be the same person? This vibrant, loving, radiant person.

"But you guys can come and visit, right? That's why you're here?"

He shook his head, and her smile faltered a bit. "Mal agreed to cover for me for the night." He leaned his forehead against hers. "I can't stay long, but I needed to see you."

God. She was so in love with him.

An idea sparked in her head, and she pulled away. "Come

live here."

Derek paused, and his brow knit. "What?"

"You and Mal can come live here. We can foster you. You can stay together even after you're eighteen."

He didn't look convinced. "I'm not sure your mom would like that."

"My mom is one of the kindest people I know. She loves you both, and she knows I love you. She would care for you like you were her own children."

He looked away and worried at his lip. She could see he didn't think it could be so easy—that it sounded too good to be true. But it was true. They could make it true.

"I want it. I want you both somewhere safe. I know there's nowhere safer than here—stay here through school. Mal can share a room with me. You can have your room."

He stared at her, searching her face for some sort of lie. There was none, of course. She meant every word.

Slowly, his uncertainty gave way to a grin, and he looked down at her lips. "Or Mal could stay in her own room, and I share with you," he suggested, huskily.

Becca's heart skipped, and the heat from his stare went down her entire body. She shifted on her feet. "Don't be gross."

"Gross?" He raised a brow and his hands around her lowered, sensually moving down the sides of her body until they passed her waist, then settled on the back of her hips. He took a small step forward, until their chests were flush together.

Becca blinked and swallowed.

"I love you, Becca. I am so ridiculously in love with you that the thought of anything else pales in comparison. I would sleep next to you forever, *love* you forever. I don't think that's gross." His head lowered with each sentence, and when he was done, his lips were nearly touching hers. His breath brushed over her face.

Her breath caught, and without another word, he closed the minuscule distance.

It was slow and tender, his mouth working hers with such

care, her heart melted in her chest. It grew deeper, his fingers digging into the fabric of her pants.

Again, her arms wrapped around his neck, and her lower half pressed against him. She sighed into him.

"Please," he mumbled into her mouth, "let me love you."

He asked her permission, and she granted it.

Becca nodded eagerly, and Derek moved to pull her legs up, so they wrapped around his waist. She gasped in surprise, then chuckled without breaking the movement of their lips as he started forward.

He climbed the stairs and entered her bedroom. The lights were off, so he flicked them on as he walked past, and then carried her to the bed.

His fingers grasped desperately at the flesh below her hips, and he knelt on the bed and lowered her softly so her back lay on the pillows.

Pulling away, his eyes followed the path from her mouth… down, down, down every inch of her body. His irises were blown out black, and Becca matched the desire she saw in them.

She bit her lip and let her own eyes dip down his body. Her breath caught at the sight of his tented pants.

"I'm going to show you…" he said, leaning forward again so his hands were positioned on each side of her head. His face came down, gently encouraging her neck to expose itself. "Just how much I love you."

She would never forget the way Derek Stokes loved her.

His hands brought her to life and made her feel things she never knew were possible.

This boy, that had once been a stranger on the side of the road, was the only thing in this world that could make light spark on the back of her eyelids with his lips and his hands. He touched her bare skin like she was the most precious thing in the world, and when they collapsed, panting, she held him tight in the soft moments afterward because she *knew* he was.

One of his hands brushed the side of her cheek, as his eyes closed. A small smile lingered on his face.

She never thought she'd be able to love someone the way she loved him. Never considered it would happen with someone who'd been by her side for so long.

Her own hand came up and stroked his upper lip.

He was gorgeous, lovely, kind. How did she become so lucky?

"Will you be my girlfriend?"

Becca gasped and laughed. She smacked him playfully on the shoulder. "Isn't that something you're supposed to ask *before* we have sex?"

He opened his eyes and positioned himself so he was leaning over her on his forearms. "I was going to, but then I got a little distracted."

She laughed and reached her hands up to his face. "You're so lucky I love you." She pecked him on the lips.

He bit his lip and ducked in again for another, longer kiss. Soft and content.

When he pulled away, Becca pushed strands of his hair behind his ears so she could see him clearly. "Stay here, Derek. I'll talk to my mom. It can be just until you figure out what you want to do. You both have a home here, if you'll take it."

He cupped the side of her jaw and grinned down at her. God. He was beautiful. And he was all hers. He nodded. "Okay."

MARCH 1986

"I told you not to worry about it." Derek frowned and looked at the gift bag with tissue paper sticking out the top that Becca held out to him.

"You might have gotten away with it last year, but there is no way in hell I'm missing your birthday gift this year."

She'd been planning this for weeks. He'd said over and over that all he wanted to do for his birthday was exactly what they did last year.

That's why they were currently parked outside the same small ice cream parlor at 9:30 at night, both with chocolate cones in their hands, but she wasn't going to miss out on getting him a gift just because he said not to. Anyone who says they don't want a birthday gift is lying.

He shook his head, but smiled as he carefully set his cone down and accepted the present.

Becca licked happily at her ice cream and watched him with eager eyes.

He glanced up at her through his lashes, then tugged the tissue paper out. He reached in and pulled out the brand-new leather jacket that Becca had carefully folded before placing it in the bag.

She smiled sheepishly. "I know it's not much, but you were complaining about the other one getting too old, and I thought you could have this one, and I could have your old one and—"

He cut her off with a kiss that tasted like chocolate and

cigarettes. Her eyes drifted closed, and she felt a drop of ice cream hit her hand.

He pulled away after a moment, and Becca blinked her eyes open, dazed. "It's perfect. I love it."

She grinned and licked the melted cream off her hand.

Content, he smiled and put the gift back in the bag for safekeeping and moved it out of the way of the melting ice cream.

Becca glanced over at the small envelope she had stored in secret in the side door compartment. It wasn't a birthday gift, and it wasn't necessarily about Derek, but it had arrived today, and she wasn't sure if she should bring it up now or later.

"What is it?" He caught her eyes wandering and followed her gaze to the envelope. "What's that?"

Becca bit her lip. She was excited to tell him, but this was his day, not hers. "It's nothing."

He raised a brow. For a second, she thought he would drop it, but then he suddenly reached across her lap and grabbed it. She couldn't catch him in time before he turned his back to her and opened the envelope.

"Wait. Derek, let me—"

He smiled and read the words on the letter out loud. "*Dear, Rebecca Lewis. Congratulations! It is my pleasure to inform you that you have been…*" His words trailed off as he continued reading and it clicked in his head.

She sat still, anxiously waiting for whatever he might say next.

He looked at her. "You got in?"

He knew how important this all was to her. After he and Mal moved in with her and her mom, he'd sat with her at the kitchen table as she worked her way through the colleges she'd applied to and tried to pick which would be best for her future career as a nurse like her mom.

Eventually, she, with Derek's help, had decided that this university in California would be her top choice.

"It came while we were at school."

He grinned so brightly it was like he was the one who had been accepted into college. "I never doubted you for a second." He leaned in and kissed her lips again.

Becca's heart soared.

But that wasn't the only reason she was worried to bring it up on his birthday.

Now she knew she would be moving to California in a few months.

And yet, the conversation about what Derek would do had remained inconclusive. She knew it agonized him trying to make a choice. Follow her across the country to his home state or stay in Highburg.

On the surface, it might look easy, but it wasn't.

She'd been waiting for this letter to arrive to bring it up. Pretty soon, she would need to accept her enrollment and make living arrangements. To do that, she would need to know what Derek was thinking.

They'd daydreamed about leaving Highburg together, starting brand new somewhere else, without the gossip that followed them. But it all felt more complicated than that now.

"Derek. I know it's your birthday, and I don't want to ruin it, but…"

He stared at the letter. He already knew what she wanted to ask. "But am I going with you or staying here?"

Her breath caught. The idea of being so far from him already made her heart ache. "Yeah."

He was quiet for a moment. Both of their ice creams were almost gone. The cone caught all the melt and kept it from dripping.

Folding the letter up, he slipped it into the envelope and handed it back to her. She took it between her fingers.

He took a deep breath. "I need to stay here—for Mal." He said it quickly. It was clear from the pained, but determined, look on his face that he'd decided this a while ago and just now had the courage to say it. "She needs someone right now more than ever, and I can't just leave her behind. I'll stay here and get a job as a mechanic or something. She'll need a few years to graduate, but we'll figure it out."

Becca smiled sadly and nodded. "Good."

He blinked. "What?"

"I said good. If you had said you were coming with me, I would have talked you out of it." Becca took his hand. "You're absolutely right. Mal needs you more than I do. Not that I *don't* need you, but I am perfectly capable of handling myself." She smiled.

Derek chuckled, and his hand rose to Becca's cheek.

She knew this was coming. She also knew that Mal was having a hard time, and if Derek left her behind, it would be even more difficult for her. Becca decided for Derek that he needed to stay here with Mal a long time ago, even if she hadn't told him that.

She nuzzled into his palm.

Even if she knew it was for the best, there was still a parting sadness, months in advance.

She'd get used to the idea when August came around. They weren't kids anymore. They were adults who could take on hard things. Hell knew they'd endured worse.

"You can handle anything, sweetheart," he said.

"I know." She grinned.

"I'll still be right here."

"I know."

He leaned in. "I love you."

She smiled as their lips touched. "I know, and I love you."

There was no possible way to tell what the future held for them.

Their timeline of the past and present came as one of chance, but its marks still held her tightly. Some were deep and cutting, but some were her most cherished moments. Those gifts wouldn't be lost so easily.

They were right where they needed to be—Becca and Derek. They were happy, and they were safe.

Even apart, they would both put up one hell of a fight before they let anything come between them.

If the past was any true indicator of their capabilities, then they would be just fine.

THE END

MEET THE AUTHOR

Talia Aden, an indie romance author, fell for reading and romance at an early age. Shortly after, she found a love of storytelling and put her romantic and creative mind to work. Envisioning book publication since ten years old, her debut novel "All in Good Time" is the first of many daydreams turned into a reality.

Stay connected with Talia through social media.

 @TaliaAdenAuthor

 @TaliaAden

 www.TaliaAden.com